## To Hell in a Handcart

Richard Littlejohn is an award-winning journalist and broadcaster, outspoken, controversial and funny. He has a twice-weekly column in the *Sun* and has written for the *Daily Mail*, *Evening Standard*, *Punch* and *The Spectator*. He has presented TV shows for LWT, Carlton, Channel 4 and Sky and radio programmes for LBC and the BBC, for whom he currently hosts the top-rated football phone-in *6-0-6*. His highly acclaimed non-fiction book, *You Couldn't Make it Up*, tore apart the Tory years. *To Hell in a Handcart*, his first novel, does the same for Blair's Britain.

Praise for Richard Littlejohn:

'Irascible, irreverent and totally compulsive.'

*Daily Mail*

'Wounding, funny, mocking, unfair and a tonic . . . I admire Littlejohn, love his writing and am amazed that 1990s Britain has only produced one such satirist.'

Matthew Parris, *The Times*

'The only serious competitor P.J. O'Rourke has.'

*Independent*

For Wendy

# To Hell in a Handcart

**Richard Littlejohn**

📖 HarperCollins*Publishers*

HarperCollins*Publishers*
77–85 Fulham Palace Road,
Hammersmith, London W6 8JB

www.**fire**and**water**.com

A Paperback Original 2001
9 8 7 6 5 4 3 2 1

Copyright © Richard Littlejohn 2001

The Author asserts the moral right to
be identified as the author of this work

A catalogue record for this book
is available from the British Library

ISBN 0 00 710613 0

Typeset in Meridien by Palimpsest Book Production Limited,
Polmont, Stirlingshire
Printed and bound in Great Britain by
Omnia Books Limited, Glasgow

## Acknowledgements

My thanks to Mike Kemp, for his invaluable help, inspiration and getting me home from Gerry's in one piece; to Adrian Bourne, Nick Sayers and Tim Waller at HarperCollins; and to Eddie Bell, for being crazy enough to commission this book in the first place.

# One

## The Tigani, Romania

The Tigani doesn't feature on many maps. It isn't sign-posted. The Tigani doesn't advertise. Strangers are rare in these parts.

The Tigani – Gypsyland. Bandit country, home to six hundred close-knit families.

The police never ventured here. There had been no official law enforcement since the fall of Communism and the death of the dictator Ceauşescu. When the men in the black Mercedes S500 had stopped en route to ask directions, the non-gypsy locals questioned their sanity.

Their $100,000 limousine passed silently along the dust road, its computer-assisted air suspension soaking up the potholes like a sponge absorbing spilt milk. The trademark double-glazed smoked glass of the Daimler-Benz company concealed the faces of the driver and his three passengers.

It had cost the men in the Merc $100 and a carton of Marlboro to persuade a taxi driver from a town thirty miles away to lead them to the turning for Gypsyland. They followed his rotting Romanian-built Renault saloon for over an hour before he pulled off the single carriageway, pointed them towards their destination and wished them good luck. Then he was off in the opposite direction in a cloud of dust.

It had taken them just over three hours to cover the ninety miles from the Romanian capital of Bucharest, the final leg of a journey begun in Moscow.

As the car made its stately progress along the unmetalled lane, it was surrounded by raggedy, bare-footed, snot-nosed children and their semi-feral pets. Further back stood a gaggle of women aged from fifteen to seventy-five, wearing traditional Romanian peasant costume, long skirts, woollen jackets and headscarves. The younger women clutched babies in swaddling clothes.

They passed a group of men, all dressed in the familiar Eastern European uniform of denims, sweatshirts bearing the names and logos of provincial English football clubs, trainers on their feet. They pulled on untipped cigarettes and watched, warily.

Behind them loomed a derelict cement factory, which had closed eleven years earlier, a monument to the futility of central planning. There was real poverty here. Families of seven and eight sharing two rooms, with bare floors and a few sticks of furniture, heated inadequately by a simple log fire.

Yet at one end of the village stood a few new houses, red and white brick-built, with one or two cars in the driveway. These were home to the Popescu clan, the town's ruling Roma gypsy family.

The Mercedes approached the biggest house in the street, a neat two-storey construction, with uPVC windows, a bright red front door and a paved driveway, upon which stood a Toyota pickup truck, with heavy-duty towing attachment, and an old-model BMW 525i. There were flowers in the garden, in stark contrast to the barren patches of yard elsewhere in the town.

This was the home of Marin Popescu, leader of the Roma clan, the self-styled *Bullybasa*, whose word was what passed for law in the Tigani.

The driver pulled into the paved driveway and brought the Mercedes to a halt behind the BMW. He popped the central locking.

Three men in Armani suits and Gucci loafers got out. They were all wearing immaculate black, collar-less shirts and sunglasses. The humidity stuck to them like warm glue, in stark contrast to the filtered, constant sixty-eight-degree, humidified air in the Mercedes. A small crowd of peasants

2

watched from a distance as two of the three Russians approached the front door. There was no movement from within the house.

The biggest of the group pulled the wrought-iron handle of a bell hooked up to the door and waited for a reply.

He stepped back and surveyed the front aspect. Not a curtain twitched.

'Marin Popescu,' he called.

Nothing.

The smallest of the three men returned to the car and rapped his knuckles on the driver's window. The boot lid eased open with a gentle clunk. He walked to the back of the car, bent over the boot, reached inside, removed a tarpaulin and retrieved a Soviet Army-issue, hand-held, anti-tank grenade launcher.

'Marin Popescu,' the big man called out again.

Silence.

The big man and his other companion strolled around to the back of the Mercedes. The small man moved to one side and took up position on one knee about thirty feet from the front door.

The crowd withdrew and scattered for cover. The other two men climbed back in the Mercedes and the driver reversed slowly.

The small man squeezed the trigger, propelling an armour-piercing grenade in the direction of the front door. It hit the target, shattering the reinforced steel behind the wooden façade, passing along the hall and exiting via a kitchen window. It slammed into a tractor parked at the rear and exploded, igniting the tractor's fuel tank, sending it thirty feet into the air in a spectacular, incandescent fireball, shattering every window at the back of the house, melting the uPVC frames like putty.

The small man put the grenade launcher back in the boot of the Mercedes and replaced the protective tarpaulin, like a mother covering her precious, newborn baby.

The other two men got out of the car, clutching

Kalashnikovs. The small Russian took a machine pistol from a holster under his left armpit. They waited for the smoke to clear, then walked towards the house.

As the smoke parted, they could see the figure of a man, 5ft 9ins, medium build, greasy, greying hair, walking towards them, his arms outstretched towards the heavens.

The *Bullybasa* was a less impressive figure than they had expected, even though he was immaculately dressed in designer trousers and silk shirt, with an expensive watch on the wrist of his extended left arm.

He was in his late forties, with a weathered complexion, typical of the Roma people. His nervous smile revealed a gold front tooth.

He had already been humiliated in front of the town. Even if he came out of this alive, he might never be able again to command fear and respect in the Tigani. It was time to negotiate.

'Gentlemen. I am Marin Popescu,' he said in the pidgin Russian he had picked up as a result of his involvement in the car-smuggling racket. 'No more, please. Not in front of my people. Follow me into the house. We can resolve this. Come.'

He backed into the smouldering hallway, past the remnants of some expensively embroidered wall hangings.

Marin Popescu led his three visitors from Moscow into a large sitting room, furnished with plush Persian rugs, upholstered leather and mahogany sofas and matching footstools. A 46-inch back-projection Sony home cinema TV stood in one corner, its cable leading outside to a large satellite dish, like a giant wok, now containing one molten tractor.

The big man spoke.

'Where is he?'

'Gentlemen, we should talk.'

'We have nothing to discuss.'

'Where is he? Where is your son, Ilie?'

'I am not able to tell you that. I do not know.'

The big man levelled the muzzle of his Kalashnikov at Marin's head.

'No, please,' Marin pleaded.

The big man swivelled left and unloaded ten rounds into a wall hanging hunting scene above the fireplace.

'For the last time. Where is he?'

'He is not here.'

'We know that.'

'He has not been here.'

The big man raised the Kalashnikov and smashed Marin round the temple. The *Bullybasa* collapsed in a heap on the marble tiled floor.

'OK,' he said. 'Enough. He has been here. He was here three weeks ago. But he is not here now. He is very afraid. He has run. He has gone. But he told me to say you will get your money. He is very sorry, it was not his fault.'

'Where is he?'

'He has gone to England, to get your money.'

'Where in England?'

'London, maybe. I'm not sure. But he will be back with your money. He will steal cars, ship them to me. I will sell them, give money to you.'

'Not good enough.'

The big man put the Kalashnikov to Marin's head. He pressed his Gucci loafer into his throat.

The second Russian reached into the pocket of his Armani linen suit, took out a chamois leather pouch and removed a pair of silver-plated pliers.

'You know what they say about Russian dentistry?' The big man smiled for the first time. 'It's all true.'

As he pressed his foot into Marin's Adam's apple, the second Russian knelt beside him and squeezed the *Bullybasa*'s streaming nostrils. Marin gasped for breath.

The second Russian clamped the pliers onto Marin's golden front tooth and yanked. Marin let out an agonized, terrified screech and his tooth was wrenched from its roots, ripping his gum and top lip in the process. He writhed in

5

agony on the floor as the big man released his grip. His mouth was a claret gash. The blood poured through his fingers. The pain was excruciating.

'We'll call that a down payment,' said the big man.

Marin cried out in pain, like a wounded fox caught in a snare.

'London?' mused the big man, wiping his forehead with a silk handkerchief.

'He will get your money,' Marin tried to reassure the Russian, even though he was gagging on his own blood.

'Money?' laughed the big man. 'It's gone beyond money.'

He lowered the Kalashnikov and pumped two bullets into Marin's skull, one in each eye, putting the *Bullybasa* out of his misery.

The three Russians walked out of the house and settled back into the Mercedes.

The driver reversed, engaged Drive and motored slowly out of town. There was no reason to hurry. The *Bullybasa* was dead. The car was bulletproof. And the police never come within twenty-five miles of the Tigani.

As they drew onto the road to Bucharest, the big man picked a satellite phone from the centre console and punched in a number.

Seconds later, a voice in Moscow answered.

'Sacha, it's me,' said the big man. 'Who do we know in London?'

# Two

## London

Mickey French handed over two £50 notes and trousered his £2 change. Petrol had hit a tenner a gallon during the last fuel blockade and what went up never seemed to come down again.

He walked back to the car, turned the key in the ignition and pressed the pre-set button on the radio.

*'You're listening to Rocktalk 99FM. I'm Ricky Sparke and these are the latest headlines. In Kent, another thirty-five Romanian nationals were found wandering along the hard shoulder of the A2. Police officers gave them meal vouchers and rail tickets to Croydon, where they will be able to register for free housing and social benefits. It brings to over 150,000 the number of asylum-seekers currently waiting for their applications to be processed.*

*'Fighting broke out on the Chiswick flyover in west London as motorists abandoned their vehicles to escape a five-hour, ten-mile traffic jam caused by the new 25 mph speed limit on the M4, which is being rigorously enforced by cameras and satellite technology.*

*'Police made more than two hundred arrests, three for assault, two for threatening behaviour and the rest for exceeding the temporary 15 mph speed limit on the elevated contraflow section.*

*'The trouble was witnessed from above by the Deputy Prime Minister who was flying by helicopter to Norwood, where an RAF jet was waiting to transport him to Acapulco for a seventeen-day fact-finding conference on the future of the lesser-spotted Venezuelan swamp vole.*

*'More news later. This is Madness.'*

You can say that again, old son. Complete madness. Mickey French shook his head, smiled a resigned smile and drummed his fingers on the steering wheel as his old drinking mate, Ricky Sparke, fired up the opening bars of 'House of Fun'.

'Thank Christ I'm out of it,' he said to his wife Andi, perched beside him on the passenger seat of his pearl-white M-reg Scorpio Ghia.

'How many times have I heard that? I'm still not sure you really mean it,' she said, as he pulled off the forecourt and forced his way into the right-turn-only lane to avoid the half-mile queue for the pumps in either direction.

'Honest, love. I do mean it. Cross my heart, on our babies' eyes.'

The babies in question were sitting in the back seat, oblivious to their parents, to each other, to the outside world.

Katie was now fifteen and had a portable stereo permanently glued to her head. Occasionally she paused to change her chewing gum or call a friend on her pay-as-you-go mobile.

Her semi-permanent pout could not, however, obscure her looks. Katie was destined to break a few hearts. She was a pretty girl, dark-haired, olive complexion, slight, boyish figure, pert nose, just like her mum, who was of Greek Cypriot extraction, maiden name Androula Kleanthous, known to all as Andi.

Katie would sometimes complain that she wasn't as full-hipped or ample-breasted as her classmates, but Andi reassured her that she'd be grateful for that in twenty or thirty years' time.

Andi herself could still squeeze into a size ten at forty-plus and compared to some of the grotesque, lard-arsed old boilers outside the school gate, looked like a movie star. That's what Mickey told her, at any rate.

And he meant it.

Young Terry, just coming up thirteen, was built like Mickey. He was already 5ft 9ins, just four inches short of his dad, and weighed in at eleven stone. He adopted the same cropped haircut as his father, but unlike his dad not out of necessity.

Mickey's fighting weight was fifteen stone, but he'd gone to flab since he left the Job. Not so as you'd notice, mind. He came from a long line of dockers, brick-shithouses of men who could carry a few extra pounds. But Mickey knew.

Terry pulled down the peak of his baseball cap to obscure the light shining on the screen on his Gameboy.

They were driving from their home in the village of Heffer's Bottom on the Essex borders to Goblin's Holiday World on the south coast for a long weekend.

Driving would perhaps be overdoing it. Inching forward in a southerly direction might be more accurate, that's if you didn't count the regular periods of complete standstill.

Despite Katie's initial protestations, she was looking forward to the holiday. She doted on her dad and vice versa. They didn't see much of each other, never had really, what with Mickey's work when she was growing up. He was always there, though, when it mattered, and she appreciated that.

Her friends had parents who were always going on about spending 'quality time' with their children, but Katie could tell they only ever thought of themselves.

Who needs quality time when you've got quality parents?

Apart from the metallic leakage from Katie's Walkman, the occasional 'cool' from Terry as his micro-electronic alter ego slayed some more aliens and the Rocktalk 99FM soundtrack on the radio, all was peaceful and cordial.

'You still don't believe me, do you?' Mickey said.

'If you say so.'

'No, love, this is important to me. I don't want you to think that I'm still pining for the police.'

'Yeah, yeah.'

'What's with the yeah, yeah?'

'Mickey, you were married to the Job for as long as you've been married to me. You were like a bear with a sore head for months after you put your papers in.'

'Not any more. The game's not worth the candle.'

'I never thought I'd hear you say that.'

'Me, neither. It's just, well, you know.'

'What?'

'For instance, take that last news bulletin.'

'I thought your mate read it very well. For once. He didn't stumble. Or swear.'

'Come on, Andi. Be fair. Ricky's cleaned up his act.'

'About time.'

'Case of having to. Anyway, it's not how he read it, it's what he read.'

'What about it?'

'Two news items, right? Between them they just about sum it all up. On one hand, we've got waves of so-called asylum-seekers pouring into Britain, scrounging, thieving . . .'

'You can't lump them all together as crooks and scroung-ers,' Andi interrupted. 'My family are immigrants. We came here to make a better life, too, just like some of these people. You don't think we're all scroungers and crooks.'

'I know that, love. But there's a world of difference between your people and what we've got now. Your family came prepared to support themselves, brought skills, started businesses. Look at your dad. Asked for nothing, built a chain of restaurants from scratch.'

'So what's your point? How do you know we won't have a Romanian or a Kosovan restaurant on every High Street in ten years' time?'

Mickey laughed. 'Don't hold your breath. OK, so some are genuine, I'm not denying that. But there's a fair share who have just come to take, not give. Beggars, pickpockets, all sorts. We're talking organized criminal gangs from East-ern Europe. Interpol know who they are. The Branch know who they are. And what does Old Bill do about it?'

'What are they supposed to do, Mickey? It's the govern-ment letting them in.'

'Yeah, OK. But the chief constables bleat about lack of resources, yet they're never short of money – or "ree-sor-sis" as they always call it – when it comes to those poor sods on the M4, just trying to get to work, visit their gran in hospital, who knows? They crawl for ever at about 5 mph, then the moment they find themselves out of the woods they're nicked for doing more than 15 mph, pulled over, random breath-tested, tyres checked. How much does all that cost?'

'Oh, I forgot to tell you,' Andi interrupted. 'Mum got a ticket the other day. A foot over a zigzag line, outside the chemist's, picking up her prescription.'

'Bastards. There you go,' said Mickey. 'Yet at the same time, there's gangs of bandits heading for the West End with rail tickets paid for by the good old British taxpayer. And even if they are caught, they get a slap on the wrist and a pound from the poor box.'

'That's not the police, Mickey. That's the courts.'

'Accepted. But there's never any leniency when Muggins in his Mondeo gets another three points on his licence, a thousand-pound fine and another few hundred quid on his insurance. We're letting off real villains and at the same time turning as many decent folk as possible *into* criminals. That wasn't what I joined the police for. And you know what really pisses me off?'

'Go on, you're going to tell me anyway,' Andi chuckled.

'I know most of this is the fault of the politicians. But there are plenty of Old Bill who not only go along with it, they abso-bloody-lutely love it. From the Black Rats in the jam-sandwiches to the fast-track fanny merchants at the top. That's why I'm well off out of it. Now do you believe me?'

'Every time, lover.' She squeezed his hand and smiled. It was a while since they'd been away as a family and nothing was going to spoil this holiday. 'You all right?'

'I'm fine. Sorry to bang on, love. It's just, you know, every now and then.'

'Sure, I know. And I'll tell you something. I'm glad you're out of it, too. I wasn't certain how you'd be, at first. There were a few difficult days, you know.'

'Yeah, I'm sorry. It took me a while, that's all.'

'It was bound to. I did understand. If I got a bit agitated sometimes, it was only because I was worried about you. After the, well, you know, after that, after you were shot, not knowing whether you were going to make it. Then not knowing if you'd walk again. Or work again. Not that that mattered. I'd have got a job, we'd have been all right, really we would.'

Mickey squeezed her hand back. Funny, they didn't talk about it much at home. Too painful, maybe.

They weren't like those couples who were always talking and touching for fear of what might happen if they stopped. They didn't need to. So much between them went unspoken.

But he found it easy to talk to Andi in the car. It wasn't that he dreaded eye contact. He adored eye contact with her, especially when they were making love. Conversation came easier when he was in the motor, that's all.

Maybe it was a legacy of all those stakeouts, all those long nights in smelly squad cars, full of stale burgers, flatulence, boredom, anticipation and, yes, fear, real fear. He never knew whether the target would be tooled up, how he would react. He'd been trained, programmed, honed, briefed, but when push came to shove, fear and adrenalin kicked in.

And when it happened, there was farce and fuck-up, too. Like on the night he stopped the bullet which nearly killed him.

'We don't need to import criminals. We've got enough scum of our own,' Mickey reflected, as the traffic again ground inexorably to a standstill.

*　　*　　*

It was a routine stakeout. Mickey and his colleagues from the armed response unit were parked up outside the Westshires Building Society in Hornsey, north London.

They'd been in this situation dozens of times, acting on information received that rarely came to anything. For once, it was game on.

Chummy strolled round the corner and into the building society, wielding a shotgun, blissfully unaware that the police were lying in wait, courtesy of a friendly, neighbourhood grass who offered him up over Guinness and Jameson's in the back bar of the Princess Alexandra in exchange for a bit of leeway on a handling charge he was facing in the not too distant.

Challenged by armed officers inside the building, the robber turned and ran. Mickey and two other firearms officers chased him through an industrial estate and onto the railway line.

He was a big lad, out of Seven Sisters, strapping, gangling, six foot tall, and, still clutching the shooter, he ran, ducking and weaving through the parked cars, dodging between the railway carriages.

The police got lucky when he caught his left size-twelve Timberland mountain boot in a badly maintained bit of track, snapped his ankle like a Twiglet and could only crawl underneath a derelict wooden goods van, which hadn't moved since Dr Beeching.

Trapped, frightened, fuelled by cocaine, he started firing. He wasn't much of a shot and Mickey and the lads fell back on their training, took cover and followed procedure, which was to lie low, not return fire and wait for the negotiator to arrive.

The temptation, the natural inclination, was always to storm the blagger and stick a shooter up his nose. But as a specialist weapons officer, Mickey knew to play the long game, the waiting game. It usually worked. Only very occasionally did someone get hurt.

When it went wrong, it went horribly wrong. Mickey had been on the Libyan Embassy siege when a gunman started firing out of the window into St James's. He was only yards away from WPC Yvonne Fletcher when she went down.

The bastard who fired that fatal shot got diplomatic immunity and walked free. It still riled Mickey all these years later.

He had been in Tottenham, too, the night PC Keith Blakelock bought it at Broadwater Farm, hacked to death, his head severed and paraded on a pole.

In the railway siding, Mickey had bided his time, even though five minutes seemed like a lifetime in these circumstances. Then he saw one of his colleagues, Jimmy Needle, leap up and start to run in the direction of the embankment. Two young boys had wandered onto the line from the nearby playing field to see what all excitement was about and had stumbled straight into the line of fire.

As Needle ran towards the boys, the blagger, Lincoln Philpott, he was called, panicked and loosed off a couple of shots.

By this time Mickey was on his feet. Philpott fired wildly and inaccurately, blasting anywhere. Mickey felt a sudden, almost dull, thud in his back, then a burning, piercing sensation, like acute kidney pain.

The next thing he was lying face down, paralysed in agony. One bullet had ricocheted off a carriage and thudded into Mickey's lower back, smashing his discs.

I can't feel my legs, he thought. For some reason the first thing that came into his mind was that old hospital joke.

'Doctor, I can't feel my legs.'

'That's because we've had to cut your arms off.'

Mickey, despite the pain, smiled inwardly. They say that from adversity comes humour. Something like that, anyway. And Mickey spent his life trying to see the funny side. If you didn't, you'd end up like the Michael Douglas character in that movie, *Falling Down*, roaming the streets firing at random.

They put him back together in the spinal injury unit at Stoke Mandeville, but he was out of the game in plaster and traction and therapy for the best part of nine months.

They offered him counselling, but Mickey declined politely. He would have declined impolitely had they insisted.

Some time afterwards, he was talking about it with Ricky

Sparke over a couple of large ones in Spider's Bar, a downstairs drinker in Soho, run by a dubious Irishman called Dillon.

'You know the worst thing about it, Rick?'

'The pain?'

'Nah, nothing like that.'

'What then?'

'Michael Winner.'

'Michael Winner, what's he got to do with it?'

'He runs this police trust thing, for coppers who get shot on the job.'

'And?'

'Well, I'm lying there in Stoke Mandeville, minding my own, head down in a George V Higgins, more plaster than Paris, and in walks Winner with a posse of Fleet Street's finest and a couple of film crews from the TV. He's come to present me with an award.'

'That must have been nice for you.'

'I'd have done a runner but I couldn't move. And the next thing I knew, he was on me. All that cigar smoke, all those dinners. After he'd gone I asked the nurse to give me a bed-bath – though it would have taken a fortnight in a Jacuzzi full of Swarfega to do the job properly.'

Dillon sent over a couple of glasses of his own special concoction – Polish spirit and schnapps marinaded with chilli peppers for a month in the deep freeze.

They swallowed the glutinous liquid whole, Eastern European-style. It was the only way. Otherwise it could strip the enamel off your teeth. If there had been a fireplace they would have thrown their glasses into it. There wasn't, fortunately, just a battered sofa where the fireplace would have been, containing an actor who used to be in a cat food commercial sleeping off a three-day hangover.

'Actually, Winner wasn't the worst thing, mate,' said Mickey, as the drink brought about its inevitable melancholic meta-morphosis.

'No? What's worse than Michael Winner?'

'Not much, it has to be said. But it wasn't just being shot. I half-expected that. It wasn't even Philpott walking on a technicality, much as that churned my guts. It was the way his brief told it, made it sound as if we'd planted the gun on him. He painted Philpott as the victim in all this and us as the villains of the piece. That's what hurt.'

'First thing we do, let's kill all the lawyers. That was what Shakespeare wrote, if my O-level English serves me. Hal to Dick in Henry the Something, part, oh I dunno, let's have another drink,' Ricky mumbled.

'Fromby.'

'Eh?'

'Fromby. Philpott's brief. Smug, self-righteous bastard. Justin fucking Fromby.'

'Mickey. Mickey. Mick-ee!' Andi prodded him in the ribs. 'Wake up, Mickey, the traffic's moving.'

'What? Oh, sure. I'm sorry love, I was miles away,' he replied, easing the Scorpio into Drive and resuming their journey.

'Anywhere nice?' she asked.

'Nowhere I'd want to take you and the kids,' he said. 'Nowhere I want to go again in a hurry.'

Mickey checked his watch, a silver Rolex presented to him at his leaving do. Mickey joked it was the best fake Rolex he'd ever seen. Everyone laughed, although he noticed the detective in charge of the whip-round could only manage an embarrassed grin. Mickey didn't ask and he didn't check subsequently, either. It was the thought. And the watch told the time and hadn't gone rusty, not like some of the moody kettles he'd seen over the years.

'Wossamatter, Dad, why aren't we moving?' Terry asked, looking up from his Gameboy.

Mickey explained that the annual festival of digging up the roads used to run from February until the end of the financial year at the start of April. Now you got roadworks all year round, like strawberries. They used to be seasonal, too. That's progress.

On Rocktalk 99FM, Ricky Sparke was back-announcing 'The Guns of Brixton' by the Clash prior to reading out another bunch of delays. He could only hope to scratch the surface. So many roadworks, so little time. He hadn't even mentioned the little local difficulty Mickey currently found himself in. Any delay less than an hour was hardly worth the bother any more. People had come to expect it.

Still, that was then. Whenever he felt bitter, Mickey took stock of his life. He was at least alive, he had a reasonable pension, around £25,000 a year, which he supplemented driving Ricky Sparke around and doing the odd job for a local chauffeur firm. He had a beautiful wife, two smashing kids and his mortgage was paid off. And now they were on their way to Goblin's Holiday World. Life could be very much worse.

Now they were on the move again, through the waste-lands of north-east London on a new swathe of road for which hundreds of solid, Victorian artisans' cottages had given their lives.

There were GATSO speed cameras every eight hundred yards or so, rigidly enforcing a totally unnecessary 40 mph speed limit. Even though Mickey knew the odds were that only about ten per cent of them were likely to contain any film, he wasn't taking any chances and drove at a constant 39 mph in the middle lane. He didn't need any more points on his licence and, anyway, they were bringing in the new digital cameras which didn't need film, nicked you for fun.

Driving was what he did for a living these days. How else was Ricky Sparke going to get home from Spider's of an evening without getting mugged or arrested if Mickey and his Scorpio were off the road?

Either side of him, cars, vans and lorries hurried by, accompanied by a flashing of camera bulbs which would have done credit to the paparazzi outside a West End premiere. Their drivers saw spot fines and suspensions as an occupational hazard, in much the same way old-time villains did their bird without complaint even if they'd been fitted up. If they get caught this time, it's outweighed by all the times they weren't. It comes with the turf, or, rather, the tarmac.

Mickey couldn't see the point. In a mile or two the shiny new freeway would end abruptly and all three lanes would be funnelled into two, then one. Why risk three points and a couple of hundred quid just to be two or three minutes earlier to the traffic lights or next set of roadworks?

He plucked another wine gum from the packet on the dashboard and popped it in his mouth. Soon three lanes became two, 39 mph became 20 mph became 10 mph became stop. Mickey found himself at the head of a new queue at a red light, halting traffic at the start of a single lane, cordoned off with the inevitable cones and, unusually, tape, the kind police use to seal off a scene of crime.

Suddenly he was aware of a swarm of bodies around the car, filthy water being sloshed on his windscreen, knuckles rapping on the side windows. Mickey waved them away to no avail.

He could see the faces pressed against the glass, foreign faces. There must have been ten or a dozen, swarthy, olive-skinned young men with gold teeth in designer clothes, women in shawls and headscarves with babies in arms, thrusting their hands towards the car.

'Money, money, give me money, English. Hungry. Help. Give. My baby starving.'

'Dad, Dad, make them go away,' Katie implored him in panic.

'Don't worry, darling, we'll be on the move soon. Stay calm.'

'But they're frightening me, Daddy.'

'Just ignore them,' said Mickey, checking the central locking and securing the windows of the Scorpio.

A woman threw herself across the bonnet, pleading,

18

cajoling. 'Money, English. Give. Hungry. Refugee. Money.'

'Get off the car. I said, get off the car,' Mickey shouted at her.

Terry started hammering on the inside of the rear passenger window, where a menacing face thrust itself towards him. 'Fuck off, fuck off, just fucking FUCK OFF,' he shouted.

'TERRY! Stop that. STOP IT. You'll only make things worse,' screamed Andi, freaked by the stifling, claustrophobic atmosphere inside the Scorpio.

'Change, you bastard, CHANGE,' Mickey hollered at the red light. But the red light stared back defiantly.

'DADDY! DADDY! They're trying to get in the car,' Katie called out hysterically. Mickey could hear the sound of the rear hatchback being jemmied open. All their luggage, Andi's jewellery, their holiday money in Mickey's travelling case. It was all in there.

There was a deafening crash to his left. One of the gang had taken a crowbar to the front passenger window. Mickey looked across to see his wife showered with hundreds of shards of glass, cowering in her seat. The assailant tried to force the door, but the Ford central locking held.

Andi was petrified, clutching her handbag as an arm reached through and grabbed for it. Mickey couldn't hear himself think. The shattered window had triggered the alarm, which pierced the air.

Terry lunged forward and seized the arm, wrenching it away from his mother. Mickey saw a gleam, a flash. He knew instantly it was a blade. He dived across and grabbed the attacker's wrist as the knife flashed just inches away from Andi's cheek.

The fist dropped the blade into Andi's lap. Mickey picked it up and, instinctively, plunged it into the hirsute forearm being gripped by his son.

He could hear the scream of the attacker above the cacophony of the car alarm. Both arms withdrew, blood

19

spurting everywhere, splattering on the inside of the wind-screen, erupting over the dashboard. More beggars threw themselves at the vehicle.

Mickey wrenched the car into reverse and stamped on the accelerator. There was another agonizing screech as the legs of the man attempting to jemmy open the rear tailgate were crushed against the reinforced front bumpers of the car behind, a blue Volvo 740 estate, driven by an Orthodox rabbi from Stamford Hill.

Mickey jammed the gear lever into first and stood on the gas pedal. The car surged forward through the tape, scattering the cones, mounting the pavement.

Mickey's vision was obscured by the blood on the wind-screen. He tried to wipe it away with his hand, but it smeared. Steering with one hand, he cleared a patch in the claret.

As he did so, he saw the crazed figure of a small, dark-haired woman, arms outstretched, holding her child before her, gesticulating in his direction, screaming hatred. Mickey threw the wheel left in an attempt at evasive action.

Too late.

The woman was hurled backwards and a small body propelled through the air. It bounced once on the bonnet, slammed into the windscreen, rolled under the front nearside wheel and was gone.

Mickey shuddered to a halt.

'What are you DOING?' Andi cried, her face dripping with blood. 'Just DRIVE, Mickey. Get us *OUT OF HERE!*'

'But the baby.'

'Fuck the fucking gypsy baby. What about your babies? DRIVE!'

# Three

Mickey swung the Scorpio into the car park of a huge, half-timbered Thirties roadhouse, now plying its trade as an American theme restaurant, at least a mile from the scene of the ambush.

He looked across at his wife, who was shaking and crying uncontrollably. He turned to his kids in the rear seat. Katie was screwed up in a ball, in the fetal position, sobbing.

Terry was bouncing, his eyes on stalks, popping out of his head, blood all over his sweatshirt and on the underside of the peak of his baseball cap. The adrenalin was still pumping. He was punching the roof lining of the Scorpio and roaring like a young lion after his first kill.

'Yes, yes, YES!' Terry cried, triumphantly.

'Terry, son. It's all right. Calm down. You did well. Just, you know, chill. Cool. Whatever you call it,' said Mickey soothingly.

He put his arm round Andi and pulled her close. 'Are you hurt?'

'No, I don't think so,' she replied, fumbling inside her handbag for a wet-wipe. 'It's not my blood, lover. I'll live.'

They both turned to Katie, shivering on the back seat, her arms across her head, trying to shut out the horror of it all.

Mickey disengaged the central locking, silenced the alarm and got out of the car. He walked round to the rear passenger side, opened the door, picked up Katie and cradled her in his arms.

'Katie. Katie, darling. It's all right. We're all fine. It's all over.'

She threw her arms round his neck. He could feel her warm tears on his face, could taste her terror. She whispered in his ear: 'Daddy, make it better.'

Mickey looked at the Scorpio. Or rather what was left of it. The lunchtime trade arriving for overcooked burgers and rancid ribs surveyed the devastation.

'My God,' said Mickey. 'The baby.'

'What?'

'That woman's baby. I think I killed it. I've got to go back.'

'You can't be serious,' Andi said.

'Deadly. Look, take the kids inside. Clean yourselves up. I have to go back. I used to be a police officer, for God's sake. Can you remember that? Please.'

He went to call the police on his mobile, then realized someone would have done it already. But Mickey had to return to the scene. He was looking at failing to stop, failing to report an accident, malicious wounding, death by dangerous driving, even, and God knows what else.

OK, so there were mitigating circumstances. Self-defence, reasonable force. But these things had to be done by the book.

'I won't be long. Promise. I have to do this. Get the kids a burger or something.'

Andi knew resistance was futile. He would do the right thing. That sometimes infuriated her, but that's why she loved him.

Mickey got back in the car, which looked like a left-over from a demolition derby. He turned the key in the ignition, selected Drive and rolled the car back onto the main road.

He drove slowly, unsure of just how far he had come. In the distance he could see the flashing blue light of a patrol car. As he approached, he saw an officer in a fluorescent yellow jacket in animated conversation with a rabbi.

But something was missing. Where were the roadworks? There were a few lengths of tape, fluttering in the breeze, but nothing else.

He pulled in to the kerb, walked over to the officer and introduced himself. 'I think you're looking for me.'

'I've just been hearing all about it from this gentleman here,' he said, indicating Rabbi Chaim Bergman. 'Are you all right, sir?'

'Er, yes, I suppose so. In the circumstances.'

'And the family?'

'I left them at that burger place down the road. You'll be wanting a statement from me.'

'That won't be necessary, sir.'

'Won't be necessary? This was like a fucking war zone twenty minutes ago.'

'So it might have been, sir. That was twenty minutes ago.' He looked at Mickey. 'I know you, don't I? You were an instructor at Hendon. Weapons, right? Sergeant French, correct? You got shot, over in Hornsey?'

'Um, yes. And it's *former* sergeant. I put my papers in. It's plain mister now.'

'You don't remember me. PC Cartwright, Tony.'

'Now you come to mention it,' said Mickey, looking around him, puzzled.

'Yes, you failed me.'

'Sorry about that.'

'No hard feelings. I did an advanced driving course and landed the area car. You probably did me a favour.'

'Glad to hear it. But I don't understand what's going on here.'

'The good rabbi was just explaining. Apparently, after your contretemps with our Eastern European guests, they gathered up their wounded and ran off through that council estate over there.'

'But where are the traffic lights? The cones? The rest of the tape?'

'They took that, too.'

'WHAT?'

'We had heard rumours, but we've never caught them at it.'

'At *what*?'

'They bring the traffic lights with them, in a van. Then they set up a fake set of roadworks. The tape makes it look official. Gives them a captive audience. They're very well organized.'

'So none of this . . .'

'Apparently not, sir.'

'But what about the fella with the knife? I mean, I . . .'

'Now then, Sergeant, sorry, *Mister* French. I'm sure I don't have to tell you the inadvisability of incriminating yourself. The way it looks to me is that with no victim, there's been no crime. No crime, no complainant, no report, no problem. Unless, of course, you wish to make a complaint?'

'Er, no, forget it. Thanks.' Mickey turned to go. 'Hang on, what about the baby?'

'Ah, yes, the baby,' said the PC. 'Come with me.'

He led Mickey over to the side of the road where a small, crushed figure lay crumpled in a bundle of blankets.

He kicked it.

The blankets fell open to reveal . . . a life-size doll.

'I'm sure they can afford another baby, sir. Mind how you go.'

# Four

**Then**

'You're WHAT? You can't be serious?' Justin Fromby unscrewed the top of another bottle of Bulgarian Beaujolais and filled a dirty half-pint mug to the brim. He scratched his balls and adjusted his flaccid dick. His Y-fronts had seen better days.

'Oh, I'm serious, all right. I have never been more serious in my life.' Roberta Peel rolled over on her grubby futon, reached for a cigarette from a pack on the sticky glass-topped coffee table, lit it and drew deep.

'But what about your work?'

'It *will* be my work.'

'I mean, the law centre. You can't turn your back on that.'

'I can do whatever I please, or do you only pretend to believe in women's lib?'

'Of course not. That's not fair. You know I'm committed to the Project. That's why I'm doing it.'

'But, the *police*, for God's sake. They're the enemy. You've always agreed on that. You saw what they did to the gay rights marchers. You were on that picket line at the power station. They're animals, pigs.'

'Precisely,' Roberta replied with a self-satisfied smirk. 'And what do you do with animals?'

'Liberate them?'

'Don't be daft, they're not smoking beagles or laboratory rats.'

'What then?'

'You train them.'

'Train them?'

'Haven't you ever heard the expression, if you can't beat 'em, join 'em?'

'Sure.'

'Well, we're never going to beat them. Not by marching and demonstrating. That's for students and idealistic dreamers. It's wanking in public.'

'But we've had some successes.'

'Such as? A few occupations, petitions? Stopping the traffic outside the Old Bailey? Gestures. You can't beat the system from without. You have to be within it to make any real difference. We have got to capture the institutions.'

'But that could take years.'

'About twenty, I reckon. Maybe twenty-five years at the outside.'

'But that's an entire lifetime.'

'Only if you're in your twenties. Look at the bigger picture, Justin. You've got a brain, use it. Ask yourself who, eventually, is going to have the biggest influence on the way society works – a 45-year-old overgrown student activist, pissing around on the fringes? A middle-aged trades union leader, locked outside the factory gates? A 45-year-old journalist churning out agitprop bollocks in a small circulation revolutionary newspaper on sale outside Woolworth's? A 45-year-old lawyer up to his arse in housing benefit applications and claims for wrongful arrest? Or a 45-year-old judge, a 45-year-old Cabinet minister, a 45-year-old editor of a national newspaper, a 45-year-old Commissioner of Police?'

'Hmm,' mused Justin, downing his rough red wine and pouring another from the bottle on the mantelpiece, perched next to a six-inch bust of Karl Marx, under the watchful eye of a Che Guevara poster on the voguish mud-brown wall. He wiped a tumbler with his discarded T-shirt, filled the glass and handed it to Roberta, still lying naked on the futon.

Two middle-class kids with law degrees, fresh out of university, sharing a top-floor bedsit in shabby Tufnell Park, their lives stretching out before them. It was a nowhere district between the Holloway Road and Kentish Town, north London, a tube station between King's Cross and Finchley Central, two and sixpence, Golders Green on the Northern Line. And it didn't have a park.

Roberta was plain, but that's the way she liked it. At 5ft 7ins, she was stocky, not fat, with full hips and firm tits like rugby balls, and had nipples you could hang a child's swing on. She favoured kaftans and sensible shoes. Daddy was a vicar, the Rev Robert Peel, in an affluent part of Surrey. He had wanted a son, so Roberta was named for him. Mummy something in the WI, a parish councillor and magistrate. Roberta was an only child and she was pampered, at least to the fullest extent of a parson's C of E stipend.

They were thrilled when she left her all-girls grammar school and went off to university to study law. Roberta was sad to leave St Margaret's, not because she was loath to shed the shackles of school. She had a crush on the games mistress.

Justin was the son of Edward Fromby, sole proprietor of Fromby & Fromby, the biggest retail coal merchant in Nottingham-shire, and, as he always referred to her at the Round Table cheese and wine evenings, his lady wife Mary.

Justin was christened Edward Albert Fromby, like his father, his grandfather and his father before him. Mr Fromby Snr wanted his only son to follow him into the coal and smokeless fuel business. But Edward Jnr persuaded him that the discovery of North Sea oil and gas would spell the end of the retail coal business.

After the miners' strikes of 1972 and 1974, no government was ever going to allow the nation to be almost wholly dependent on a dwindling resource subject to frequent interruption on the whim of a union run by Communists. He was very convincing. Secretly young Edward admired the Communists who ran the National Union of Mineworkers, but was too scared of his father to mention the fact.

Edward Fromby Snr was nothing if not a pragmatic man. 'I'm nothing if not a pragmatic man,' he said frequently. 'You don't succeed in the retail coal business without a healthy helping of pragmatism.' He acknowledged the merit in his son's argument and, after unsuccessfully trying to persuade him to go into the North Sea oil business, agreed that he should go to university to study law, hoping that he would return and get himself articled to the town's leading firm of solicitors, perhaps one day becoming senior partner.

Young Edward had a different compass. Wills and conveyancing held no attraction for him. He wanted to be a street lawyer, fighting for the rights of the downtrodden, the workers, the oppressed minorities. He wasn't going back to Nottinghamshire. He was going to London.

As soon as he got to the LSE, he dropped the Edward Albert and adopted Justin as his given name. Very Seventies, he thought. And if anyone asked about his family, he simply said his dad worked in the Nottinghamshire coalfields. He was careful not to lie but not to tell the whole truth, either. He must have been cut out to be a lawyer.

'Justin. That's a funny name for a coal-miner's son,' Roberta remarked when they were introduced.

'Hmm, yes, I suppose so. I wasn't christened Justin actually, but whenever I came home from school, my mother would call out "You just in, are you?" and it sort of stuck. A bit of a family joke,' he claimed. He almost believed it himself.

'So what were you christened?'

'Oh, it doesn't matter.'

'You're right. It doesn't matter. What's in a name? This is the 1970s. We can be who we want to be. If you want to be Justin, that's fine by me.'

Their friendship was forged at university. They weren't so much lovers as good friends who had sex sometimes, usually unsatisfactorily for both of them. But neither was experienced and neither was sure what to expect. Perhaps that was all there was to it. Roberta had been cloistered in an all-girls school and opportunities for adventures with the opposite sex were limited. Justin, or Eddie as he then was, had been an awkward, lanky youth. His overbearing mother had discouraged him from forming relationships with girls.

At university, Roberta experimented with other men, but they were usually pissed and it didn't seem much of an improvement on what she had with Justin. For his part, Justin didn't seem to mind who she slept with. Their friendship transcended the sexual.

He contented himself with his studies and increasing involvement in student politics.

Their relationship was more brother and sister, even if it was occasionally incestuous.

They were at ease with each other. They squabbled but had few hang-ups. They were not embarrassed to be naked together, or to bare their emotions.

Justin and Roberta lay on the futon and drained the last of the Bulgarian Beaujolais. Justin rolled a joint, which he liked to smoke with cupped hands, Rastaman style.

'Hey, stop hogging that,' Roberta complained. 'Pass it here.' She sucked hard and inhaled the weed, holding her breath for several seconds before releasing the smoke.

'This will have to stop, you know.'

'What?'

'Dope, booze. If you join the police.'

'There's no *if* about it. I *have* joined. I start two weeks on Monday.'

'Better make the most of it, then.'

He passed her the joint again. She took it, greedily.

'You sure it's worth it?'

'One hundred and fifty per cent certain. You are sharing a joint with the future commissioner of the Metropolitan Police,' she wheezed.

'Get real.'

'This *is* real. You watch me. And if you take my advice, you'll get out of that law centre and find yourself a proper job with a real law firm. Make a difference, Justin. Make a difference. You can do your *pro bono* social work in your spare time. We've grown out of "the revolution starts when this pub closes" stage of our lives. The revolution starts now.'

'If you're serious about this police thing, you're going to need me. You're going to have to make compromises, bite your lip, never let go in public. But there will always be somewhere for you to come. I will always be here for you. I will keep your secrets and never betray you. I do love you.'

'Then make love to me,' she demanded.

This was the bit Justin was dreading. He adored Roberta, loved to lie naked with her, but somehow the sex thing didn't really work for him. Still, he tried.

He rolled on top of her and kissed her dirigible breasts, almost choking on her rigid nipples.

'Fuck me. Fuck me hard,' she pleaded. 'Inside me, now.'

They'd already made love once that evening and it had been over in an instant. He'd taken her from behind. He found that doggy-fashion, in the dark, was the only way he could muster any enthusiasm. Twice in a night was asking a bit much and this time she wanted it on her back, with the light on.

Roberta reached down, ripped off his pants and squeezed his balls, but the best he could manage was a lazy lob.

By now she was frenzied, as the alcohol and narcotics kicked in, maybe for the last time in her life.

She grabbed his cock and pulled it towards her, willing him to harden. But it was no good. It was like trying to push a marshmallow through a letter box.

'Sorry, sorry, sorry,' Justin kept repeating. 'It must be the dope, or the booze or both. Just give me a minute.' He so wanted to please her.

But Roberta didn't have a minute to spare.

She reached up and lifted the six-inch bust of Karl Marx off the mantelpiece.

She lay back on the futon, raised her sturdy arse, parted her knees and thrust the father of international socialism head-first between the thighs of the future Commissioner of the Metropolitan Police.

# Five

## Now

'You're listening to the Ricky Sparke show on Rocktalk 99FM.
Let's go to George on line one. Morning, George. Good to have
your company today. What can we do for you?'

'Hello?'

'Hello.'

'Can you hear me?'

'Loud and clear, George.'

'Er.'

'Fire away, George. We're waiting.'

'You can hear me?'

'Yes George. You're live on air.'

'Is that you, Ricky?'

'No, it's the Samaritans, George.'

'What?'

'George, you're live on Rocktalk 99FM. You rang us. A
nation awaits your pearls of wisdom.'

'Well, like, what I wanted to say was, er . . .'

'Get on with it, George. I can't wait much longer. I'm losing
the will to live.'

'Well, you know, it's about these beggars, like.'

'What about them?'

'Well, er, something should be done.'

'And what precisely do you have in mind?'

'Dogs.'

'Dogs, George. I see.'

'They should set the dogs on them.'

'What dogs?'

'Police dogs, I dunno. Any kind of dog.'

'Alsatians?'

31

'Yeah. And Dobermans and Rottweilers.'

'Yorkshire terriers, miniature poodles?'

'Are you taking the piss?'

'Perish the thought, George. It's just that, well, don't you think dogs are a bit drastic? How about firehoses?'

'Firehoses. Yeah, why not? That's a great idea.'

'Flamethrowers?'

'I don't care, I just want them off the streets and back where they came from. It's not safe for a little old lady to go out of the house without being mugged or raped by these beggars . . .'

'Ah, yes . . . I was wondering when the little old lady would turn up. She normally makes an appearance whenever anyone runs out of rational argument. Tell me, George, when exactly was the little old lady in question last mugged or raped by a beggar?'

'I'm not taking anyone pacific, like.'

'Specific.'

'What?'

'Specific. The Pacific is an ocean.'

'Anyway, it could happen if something isn't done. These Romanians are a bloody menace. They should be rounded up at gunpoint and sent back to Rome where they belong.'

'Goodbye, George. Don't bother ringing us again. It's coming up to midday. That's all we've got time for today and this week, thank God. Join me again at the same time on Monday for another unbelievable assortment of losers and lunatics live on Rocktalk 99FM. Until then, this is Ricky Sparke, wishing you good morning and good riddance. We are all going to hell in a handcart.'

Ricky removed his headphones and threw them onto the console next to the cough-cut button and a rack containing eight-track cartridges. The red on-air light was extinguished, indicating his microphone was switched off. He put his feet up on the desk, lit a cigarette and leaned backwards.

Where on earth do we find these people? It was the same

every day, a telephonic procession of inarticulate imbeciles, radio's answer to the fish John West reject.

Ricky had one underpaid, overworked producer in charge of everything from the running order to making the tea and working the fax machine. His only back-up was a girl on a work experience scheme who couldn't operate the phones properly and appeared to be clinically dyslexic.

Rocktalk 99FM was the latest incarnation of a station which had started life eight years earlier as Voice FM. Its founders had won the franchise by persuading the Radio Authority they planned to broadcast a cerebral schedule of original drama, discussion, debate and documentaries dedicated to politics, humanitarian issues and the arts. It was going to sponsor live concerts and forums and gave a solemn and binding guarantee to recruit at least forty per cent of its staff from the ranks of the ethnic minorities.

That was the theory, anyway. The 'promise of performance' document managed to impress the assorted worthies who make up the Radio Authority, which regulates the commercial sector, and Voice FM was awarded a ten-year licence.

Six weeks before the station went on air, the founding fathers received an offer they couldn't refuse from an Australian consortium desperate to break into the British market. They trousered the thick end of £15 million between them and withdrew to spend more time with their mistresses.

When Voice FM was launched, it bore little resemblance to the original pitch. Having spent most of their money actually buying the licence, the Australians had virtually nothing left over to spend on content. Out went original drama, documentaries and live concerts.

There was certainly discussion and debate, if that's what you call cabbies from Chigwell complaining about cable-laying and bored housewives ringing agony aunts with their mundane grievances and PMT remedies.

As for recruiting from the ethnic minorities, that promise

was kept, up to a point. The security officer was Bosnian and the cleaners were all illegal immigrants from Somalia.

Two years on, Voice FM was relaunched as Bulletin FM, a cheap-and-cheerful rolling news station, hampered by the fact that it didn't actually employ any correspondents, just a roster of failed actors hired to read out agency reports and stories copied out of the newspapers and off the television by kids on work experience.

The traffic reports were delivered by one Ronnie Dugdale, an alcoholic ex-bus driver who had once enjoyed fifteen minutes' fame as a contestant on *Countdown*. He was the first player to score nil points, failing to muster any word over four letters and missing the target on the numbers board by more than two hundred. After the show he was escorted from the green room by security for attempting to grope Carol Vorderman, the show's attractive co-presenter. On the way home he was breathalysed, disqualified from driving for two years and sacked from the bus company. Still, it made him a minor celebrity and minor was all the celebrity Bulletin FM could afford.

When the motoring organizations withdrew co-operation because they hadn't been paid, Ronnie took to making up his traffic reports, which became increasingly bizarre as the day wore on and he shuttled backwards and forwards between the Bulletin FM studios and the Red Unicorn over the road. One afternoon, he arbitrarily announced the closure of half a dozen main arteries and advised drivers to avoid Westminster and Waterloo Bridges because of a fictitious demonstration and march by 20,000 dwarves, demanding equal rights for the vertically challenged.

Unfortunately, thousands of drivers took him at his word. It caused gridlock in central London on an unprecedented scale. The Strand was still jammed at two o'clock the following morning. He was fortunate charges were not preferred.

That was the end of Ronnie's radio career. Last heard of he was awaiting trial for driving a minicab through the front of a halal butcher's shop while several times over the limit and while still serving a suspended sentence for driving while disqualified, without insurance, road tax or a valid MoT certificate.

It was also the end of what passed for Bulletin FM's credibility. The station's owners decided that rolling news was not the way ahead and convinced themselves that sport was the next big thing. Having seen the success of Sky, they decided to launch a dedicated football station, Shoot FM. Not actually having the commentary rights to any live football, they were reduced to inviting listeners to call in match reports on their mobiles from the back of the stands. This lasted about six weeks, until the lawsuit landed from the Premier League. Shoot FM struggled on, covering non-league football and commentating on the Spanish Primera Liga, until Sky realized it was being ripped off and the commentator was in fact sitting in Shoot FM's studio watching the game on Sky Sports Three.

With three years left on the licence, the Aussies played their last card. Scouring the franchise document they discovered it allowed them to play forty per cent music by content. They decided they could always fill the other sixty per cent with phone-ins and thus Rocktalk 99FM, a mixture of classic rock and pig-ignorance, was born.

It coincided with Ricky Sparke, controversial columnist, being shown the door by the ailing *Exposer*, a downmarket tabloid aimed primarily at the illiterate and famous for being the first Fleet Street publication to feature full-frontal nudity.

The *Exposer* was Ricky Sparke's last-chance saloon as far as newspapers were concerned. He'd blown more jobs than Linda Lovelace, largely through drink and an inability to tolerate fools. He was a gifted polemicist but had a history of throwing typewriters through windows if some lowly sub-editor changed so much as a single syllable of his prose.

For once, drink and madness played no part in Ricky's downfall. His contract had run its course and the editor decided there was no longer any point in paying £100,000 a year to a wordsmith for a once-a-week column, given the fact that few of his readers could actually read.

Ricky was replaced by a former lap-dancer who dispensed sex advice in the form of a comic strip with voice bubbles, *True Romance*-style. When her first column appeared, readers were invited to take part in a competition to describe in no more than twenty words why they'd like to give her a bikini wax. The winner got to give her a bikini wax. Ricky entered under a false name and came second.

Ricky had frequently appeared on Voice FM, Bulletin FM and Shoot FM as a guest pundit, filling the voids between callers with sarcastic banter and mock outrage. It didn't pay much but there was always a steady supply of drink in the studio, which Ricky reckoned at least saved him a few bob. He was quite good at it, too.

When Rocktalk 99FM was launched, Ricky received a call from Charlie Lawrence, the programme director, who offered him a job as the mid-morning presenter.

Lawrence was a former salesman who started off selling solar-powered boomerangs to tourists at Circular Quay in Sydney, wound up in newspaper telesales and graduated to promotions manager at an ailing talk-radio station.

He transformed the station, turning it into Down Under AM, Australia's first all-gay on-air chatline.

Lawrence shipped up in London, headhunted by Rocktalk FM's Australian management in an act of desperation.

'We need controversy, we need to provoke people. We need someone who's not afraid to speak his mind. You're the man, mate,' Lawrence had insisted over a bottle of Polluted Bay Chardonnay.

Ricky didn't take much persuading. He was also available. What Lawrence didn't know was that Ricky had already been told his contract at the *Exposer* wasn't being renewed and that he had nowhere else to go.

Ricky was almost potless. Although he had always been handsomely paid, his prodigious thirst and the mortgage on his flat in a mansion block at the back of Westminster Cathedral swallowed his earnings. He could just about manage to service his credit cards and his extended bar bill at Spider's.

He could have lived somewhere cheaper, but he needed to be at the centre of town. He also liked being driven, especially since the London Taxi Drivers' Association had blacklisted him following a column in praise of minicabs. Ricky only discovered this when he clambered into the back of a black cab in Soho one night and asked to be taken home.

The driver looked at Ricky in the mirror and checked. He took a newspaper cutting off his dashboard, held it up to the vanity light, inspected it and turned to get a better look at his dishevelled passenger.

'You're him, aren't you?'

'Eh?'

'Sparke. You look older in real life. And fatter. But I can tell it's you.' The driver was clutching Ricky's picture by-line, torn from the pages of the *Exposer*. It had been taken some years earlier in a professional studio and enhanced by Fleet Street's finest photographic technology. Although Ricky had worn badly over the years, it was still recognizably him.

'OK, so it's me. Give the man a coconut. Now take me to Westminster.'

'You must be kidding, mate, after what you said about us. You're barred.'

'Then take me to the public carriage office. You can't do this.'

'I can do what I like. Now get out. Go on. Out!'

Ricky stumbled out of the cab and retraced his steps downstairs into Spider's. Dillon laughed when Ricky told him the story, gave him another one for the strasse on the house and called a local chauffeur firm to take him home.

When the car turned up, it was being driven by former police sergeant Mickey French, an old mate Ricky had known since the Seventies, when he was a local newspaper reporter and Mickey was PC at Tyburn Row, although he hadn't seen him for a couple of years. Mickey took him back to his flat, declined an offer of a drink and said he'd call Ricky in the morning. Since that night, Mickey had been Ricky's regular ride around town.

Not today, though. Mickey had taken the family off for a long weekend at Goblin's Holiday World and Ricky was left to his own devices. Lunch loomed. Ricky had no wife to go back to. He was married once, to a copytaker on his first newspaper, a printer's daughter from Lewisham, south-east London.

But it wasn't going anywhere. Ricky refused to go south of the river and she could never settle north. Since he never came home, it didn't really matter where they lived. She moved out, filed for divorce after less than a year of marriage and ended up with a used-car dealer in Eltham, three kids, a facelift, a tummy tuck and a villa in Marbella, where three times a year she topped up her fake tan with the real thing.

Ricky never remarried, was never bothered about children, rather liked his bachelor existence. The booze had taken its toll over the years, but had never taken over. Ricky prided himself that he always got up for work, no matter how rough he felt.

'I'm a milkman. I deliver,' was his proud boast. And he did deliver. Abuse and insults by the bucketloads, tipped over the heads of the great and the gormless, the rich and fatuous in a succession of newspapers. He'd always been good for circulation but his off-the-ball antics cost him a string of jobs, right back to the time when still in his teens he clattered the long-serving chief reporter of the long since defunct *Tyburn Times*, sending him tumbling downstairs, in a heated dispute over punctuation, and caused his first employer to tear up his indentures.

A quarter of a century later, he had mellowed, rather like a top-class single malt. Probably because of single malt.

His fighting days were over, ever since he had mistakenly stripped to the waist on the Central Line and offered violence to half a dozen Millwall fans making a nuisance of themselves on the way to Loftus Road. He spent three weeks in hospital as a result of that piece of foolhardiness. It cost him three teeth, replaced with some expensive bridgework. Ricky had been knocking off a divorced dental hygienist at the time and had been able to negotiate a discount for cash from the South African dentist with whom she shared a surgery. She eventually gave up on Ricky, hooked up with the dentist and moved to Jo'burg, where she was killed in a drive-by shooting. Some people never know when they're well off, Ricky remarked when he heard the news.

'How's it going, mate?'

Ricky looked up and saw Charlie Lawrence standing in the studio doorframe.

'This isn't a job for grown-ups,' he replied, running his fingers roughly through his hair, massaging his scalp as he did it, trying to relieve the tensions of dealing with the great unwashed and their uninformed, unfocused view of the world, three hours a day, five days a week.

'You look plenty grown up to me, mate. A little too grown. Not so much grown up as grown out. You should take up squash,' said Charlie, indicating Ricky's middle-age spread.

'You must be joking,' Ricky said. 'Anyway, this is all bought and paid for. Once you're older than your waist size, it's not worth the bother.'

'Oh, no? Take me, mate. We're, what, about the same age? I've still got a six-pack.'

'So have I. It's in my fridge and it's full of Guinness.'

'You should take more exercise. It'll do your temper good, too.'

'There nothing wrong with my fucking temper.'

'That's not what it sounded like to me this morning.'

'What are you going on about, Charlie?'

'I thought we were a little bit on the grumpy side today.'

'We? You mean me. Well, it's all right for you sitting in your strategy meetings. I'm the one who has to handle all these fuckwits. Who needs them?'

'That's where you're wrong, mate. They may be fuckwits, but they're *our* fuckwits. And we've got fewer of them by the week. *Who* needs them? *We* need them. The *advertisers* need them. *You* need them, mate. You *definitely* need them.'

'And what's that supposed to mean?' snapped Ricky, swivelling on his chair, his right arm colliding with his Rocktalk 99FM mug, sending stale, cold coffee cascading over the console.

'Can we have a word?'

'That's what we are doing, isn't it?'

'I mean an official word. In my office.'

'This is *my* office. Say what you've got to say.'

'I've just got these, mate. Take a look.' Charlie threw a stack of ring-bound A4 paper on the console. Ricky picked it up and studied it. Numbers, figures, graphs.

'What is this?'

'The RAJARs, mate. The official listening figures for the last quarter. We have been experiencing some very serious churn.'

'Since when have you been running a dairy?'

'You're the one who's always boasting about being a milkman. I'm afraid you're not delivering.'

'I'm here every day. I've never let you down.'

'We're not talking attendance here. You don't get a silver star for turning up. This is what matters,' said Charlie, pointing to the bottom line on the second sheet of paper.

'And what does it say?'

'It says that between nine and noon we are down almost thirty per cent. And who's on between nine and noon?'

'That's only to be expected. I'm new to the station. People have got to get used to me. You have to figure that it will take time to win people round. Three months ago, before I started, this was a football station, with no fucking football. I've had to start from scratch.'

'You can't argue with a fall of thirty per cent.'

'I can. Three months ago, the only listeners you had were a bunch of soccer-mad morons too stupid to find Radio Five.'

'That's as maybe, but there were thirty per cent more of them.'

'Of course, that stands to reason. The kind of terrace plankton you had listening to you then are hardly going to stay tuned for adult-orientated rock interspersed by saloon-bar pontificating.'

'I know that. But if you look at the figures more closely, you'll find that the new audience is falling away, too. It's down ten per cent over the past two weeks, according to our tracking.'

'You picked the format. And you picked the presenter. Me.'

'True. But I didn't know you were going to go out of your way to piss off the listeners.'

'I don't.'

'You do, mate.'

'Don't.'

'What about George just now?'

'The man was a fucking idiot. Turn the dogs loose on beggars? For fuck's sake.'

'A lot of people out there agree with him.'

'A lot of people want to bring back hanging, drawing and quartering.'

'Look, Ricky, all I'm saying is lighten up. Cut them some slack. Don't be so short with them.'

'Short is what I do.'

'So you've got to do something a bit different. Look on the audience as our customers. Be nice to them once in a while. Play to their prejudices. Don't sign off by dismissing them as a bunch of losers and lunatics. God knows what message that sends to the advertisers.'

Ricky got up and pulled on his coat from the back of his chair. He picked up his bag and headed for the door. Charlie didn't move.

'Excuse me, Charlie. I don't need this after a long week. I'm off to get pissed.'

Charlie's eyes hardened. His corporate smile faded.

'I don't think you've been listening to me, Ricky.'

'Sure I have.'

'Oh, I don't think so.'

'So what's your point?'

'My point is that this station, particularly in this time slot, is going down the dunny. I'm paying you a lot of money. Too much money. I'd never have given you so much if I'd known you'd already been kicked out of the *Exposer*.'

'I wasn't kicked out. I just, er, left.'

'Don't lie to me. They didn't renew your contract. And they replaced you with the Picture Book lady. I should have fucking hired her myself.'

'And what, exactly, is that supposed to mean?'

'It means that if these figures don't show a serious upturn, you're finished.'

'See if I care.'

'Oh, but you do care, Ricky. This is the last train to Clarksville for you, mate. There's not a newspaper left in London would hire you and if you screw up this gig, there's not another radio station would touch you either. Just you think on that when you're diving headfirst into the European wine lake in ten minutes' time. Think damned hard. Think about your bar bills and your monster mortgage on your funky little bachelor pad. You've got to raise your game. If we're not up at least thirty per cent, back to where we were, by the next survey, you're dead meat. You've got three months.'

# Six

Mickey French dropped Andi and the kids at her mum's house in Palmers Green. They'd driven straight there, round the North Circular. It was nearer than their home in Essex. Andi and the children went inside to change out of their blood-spattered clothes. Andi stood in the scalding shower for a good ten minutes, scrubbing her skin with a loofah, scraping away every trace of the red-hot gypsy blood, which had turned cold and caked in her hair.

'No, Mum, we're not hurt. Yes, Mum, we'll be fine.' If she said it once, she said it a dozen times as her mother fussed and fretted, while at the same time maintaining a steady stream of strong, dark, bitter coffee and rich Greek pastries.

'No, we're not going to the police. Mickey's dealt with it. We just want to put it behind us. Please, Mum, let's just forget it. We haven't lost anything, we're all in one piece.'

Terry stuffed his face with Nana's filo fancies and relived the adventure for Andi's mum's benefit. If it was possible to embellish their ordeal, Terry managed it. He couldn't wait to get back to school to tell his mates. This wasn't a playground punch-up, this was for real. As far as Terry was concerned it had been as big a step on the road to manhood as his first crop of pubic hairs.

Katie hugged her grandmother and let it all come out. After a long soak in a foaming bath, she dressed in the new jeans and spangly boob tube she had been saving for the first-night disco at Goblin's. With a bit of make-up she could pass for eighteen, she told herself. It made her feel better and helped her forget.

Mickey took the car to his cousin Roy's body shop in Crouch End. Roy replaced the broken window and rear tailgate lock with identical parts from another Scorpio, which he had towed in at the request of the police and was in the process of cannibalizing. It had been written off when it was wrapped around Crouch End clock tower by a team of joy-riders.

Roy said he agreed with Ricky Sparke's last caller that day. They should set the dogs on these bastards. You couldn't move in north London for gangs of gypsies, begging, mugging, burgling.

To make matters worse, Roy complained, the local council had spent a fortune housing them, yet his sister had been on the waiting list for twelve years without getting any nearer a ground-floor flat.

Mickey shrugged. He was all angered out.

'He's a mate of yours, isn't he?'

'Who?'

'That Ricky Sparke.'

'Yeah. I've known him for years.'

'How did you meet him?'

'It was when I was at Tyburn Row. I was a young DC on the Great Harlesden Cheese Robbery. Ricky was covering it for the local rag.'

'I vaguely remember that.'

'It was bloody hilarious. They were the most inept bunch of crooks I've ever come across. It was an inside job. The foreman and his brother-in-law did it.'

'How did you know it was an inside job?'

'Elementary, my dear Roy. They'd tried to make it look like a break-in. The foreman claimed the thief must have got in through a side window. But when I examined the scene, all the broken glass was on the outside. You didn't have to be Columbo to work it out.'

'Did he confess?'

'Not at first, only after we nicked the brother-in-law. You see, they hadn't lined up a buyer. They'd half-inched it on spec. And there isn't a ready market for several hundredweight of catering packs of processed cheese. The brother-in-law tried knocking it out round the pubs, but most of the landlords didn't want to know. We finally felt his collar when he walked into one boozer carrying a piece of Cheddar the size of a breeze block and offered it for a fiver to an off-duty police dog handler, who was in there having a quiet pint. He'd stashed it in his spare bedroom and it had started to go rancid. He'd forgotten to turn off the storage heaters. You could smell it two streets away.

'Ricky got to hear about it, I filled in the details and he wrote me up on page one of the *Tyburn Times* as some kind of latter-day Sherlock Holmes. It made the nationals. Ricky sold it to the *Sun* for £100 and gave me half.'

'Did you take it?'

'Yeah. I know I wasn't supposed to, strictly speaking, but it wasn't as if I was bent. Christ, you should have seen some of the coppers at Tyburn Row in those days. Bent as a pig's dick, most of them. Sure, I pulled a few strokes, cut a few corners, cocked a deaf 'un once in a while. But I wasn't on the take like some of them, so I looked on it as a kind of reward. I took Andi on a dirty weekend to Southend with it.'

'So that's where you got the money from. Her old man went spare, I seem to remember.'

'Yeah. Christ, it was like crossing the Corleones. The Bubbles can be just as grumpy when they put their mind to it. Insisted I married her. I was going to anyway.'

'You always were a sentimental old fucker,' Roy teased him. 'Go on. Get out of here. On your way.'

Mickey drove back to his mother-in-law's detached house, a substantial Thirties mock-Tudor with added Doric columns on the front porch. It had been bought outright from the proceeds of her late husband's kebab house empire.

Palmers Green was where successful Greek Cypriots settled, just as the Jews had earlier colonized Golders Green when they started to make their fortunes.

Mickey wondered where second-generation Romanian beggars might end up.

'All fixed,' he announced as he walked into the sitting room. 'Let's go home.'

'Mickey,' said Andi. 'We've been talking. And we've had a vote, haven't we kids?'

'A vote?'

'Yep. And we don't want to go home. We want to go on. We want to have our holiday.'

'Are you sure? Absolutely sure?'

'Uh-huh.'

'Terry? Katie?'

'Sure, Dad. It was unanimous,' Katie walked towards him and gave him a hug.

'Mickey, it's all bought and paid for. You've worked hard for this. We've all been looking forward to it.'

'Ma?' he said, looking at his mother-in-law.

'I tried to talk them out of it, Mickey. But you know my daughter. Determined, like her father, God rest his soul.'

Mickey smiled. 'OK, then. Let's go.'

They got back in the Scorpio. Mickey slipped his favourite Blues Brothers tape into the cassette deck and pulled on his Ray-Bans.

'Right, then. It's sixty miles to Goblin's Holiday World. It's getting dark and we're wearing sunglasses. Hit it.'

Their laughter was drowned out by Sam and Dave.

It was as if nothing had happened.

They weren't to know then that nothing would ever be the same again.

# Seven

**Then**

As a graduate entrant, with an honours degree in law, Roberta Peel sailed through the Metropolitan Police training school at Hendon. Next stop was Bramshill, the officers' academy. She had been singled out for fast-track promotion. But for the time being she found herself as a probationary WPC, stationed at Tyburn Row, attached to the juvenile bureau.

It was a typical old red-brick London nick, the sort of place Dixon of Dock Green would have recognized, scheduled for closure in two years on the planned amalgamation of three divisions in a purpose-built new station.

WPC Peel was working the night-shift, sipping tea and reading the *Guardian*, when she was summoned to the custody area. Another constable, Eric Marsden, had brought in a 15-year-old boy on a charge of malicious wounding.

He was a wiry, black youth, about 5ft 9ins, with an ebony complexion and afro haircut. He wore a leather bomber jacket, plain green T-shirt, flared denims and a pair of red Kickers.

He was being held in an adult cell, as there were no separate juvenile facilities. Roberta could see he had clearly been roughed up.

Eric Marsden was a beat cop of the old 'clip 'em round the ear' school. Except that he didn't always confine himself to clips round the ear. The boy had a split lip and there were signs of swelling around his right eye. As Roberta entered his cell, the boy was clutching his ribs.

It was alleged that he was part of a gang involved in a fight with some local white skinheads outside a chip shop. One of the white youths had been slashed with a blade and Marsden had recovered a knife which had been bagged and was awaiting a fingerprints examination. The white youth had identified the boy in custody as his assailant.

'Are you all right?' she asked him.

The boy stared at the floor.

'Who did this to you? Was it the arresting officer?'

'No it fucking wasn't,' a cockney baritone voice boomed. Roberta turned to discover Eric Marsden looming up behind her. He was a big man, 6ft 1ins, a couple of stone overweight.

'You better watch that mouth of yours, my love.'

'I am not your love. I am the juvenile officer responsible for this suspect's well-being. I am trying to establish the truth here.'

'He's been in a gang fight. You should get your facts right, sweetheart, before you go making allegations.'

'I am not making any allegations. I am making inquiries.' She decided to let the sweetheart pass for now.

'Well you can start by inquiring as to what his fucking name is, for a start. I'm going to the canteen. We can't interview him until his parents or a responsible adult get here. And that can't happen until we establish exactly who he is. He's all yours, darling.'

'I am not your darling, either.'

'I suppose a gobble's out of the question?' Marsden laughed out loud, turned on his heel and headed for the canteen, where he could slag off Miss Prim and Proper fucking fast-track graduate entrant to his mates over a bacon sandwich.

'What's your name?' she asked the boy. 'It will be better for you if you tell me. The sooner we can notify your parents, the sooner we can interview you, the sooner you can go home.'

'I don't want my parents. I want a brief.'

'I'll call a duty solicitor.'

'No. Get me Mr Fromby.'

'Mr Justin Fromby?'

'You know him.'

'I've heard of him. Doesn't he work at the law centre?' said Roberta, anxious not to let on.

'Yeah.'

'I'll see what I can do.'

Roberta left the cell door open and walked along the corridor.

'He wants a solicitor,' she told the station sergeant. 'He's asking for Justin Fromby.'

'That's all we fucking need, that Trotsky wanker,' said the sergeant. 'You won't find him at this time of night.'

'Oh, I think I might be able to find a number for him.'

'How are you going to manage that?'

'I'm supposed to be a police officer, aren't I? The phone book might be a start.'

Roberta slipped into a side office and dialled Justin's number from memory.

He answered after a couple of rings.

'Justin, it's Roberta.'

'Hi. You coming over?'

'No. I'm at work. Can you come here?'

'I'd rather not. I've just got back from the RAC rally.'

'RAC rally? You don't even drive.'

'Not the RAC, the *RAC* – the Rock Against Capitalism rally at the Roundhouse. The Jam were top of the bill. Your American friend, Georgia Claye, was there. You should have seen the state of her. Out of her skull on something. She tripped over pogoing to "Eton Rifles" and smashed her head on the side of the stage. I helped carry her out.'

'Never mind her, Justin. She'll end up living in a cardboard box the way she's going. You know her husband's left her already?'

'The Italian guy, medical student?'

'Yeah, anyway, I haven't rung you to discuss Georgia Claye's problems. This is important. We've got a boy in custody and he's asking for you.'

'For me? What's his name?'

'He won't tell us.'

'What does he look like?'

'Black, slim, 5ft 9ins, afro, age about fifteen, I should think.'

'Hmm.'

'Do you know him?'

'Maybe.'

'Well he knows you.'

'What's he in for?'

'Malicious wounding.'

'OK. I'm on my way.'

Justin Fromby called a cab and arrived at Tyburn Row three-quarters of an hour later.

The desk sergeant needed no introduction. 'Evening, Trotksy,' he said dismissively. Justin didn't rise to the bait.

Roberta appeared from the corridor.

'This is Mr Fromby,' the sergeant told her.

'Pleased to meet you, Mr Fromby,' she said, without the slightest hint of recognition. 'I'm WPC Peel, from the juvenile section. If you would be kind enough to follow me, I'll take you to your client.'

Roberta showed Justin into the cell.

'Hello, Trevor,' said Justin, immediately.

'Hello, Mr Fromby.'

'You two obviously know each other.'

'Yes, WPC Peel, we do. This is Trevor Gibbs. He lives on the Parkgate Estate. I know his father.'

'Don't tell my dad, please Mr Fromby.'

'OK, but they'll need your name and address. I'll handle it.' He turned to Roberta. 'The law allows my client to be interviewed in the presence of a parent or responsible adult. I shall sit in for his father.'

They walked out of the cell and back to the custody area.

'The boy's name is Trevor Gibbs,' she told the sergeant. 'He is ready to be interviewed. Can you call PC Marsden?'

'I'll fetch him from the canteen. I fancy a cup of tea. The walk will do me good,' the sergeant said.

Once the sergeant had left the custody area, Roberta ushered Justin into an ante-room.

'Well? Who are we dealing with?'

'His dad is Everton Gibbs. He's the community leader on the Parkgate. A good man, standing for the council. What about the boy? What have you got on him?'

'He's alleged to have cut another boy, a white youth, in a fight outside the chip shop. Marsden found a blade and he's bagged it for prints.'

'That's unfortunate.'

'What do you mean?'

'Three weeks ago, in this station, I represented him. He was cautioned for possession of a knife. On the day-shift. I forget the name of the arresting officer off the top of my head. Young chap, maybe twenty-three or -four. Trevor's father doesn't know. If any of this came out it could seriously undermine his position. He might even lose the election. We need men like him on the council. We've got to prevent Trevor being charged.'

'How the hell are you going to do that? Marsden brought him in, he'll be the interviewing officer. I'll only be sitting there.'

'I can handle Marsden. But you'll have to lose the knife and his form.'

'I can't do that, for God's sake. What if someone found out?'

'They had better not. Look, it's late, there's hardly anyone around, no one will know.'

'Marsden will.'

'He's a lazy bastard. I've come across him before. A bit too handy with his fists. I'll deal with him.'

When Marsden appeared five minutes later, Roberta retrieved Trevor Gibbs from his cell and led him into the interview room.

Justin spoke first. 'I would like to place on record that this is an unlawful arrest. My client has been subjected to a racially motivated assault. He is the victim here. Furthermore he alleges that you, PC Marsden, beat him up. I am preparing a formal complaint.'

'Oh, do fuck off, Fromby. I've heard it all before. All the spades pull that stroke.'

'I won't listen to racist language,' Roberta interrupted.

'You'll shut up and do as you're told, petal. Or have you been promoted while I've been in the canteen?' Marsden barked back.

'This young man's father is a respected figure in the community, a personal friend of your commanding officer. You, on the other hand, have a reputation for, shall we say, heavy-handedness. Given the choice between a frightened, fifteen-year-old boy from an oppressed minority and a fat thug like you, I think I know who people will believe.'

'This interview is suspended right now,' Marsden said. 'Take him back to his cell,' he told Roberta. 'We'll resume later.' Marsden returned to the canteen to consider his options. Justin went outside for a long smoke.

As Roberta led Trevor Gibbs through the custody area, another young officer was bringing in a prisoner, a drunk and disorderly.

PC Mickey French smiled at Roberta, then looked at her prisoner. As they passed, Mickey grabbed hold of Trevor's arm, spun him round and took another good look.

'OK,' he said.

'Mickey?' said the desk sergeant.

'Nothing, sarge. Let's get this geezer booked in, D&D. Complaint from the landlord of the Dun Cow.'

Roberta put Trevor back in his cell and left the custody area. She walked along the corridor, past the canteen, up the stairs and into the juvenile bureau. She switched on an anglepoise lamp and walked over to a filing cabinet. It was unlocked. Under G, she found it. Gibbs, Trevor, possession of an offensive weapon, to wit, one knife. First offence. Caution administered and recorded. Arresting officer, PC107 French.

Fuck it.

'Found what you were looking for?'

Mickey French startled her.

'Er, yeah.'

'And what are you going to do about it?'

'What do you mean?'

'I've been talking to Eric Marsden.'

'And?'

'Fromby's trying to fit him up on an assault on the prisoner.'

'I reckon he did beat him.'

'Eric denies it. Says he got the injuries in the fight outside the chip shop. Sounds about right. I nicked Gibbs the last time. He's a nasty little fucker. You going to charge him?'

'Mr Fromby says that if we charge Gibbs, he'll make a formal complaint against Marsden.'

'If this caution comes to light, you've got no option but to charge him.'

'What should I do?'

'That's up to you, girl.'

Roberta thought that this was no time to raise the issue of inappropriate sexist language. Actually, she rather liked Mickey. He wasn't as much of a bastard as the older Plods.

'Fromby knows about the previous. He wants me to lose it. And the knife,' she blurted out in panic.

'What, this one?' said Mickey, waving a plastic bag above his head containing the knife Marsden had confiscated from Trevor Gibbs.

'Where did you get that from?'

'Never you mind. What are you going to do with the previous?'

'The way I see it is that everybody wins here. Fromby gets what he wants, Marsden's off the hook. Everybody's happy,' she replied, nervously.

'And what if I don't give a fuck and turn you in?'

Roberta froze.

Mickey raised his other hand. It contained a small cassette recorder. It was still running.

Shit.

'Give me that,' he said, motioning his hand towards the folder Roberta held under her arm. 'You're a lucky girl.'

'Lucky?'

'There's two copies still in here. Usually we keep one and send the other to central records at the Yard. This hasn't gone off yet. I must have forgotten.'

'So what happens now?'

'You're a silly fucking cow. Old Eric Marsden may be a cunt but he's only got a year left to his pension.'

Roberta was in no position to take exception to the use of the vaginal expletive or to protest about being called a silly fucking cow. She knew she was a silly fucking cow. At least on this occasion.

'So?'

'So why wreck anyone's career here. Eric Marsden's or yours?'

'What about the sergeant?'

'He is the original wise monkey. He sees nothing, hears nothing, says nothing. He doesn't want to know. No charge, no paperwork. He's sweet. Fromby's hardly going to say anything. The boy certainly won't object to being released. Eric will stay shtoom and he'll put the frighteners on the skinhead who picked him out. He'll tell the sergeant that Gibbs is being released pending further inquiries. That'll be the end of it.'

'And you? What's in it for you?'

'I don't want Eric going down the shitter and I reckon you've got a big future.'

Nice tits, too, he thought.

'What are you going to do with all this – the knife, the file, the tape recording?' she asked.

Mickey stroked the stubble on his chin and shrugged his shoulders. 'I haven't thought about it. Nothing, maybe. Who knows?'

# Eight

Ilie Popescu knew the men from Moscow would come looking for him. His father, Marin, had set him up in the car-smuggling business and sent him to Hamburg, where he stole Mercedes, BMWs, Audis and Porsches to order and shipped them to the former Soviet Union. The hard cash he sent back to the Tigani helped finance his father's other line of business, an organized begging racket across Western Europe.

At twenty-one, Ilie was an accomplished car thief. It was easy money. In the first six months, Ilie successfully stole and despatched cars worth almost $3 million on the black market. The deal was always cash on delivery.

On a roll, emboldened by an unblemished track record, Ilie met his Russian contact and explained that in future he would need half the money up front. He had overheads, he explained. There were police officers and port security guards to be paid off.

The message was relayed to the men in Moscow, who were unhappy about the new terms and conditions. But they trusted Marin Popescu, with whom they had done business for several years since the fall of Communism. They would extend that trust to his son.

A week later, Ilie received $500,000 in advance of his next consignment, in unmarked, used notes in a leather attaché case, passed to him by his contact in a bar off the Reeperbahn. In return he was handed a list containing the marque and specification of the vehicles he was to supply, some of them destined for clients in the Middle East.

The deliveries were to be completed within one month.

Ilie would receive the balance when the cars arrived in Moscow.

That gave him plenty of time to party. He was a good-looking boy, lean, about 5ft 9ins, with short, jet-black hair, chocolate-brown eyes and a winning, slightly menacing, smile. In Hamburg, he had developed a taste for expensive clothes, nightclubbing, whores, cocaine and gambling.

Cocaine and gambling don't mix. There's calculated risk and then there's recklessness. Ilie came down on the recklessness side of the equation. In one week in the casinos, Ilie blew the thick end of $350,000 on the tables, $350,000 the Russians had given him as a down payment.

So what? Ilie told himself. It doesn't concern them. They'll get their cars and I'll get the balance.

The cocaine convinced Ilie he was invincible. It also made him sloppy.

His *modus operandi* had always been to target vehicles belonging to Hamburg's high-rollers and wealthy industrialists, importers and exporters. He stole them individually from parking lots and garages, paying off chauffeurs and car park attendants for information and silence.

Single car thefts attracted little attention from the authorities. The owners were irritated, but insured for full replacement value. Why should they worry?

Within a fortnight, Ilie had frittered the whole $500,000. He hadn't stolen a single car for over two weeks, his Russian contact was becoming concerned. Don't panic, Ilie reassured him. Have I ever let you down?

That night, his tame policeman, Jurgen Freund, called at his hotel for his regular $10,000 monthly retainer. He found Ilie in bed with two whores. The room was littered with empty bottles – champagne, Polish vodka, scotch. The whores were sharing a substantial joint. Ilie's eyes were on stalks and his nose was streaming.

'I've come for my wages,' the cop said.

'You'll have to wait. I don't have the money right now,' Ilie replied.

'Not good enough,' Freund said.

'Hey, relax, man. Have a drink. Have a smoke. Hey, baby,' he said to one of the prostitutes. 'Be nice to the man.'

'I didn't come here to get laid. I came to get paid,' Freund said angrily. 'Two weeks ago, you received $500,000 from the Russians. Do you think I'm stupid? All I want is $10,000. You owe me.'

'I said you'll get it.'

'You're running out of time. You'll never make your delivery. You haven't stolen one car in the last two weeks.'

'I'll be fine. I've got it covered.'

'Don't get careless,' Freund warned.

'I've got it all worked out. There's a car transporter coming in from Wolfsburg on Friday. Problem solved.'

'That's not the way it works.'

'It does now. Why steal cars one at a time when there's a dozen for the taking? It makes no sense.'

'Only if you've done the amount of coke you have, Popescu. You must be mad. You'll attract attention to yourself. We might be able to overlook the odd Mercedes here, the occasional BMW going missing there. But a transporter-load? No fucking chance.'

'Who's running this operation?' Ilie barked.

'You're on your own this time, my Roma friend.'

'Fuck you,' screamed Ilie, pulling a pistol and pointing it at Freund's face. The cop backed away from the gun and opened the door to leave.

'Fuck you, I don't need you. You're off the payroll. Now get out.'


Two days later, a car transporter pulled off the autobahn near Hamburg and onto a slip road. It drew to a halt at a set of temporary traffic lights.

Ilie Popescu and another Romanian, Gica Dinantu, also from the Tigani, scrambled up an embankment, scaled the side of the cab and ordered the driver at gunpoint to get out and surrender the keys.

The driver offered no resistance. He climbed calmly from the transporter and walked away with a measured step. Ilie took over in the driver's seat, Gica rode shotgun.

As Ilie engaged the gears and eased the transporter forward, the driver started to run. He threw himself over the embankment and rolled downhill.

Ilie laughed. This was a piece of piss. He pressed the accelerator and drove the giant transporter straight through the traffic lights, which he had put there fifteen minutes earlier.

Ilie Popescu had just stepped up a division and out of his league.

As the transporter rounded the first bend, Ilie was confronted with the flashing blue lights of a police roadblock. Cars and personnel carriers filled the road ahead. Armed officers crouched behind them.

Freund, the double-crossing bastard.

Fuelled by cocaine, Ilie hit the gas and charged the roadblock. A volley of shots pierced the windscreen. Ilie ducked instinctively as the first salvo somehow missed his head.

Freund had no intention of taking them alive.

'Gica, fire back man, FIRE BACK,' he screamed. His words landed on dead ears.

In the passenger seat to Ilie's right, Gica Dinantu was slumped forward. The top of his head had been shot off. Blood and brains oozed out of his skull.

Ilie ploughed through the roadblock, scattering police cars like Dinky toys. Bullets bounced off the side of the transporter and ricocheted around the cabin. Miraculously, Ilie was unscathed.

The massive bulk of the transporter was being propelled with unstoppable momentum. Despite the power steering, Ilie struggled to maintain control. The tail of the heavily laden articulated vehicle swayed violently from side to side, like an agitated alligator.

Ilie clung on as he kept his foot flat on the floor, trying to put as much distance as possible between himself and the Hamburg police department armed response unit.

In the passenger side rear-view mirror, Ilie spotted a police motorcycle gaining on him. The pillion passenger had a high-velocity rifle trained on the transporter. The cop fired twice, puncturing the front nearside tyre, which exploded and shed its rubber tread like orange peel.

Ilie hit the brakes. As he did so, the police motorcycle skidded, hit a pothole and began to cartwheel. The two officers were killed on impact as the bike sliced through the back window of a brand-new Mercedes E320 estate car, upon which an antiques dealer from Hamburg had already paid a substantial deposit.

They were ejected onto the tarmac when the transporter lurched to the right and turned turtle at 110 kmph. It skidded off the road and travelled a couple of hundred metres on its roof, crushing its top floor cargo like cigarette cartons, before spinning again and crunching to a halt, driver's side up.

Ilie had retained consciousness throughout, courtesy of the copious quantity of cocaine he had consumed before setting out on his first big-time lorry hijacking.

He tried to push open the driver's door, but the force of gravity conspired against him. He attempted to lower the window, but the electrics were dead. With his right foot, he kicked out what remained of the windscreen, unfastened his seat belt, swung from the door handle and jumped.

He landed safely and rolled, parachute-style, away from the transporter. He looked up and saw in front of him an M320 sport utility vehicle which had slipped from its berth of the lower deck of the transporter, been thrown clear and landed on all four wheels, remarkably unscathed.

Ilie yanked open the door, dived under the steering column and twisted the ignition wires together. The old hotwire routine. The engine sparked into life.

The tank contained enough gas to put maybe ten kilometres between Ilie and his pursuers, if he was lucky. The motorcycle cops were the advance guard. The rest of the posse was still some way off.

Ilie pushed the gear lever into Low and engaged the four-wheel drive. He guided the M320 about fifty metres away from the scene of the crash and turned towards the transporter, which lay motionless on its side, displaying its seventeen remaining tyres and soft underbelly.

Ilie lowered the electric driver's side window, pulled the pistol from his belt and pumped six shots into the fuel tank. As the first flames shot into the air, Ilie gunned the M320 in the opposite direction.

He was about 250 metres away when he heard the explosion. The reflection in the rear-view mirror turned bright orange. The heat from the fireball engulfed the M320 but it outran the flames. Ilie didn't look back. He knew the inferno would keep the chasing policemen at bay.

With any luck they would think he had perished along with his childhood friend, Gica Dinantu, and one million dollars' worth of Daimler-Benz automobiles.

But that wasn't all that went up in flames.

So did Ilie Popescu's chance of recovering the $500,000 he owed the Russians.


Marin Popescu had listened in silence as Ilie related his predicament. He could not believe his son's foolishness.

After abandoning and torching the M320 on the outskirts of Hamburg, Ilie had found his way back to the Tigani via the extensive network Marin used to infiltrate his gangs of professional beggars throughout Western Europe. The German police would eventually piece together what had happened and the men from Moscow wouldn't be far behind.

Marin knew they would come. There would be retribution. And first he had to break the news of the death of their only son, Gica, to his old friends, the Dinantus. They would blame Ilie, two years Gica's senior.

Marin was furious but he had to protect his son. Fortunately for Ilie, Marin didn't only smuggle cars, he smuggled people.

Ilie joined a party of Roma bound for England. Marin gave him $5,000 and told him to lose himself as soon as he got to London. He was not under any circumstances to contact his elder brother, Boban, who ran the London end of the car theft racket. They would be watching Boban, Marin warned. Nor must he attempt to phone home. Ilie would have to vanish until Marin could square things with the Russians. Marin would get word to his son when it was time.

Ilie and the other Roma, men, women, children and babes in arms, who had paid $3,000 each for their passage to England, left Romania at the town of Timisoara, on the Hungarian border. They were hidden in false ceilings in lorries and driven across Europe to Calais. Once there they were transferred to fresh vehicles and loaded on cross-Channel ferries, unhindered by the French authorities.

Ilie and the others had their instructions. Once at sea, they were to destroy all the passports and documents, anything which might identify them. Britain had a reputation throughout Eastern Europe as a soft touch, for interpreting the 1951 Human Rights Convention on Refugees more liberally than any other country. Asylum-seekers from Kosovo, Albania, Bosnia and Romania poured daily across the Channel.

Ilie and his party had been abandoned at a motorway service area near Ashford in Kent. The women had immediately started begging outside a fast-food outlet. The men banged on car windows at petrol pumps, demanding money. The children descended on the convenience store and stole everything they could carry.

When the outnumbered private security staff called the police, a single squad car arrived. The officers handed out leaflets in thirty-two different languages, many of them scribble, instructing the new arrivals to make their way to the immigration service reception centre at Croydon, in Surrey. Transport would be provided.

Ilie's instinct was to slip away. But where to? He couldn't get in touch with Boban. He needed a new identity. He boarded the luxury coach laid on by the local authority and travelled with the rest of the party to Croydon.

If he bucked the system, he reckoned, he might still be arrested and deported.

At Croydon, as a further precaution, he told the inquiring immigration officer through a resident translator that he was sixteen. His father had told him they could not deport him if he was a minor. Ilie could just about pass for sixteen from a distance. The immigration officer looked at him and shrugged. He was past caring. He was on a promise and just wanted to get home for the night.

Under 'age', he wrote 'sixteen'.

Under 'name', he wrote down the first name that had come into Ilie's head. The name of the man Ilie left dead by the roadside in Hamburg.

'Gica Dinantu.'

# Nine

> 'And in a late-breaking story, before the Deputy Prime Minister flew off to Acapulco he decreed that as part of the government's integrated transport policy the whole of central London, Birmingham and Manchester were to be pedestrianized. He also confirmed that proposals to put humps and other traffic-calming measures on motorways were being studied at the highest level in line with global warming and road safety targets. That's all for this bulletin. Next news in an hour. You're listening to Rocktalk 99FM, your first choice for classic rock and conversation. Here's Jimi Hendrix with some of that old "Crosstown Traffic".'

Mickey hit the OFF button. He'd had enough crosstown traffic for one day. Enough cross-country traffic, too. Enough motorway traffic. Enough traffic to last him the rest of his life. Full stop. But they'd made it. Four and a half hours after leaving Andi's mum's house in Palmers Green, and several light years after leaving home, the French family finally arrived at Goblin's.

As they drew up to the entrance, Mickey couldn't help noticing that the 'l' and 's' were missing. The gap-toothed neon sign above the door consequently read 'GOB IN'. It made it sound like a punk rock revival.

The car eased to a halt. Mickey put on the handbrake. No one else stirred. Terry had eventually come down to earth on the south side of the Dartford River Crossing and had collapsed into a deep sleep.

Sheer exhaustion had caught up with Andi and Katie, too. They had both slept most of the way and Mickey had to content himself with Rocktalk 99FM for company.

He only really listened to the station because Ricky Sharpe worked for it. He thought the other DJs were brainless chimps, who belonged on children's television. He liked the music, though, so he stuck with it.

'Andi, wake up love,' he said, gently shaking his wife's right shoulder. 'We're here.'

The kids were unconscious. 'Come on kids. Terry, son. Kate, love. Wake up, bambinos. The eagle has landed.'

Mickey eased himself out of the car with a modicum of difficulty and lit a Marlboro. He could feel his back. Although the doctors at Stoke Mandeville had made a fine job of rebuilding his shattered discs, his back was prone to seize up on long journeys. He had experimented with one of those seat covers made out of wooden balls, which some cabbies and bus drivers swear by. But he'd thrown it away. It had been like sitting on marbles and played havoc with his Chalfonts.

'Your back OK, Mickey?' Andi asked, with a trace of anxiety. She still feared it might snap without notice.

'A bit stiff. I need to straighten up.' Mickey stretched, rocked on the balls of his feet, supported his weight on the driver's door and attempted a couple of squat thrusts, which brought on a violent bout of coughing.

'I think you're supposed to take the cigarette out of your mouth first,' Andi joked.

Mickey smiled back. 'A Radox bath should do the trick.'

'I'll give you a nice massage, if you play your cards right.' She blew him a kiss.

'Carry on like that and it won't only be my back that's stiff.'

'Dad! Mu-um!' said Katie. 'Don't be so-oo gross.'

Mickey and Andi reddened. They'd thought the kids were still asleep.

'Only joking,' Mickey said. 'You know we're far too old for that sort of thing.'

'Old enough to know better, too,' Katie played along.

Secretly she was thrilled that her mum and dad still fancied each other. It's just that she didn't want them flirting in front of her. And they didn't usually. Although they had always been open with the kids, privacy was important, too.

Whenever they went away, even though it hoisted the bill, they always got the kids separate rooms of their own, ever since Katie had reached the self-conscious stage. They'd booked three rooms adjoining at Goblin's.

Mickey walked round to the back of the car and opened the rear tailgate. Cousin Roy had done a good job.

As he reached inside to begin unloading their luggage, Mickey heard a shout.

'Oi, you.'

Mickey looked up and saw a belligerent elf, about 5ft 11ins, in a Lincoln-green jerkin, green tights, curly boots and red felt hat, marching towards him, gesticulating like a deranged tic-tac man. He wore a green and white badge the size of a side plate, bearing the words: 'Goblin's Greeter. Here To Help You Have Fun.'

'Oi, you. Yes, you. I'm talking to you. What the hell do you think you're doing?' the elf barked.

'Excuse me. And who are you, exactly?' Mickey replied.

'Security.'

'You're kidding me. You don't look like security. You look like something that just fell off a toadstool.'

'Company policy. All employees dress like elves. Disney's got Mickey Mouse and Goofy. Goblin's has got elves.'

Whatever the outfit was supposed to achieve, the effect was spoiled by the clumsy tattoos on his forearms.

Mickey couldn't resist a loud guffaw. He thought about chinning him but decided against it. He was too tired for a start. Anyway, think of the court case. GBH on an elf. He'd never live it down. Easier to take the piss.

Mickey engaged the elf in eye contact, then slowly surveyed him, up and down, from the bell on his hat to the curly points of his pixie boots.

'And how many O-levels do you need for your job?'
Mickey asked.

'I'll have you know I used to work in a bank. But they've
shut down all the branches round here and replaced us with
hole-in-the-wall machines. You take what you can get. It
was either this or Burger King. Anyway, stop changing
the subject. You can't park here. Can't you read?' The elf
pointed to a sign indicating parking for the exclusive use
of staff.

'Just give us a minute, boss. I'm unloading my car.
I've just arrived. I'm checking in,' said Mickey, the joke
wearing thin.

'Well you can unload somewhere else,' the elf said.

'I'm supposed to be the guest here,' Mickey protested.

'Not my problem. Now move it, or I'll have it clamped.
There's a £120 recovery fee.'

'I don't fucking believe this.' A quarter of a century in
the police force and here I am being ordered around by a
fucking pixie, Mickey thought. 'This is unreal.'

'Only doing my job, mate,' said the elf.

'That's what the *Wehrmacht* claimed.'

'Eh?' said the elf.

'Ve vere only obeying orders, mein Führer.' Mickey
snapped his heels and thrust his right arm forwards and
upwards in a Nazi salute.

The elf took two paces back.

'Look, mate,' Mickey said, wearily. 'I know you've got
a job to do. But, as I said, we're the guests here, right?
We've had a long day, we're dog-tired. We just want to
get checked in, go to our rooms and sleep. So this is what
I'm going to do. I'm going to unload the car, put the bags
down here, and then, and only then, will I move the car.
Is that all right by you?'

'I suppose so.'

'Thank you.'

'Elves have feelings, too,' said the elf.

'Sure,' said Mickey. 'Tell you what, do us a favour. While

I'm moving the car, why don't you frolic indoors and get a porter to help us with our bags.'

'The porter doesn't work nights. Check-in time is 6 pm. You're late.'

'I know we're fucking late. You don't have to tell me we're late. I don't suppose you'd consider giving us a hand with the luggage?'

'Love to, mate, but I'm not insured, see. And I've got a dodgy back.'

'Tell me about it, mate.' Mickey shook his head.

Mickey dumped the bags on the kerb and Terry began to manhandle them up the steps to reception.

'That's all right, son. I'll do it when I've parked the car.'

'I can manage, Dad.'

'OK. But leave that big one. I'll fetch it indoors.' Mickey shut the tailgate and walked round to the driver's side door.

'Satisfied?' he asked the elf.

'Not quite.'

'NOW what?'

'This is a no-smoking facility. You'll have to put that out. We don't allow tobacco anywhere on the site.'

Mickey took a last puff, threw the stub on the floor and crushed it underfoot.

'And if there's anything else I can do to help, please don't hesitate to ask,' said the elf.

Fuck off and die, Mickey thought to himself. That would be a great help.

Mickey parked the car, walked back the hundred yards to reception, took the bags inside and registered.

The girl behind the counter was dressed in the same elfin uniform as the security guard.

'Check-in is 6 pm,' she said robotically, in the kind of voice employed by women in call centres.

'So we've been told.'

Mickey asked if there was any chance of getting something to eat.

67

'Sorree,' said the girl. 'Goblin's Grille closes at 9.30 pm, Monday to Saturday and 8 pm on Sunday.'

Room service?

'Sorree.'

Mickey asked if there was an all-night take-away nearby, where he might pick up some food.

'Sorree, guests are not allowed to consume food bought off the premises in their rooms. Policy. You'll find a full list of rules in the welcome pack in your room.'

Mickey would have to wait until breakfast, 7.30 am to 9.30 am, Monday to Saturday, 8.30 am to 10 am, Sundays.

The receptionist handed Mickey their room keys. 'Second floor. You'll have to use the stairs. The lift is out of order. Sorree.'

'Great,' said Mickey.

'Glad to be of assistance, Mr French. Welcome to Goblin's. Have a nice day.'

They lugged the cases up the stairs and, as Mickey settled the kids into their rooms, Andi ran him a hot bath.

'At least the water works.'

'Come on, it's not that bad.'

'No, of course not. I didn't mean it like that. It will be great, just great.'

'We'll unpack in the morning.'

'Fine.'

Mickey towelled himself dry and collapsed on the bed while Andi pottered in the en-suite bathroom.

He started to drift off, the horrors of the day subsiding.

He was on the brink of deep sleep when he felt a gentle tingle in his groin. He opened one eye and looked down as Andi ran her tongue between his balls and up the shaft of his cock.

'I'm sorry, love, I haven't got much energy,' he apologized, though he felt himself responding.

She looked up at him, doe-eyed, squeezed hard and lightly kissed the tip of his now engorged dick. 'You just lie there. This one's on me,' she said as she took him in her mouth, her eyes still locked onto his, which by now were both wide open.

'What have I done to deserve this?' he asked, desperately trying to delay the inevitable.

'Everything, lover. You've heard the expression: when in Rome?'

'Uh, uuugh,' Mickey grunted in acknowledgement.

'Well, as the lady said,' Andi smiled as Mickey's scrotum tightened, 'welcome to Goblin's.'

# Ten

## Tyburn Juvenile Panel

Wayne Sutton dug deep into his left nostril with the long nail on the index finger of his right hand, which had HAT tattooed, or rather Biro-ed, on the knuckles in erratic, pre-school letters. Wayne thought it spelled HATE. Spelling had never been his strong point, which, since he had rarely attended school, was no great surprise. He was once moved on for begging outside Tyburn tube station with a cardboard sign reading HUNGREY AND HOMLES.

Wayne dislodged a large, crusty bogey. He rolled it between his right thumb and forefinger, examined it, popped it in his mouth, toyed with it with his tongue, threw back his head and propelled it into the air.

'Wayne. Please pay attention,' said the plump, middle-aged lady sitting opposite him.

Wayne shrugged and tugged his right earring. He had the body of a man and the mind of a moron. He wore his lack of education on the sleeve of his designer shell-suit, which he had stolen at knifepoint from another kid on the Parkgate Estate. Taxing, he called it.

Ever since he was ten, he had terrorized the estate and its environs, leading a semi-feral existence. He was no stranger to the courts, but since the law granted him anonymity he was known to readers of the *Tyburn Times* only as Monkey Boy, owing to his ability to scale drain-pipes and gain entry to premises through upper-storey windows.

Wayne never knew his father, who could have been any one, or all, of a gang of bikers his mother had obliged in a caravanette in Clacton. Or a travelling salesman she had screwed on the end of Clacton pier in return for the price of a bottle of sherry.

Wayne's mum was a slag. There was no other word for it. She had stumbled through a succession of drunken, violent relationships, existing on benefits and a few extra quid selling her favours to old men in the derelict bowls club, which had been closed since Wayne's first, bungled, arson attempt.

She would meet her punters in the pub opposite the Post Office and, after a couple of milk stouts, would relieve them of their sexual tensions and a substantial part of their pension money. She even charged one old geezer an extra 50p for tossing himself off without permission while he was waiting in line.

It had been obvious to all that Wayne was being neglected and was in desperate need of a stable home environment. But social services, in their wisdom, rejected fostering on the grounds that it was best to keep the family together.

Family. That was a laugh. The only family Wayne had ever known apart from his mother was whichever feckless thug was currently punching his mum's lights out in between bouts of heavy drinking, drug taking and thieving.

'Mr Pearson, please continue,' said the middle-aged magistrate.

'Thank you, ma'am.' Mr Pearson cleared his throat.

'January 16. Abusive behaviour to staff and customers at Patel's Minimart and Video Library.

'January 22. Breaking a 14-year-old boy's arm at Tyburn fairground.

'January 23. Smashing a plate-glass window at Corkeez wine bar.

'January 28. Throwing stones from the bridge above the underpass in Nelson Mandela Boulevard onto passing vehicles.

'February 4. Shoplifting at Waterhouse's department store.

'February 7. Breaking the windows of a number of premises on the Parkgate Estate. The list is attached, ma'am.'

'I am obliged to you, Mr Pearson.'

'February 11. Setting fire to a tramp behind the Odeon.

'February 14. Abusive behaviour, criminal damage to St Valentine's flower display at Buds the florist in the High Street.

'February 21. Criminal damage to bus shelter.

'February 22. Shining a laser beam into the eyes of a cab driver in Roman Road, causing him to swerve and career into a fruit and vegetable stall, hospitalizing the stallholder, a Mr Bunton.

'March 2. Kicking over litter bins in High Street. Graffiti spraying on wall of Town Hall.

'March 6. Shoplifting in Waterhouse's again.

'March 9. Attempted burglary at SupaTalc the chemist's.

'March 17. Thrown out of Toy Town for attempting to steal Buzz Lightyear dolls.

'March 19. Threats made against cashier at Continental Stores in Market Road.

'March 25. Burglary of homes on Parkgate Estate. You have the list, once again, ma'am.

'March 31. Possession of controlled drugs, cannabis and Ecstasy tablets, with intent to supply.

'April 1. Urinating from walkway on Parkgate Estate onto the head of PC 235 Watkins, home beat officer.'

'I think we've probably heard enough, Mr Pearson. Thank you. I have read all the relevant papers and social reports.'

'Then you will see that over a five-month period this year, Wayne Sutton has committed no fewer that seventy offences, ranging from assault and robbery to taking and driving away motor vehicles, culminating in a high-speed chase through the Parkgate Estate in May. He is also in breach of a curfew order, imposed by this panel last December.'

'Indeed, Mr Pearson. I am most grateful.'

'In addition to the evidence in your file, we also have video footage of Wayne committing a large number of the offences, taken from the closed circuit security cameras in the High Street and within the Parkgate centre. In some of the footage, you will see Wayne actually waving to the camera, in the full knowledge that he was being filmed.'

Wayne smiled.

'Are you suggesting that Wayne knew the seriousness of his behaviour?'

'Without question, ma'am. He has been before this panel on a number of occasions, been subject to a series of supervision orders.'

'Yes, but does he realize what he is doing?'

'The police service are of the opinion that he does and that for his own benefit and the protection of the community at large, a custodial remedy would be appropriate and desirable. I would remind you that he has already broken an Anti-Social Behaviour Order.'

'And what do the probation service have to say on the matter, Mr Toynbee?'

Jez Toynbee looked up from the thick file in front of him. He had been christened Jeremy, but thought Jez sounded more democratic. At 5ft 8ins, he was no taller than his young charge, Wayne, sitting alongside him.

'Wayne Sutton is an averagely intelligent young man, in need of guidance and encouragement. He comes from a dysfunctional background. He has never had a father figure. His mother is an alcoholic, part-time prostitute. She undoubtedly loves Wayne, but is deficient in the parenting skills department. Wayne's only male role models have been itinerant men who formed temporary liaisons with his mother.

'We in the probation service believe that although Wayne is clearly disturbed, his offences were not committed out of wickedness but as a cry for help.

'While the panel has the power to send him to a young

offenders' institution, we do not believe that would be beneficial at this stage of his development. In fact, there is every reason to believe that it would actually be counter-productive.

'In a secure institution, Wayne would come into contact with other young offenders, which could further disrupt his personal development. We sincerely believe that he can be rehabilitated and go on to take his rightful place in society and make a full contribution.'

'Bollocks,' muttered Pearson under his breath.

'Did you say something, Mr Pearson?'

'No ma'am.'

'Pray continue, Mr Toynbee.'

'Thank you, ma'am. As I was saying, we believe that Wayne Sutton is not beyond redemption. The problem in his case has been his deprived childhood. He has not been showered with presents, like other children, which explains his thieving. He has never had the luxury of a family car, which contributed to his taking and driving away of vehicles. While his mother loves him, she has been incapable of showing him affection. He has been routinely assaulted by some of his mother's, er, male associates. He has a repressed anger, which manifests itself in assault and criminal damage.

'We believe that if Wayne can be shown the kind of affection missing in his life, can be exposed to some of the normal treats which other children expect as their birthright, he can be persuaded of the error of his ways. Before you consider a custodial solution, I would urge you to put this unfortunate young victim of society first. His welfare and his future must be paramount.'

'What, exactly, are you suggesting, Mr Toynbee?'

'The probation service, with the assistance of the local authority and the Victims' Trust, have recently established a scheme aimed at broadening the horizons of offenders like Wayne. Under close supervision, young offenders are taken beyond their immediate environs and given a glimpse of the wider world which awaits them. We find it helps them confront their criminality and makes them feel valued. In turn, this will help them reject their previous behaviour and become valued members of the community.'

'Very well, Mr Toynbee. This panel is always reluctant to impose a custodial sentence. Having read all the reports and having heard your submission, we are agreed that Wayne should be released into the supervision of the probation service. Wayne, stand up, please.'

Wayne dragged himself to his feet and stared past the magistrates and out of the window.

'Wayne, we have been persuaded by Mr Toynbee that you deserve one more chance to take your rightful, and lawful, place in society. But if you don't respond, you will find yourself locked up. You will report back here in three months. Do you understand?'

Wayne farted.

# Eleven

Ricky Sparke stumbled upstairs and, by placing one hand over his left eye, managed to locate the keyhole in the front door to his flat. He stepped over the pile of unopened mail on the doormat, threw his coat on the sofa and reached for the vodka bottle.

He unscrewed the cap and turned it upside down. It was empty. He wrung the neck, like a man strangling a chicken, but the bottle was spent.

Ricky retrieved another from the washing machine.

Since he had a laundry service, he had no need of the Indesit combined washer/drier. So he used it as storage space. Every other surface was covered with old newspapers, magazines, CD cases and LP covers with coffee mug stains on them.

Ricky picked up a dirty glass, wiped it on his shirt tail, poured a large slug of Smirnoff into it and topped it up with half a bottle of flat slimline tonic.

By drinking slimline tonic, Ricky had convinced himself that it wasn't really drinking at all.

It was his concession to fitness. He was always trying fad diets, none of which worked, largely on account of the fact that he would insist on supplementing them with vodka and Guinness.

He once went on a white wine only diet, after reading that Garry Glitter had lost three stone on it.

Ricky lost three days.

He devised his own version of the F-Plan diet. He called it the C-Plan. Ricky thought that if it worked he would market it and make his fortune.

The principle was fairly simple. You could eat anything you wanted, provided it began with C.

The diet started well on day one, Ricky eating nothing but cottage cheese and cabbage.

On day two, he dined on corn on the cob and cucumber.

Encouraged by the results, he extended the diet to his drinking habits. Two bottles of Chablis later, he moved onto Chartreuse and, eventually, Carlsberg Special Brew.

Then came champagne, chicken tikka masala, chips, cheese and onion crisps and cognac. He had completely forgotten about the chicken tikka massala until he brought it up on the platform of Upminster tube station.

Ricky had fallen asleep on the District Line, passed his stop at Westminster, slept all the way to Ealing Broadway, turned round and slept all the way back, past Westminster once more and onto Upminster at the eastern end of the line.

He was woken by a guard, turfed off the train, threw up, slipped in his own sick, smashed his head on a bench and passed out.

Ricky discovered a previously unidentified side effect of the C-Plan diet.

Concussion.

He slept the night on Upminster station and made his way back the following morning, breaking his journey at Aldgate East for an extremely painful and deeply unpleasant shit.

Since then he'd stuck to vodka and the occasional can of Nigerian lager, which had been his first news editor's pet name for Guinness.

Ricky took a slug of his vodka and slim and retrieved a can of Guinness from the fridge to chase it down with.

He made a mental note to go shopping the following morning, Saturday. He was down to his last bottle of vodka and five cans of Guinness. Oh, and some milk might come in handy, too.

Ricky slumped back on the sofa and hunted for the remote. He located it under a pile of soft-porn magazines. He didn't know why he bothered buying them any more. Half the time he was too pissed to toss himself off.

Ricky laughed. It was true. He was the one sad bastard who really did buy *Penthouse* for the articles.

Ricky hit the remote and the 33-inch Loewe TV in the corner came alive. Along with his Linn hi-fi, the state-of-the-art television was his pride and joy.

He loved his home entertainment. He was a cable junkie. And his collection of CDs and LPs, which he still played on a 20-year-old Linn Sondek LP12 turntable, was larger and more comprehensive than the record library at Rocktalk 99FM. Ricky often took his music in with him.

Charlie Lawrence didn't believe in wasting money on immaterial software, such as records. He relied on freebies. And since all the popular stuff disappeared overnight, Ricky reckoned that the only way he'd get a decent show on the air was by supplying his own CDs. Otherwise he'd be reduced to playing Lena Zavarone, Kenneth McKellar and the crass soft rock no one even wanted to steal.

Ricky flicked through the channels, hoping to stumble across some hard-core German channel.

It was always more in hope than expectation. The only porn he ever found late at night seemed to have been made in the 1970s. Before they got their kit off, all the players looked like Abba, during their 'Waterloo' period.

Ricky paused when he saw what looked like a game show come on. The spangled host grinned insincerely and introduced the programme.

'Good evening and welcome to a brand-new edition of ASYLUM!

'Today's programme features another chance to take part in our exciting competition: Hijack an airliner and win a council house.

'We've already given away hundreds of millions of pounds and thousands of dream homes, courtesy of our sponsor, the British taxpayer.

'And, don't forget, we're now the fastest-growing game on the planet.

'Anyone can play, provided they don't already hold a valid British passport. You only need one word of English:

'ASYLUM!

'Prizes include all-expenses-paid accommodation, cash benefits starting at £180 a week and the chance to earn thousands more begging, mugging and accosting drivers at traffic lights.

'The competition is open to everyone buying a ticket or stowing away on one of our partner airlines, ferry companies or Eurostar.

'No application ever refused, reasonable or unreasonable.

'All you have to do is destroy all your papers and remember the magic password:

'ASYLUM!

'Only this week one hundred and fifty members of the Taliban family from Afghanistan were flown Goat Class from Kabul to our international gateway at Stansted, where local law enforcement officers were on hand to fast-track them to their luxury £200-a-night rooms in the fabulous four-star Hilton hotel.

'They join tens of thousands of other lucky winners already staying in hotels all over Britain.

'Our most popular destinations include the White Cliffs of Dover, the world-famous Toddington Services Area in historic Bedfordshire and the Money Tree at Croydon.

'If you still don't understand the rules, don't forget there's no need to phone a friend or ask the audience, just apply for legal aid.

'Hundreds of lawyers, social workers and counsellors are waiting to help. It won't cost you a penny.

'So play today. It could change your life for ever.

'Iraqi terrorists, Afghan dissidents, Albanian gangsters,

*pro-Pinochet activists, anti-Pinochet activists, Kosovan drug-smugglers, Tamil Tigers, bogus Bosnians, Rwandan mass murderers, Somali guerillas.*

*'COME ON DOWN!*

*'Get along to the airport. Get along to the lorry park. Get along to the ferry terminal. Don't stop in Germany or France. Go straight to Britain.*

*'And you are guaranteed to be one of tens of thousands of lucky winners in the softest game on earth.*

*'Roll up, roll up my friends, for the game that never ends. Everyone's a winner, when they play:*

*'ASYLUM!'*

Was he taking the piss, or what?

Who could tell?

Ricky switched off the TV, picked up the CD remote and pressed PLAY. Randy Newman. 'Bad Love'.

Ricky drained the can of Guinness and topped up his vodka. He reflected on his earlier encounter with Charlie Lawrence.

Fuck him and his fucking job. Who needs it? Ricky's inclination was to walk away from Rocktalk 99FM. But Charlie Lawrence was right.

Actually, Ricky needed it. He'd never been out of work, he had an expensive flat and expensive tastes.

Tonight, Dillon had handed him his bar bill at Spider's. It came to £1,234.75. Ricky had to promise to pay him next week, when his salary cheque was paid into the bank.

Ricky collected the mail from the doormat.

Junk, bills, flyers, pizza menus, minicab cards.

And one registered letter, marked URGENT.

It was from the Tyburn Building Society.

> *Dear Mr Sparke,*
> *We note from our records that you are now four months in arrears with your mortgage. As of today (see date above) . . .*

Ricky looked at the letter heading. It was dated two weeks ago.

> *. . . you are deficient on your repayments to the tune of £7,240.70. Interest is accruing daily.*
>
> *Please contact us immediately and make arrangement for payment. Failure to make full restitution within twenty-one days will result in county court proceedings for recovery of the debt and repossession of the property.*

Shit.

# Twelve

Ilie Popescu swallowed another handful of aspirins to dull the pain. It had taken fifteen stitches to treat the deep wound in his right arm.

He had told the staff at North East London Memorial Hospital that he had impaled himself on a garden fork. His English was imperfect, but he could get by.

Ilie had given them the name he had adopted, Gica Dinantu, the name of his partner in crime, now deceased.

It had been accepted without question by the immigration officer at Croydon and since he had no papers, it was impossible to prove otherwise. He couldn't risk being traced.

Having registered at Croydon, he was issued with temporary papers and a berth in a hostel in Tottenham, which now housed almost a hundred asylum-seekers from Eastern Europe. It had been a dilapidated old people's home, due for closure. The local council shipped out the last of the elderly residents and spent £400,000 refurbishing the building in the style to which the migrants intended to become accustomed.

All rooms had satellite television and small refrigerators, like hotel minibars. There was a communal canteen offering a variety of food, no worse, Ilie thought, than his expensive hotel in Hamburg.

There was a snooker room and, in the grounds, a brand-new tennis court and five-a-side football pitch.

Ilie was amazed at the generosity of the British. He received free board and lodging, clothing coupons and £117.50 a week in cash, which he supplemented with the proceeds of begging and petty crime.

Ilie had struck up a friendship with a pretty Kosovar Albanian girl, Maria. They'd been hustling passengers on the London Underground when they were spotted by a gang of skinheads, roaming the West End rolling foreign tourists, putting the boot into beggars and nicking collecting tins from the homeless.

Ilie and Maria were chased up the escalators at Warren Street, through the Euston underpass and into the sidestreets at the back of the railway station.

They lost their pursuers in an alleyway behind the Exmouth, a popular pub with railway porters and guards. Panting furiously, hearts pounding, they grasped each other frantically. He hardened instantly. She reached inside his tracksuit trousers, lifted her skirt, put her arms round his neck and raised herself, straddling him. He pulled aside the gusset of her knickers and she lowered herself around him, knotting her ankles behind his back. The sex was violent and brief. They came together.

Since then they had spent every night together at the hostel. Their encounter with the shaven forces of English nationalism had not deterred their begging. Their expeditions became ever more ambitious.

Soon Ilie, or Gica, as even Maria called him, was running street crime and begging out of the hostel. There was no shortage of willing volunteers.

Using a stolen van, Ilie would transport his gang to various areas of London, where they would burgle, beg, snatch handbags and hustle drivers, posing as squeegee merchants at traffic lights.

It was Ilie's idea to steal the temporary traffic lights from the High Street and set them up at various locations. Easier to sting a captive audience. It was a variation on the idea he had used to hijack the car transporter in Hamburg, which would have worked like a dream had it not been for Freund's treachery. If he ever straightened things with the Russians, Ilie vowed, he would return to Hamburg one day and slit Freund's throat.

Ilie also came up with the idea of buying, or rather shoplifting, a doll to use as a prop. The English were mugs, he reckoned. Real suckers for a woman begging with a bay-bee.

That day they'd set up their phoney roadworks on the main drag through north-east London at the point where three lanes funnel into one.

Ilie's gang surrounded the car and went into their usual routine, banging on the windows, sloshing dirty water on the windscreen.

The driver was a big man, his wife much smaller. There were two children in the rear. A pretty little girl and a boy, younger, a scale model of his father.

Ilie tried to grab the woman's handbag, smashing the passenger window with a crowbar and reaching through with his knife to cut the straps.

The driver had grabbed the knife and buried it deep into Ilie's forearm, accelerated away, brushing Maria into the gutter.

At the hospital, they insisted on giving Ilie a powerful tetanus jab. Now his arse was sore, as well as his arm.

And for what? Nothing. They'd come away empty-handed.

Fuck it. If only he'd stuck to stealing cars. Why the hell did he have to get greedy?

Ilie made a mental note to steal a new knife. He picked up the cellphone he'd taken from a parked car in Dalston and which had been reprogrammed by a computer engineer from Montenegro, claiming to be an ethnic Albanian from Kosovo fleeing Serbian oppression.

Ilie studied the keypad.

He pulled a scrap of paper from his pocket and entered an eleven-figure number. Ilie pressed the green SEND button.

In a penthouse flat in Highgate, a stone's throw from Karl Marx's tomb, a phone rang.

Ilie's brother's phone.

# Thirteen

Mickey woke with a start. The noise jolted him bolt upright.

> *'Good morning, Goblin's gang. It's 7.30. Rise and shine. This is Radio Goblin's reminding you that breakfast is now being served in Goblin's Grille until 9 am sharp. Here's some music to get you in the mood.'*

'What the . . . ? What on earth . . . ? Jesus,' said Mickey, sitting up and rubbing his eyes, as the radio set in the bedhead tried to persuade him that everywhere he went, he always took the weather with him.

Mickey fumbled the light, located the radio and hit the off switch.

He walked to the window to see what kind of weather he had brought with him.

It was pissing down.

'Where did that come from?' Andi stirred from her slumbers.

Mickey picked up the Goblin's guide from the MFI pine dressing table and turned to the section marked In-Room Entertainment.

Under Radio, he read: 'Radio Goblin's broadcasts from 7.30 am to 10.30 pm, when it switches off automatically. Guests who do not wish to be woken at 7.30 am should set the control from AUTO to OFF.'

'Now they tell us,' Mickey said.

It was well past 10.30 pm when they'd finally made it to bed.

'You were otherwise engaged,' Andi teased, running her tongue along her top lip.

Mickey smiled, remembering his nightcap. He walked round to Andi's side of the bed, kissed her forehead, slid his hand under the cover and ran his fingers along the inside of her smooth left thigh.

'Later, lover,' she said. 'I'm starving. Wake the kids and let's get some breakfast.'

Mickey's advancing erection beat a reluctant retreat. He dialled the bambinos, first Terry and then Katie.

They were already awake. Radio Goblin's had beaten him to it.

'Fifteen minutes, downstairs in the lobby,' he told them both.

The rooms could not be described as generously proportioned, but they had made an effort.

The chainstore pine furniture was at least homely. There was a minibar and the usual tea- and coffee-making facilities and satellite TV. There was a proper power-shower and the plumbing actually worked.

Even so, the bathroom seemed to have been carved out of former cupboard space. If you were petite, like Andi, it was no problem.

If you were the size of Mickey, taking a dump meant assuming the natural childbirth position, with one leg draped over the side of the bath. But that didn't stop the other leg getting scalded on the red-hot radiator/towel rail. The only solution was to swivel round and drape both legs over the bath, putting your arse at risk of third-degree burns.

It was the first time Mickey had ever taken a shit side-saddle.

The lobby looked different in daylight.

The main building had a 30ft-high, clear-glass conservatory tacked onto the front of it. But it couldn't disguise its origins.

Goblin's had started life shortly after the Second World

War, one of dozens of utilitarian holiday camps which had sprung up around the coast of Britain.

The cheap package holiday boom of the late Sixties and early Seventies had pretty much wiped them out.

Goblin's was a brave attempt to fight back, to bring the Disney experience to those reluctant to travel abroad and to compete with foreign invaders like CenterParcs.

A Kenyan entrepreneur who had made his fortune buying up and selling on former British Railways hotels had invested millions in an attempt to transform Goblin's into a leisure experience fit for the 21st century.

He had been partly successful. The original swimming pool had been relined, heated and covered over to protect it from the elements.

The canteen had been redecorated and redesigned. It now looked like a shopping mall food court.

The concert hall had been turned into a state-of-the-art laser disco and karaoke venue.

But somehow, the DNA seeped through. The place still smelt of knobbly-knees contests, glamorous grannies, aye-aye-aye-aye conga, and risqué 'Ooo, missus' comedians.

Radio Goblin's was a throwback to the days of tannoys, 'wakey, wakey, campers' and enforced jollity.

The old Greencoats had become Goblin's Greeters and they clearly hated it. If you're going to dress grown men and women as giant pixies you need to live in an irony-free society.

The Americans can get away with it. Your average aluminum-siding salesman from Idaho has no problem conversing with a six-foot gerbil. The six-foot drama student inside the six-foot gerbil costume thinks it's his first step to Hollywood stardom. In the USA, everyone's in showbiz.

At Goblin's, the Greeters weren't aspiring actors. They were out-of-work toolmakers, redundant fishermen, unemployed bank staff and otherwise unemployable youths. They didn't see it as step one on the Yellow Brick Road.

If Disney is the Magic Kingdom, Goblin's was Surly City.

The French family wandered into Goblin's Grille, where the queues were already forming.

They'd eat first, then plan their day.

Andi might have been starving but she took one look at the full English breakfast buffet, poured herself a glass of grapefruit juice, tipped an individual packet of muesli into a bowl and topped it up with lukewarm milk.

'Is that all you want, love?' asked Mickey.

'For now, yes. You know I'm not a big breakfast eater.'

'But ten minutes ago, you were starving.'

'I've changed my mind.'

'Suit yourself. We'll get a proper lunch later.'

Katie chose black coffee, a bottle of Sunny Delight and a pot of blueberry yoghurt. After watching the chef wipe his nose on the sleeve of his green Goblin's jerkin, she decided she was watching her weight.

The congealed eggs, limp bacon, burned sausages, radio-active baked beans, cold toast and rancid butter substitute held no such horrors for Mickey. He was a veteran of police catering. Compared with the old Tyburn Row canteen, the Goblin's Grille was four-star Michelin. Which might explain why everything smelt and tasted of burnt rubber.

Terry followed suit, loading his plate like his dad and piling half a dozen hash browns on a side plate. They looked like deep-fried Brillo pads.

Mickey and family carried their food to a large toadstool in the corner and took their places on plastic seats designed to look like tree stumps.

'You can't sit there,' said a peroxide waitress, dressed in Goblin's uniform, her bulbous thighs straining her laddered green leggings.

'Pardon?'

'This section is reserved.'

'Who for?'

'Guests.'

'Guests? We're guests,' said Mickey, cutting into a saw-dust sausage.

88

'Other guests.'

'What other guests? The place is half empty.'

'*Special* guests.'

'Special? Aren't *we* special?'

'All our guests are special, sir. It's just some are, well . . .'

'Don't tell me. More special than others.'

'Not exactly, sir, just different, like,' said the waitress, who looked like a dog-rough version of Debbie Harry, Mickey thought.

'Different? What, disabled or something?'

'Or *something*, sir.'

'What kind of something?'

'You'll find out, sooner or later, sir.'

'Brilliant. Can I finish my breakfast?'

'They'll be down soon. They all come down together. Look, I'm not trying to be difficult, sir. Why don't you sit at that table over there. It's got a lovely view of Goblin's Grotto. I'll carry your meals.'

'Mickey, let's just do it,' said Andi.

'OK.'

'Thank you, sir. If I can help you further, my name's Debbee. I'm not actually a waitress. I'm a glamour model. I'm resting at the moment, though.'

And have been for the past twenty-five years, thought Mickey. Reminded him of an old Tom he'd pulled in at Tyburn Row. It could have been her, for all he knew. He wasn't going to pursue it. She was never charged. She used to give relief to half the relief in exchange for immunity from prosecution, even if not immunity from anything else.

They shifted tables and resumed breakfast.

As they did, there was a kerfuffle at the entrance to Goblin's Grille. An unruly gang of youths, all aged about fourteen, fifteen maybe, shuffled in, pushing and shoving and jeering, beneficiaries of what the probation service called 'broadening the horizons' of young offenders.

Goblin's was where Tyburn juvenile panel had sent Wayne Sutton to 'confront his criminality'.

Wayne had chosen to confront the staff, instead.

He whisked the hat off the head of a Goblin's Greeter and threw it to one of his mates. A manic game of catch ensued, with the Goblin's Greeter, an overweight, balding man in his late fifties, running around like a headless puppy in vain pursuit of his headgear.

The youths appeared to be in the charge of a man in his late thirties, about 5ft 8ins, denim shirt, cord trousers. He maintained an air of complete indifference, studying the vegetarian alternative menu.

The mêlée was broken up by Debbee, who dived in like a rugby wing threequarter and retrieved the hat.

She squared up to Wayne, quite obviously the ringleader, and grabbed him by his earring.

'Oi, you can't do that, you slag,' Wayne squealed indignantly. He knew his rights.

'Don't you call me a slag, or I'll rip your ears off, you little twat. Just behave, all right?'

'You're hurting me.'

'Good. Now calm down, get your breakfast and sit over there and eat it.'

'I'll have you.'

'Don't make me laugh, Sunny Jim,' said Debbee, throwing back her head. 'Now just do as you're told. And you,' she said to the man nominally in charge. 'Yes, you. I'm talking to you. Keep these hooligans in order or I'm calling the management.'

'Don't you take that tone of voice with me, mizz.'

'And don't you mizz me, either.'

'There's no need for violence. You could try reasoning with them.'

'And you could try doing your job and controlling them.'

Debbee turned on the heels of her pixie boots and marched off. The youths made barking noises as she left.

'Marvellous,' said Mickey, watching from a distance.

'What do you mean?' said Andi.

'That's all we need.'

'Oh, come on, Mickey. It was only high spirits. They're just kids. Lighten up, we're on holiday. So are they. You know what kids are like.'

'Everything all right, folks?' It was Debbee, back to clear away their plates.

'Yeah, fine,' said Mickey. 'You're a bit tasty in a ruck.'

'So I've been told.'

Andi scowled. Debbee might be a dog, but she didn't like Mickey flirting with another woman.

'Who are that bunch?' asked Mickey.

'Oh, they're, like, deprived kids or something. They're here for a week on holiday. That bloke is a social worker, I think. He's a bit of a wanker, if you'll pardon my French. He can't control them. Look at them now.'

The gang of youths was gathered around the table in the corner which the French family had recently vacated.

It was like feeding time at the zoo. They tore at their meals with their hands. They threw bits of food at each other.

'That's why I put them in the corner, well out of the way,' Debbee explained. 'You don't want a face full of fried egg, do you?'

Terry thought it looked a bit of a grin. For two pins he'd have joined in.

Mickey was less than impressed.

At the centre of the group, Wayne Sutton held court. He had plans for the rest of the day. And they didn't include water polo or crazy golf. He'd tell them later.

The food fight subsided. Wayne sat under a large, green and white No Smoking notice, and lit a cigarette.

Jez Toynbee, social worker, buried his head in the *Guardian*.

'See?' said Debbee. 'Hopeless.'

'That kid in the middle,' said Mickey. 'I've seen his type before. He's a wrong 'un. It's written all over him.'

'I dunno, Dad,' said Katie, polishing off her blueberry yoghurt. 'He's kinda cute.'

'Yuk!' spluttered Terry, mopping up the last of his breakfast with a cold piece of toast.

'What?' said Mickey.

'That boy in the middle. He's quite good-looking, don't you think, Mum?'

'Well, um.' Andi knew what was coming.

Mickey put down his mug of tea, very slowly. Always a bad sign.

'Now you listen to me, young lady.' He looked his daughter straight in the eye. 'He's trouble. I don't want you going anywhere near him. Understand?'

Katie averted her gaze.

'I said, do you understand?'

She muttered something under her breath.

'Hey, I'm talking to you. Do you understand?'

'Yes, Dad.'

# Fourteen

Radio Goblin's blared out of the loudspeakers concealed in every ceiling. There was no escape, short of poking your eardrums out with a knitting needle.

Agabloodydoo.

'Come on, love. Let's get a drink,' Mickey said to his wife.

Katie and Terry had gone swimming.

Mickey and Andi strolled into Goblin's Goblet, decorated in the same elfin style as the rest of the public space.

'Large VAT and a white wine spritzer, please, chief.'

The barman was kitted out in the same uniform as the rest of the staff. He was distinguished by the ring in his nose. Mickey had never seen one like this before. Most dedicated nose-ring enthusiasts favour one or other nostril. This one was dead centre, like a prize bull. Mickey wondered if they tied him to a rail of an evening.

He poured their drinks into two wooden Goblin's goblets, like halved acorns.

'Any ice?' asked Mickey.

'The machine's broken,' explained the barman, in a broad Brummie accent.

'Do us a favour, chief. Turn the music down a bit,' said Mickey.

Agabloodydoo had given way to GerisoddingHalliwell.

'Love to mate, but I'm not allowed, like.'

'Why not?'

'Policy. The customers like it.'

'We're the only customers in here.'

'No can do, boss. It all comes from a central control,' said the barman, half-apologetically.

Andi picked a splinter out of her mouth.

'Sorry about that, madam,' said the barman. 'Bits come off in the dishwasher.'

'Worked here long?'

'A few months. I came down from Brum. I got the old tin-tack when the Krauts pulled out of Longbridge. I used to be a skilled man, you know.'

Another customer walked in.

'Do you have any Chardonnay?' he inquired.

'We've got white wine. I don't know what sort,' said the barman.

'It's not Chilean, is it?'

'I'll have a look.'

The barman picked up the bottle and read from the label. 'Produce of grapes from the European Community.'

'I'll have half of lager.'

Jez Toynbee nodded back, settled on the next bar stool and took a sip of his lager from his wooden goblet.

'I saw you at breakfast,' Mickey said. 'You're with that bunch of young hooligans.'

'I am with those young *men*, if that's what you meant to say.'

'No offence, chief. But they looked a pretty unruly bunch to me.'

'High spirits, that's all.'

'That's what *I* said,' Andi chipped in.

'So what brings you – and them – here?'

'Same as you, I imagine. Vacation.'

'I take it you're not their dad. Not all of them, anyway.'

'Funn-ee. No, but they're in my care.'

'Probation officer?'

'That's not a term we use much these days, even in the probation service. I'm their mentor.'

'Mentor, eh?'

'Sort of big brother. It's my job to help them overcome their disadvantages.'

'And what kind of disadvantages might they be?'

94

'Difficult family situation, behavioural irregularities.'

'Irregularities?'

'These young men, my clients, are suffering socio-economic deprivation and have lacked guidance.'

'I've come across a few like them in my time, climbing out of people's windows with a pocket full of jewellery, that sort of, er, whatchacallit?, behavioural irregularity.'

'Oh?'

'Ex-Job.'

'I see. I might have known.'

'What's that supposed to mean?'

'Leave it, Mickey.' Andi touched his arm.

'No, love. *What* might you have known, chief?'

'That you'd be judgemental. I've brought them here to get away from that kind of prejudice.'

'Prejudice. Fucking *prejudice*? You'd be prejudiced if you'd had to deal for years with some of the lives little bastards like this have wrecked.'

'That's unfair. You can't lump them all together.'

'So, enlighten me. What have this bunch done between them?'

'I am not at liberty to discuss individual cases.'

'Let me guess. A bit of TDA?'

'TDA?' inquired the barman, who was enjoying the excitement.

'Taking and driving away. Nicking cars, in English. Robbery, burglary, spot of criminal damage?'

'Whatever they have done,' protested Jez Toynbee, 'is behind them. They deserve the chance to become fully rounded, integrated citizens.'

'No fucking chance.'

'They certainly wouldn't have any chance if the system left it to people like you.'

'And you know best, do you?'

'I'm prepared to make an effort. That's what this programme is designed to achieve.'

'Programme?'

'Yes, we call it the Better Way project. It is aimed at showing these unfortunate young men that there is a better way. To give them hope, to include, rather than exclude, them.'

'And that's what they're doing here, is it?'

'We believe that if they can be exposed to the rewards of life they will be able to confront their behavioural disadvantages.'

'And what about the kids who don't have, er, behavioural disadvantages? Who don't rob and burgle and destroy.'

'That's not my problem. My job is to nurture and mentor my clients on behalf of society, people like you.'

'Well, thanks a bunch. It's come to this, hasn't it?'

'To what?'

'Nick a video and win a holiday.'

# Fifteen

The spark plug hit the side window of the Vauxhall Cavalier, shattering it into a thousand shards.

Good. No alarm.

These older models were a pushover.

Wayne Sutton reached inside, flipped the lock and crawled onto the front seat. He rifled the glovebox. Nothing much. A half-eaten bag of wine gums, a couple of Celine Dion cassettes. He pocketed about £10 worth of coins the owner kept in the car for the purposes of feeding the meter.

Nothing else worth nicking. Not even a mobile.

Wayne slid out of the car and walked away nonchalantly. The rest of the gang kept watch as he approached a Land Rover Discovery. On the dashboard, the telltale red LED flickered, indicating that the anti-theft mechanism was armed.

Wayne peered into the car. In the luggage bay, a set of golf clubs. Back home he'd have had them away in an instant. They'd have been fenced in a couple of hours. Here, Wayne reckoned, he might look a bit conspicuous, hawking a set of precision Pings around the tables in Goblin's Grotto.

Wayne was after cash. High-end stereo cassette players, common currency on the streets round Tyburn Row, were no use to him here. Non-convertible.

'Let's knock this on the head,' he said. 'There's nothing here for us.'

It was always a long shot. The Goblin's holidaymakers were unlikely to leave large sums of money lying about in their motors, but it was worth a punt.

The rooms were favourite, but not right now. Not in broad daylight. He'd wait until they were all at dinner tonight, or pissing it up at the Goblin's Groove, the camp's laser-disco.

The rain started to fall again. Time to mooch back inside.

Wayne and the chaps retrieved their swimming costumes from their rooms and made their way to the pool. As they passed the bar, they acknowledged Jez Toynbee, who waved cheerfully. 'Having a good time, boys?'

'Yeah, wicked.' Wayne smiled back. 'Tosser,' he said under his breath, through a clenched grin.

The boys changed and threw their clothes into a loose heap. In their trunks, they were diminished. The South Central Los Angeles fashions, the trainers the size of cross-Channel ferries, added swagger and menace.

Stripped of their combat uniforms, they looked what they were – a bunch of awkward, sprouting schoolboys. Or would have been, if any of them had ever bothered going to school.

Despite his surly demeanour and spiteful eyes, Wayne was a pretty boy. He had the androgynous appeal of the young models favoured by the fashion industry.

Wayne thought about wrenching open a few lockers, but the vigilant presence of one of Goblin's security staff deterred him. The guard was dressed like all the other workers at the holiday world, except for a thick leather belt, with a heavy torch and a two-way military-style personal radio dangling from it, and a tin star on his lapel.

The guard detached the torch and twirled it like a six-gun. 'You can't hang around in here. Come on, out of it.'

Wayne and his posse shuffled off, pushing and shoving each other. Two of the other boys picked up the smallest member of the party and heaved him into the deep end, next to a notice reading 'No Horseplay'.

Wayne dived in. He was a strong swimmer, self-taught in Tyburn Reservoir, where he'd retreat for a joint and a dip on hotter days. One afternoon he'd stumbled across his mum, servicing an itinerant tarmacing gang in the pump house. He didn't go home for three days. She hadn't reported him missing. Probably hadn't even noticed.

As Wayne surfaced, his attention was drawn to a petite,

dark-haired girl in a skimpy bikini, perched on the edge of the pool, with her legs dangling in the water.

The rest of her was bone dry.

Wayne saw a heavily built lad, a couple of years younger, maybe, with cropped hair, creep up behind her.

'No, Terry. No, don't you dare. You know I . . . Terry!' she cried out.

It was too late. He pushed her square between her shoulder blades and she lost her balance and tipped into the water.

As the girl came up for air, the boy ran towards the pool and launched himself into the air. He raised his knees to his chest, clutched them in his arms and hit the surface like a depth-charge.

The wake knocked the girl off balance again and submerged her.

'Terry. You sod. You sodding, sodding, sod.'

Terry laughed.

'That'll stop you posing. Little miss bathing beauty.'

'I'll get you for that,' his sister screamed, lashing out at him.

Terry felt an arm round his neck. It started to choke him and dragged him underwater. Terry thrashed about in panic as his nostrils began to fill with chlorinated liquid.

Wayne Sutton tightened his grip. Terry kicked out. He couldn't breathe.

'Stop that. Stop that NOW,' Katie screamed, launching herself at Wayne. She scratched his face, causing him to loosen his grip long enough for her brother to struggle free.

'BASTARD. Leave him ALONE.'

Wayne turned and raised his arm. The girl looked up at him, soaked and bedraggled. Wayne stopped mid-swing.

'He's my brother. Just leave him.'

'But I thought he was hurting you.'

'He was just being a stupid kid. There was no need to half-kill him.'

'I was only trying to . . . oh, fucking forget it.'

'OI, you. OUT. Out of the pool, this instant.'

It was the jolly green swimming pool attendant, swinging his torch and barking for assistance into his radio.

'Wossupwiv you?' Wayne screamed back.

'No Horseplay. Them's the rules. Someone could get drowned.'

Katie intervened.

'Just a misunderstanding. A bit of fun that got out of hand. It won't happen again, will it?'

The colour was returning to Terry's cheeks, though he was still coughing and spluttering.

'Will it?'

'Nah,' coughed Terry.

'Will it?'

'If you say so,' said Wayne Sutton.

'Last warning,' said the pool attendant. He turned on the heels of his pixie boots and marched off to sort out a drunken thirty-something sliding headfirst down the under-fives' novelty water-chute.

'And, well, thanks,' said Katie.

'Yeah, right.' She could have sworn that Wayne Sutton actually blushed.

'Laters.'

'Laters.'

He swam off.

'He coulda killed me,' Terry whined.

'Serves you right.'

'I'm telling Dad. He told you not to have anything to do with those boys. And him in particular.'

'You do that and I'll tell him you tried to drown me. Now just leave it. I'm starving. Let's get some chips.'

Across the pool, she could see Wayne Sutton hoisting his lithe frame out of the water. He glanced back in her direction. She pretended not to notice.

A bit of a show-off, a bit hot-headed, but boys were like that, Katie thought.

Just as she'd thought at breakfast.

Kinda cute, too.

# Sixteen

Ricky Sparke turned down the sound on *Sports Report* and answered the phone.

'There you are.'

'Where else would I be?'

'This time of day, the Marquis of Granby would be the obvious bet.'

'I thought you were supposed to be on holiday.'

'I am.'

'Then what are you ringing me up for?'

'How'd Spurs get on?'

'Haven't you got a wireless down there?'

'Yeah, but it only receives Radio Goblin's.'

'What?'

'You don't wanna know.'

'What about the car radio?'

'It's pissing down. I can't be bothered to get wet.'

'No TV?'

'It's piped in and at the moment it's a choice between monster truck racing and CNN Asian Business Report.'

'Sky?'

'They're too mean to pay the subscription.'

'What kind of place you staying at – Whitemoor prison?'

'Not as good as that, mate. They've got Sky. The food's probably better, too. And there are more criminals in here.'

'Eh?'

'Team of young tearaways with some iron in tow. The Better Way project.'

'What's all that about?'

'I'll tell you when I see you. How'd Spurs get on?'

'Lost two-nil.'

'Doesn't surprise me.'

'When you back?'

'Tuesday night. I'm back on the case Wednesday morning.'

'You all right for a job Friday night?'

'Yeah, don't see why not. Anything special?'

'I've got a date.'

'Been hanging round Battersea Dogs' Home again?'

'Oi, leave off. She's OK.'

'Were you pissed when you pulled her?'

'I'd had a couple in Spider's.'

'You given her one yet?'

'Nah, but you never know.'

'What's she look like?'

'One of the Gladiators.'

'Which one?'

'Kirk Douglas.'

Mickey roared with laughter. 'See you Wednesday, super-stud.'

'What's so funny?' Andi emerged from the bathroom.

'Have I told you lately that I love you?'

'What's with the Van Morrison?'

'Ricky.'

'Eh?'

'His love life.'

'What love life?'

'Exactly. Grab-A-Gremlin night at Spider's is about as good as it gets for him. I couldn't face that. Trying to get inside the drawers of some old boiler with her lipstick on sideways.'

'I should think not. You're a married man.'

Andi let her towel drop, slowly and deliberately.

'Come here.'

There was a loud knock at the door.

'Mum, Dad. You coming?'

102

'It doesn't look like it.' Mickey shook his head.

'We'll be down in a minute, son,' Andi called out. 'Meet us by the fruit machines.'

Mickey swung his legs off the bed. He stroked Andi's pert arse as he took his clothes from the wardrobe.

'This could just be your lucky night.'

# Seventeen

GerisoddingHalliwell had given way to Sade, the Lightning Seeds and Andy Williams. Radio Goblin's came over all easy listening in the evening.

The boys watched the girls as the girls watched the boys that watched the girls go by. Or was it the other way round? Mickey wondered as he loaded his plate with spag bol.

Never could stand the bloody record.

'How's your dinner?' he asked no one in particular.

Terry was on his third slice of pizza – Pixie's Pizza Palace forming part of Goblin's Grotto food court. He gave his dad the thumbs up.

'A damn sight better than I expected, to be honest,' said Andi, even though her vegetarian moussaka wasn't up to her dad's standards. He'd won prizes for it.

'This is OK, too,' Mickey agreed, pouring himself another wooden tumbler of Chianti.

'We'll dance it off.'

'What, with my back?'

Katie looked a picture. Made up, she was right, she could pass for three years older.

She picked at a barbecued chicken breast. Her mum poured her a glass of Soave.

'Go on, love. Have a drink.'

'You sure? Dad?'

'Of course, love. We're on holiday.'

Andi took a sip.

'Can I have a beer?' asked Terry.

'You can have one out of the minibar in our room later.'

'Yeah? Great.'

'OK, team, so what's the plan?'

'I'm going to play snooker,' Terry announced. 'You wanna game, Dad?'

'Your mum and me are going for a nice drink.'

'I thought you were going dancing,' Katie said.

'Not me, love. I'll tell you what. Me and Terry will have a couple of frames of snooker, you two girls go and shake a leg and we'll meet back in the bar in, what, say an hour.'

'Sounds good.'

'Great.'

'Come on, Ronnie O'Sullivan,' Mickey said to Terry, who grabbed a last slice of cheese and pepperoni.

Andi and Katie headed off to Goblin's Groove for a bop.

Although the records were all recent releases, most of them were remakes and Andi knew all the words.

The DJ was the same irritating git who'd woken them at 7.30 that morning.

Katie danced opposite her mum, but her mind was elsewhere and her eyes scanned the room.

There was no sign of him.

'Looking for someone?' her mum asked.

'No, just curious.'

'Checking out the talent?'

'Don't be daft.'

'See anyone for me?'

'Stop it, Mum.'

Still no sign of him. No sign of any of them.

'Come on, let's go and meet your dad.'

Mickey and Terry were sitting at a toadstool in the bar.

'Two-*NIL* to the champion,' sang Terry, jubilantly.

'He wiped the floor with me. Wanna drink?'

'Yeah, drywhitewine, alloneword,' Andi laughed.

'Katie?'

'No thanks. If you don't mind, Mum, Dad, I thought I might go to bed. I'm tired.'

'No, that's fine, sweetheart. Off you go.'

'Night, everyone.' Katie glanced at her brother. 'Come

on, Terry,' she said, 'let's leave the crumblies to it.'

'Bloody cheek,' said Mickey.

'I don't wanna go to bed,' Terry protested.

'You don't have to. Here's the key to our room. There's bound to be something on TV – there's a Greek channel if all else fails. They were showing *Dallas* earlier. And you can have that beer from the minibar I promised you.'

'Cool.'

'Just the one, mind.'

'Yeah, yeah.'

Terry raced for the stairs. Katie kissed her mum and dad on the cheek and followed him.

'Good kids,' Mickey said.

'The best, lover.'


Wayne Sutton drained his third can of extra-strength cider and stubbed out his spliff.

He'd found a better way, all right.

A better way to pass his time than playing snooker, or fannying around on fruit machines, or playing five-a-side football or going dancing with Jez Toynbee.

Some of the chaps had formed an escape committee and broken for the border. Or rather, they'd stolen a car from Goblin's car park and driven off in the direction of the seaside. Jez Toynbee hadn't even noticed they'd gone.

Wayne wasn't bothered. He'd headed for the nearest offie and half-inched a six-pack of Old Mummerset Brain Damage while the owner was out in the yard tackling a small fire in his dustbin. Which Wayne, naturally, had started.

In the background, the relentless thump-thump from Goblin's Groove disturbed the calm of the night air.

He could hear the twats getting louder as the night wore on and the alcohol went ahead on away goals.

'Hi-Ho Silver Lining'.

While the twat's away, the lice will play.

And Wayne had already taken advantage. He'd turned over

three chalets, netting a couple of watches, a necklace and nearly £700 in cash. Just lying there, on the bedside table.

These people deserve to get robbed.

One more and he'd call it a night.

Wayne stashed the money and jewellery in a sports bag, which he hid in a shed in the grounds. He figured the gardeners didn't work weekends.

He walked around the back of the main block. There were lights on in some of the rooms, but most of the happy campers were either bopping or propping up the bar.

On the second floor, he noticed a window, wide open. The curtains were only partly drawn and there was no light inside. Wayne hoisted himself up on a dumpster and shinned up the drainpipe.

He eased open the window and lowered himself into the cramped en-suite bathroom. There was no sound from the adjoining bedroom as he eased the door ajar.

Wayne stepped inside.

He could hear breathing, light breathing.

Outside, voices were raised. A couple of drunks were weaving their way back to their chalets. The music from the disco fell silent.

There were footsteps in the corridor.

Wayne froze.

He retreated into the bathroom and looked out of the window. A man and a woman were going at it like rabbits up against the dumpster. The woman's knickers were round one ankle, her frock pulled up above her waist. Her companion's strides were half-mast and he was struggling to keep his footing. Every time he thrust forward, his feet slid upon the wet mud left by the day's downpour. The woman was squealing like a stuck pig.

Wayne thought of his mum.

'Who's there?'

A voice, a young woman.

'Is that you, Terry? Stop larking about.'

It was her. The girl from the swimming pool.

107

He pushed open the bathroom door.

'You. What the hell are you doing here?' She sat up in bed.

'Shhhh.'

'I'll scream.'

'No, don't. I can, um, listen, um, let me think.'

The dope, the Brain Damage, the humping couple, his mum. It addled his brain.

'Just shut up.'

'I'm getting my dad.'

'No. NO.'

Katie jumped out of bed and tried to push past him.

Wayne pulled something from his pocket.

'I'll cut you. I'll cut you.'

He grabbed her hair and she felt something metal and sharp against her cheek.

He forced her back onto the bed. She drew her knees up to her chest. She was wearing a cotton T-shirt and nothing else.

'Just shut up. I'm thinking.'

'Get out of here, right now.'

Wayne had no way out. The copulating couple blocked one exit. The main door was too risky.

'I'll just have to stay here.'

'You won't.'

'Shut up, you spoilt bitch.'

He slapped his palm across her mouth and she could glimpse the glint of steel in his other hand.

Katie felt his hand pressing against her lips. She opened her mouth and snapped her jaw shut around his index finger.

Wayne screamed.

'AAARGH! BITCH.'

Katie kicked out. Wayne stumbled backwards, clutching his hand.

Downstairs, next to the dumpster, the startled lovers rearranged their clothing and ran like hell. Coitus had been well and truly interrupted.

Katie made the door and forced it open. There was Terry, alerted by the scream, still clutching the bottle of Beck's he'd taken from his dad's minibar.

Terry saw Wayne doubled in pain and took his chance.

He launched himself at Wayne and using his full force brought the bottle crashing down on his head. The bottle smashed, Wayne's skull split.

As he fell, Terry kicked him hard.

'Run for it, sis.'

Katie turned to flee just as Mickey and Andi were reaching the top of the stairs.

'What the . . . Katie.'

'DADDY!'

Mickey rushed towards the bedroom as Andi comforted her distraught daughter.

'OK, Terry. Stop.' Terry was still putting the boot in.

Mickey hit the fire alarm. That would bring security running.

He pulled Wayne to his feet. The boy was pumping blood from his finger and his head. Mickey pushed his arm halfway up his back.

'What are you doing here, you bastard? If you've hurt my daughter, I'll fucking kill you.'

'Dad, Dad. I'm fine.'

'Did he touch you?'

'What do you mean?' Katie trembled.

'Touch you. You know, *TOUCH* YOU!'

'Mickey, you're frightening her.'

'DID he?'

'Not like you mean, Dad, no.'

'Then what the fuck was he doing here?'

By now, every room in the place had been evacuated. The corridor was full of guests in various states of undress.

Goblin's security turned up in force. Both of them, followed by Jez Toynbee.

Mickey still had Wayne in a half-nelson, his face pushed against the wall.

'Leave him alone, you fascist bully,' screeched Toynbee.
'You what?'
'Look what you've done to him.'
'I haven't done anything.'
The Goblin's security guard stepped in. 'Whatever has gone on here, this, er, young man is clearly in need of medical attention. And I think I had better call the police.'
'Young man, young man,' said an elderly lady to the security guard. 'I think you better had. I've been robbed.'

Two more guests came forward to say their rooms had been burgled.

The security guard was all for searching Wayne Sutton's room, but Jez Toynbee protested with such vehemence that it would be an illegal search that he decided to wait for the police.

By the time the boys in blue arrived forty-five minutes later, Jez had already spirited Wayne to hospital in the Citroën people carrier in which he had brought his party down from London.

He refused to allow anyone to ride with them.

Mickey French was insistent that Wayne be detained until the police turned up. But the camp manager over-ruled him after Jez started making threatening noises about lawsuits and compensation.

Wayne was given first-aid and allowed to leave with his mentor.

Halfway to hospital, Wayne told Jez to stop the van. He needed to be sick.

Clutching his bloodied hand with the other, he ran into a copse at the side of the road and disappeared out of sight. Jez could hear the ghastly retching sounds.

He didn't see Wayne take a chisel from the left hand patch pocket of his combat fatigues and hurl it fifty yards into a lake.

110

# Eighteen

Katie sat on her mum and dad's bed, sobbing. Andi wrapped her in a dressing gown and made sweet tea. Room service had gone home. The ubiquitous tea- and coffee-making facilities and long-life milk came into their own.

Mickey tipped a large measure of scotch from a minibar miniature into a tooth mug.

'Why is this happening to us, Dad?' Katie asked, plaintively.

'I don't know, sweetheart. I really don't know.'

'First the car. Now this.'

'Listen, love, I need to know exactly what happened. Before the police get here. They'll want to talk to you.'

'OK.'

'What was that boy doing in your room?'

'I don't know.'

'How did he get in?'

'I don't know, do I? He was just there.'

'Now listen carefully. Did you let him in?'

'Mickey,' Andi said.

'The police are going to ask her.'

'No I didn't. Honest, Dad.'

'Did you speak to him at all, at any time yesterday?'

'Go on, tell him,' said Terry.

'Tell me what?'

'She fancies him,' Terry mocked.

'Shut up. *Shut up*, you little sod.'

Katie dropped her head.

'She was flirting with him at the pool. She said she'd see him later.'

111

'No I didn't, liar.'

'You did, I heard you. He tried to drown me.'

'And I stopped him. It wouldn't have happened if you hadn't pushed me in.'

Mickey stood up and swallowed his scotch.

'Hang on. Let's get this straight. What the hell has been going on? I told you not to have anything to do with those boys, particularly him.'

'I didn't. I DIDN'T.'

Andi pulled her close. 'It's all right, love. Don't upset yourself any more.' She turned to her husband. 'Mickee.'

'Look, this is important. I must know the truth.'

'I'm trying to tell you, Dad. Terry pushed me in the pool and that boy – I don't even know his name – thought he was bullying me. So he dived in and went for Terry. I broke it up. That's all.'

'Did you say you'd see him later?'

'NO!'

'I heard you,' Terry insisted.

'No you didn't.'

'I did. You said "Laters."'

'That doesn't mean anything. It's just like, like, you know . . .'

'What?' asked Mickey.

'Like saying "See ya."'

'See you later?'

'No. It's just something you say.'

'You sneaked off early tonight.'

'I was tired. Mum had given me that wine. I went to bed. Stop it, Dad, please, stop it.'

'Mick-ee,' said Andi again.

Mickey heaved a sigh. 'Sorry. Sorry, really I am. Of course I believe you, darling. Of course I do. But we, rather the police, have to be sure.'

'You're not in the police any more.'

'No, but I still know how they work.'

112

There was a knock at the door.

'Mr French?'

A young constable and a WPC stood in the corridor.

'The security guard has filled us in. Perhaps we can have a word with your daughter and your son.'

'Sure, come in.'

Katie told it as it happened, the intrusion, the knife, the threats. How she'd bitten him and Terry had rescued her.

The WPC inspected Katie's room.

'It looks as if he got in through the window. There are muddy footprints on the sill and in the bath.'

'Find the knife?' Mickey asked.

'Nothing.'

'It must be there,' Katie said.

'Did you see him drop it?'

'Well, no. It all happened so quickly.'

'Are you sure it was a knife?'

'It was metal. It was sharp.'

'Could he still have it?'

'It was dark. It all happened so quickly. I dunno.'

'Look,' Mickey said. 'She's had a rough night. Can we do this in the morning?'

'Fine, Mr French. We've got a couple of burglaries to be looking into before we go. And we're due at the hospital. But we'll need to speak to all of you at the station tomorrow.'

'I know the drill.'

# Nineteen

The young constable showed Jez Toynbee and Wayne Sutton into an interview room, where an older man, fortyish, stocky, swept-back hair, shiny suit, was waiting.

'This is Detective Sergeant Armitage. He'll be conducting the interview.'

Jez and Wayne took their seats opposite.

The constable hit the record button on the dual tape recorder.

'Interview commenced 10.55 am. Present DS Armitage . . .'

'PC 234 Oswald,' said the young constable.

'Mr Wayne Sutton and Mr, er . . .'

'Jez Toynbee.'

'Jez?'

'Short for Jeremy,' Jez enlightened him.

'Mr *Jeremy* Toynbee, Mr Sutton's, er, what exactly are you?'

'Mr Sutton's mentor.'

'Mentor? I see. And you are the responsible adult?'

'I am.'

'Mr Sutton, you are not being charged at this stage, but we have to interview you in connection with an incident at Goblin's Holiday World last night. This will be conducted under caution. Constable Oswald.'

The PC read Wayne his rights.

Jez leant forward.

'Before we go any further, detective sergeant, my client does not wish to be interviewed without legal representation.'

'That is his right. Would you like me to arrange for a duty solicitor?'

'That won't be necessary.'

'Oh?'

'My client has a solicitor.'

'And who might that be?'

'Mister Fromby,' said Wayne.

'Fromby?'

'Mister Justin Fromby,' said Jez confidently. 'I believe you may have heard of him.'

'Interview suspended 10.57 am,' Armitage noted, deadpan. 'If you let me have his number, I'll contact him for you.'

'Don't bother.' Jez smiled. 'He's on his way.'

'You're kidding me.' Mickey French clattered his tea mug onto the Formica table top in the station canteen.

'Seeing as you used to be in the Job, I thought you ought to know,' said Armitage.

'Thanks, mate,' said Mickey.

'What I want to know, is what is his connection with this case? What's he doing travelling all the way down here on a Sunday to represent some little scrote?'

'Search me,' said Mickey, wondering the selfsame thing.

'You know I'll have to play this right by the book. Fromby's fucking trouble,' said Armitage. 'Something tells me this is going to get messy.'

'Yeah, right,' Mickey acknowledged him.

Armitage sipped from a chipped coffee cup. 'You ever come across Fromby, in a professional capacity, like?'

'Donkey's years ago.'

'He remember?'

'Doubt it. I was a young PC, he was making his name in the local law centre. I always had him marked down as an iron. I'm sure, at the very least, that he helps 'em out when they're busy. But he's discreet, I'll give him that.'

'Well, well.'

'This mentor character, Toynbee, he's got brown-hatter

written all over him. You reckon he's, you know, one of Fromby's *friends*?'

'Possible.'

'That might explain it.'

'Might do. Might not. He's a funny fucker. One thing I do know, any excuse to hammer the Old Bill.'

'Not many. Hey, I'd better get back. In case.'

Mickey raised his mug.

'Cheers, mate.'

'Don't mention it,' said Armitage, turning to go. 'Look, this is none of my business, but if Fromby's on the case you might want a brief of your own. In the circumstances, like.'

'Thanks for the concern,' Mickey said. 'But I can handle Fromby.'


Justin Fromby, senior partner Fromby, Hind & Partners, Grays Inn Road, was running late.

One of his conceits was that he had never learned to drive. Went down well with his clients in the public transport unions.

He insisted on travelling by train. Which is why he was running late.

After Roberta told him to get a proper job, Justin joined Hind & Partners as a junior solicitor.

The practice was built on impeccable left-wing principles, some said funded by Moscow gold. Among old man Hind's clients were a number of trades unions run by the Communist Party. He had gained a degree of notoriety in the 1960s, acting for alleged Russian agents and campaigning for the legalization of homosexuality.

By the time young Justin arrived, Harold Wilson had handed over the reins of his second term to Jim Callaghan. Michael Foot and the Labour cabinet were filling the statute books with new employment and equality legislation. Naturally, the plum cases fell into Hind's lap.

The practice grew fatter still on trades union compensation and industrial injury claims. Justin's reward was to be made a full partner.

When the old man retired in the mid-1980s, after being kicked in the head by a police horse on the Orgreave picket line while showing solidarity with Arthur Scargill's striking coal-miners, Justin, though still in his early thirties, was made senior partner.

Now his client list was a roll-call of agitprop chic, European human-rights cases, anarchists, rioters and terrorists. Fromby was both the darling and one of the pillars of the New Establishment, the toast of late-night TV studios, broadsheet comment pages, Islington salons and the army council of the Provisional IRA.

Yet once a fortnight, alternate Saturday mornings, he returned to the law centre at Tyburn to offer his advice gratis to the poor, the dispossessed and the repossessed.

Which is where he met Wayne Sutton.

Fromby took a cab to the police station and swept inside. He cut an impressive figure. Greying at the temples, hair like a mane, brushed back over his collar, in need of a wash, as was the fashion in the legal trade.

He wore a bold red and white striped shirt, no tie, a sports jacket, jeans and suede brogues.

'Fromby,' he announced grandly to the desk sergeant.

'Good afternoon, sir. We've been expecting you.'

It was a long time since any old sweat of a copper had called him Trotsky. To his face, anyway.

'Here to see my client, Wayne Sutton.'

'Yes, sir. If you'll just take a seat.'

'I'll stand,' said Fromby, admiring himself in the glass partition.

'Very well, sir. I'll tell DS Armitage that you're here.'

Armitage opened the door to reception and held out his hand. 'Mr Fromby, sir.'

Justin ignored the proffered handshake.

'This way, sir.'

He showed Justin into an interview room. 'I'll just fetch your client.'

Wayne ambled into the room, followed by Jez Toynbee.

'Who are you?'

'Jez Toynbee, Mr Fromby. May I just say I'm a great admirer of . . .'

'You rang me?'

'Yes.'

'Thank you. That will be all.'

Justin had picked up a certain grandeur, hauteur even, over the years.

'Sorry, I don't understand. I'm Wayne's mentor. I'm his responsible adult.'

'Well, you've done a great job, haven't you? I'm now representing Wayne. You can wait outside with the sergeant.'

'But . . .'

'Sergeant, get Mr, what was it?, Toynbee, I should have remembered, any relation?'

'Er, no,' said Jez.

'Sergeant, get Mr Toynbee a cup of tea, would you be so kind? I'll have an Earl Grey if you've got one.'

'Bone-china cup?' said Armitage.

'Mug will do, sergeant.'

'I'll have a word with chef, sir. Will that be all?'

'No, if you two wouldn't mind leaving, I need to consult my client. Alone.'

'Come on, Mr Toynbee. Better do as the man says,' said Armitage.

The interview room door closed.

'Now then, Wayne,' said Fromby. 'What have you been up to?'

# Twenty

'Michael Edward French, you are not obliged to say anything, but it may harm your defence if you fail to mention, when questioned, something which you later rely on in court.'

'WHAT?'

'Anything you do say may be taken down and used in evidence.'

'What the fuck is going on here?'

'Sorry,' said Armitage, shuffling uncomfortably and avoiding eye contact.

'Are you charging me? And if so, with what?'

'You're not being charged, but I have to caution you. I'll need to speak to your boy again.'

'I don't believe this. I thought you had come out to tell me about this Wayne, wossisname?'

'Sutton.'

'Yeah, whatever. Are you charging him?'

'No one is being charged here, yet.'

'So what the Christ is all this about?'

'Look, I've got to do this by the numbers,' Armitage apologized. 'It's Fromby. He's raising a shit storm. Talking about dragging the chief constable away from his Sunday lunch and filing for wrongful arrest.'

'Wrongful arrest?'

'Yep.'

'Where does he get that from? I mean, the kid was caught bang to rights. He broke into Katie's room, attacked her; what more do you need?'

'That's not how Fromby tells it.'

'You've got the footprints on the windowsill and in the bath.'

'He's not denying that.'

'What, then?'

'He claims your daughter invited Sutton to her room.'

'He FUCKING WHAT?'

'That's what he claims.'

'That's bollocks.'

'Look, I'm telling you what he's alleging.'

'OK, OK,' said Mickey, counting to ten and regaining his composure.

'Fromby says that your daughter, Katie, yeah? He says they met at the swimming pool and that she arranged to entertain him in her room later.'

'Why would she do that?'

'For sex.'

Mickey clenched his fists and swivelled on his heels. He took a deep breath.

'SEX? She's fifteen, for Christ's sake.'

'So's the boy.'

'OK, let's play the game for a minute. If what he says is true, why did he gain entry through a bathroom window?'

'So as he didn't get spotted. He says she told him to.'

'That's absolute shite.'

'That's what he says.'

'And if she'd asked him up there, why would he attack her with a knife?'

'Who says he did?'

'My daughter, that's who.'

'Her word against his.'

'But we caught him there.'

'You're getting ahead of yourself.'

'Have you found the knife?'

'Not as such.'

'What's that supposed to mean?'

'No.'

'It's got to be around somewhere. Could Toynbee have taken it off him?'

'Possible, but how do we prove it?'

'Put him up against a wall and kick the truth out of him.'

'I don't think PACE covers that.'

'Look, I'm sorry.'

'No, that's all right. None of this is on the record, but I believe you. It's just that, well, you know, with Fromby making himself busy. You know what he's capable of.'

'Yeah. I'm not having a go at you. Could they have dumped the knife on the way to the hospital?'

'Toynbee says they drove straight there. We haven't got the manpower to search every inch of the route.'

'So we're fucked.'

'It gets worse.'

'Terrific.'

'Fromby wants you and your boy charged with GBH. He's even making noises about attempted murder.'

'He's WHAT?'

'Just calm down. I told you, I'm not charging anyone right now. But this is what he claims.'

'What?'

'There was that business in the pool.'

'Yeah, Terry told you about that. Sutton nearly drowned him.'

'That's just the point.'

'Spit it out.'

'Fromby claims that Katie lured him to her room so that Terry could attack him with a bottle in revenge for what happened at the pool. And then you arrived and weighed in.'

'This is fucking priceless.'

'Look at it from where he's standing.'

'I'd rather not.'

'Who was the one taken to hospital?'

'So?'

'Head wounds, his finger half bitten off.'

'That was self-defence.'

'Reasonable force? You know the score.'

'He had a knife.'

'Correction. Your daughter says he had a knife.'

'I believe her. Don't you?'

'He says, she says. Bill or Monica. Take your pick.'

'What about the other rooms he turned over?'

'Who says he did?'

'Stands to reason.'

'Slightly different MO.'

'How d'ya mean?'

'The doors of the other rooms were forced with a chisel, maybe. From the corridor, while everyone was at dinner. He gained access to Katie's room through the window, much later.'

'You had the SOCO down there?'

'Nothing positive. Prints get smudged. Maybe he, who-ever, wore gloves.'

'He didn't have gloves on in Katie's room.'

'True, but that fits with his story. That she invited him. If he was there as a guest, why would he need gloves?'

'You found nothing in his room?'

'A bit of blow. Personal use.'

'Nothing else?'

'Nah.'

'Fuck it.'

'My hands are tied.'

'Why would anyone believe him? He's presumably got a record going back, how long?'

'Long enough. More form than Desert Orchid.'

'So why would anyone take his word over my daughter? Or me, for that matter?' reasoned Mickey.

'You're an ex-cop. They don't even believe serving cops, these days, let alone ex-cops,' said Armitage, ruefully.

'So what are we looking at here?'

'I'll do what I can, but I've got to remain strictly neutral.

That's all we can do these days. Everyone's got rights. Crime management, they call it.'

'Jesus.'

'Fromby will start raising merry hell in a minute. He wants you charged and his client released.'

'You gonna do that?'

'It's about to be taken out of my hands. I've called my inspector. He's on his way in.'

'Let me talk to him.'

'Who, the inspector?'

'No, Fromby.'

'I don't think he'll do that.'

'I think he will.'

'Why?'

'We've got history.'

'He didn't mention it.'

'He wouldn't.'

'Wouldn't?'

'Let's put it this way, he wouldn't want to.'

'What am I getting into, here?' Armitage sounded wary, counting his pension.

'Nothing,' Mickey reassured him. 'But you might just be about to get out of it.'

'Eh?'

'Tell Fromby I want to talk to him. In private. He'll go for it.'

'Why?'

'Just tell him PC French wants to see him. PC Mickey French. From Tyburn Row.'

# Twenty-one

'Five minutes. Tops. Then you're out of there,' said Armitage. 'Oh, and this never happened.'

'Cheers,' said Mickey, opening the door to the side office, where Justin Fromby sat behind a chipped wooden desk, studying some papers. His client had been returned to his cell.

'Wotcha, Trotsky.'

Fromby looked up and peered over his half-moon glasses. He didn't need them, they contained clear glass. But he thought they added a theatrical touch.

The figure in front of him looked vaguely familiar.

'Another lifetime, eh, Trotsky?'

'Look, I don't know what this is about. I have agreed to this meeting, without prejudice, to oblige Detective Sergeant Armitage. What is it I can do for you?'

'What's your fucking game?'

'I beg your pardon? I have to remind you this is most improper.'

'So why d'ya agree to see me?'

'In the interests of truth and justice.'

'You can drop the Rumpole act, Trotsky.'

'And you can show me a little more respect.'

'Respect? Do me a favour. This is a crock of shit and you know it.'

'I know nothing of the sort.'

'Wayne Sutton is a little scumbag. I don't know what your angle is here, but trying to fit me and my boy up for GBH and attempted murder is stronging it even by your warped standards.'

'I don't have to listen to this.'

'Oh, you do.'

'You'd know all about fit-ups, being an ex-policeman.'

'I know all about bent briefs, too, Trotsky.'

'If you're implying, I shall terminate this interview immediately.'

'You haven't changed much. Greyer, a bit more pompous. Still the same old devious bastard.'

'If you've got me in here to insult me, I shall call the sergeant.'

'Go on, then.'

Fromby sat fixed to the seat.

Mickey stared him out. 'This stops now, understand?'

'That's not my call.'

'Oh, yes. Oh, yes, it is.'

'Why should I put up with this?'

'Let's just say you still owe me one for Lincoln Philpott.'

The penny dropped, as Fromby remembered where their paths had met before.

'I owe you nothing for Philpott,' he said. 'I was doing my job in the best interests of my client.'

'Course you were, Trotsky.'

'I should have demanded that you were prosecuted for unlawful wounding back then.'

'And I should have brought your playhouse tumbling down.'

'What are you talking about?'

'Ask your girlfriend.'

'Who would that be?'

'Bobby the bobby.'

'You're talking in riddles.'

'Roberta Peel. Deputy Assistant Commissioner Peel.'

'What about her?'

'Formerly, probationary WPC Peel, Tyburn Row. Ring any bells?'

'Go on.'

Fromby sat poker-faced, but he was paying rapt attention.

'WPC Peel, juvenile bureau liaison officer.'

'And?'

'Wasn't there a young lawyer back then, Trotsky? An idealistic law centre volunteer, Justin Someone. Fromby, that's it. Any relation?'

'I repeat. Where, exactly, is this leading?'

'Trevor Gibbs, son of Everton. You remember Everton, nice man, God-fearing. Used to be on Tyburn council. Now a Commissioner for Racial Equality. Whatever happened to young Trevor?'

'How should I know?'

'It was your firm that represented him at his last trial, wasn't it?'

'Fromby, Hind & Partners represents a lot of people.'

'Yeah – the IRA, the Yardies. Trevor's given you enough business over the years, hasn't he? Extortion, drug-running, pimping, clubs, drive-by shootings. Wasn't it Trevor who walked into that boozer in Dalston and blew off Bunny Martin's head? You remember, Trotsky.'

'The jury found him not guilty.'

'Now there's a surprise.'

'Look, French, I'm getting tired of this. What's your point?'

'My point is this. Trevor Gibbs, juvenile delinquent, caught slashing another kid outside a chip shop. Eric Marsden, arresting officer. Good copper.'

'He was a violent racist.'

'Oh, so it's all coming back to you, is it? Anyway this young lawyer, Fromby, makes a bunch of false allegations against Marsden and persuades his bird, WPC Peel, to make the knife disappear. Trevor Gibbs walks. Maybe if he'd gone down then, Bunny Martin and a few others, unproven, would still be alive today and hundreds of other lives wouldn't have been ruined by drugs and prostitution.'

'This is all very interesting, but where's your proof?'

'Wouldn't you like to know?'

'You can't make anything stick, not after all these years.'

'Try me, Trotsky. I've got the knife and I've got it all on tape.'

'What on tape?'

'A shit-scared young WPC Peel telling me all about it. I caught her removing the files from the juvenile bureau at Tyburn Row. I've got them, safe and sound.'

'You're bluffing.'

'She didn't tell you, did she? She didn't fucking *tell you*.' Fromby shook his head.

'So what *did* you think had happened to the knife and the records?'

'I assumed she'd disposed of them.'

'And she has never, ever, mentioned that I caught her in the act? Or that I've got it all on tape?'

'No, never.'

'You know what, Trotsky, I almost believe you.'

'But why should I believe *you*, French? If you thought you had something on me, why not confront me with it during the Lincoln Philpott case? Why wait until now?'

'Good question. I was still in the Job, then. I'd have gone down with you. I wasn't particularly proud of what I'd done. Eric Marsden was still alive then, enjoying his police pension. He didn't need an inquiry any more than we did.'

'So what's different now?'

'Eric died the year before last.'

'There's still the question of your involvement.'

'I don't give a shit any more. I'll do whatever it takes to stop you. Last time you were only fucking *me* about. This time you've got my boy in the frame. Big, big mistake. You fuck with my family and I'll take your legs off. You've got a lot to lose here. So's your girlfriend.'

'She's not my girlfriend.'

'Not your type, eh?'

Fromby ignored the remark.

'Thought so. That's your business. But I keep reading that *Mizz* Peel is heavily tipped to be the next Commissioner. I imagine perverting the course of justice could put the kibosh on that. And it could seriously fuck up your chances of a peerage.'

'Why should I go for this? It would ruin you, too, if it came out,' said Fromby.

'You think I haven't thought of that? Do you think I'm fucking *proud* of what I did back then?'

'You're part of the conspiracy, too. You could go to prison. Where would that leave your family?'

'What do you know about fucking family, you jumped-up little cunt? This *is* about my family. I wouldn't even be contemplating this if it wasn't about my family. And it fucking stops now, you understand? Right here, right now. We walk out.'

'And my client?'

'Your client is lucky he can still walk.'

'What about the charges?'

'Leave that up to Armitage. There won't be any.'

'So if I drop the charges against you, you won't take it any further?'

'I can't speak for the people he robbed at Goblin's.'

'Allegedly robbed.'

'Oh, do leave off.'

'And the, er, the, um, Tyburn Road business?'

'That will be our little secret.'

'And how do I know you won't use it?'

'You don't, Trotsky. You'll just have to trust me.'

'That's not good enough. I want you to hand over the evidence, the knife, the tape, everything.'

'No can do.'

The door opened.

'You've had more than your five minutes. Time's up. The inspector will be here soon,' said Armitage.

'I think he'll have had a wasted journey,' Mickey remarked.

'Mr Fromby?' said Armitage.

'Your call, Trotsky,' said Mickey.

'Ah, yes, sergeant,' mumbled Justin, gathering his composure. 'There's obviously been a misunderstanding here.

128

On reflection, I will not be pressing charges against either Mr French or his son.'

'Mr French?'

'As you said, no evidence, no charges. Look on the bright side, no paperwork, either. No call to the chief constable. We've all got a result.'

'The inspector's not going to like this.'

'He'd have liked even less a state visit from the chief constable, dripping gravy down his golf jumper.'

'You'll both have to sign a withdrawal statement.'

Mickey and Fromby nodded together, like toy dogs on a parcel shelf.

'Look,' said Armitage, 'I don't know what's been going on in here.'

'You don't want to know,' Mickey told him. 'As you said, this meeting never took place.'

'Mr Fromby?'

'Absolutely.'

Armitage went to fetch Wayne Sutton from his cell.

Mickey collected the family.

'I'll explain later,' he told Andi. 'Let's get out of here.'

Fromby and Wayne emerged from a side door.

Mickey and Justin stared at each other.

'Goodbye, Mr French,' said Fromby.

'Be lucky, Trotsky. Oh, and give my love to your girl-friend.'

# Twenty-two

The Bose Wave clock/radio woke Ricky Sparke at noon. As Ricky came round, Michael Parkinson was reminiscing about Fred Astaire and Skinner Normanton and cueing Ella Fitzgerald.

Ricky always had his wireless tuned to BBC Radio 2 at the weekends. It was bad enough having to work for Rocktalk 99FM. Ricky was buggered if he was going to listen to it on his day off.

As Ella took Manhattan, the Bronx and Staten Island, too, Ricky took a couple of Nurofen.

He'd also recently discovered Milk Thistle herbal supplement tablets, an antioxidant supposed to flush the livers of those whose alcohol intake exceeded the government's recommended weekly limit. Ricky's daily intake exceeded the government's weekly limit.

He kept a bottle of Milk Thistle next to the bed. The label said take between one and three tablets with meals. Ricky took half a dozen and washed them down with a Bloody Mary.

He showered, thought about shaving, thought about it again, dried himself off and dressed.

It was too late for breakfast and too early for lunch. Ricky decided to go for a pint and take a view.

Sunday was his favourite day in London. The commuters were back in the suburbs, cutting their lawns, cleaning their cars, lighting their barbecues, patching up their marriages.

If you kept out of Covent Garden, the pubs were reasonably empty and the traffic was light.

Ricky decided to stroll to his favourite pub, the Passport,

in Pimlico, for a little light refreshment. There were always a few locals to talk to, middle-aged men like him, with nothing better to do on a Sunday, a couple of dowagers toying with a small sherry.

First he had to stop at a hole-in-the-wall bank machine and collect some cash and a set of Sunday papers.

Tourists and day-trippers spilled out of the park in search of sustenance. Pizzas, burgers, hot dogs peddled from illegal barrows run by illegal immigrants with links to Turkish terror groups.

Ricky walked over to a cashpoint next to the Army & Navy stores, where, from a steel trolley stained with pigeon shit, a Kosovan asylum-seeker was selling botulism on a bap to a Japanese tourist for £2.50.

Ricky stepped up to the machine, took his cash card from his wallet and inserted it.

As he punched in his PIN number, he was aware of a young woman at his side.

'You press, give money,' she said, excitedly, in a thick, Eastern European accent.

'Oi, leave it out, will you?'

Another girl joined in. 'Hungry, me. Give.'

'Just piss off,' said Ricky.

'Give money, you press,' said the first girl.

'I said, piss off.'

Ricky felt a kick in his kidneys. He doubled up and, as he fell, a young man stamped on his right hand.

Ricky looked up and saw the girl punch the keyboard again. A boot caught him under the chin. Ricky felt the blood well up in his mouth as his teeth punctured his tongue.

He rolled over to see a young man and two women running off in the direction of Victoria Station. One of the young women broke away and ran towards St James's Park. The other two vanished into the plaza at the side of McDonald's which opens on to Westminster Cathedral.

Ricky picked himself up and lurched towards the cash

machine. He hit the Eject Card button. Miraculously, it was still there.

Ricky pushed it back into the slot and punched in his PIN for the second time.

The screen came to life. It asked him what service he would like. The police would be nice, thought Ricky, but what was the point?

He pressed withdrawal.

The machine asked him how much?

He pressed in a 2, a 5, and a 0: £250, his daily limit. That should keep him going until pay day.

The machine replied: Current balance £3.47.

Eh?

Ricky fumbled in his pocket and pulled out his last withdrawal slip, from Friday night. It read: £250 withdrawn, balance remaining £253.47.

He hadn't been near a cash machine since Friday. He hadn't written a cheque in Spider's. Even if he had, and was too pissed to remember, it wouldn't have cleared yet.

Ricky re-entered his PIN and again asked for £250.

'You have already withdrawn your daily limit,' the machine told him.

A small white withdrawal slip was poking out of the front of the machine.

Ricky pulled it out and held it up to the light.

Withdrawal, £250, balance remaining £3.47. It was timed 1.03 pm. Three minutes earlier.

The girl had waited until he punched in his PIN and then, when her young accomplice kicked him to the ground, she had entered £250 and had it away with the cash.

Round the corner, out of sight, in a doorway at the back of the Cardinal's House, Ilie Popescu and Maria counted out Ricky's money.

# Twenty-three

In a penthouse flat in Highgate, a black digital telephone rang on a marble coffee table.

Boban Popescu picked it up.

'Yes?'

'Boban, that you?'

'I told you last time. Don't call me.'

When Ilie rang from the hostel, Boban had put the phone down instantly.

'Wait, please wait,' pleaded Ilie.

'This is not safe.'

'It's OK. I'm on a mobile. It has been re-programmed. No one can trace it.'

'They can trace me.'

'Have they visited you yet?'

'No, but they will.'

'They don't even know I'm in London. I was careful to cover my tracks.'

'Don't you believe it.'

'If they knew I was here they would have come to you, looking for me.'

'Not necessarily.'

'You worry too much, Boban.'

'And you don't worry enough, little brother.'

'I need to see you.'

'Forget it.'

'I need money.'

'Don't we all?'

'I'm riding my luck out here.'

'I thought your luck ran out in Germany.'

'Just a temporary setback.'

'There are some men in Moscow who would like to make it permanent.'

'So, I need to put things right. I need to raise some money to pay them back. I can't go on living on petty thefts. Let me work for you.'

'Impossible. You're trouble.'

'I'm your brother. Your father's son.'

'You haven't heard?'

'Heard what?'

'Father's dead.'

There was a stunned silence. Ilie slumped backwards against a wall, the phone in his right hand, dangling by his side.

After a few moments, he raised it.

'Boban?'

Boban told him the story.

Ilie wept.

'I'm so, so, sorry.'

'You should be. You killed him.'

'NO!'

'He died defending you.'

'I didn't want that. I didn't think . . .'

'That's your trouble, little brother. You don't think. You never think.'

'But . . .'

'You might just as well have pulled the trigger yourself.'

'Boban, please. He was my father, too. I must see you.'

'No.'

'I must. You are my brother.'

'OK, but you can't come here.'

'Where then?'

'You know Highgate village?'

'I'll find it.'

'It's on the Underground. Northern Line.'

'No problem.'

'Go out of the station, cross the main road and turn left

towards the village at the traffic lights. Walk up the hill. At the top there's a pub called the Prince of Wales. It's straight opposite. Meet me there.'

'When?'

'Where are you?'

'I'm near Victoria Station.'

'Take the Underground, change at Euston. Make sure you get the High Barnet train. I'll be there in an hour.'

'I've got someone with me.'

'Who?'

'A friend. A girl.'

'No friends. Just you.'

'OK.'

'One hour. Be there.'

'I will.'

Ilie gave Maria a £20 note from the money they'd stolen from Ricky Sparke and told her to make her way back to the hostel at Tottenham. The man at the cashpoint may have called the police. They had to split up. He'd catch her later.

Forty-five minutes later, Ilie emerged from Highgate tube station and followed his brother's directions.

The Prince of Wales was where Boban had said it would be.

Ilie stepped through the doorway into a low-ceilinged room, yellowing walls, bare wooden floorboards. The place had a Dickensian feel. The lunchtime crowd had headed home. There were a handful of drunken stragglers hanging round the cramped bar, laughing theatrically at jokes they'd told each other a hundred times before.

In the left-hand corner, by the Ladies, he spotted Boban, nursing a large Jameson's.

It was a while since he had seen his brother. Boban looked prosperous, as befitted a high-class car thief. He was four years older than Ilie, plumper, an inch shorter.

He wore a jet-black calfskin blouson, Armani jeans and an obvious Tag Heuer wristwatch.

His clothes marked him out from the regulars, an assortment of actors, lawyers, teachers and broadsheet journalists, who favoured the studied scruffy look of the North London intellectual – cords, threadbare jumpers, suede footwear.

Ilie's shell-suit stuck out like a donkey's dick.

'Boban,' he said, walking towards his brother with outstretched arms.

'Sit down and shut up. Want a drink?'

'Beer will do.'

Boban stepped up to the bar and ordered a lager from the barman, a 'resting' Welsh thespian.

'It's good to see you,' said Ilie. 'I'm so sorry about Dad.'

'He would still be here if you hadn't fucked up in Hamburg.'

'I know. I feel bad about it.'

'So you should . . .'

'I can't undo what's been done. But I can try to make it right. Let me work with you. I can steal cars. I'm good at it. I can get the money to repay them.'

'It's gone beyond that.'

'What do you mean?'

'These Russians value honour more than money. They want you dead.'

Ilie took a deep draught of his lager.

Boban seized hold of his brother's arm and gripped it tightly. 'You are not even safe here in London. You must leave.'

'I can't. I have nowhere to go. Anyway, you can't be sure they even know I'm in London. Dad wouldn't have told them.'

'He may have had no choice.'

'But they haven't contacted you. Surely you're the first place they would have looked?'

'They are not stupid.'

'I've changed my identity. They can't trace me.'

'Don't fool yourself.'

136

'You must help me.'

'Fuck you. You killed my father.'

'Boban.'

'You fucked everything.'

'No. Help me, please.'

'I can't help you. No one can help you. Now go.'

'But Boban.'

'Drink up and go. And leave by the back door. I may have been followed.'

Boban leaned over and kissed Ilie on the cheek.

'Goodbye, little brother.'

Ilie walked slowly towards the rear of the pub. He didn't look back.

If he had, he would have seen his brother take out his mobile phone and press the redial button.

'He's coming out now,' Boban said quietly and deliberately into the mouthpiece.

Across Pond Square, a black Mercedes with smoked windows was parked outside a mansion block.

Ilie Popescu descended the steps at the back of the Prince of Wales, looked both ways and turned right, towards another pub, the Gatehouse. He walked down a narrow alley and retraced his steps to Highgate tube station.

The big Russian in the front of the Mercedes turned to his companion in the back. 'That's him. Go. Moscow said just follow him for now. This isn't Romania.'

Inside the Prince of Wales, Boban Popescu swallowed his whiskey.

'Fuck him, he killed my father,' he said to himself. 'And I've got to work with these people.'

# Twenty-four

'*Welcome to a brand-new week on Rocktalk 99FM. In Swindon, gangs of Kosovan asylum-seekers fought pitched battles in the town centre, using a variety of weapons, including swords, knives and baseball bats. Shoppers fled in terror. Three people were taken to hospital. The fighting is reported to be related to a turf war over drugs and valuable begging pitches.*

'*The police should have turned the flamethrowers on them.*'

Ricky's producer threw his head in his hands. 'Stick to the script. Stick to the fucking script,' he yelled. Ricky smiled and gave him the thumbs-up.

'*Elsewhere, a lorry driver has been arrested for eating a Yorkie bar on the M25. It is part of a nationwide zero-tolerance clampdown on drivers who consume confectionery on the move and has the support of road safety campaigners and the Department of Health, which is spending £200 million on a drive to cut the nation's cholesterol.*'

Ricky's producer relaxed. He really wasn't making that one up.

'*Meanwhile, gangs of Eastern European criminals are free to roam central London, begging, mugging and robbing people at cashpoint machines of their last £250, which was all they had left for the week. Police were nowhere to be seen, naturally.*'

Where the hell did that one come from?

'That's all for this bulletin. Call me with your comments now on the usual number. First caller today is Del, from Collier St James. Morning, Del. You're on the Ricky Sparke show.'

'All right, Ricky? It's what you were saying, like about them gyppoes.'

'What in particular?'

'Well, Ricky. It's like this, see. Me and the missus were sitting at home the other night when there's this knock at the door. I get up and there's this woman, gyppo, like, demanding money. She's got this baby and she keeps saying she's hungry. Any road, I'm telling her to push off and try to shut the door and she shoves her baby in the way. If I shut the door I'm going to hurt the baby and she's screaming at me in some foreign language. The missus comes to see what all the fuss is about when we hear a crash at the back of the house. This bloke has kicked in the kitchen door, he's grabbed the wife's handbag, I've run towards him, but I'm not as young as I was. I go to grab him, but he gives me a right-hander and he's away on his toes, like. The bird with the baby spits in my wife's face and they're off.'

'Did you call the police?'

'Course I did. Straight off. Anyway I gets through to this machine which tells me I'm being held in a queue. I'm hanging on for, what, I dunno, five, ten minutes, then this voice gives me a range of options, press star for this, hash for that, whatever the hell a hash is.'

'Some sort of drug, Del.'

'Might just as well have been. Any road, about fifteen minutes later this woman comes on and I start to tell her what's happened. So I gives her the address and she's never heard of it. Turns out she's in a call centre forty miles away and hasn't got the faintest where Collier St James is. I finally get put through to a sergeant who says there isn't enough to go on and would I like to go to my nearest police station in the morning and they'd give me a crime number for the insurance.'

'Did you?'

'I would have done, but our local police station closed five years ago and the nearest one in the next town only opens between 10.30 am and 4.00 pm alternate Tuesdays.'

'There's never a cop around when you need one. How many times have we heard that on this programme?'

'Unless you happen to be driving at 32 mph on your way home from the boozer, Ricky. But I'll tell you what, mate, if the Old Bill won't do anything about it, I'm getting a gun and if it happens again, I'll blow the bastard's head off. You have to protect yourself these days.'

'Give 'em both barrels for me, Del.'

'Bloody right, Ricky, great show, mate.'

'Thanks, Del. This is Rocktalk 99FM. I'm Ricky Sparke. We'll take some more calls after we've heard from the Jam.'

Outside the studio, the switchboard was going mental.

Ricky sipped a Diet Coke. Through the glass he could see the figure of Charlie Lawrence, beaming from ear to ear.

'Great show, mate,' said Lawrence through the talkback.

Ricky acknowledged his boss but didn't have time to speak. The last chords of 'That's Entertainment' were fading.

'Welcome back. This is Rocktalk 99FM. Who's next? Let's go to Dave, from Tyburn Row, on line two. Hi, Dave.'

'Ricky?'

'Yes mate.'

'We've been burgled eight times in the past eleven months. The police know who's responsible, it's not just us, everyone's been turned over. It's that Monkey Boy what was in the papers a while back, one-man crime wave here at Tyburn Row. He should be behind bars, but I've heard, from a bloke in the boozer, like, that he's been taken away on holiday by his social workers.'

'Typical, Dave. Thinking about that last call, Del, wasn't it? Here's an idea. Let's have a competition of our own. Shoot a Burglar and Win a Million. My boss is in the control room. Morning, Charlie. How 'bout it?'

Charlie Lawrence clapped his hands in glee. He hadn't been so excited since he shifted a van-load of dodgy didgeridoos to a party of Japanese tourists.

*'Dave, I think he likes Shoot a Burglar, it's the Win a Million bit he's not so keen on.'*
*'Forget the million, Ricky. I'll do it for nothing.'*

# Twenty-five

'I've been racking my brains trying to work out where Sutton got hold of Fromby,' said Mickey, as they queued at the Dartford Tunnel, Rocktalk 99FM chattering away. 'I mean, a little scumbag like that and a top celebrity brief.'

'And?'

'Tyburn Row.'

'What about Tyburn Row?'

'That last caller, Dave, on Ricky's show.'

'Yeah.'

'When he mentioned Monkey Boy, one-man crime wave at Tyburn Row. That has to be Sutton.'

'You sure?'

'It fits. That's where I know Fromby from.'

'Tyburn Row, when you were stationed there?'

'Yeah, Fromby worked at the local law centre. Had a girlfriend on the force. Well, I say girlfriend, I always had him down as an iron. But they were thick as, I was going to say thick as thieves, but you know what I mean.'

'Carry on.'

'Well, Fromby was always turning up at the nick, representing the local toerags. That's where I came across him.'

'That was donkey's years ago.'

'Yeah, but I seem to remember reading that Fromby still works part-time at the Tyburn law centre, keeps in touch with his roots, you know.'

'So that's where he met Sutton?'

'Figures, doesn't it?'

Andi peeled a packet of Polos, popped one in her own mouth and one in Mickey's.

Rocktalk 99FM went quiet as their car progressed slowly through the tunnel.

'Mickey?'

'Yes, love.'

'What went on at the police station?'

'You know what happened. It was a score draw. Fromby dropped the charges, so did we.'

'I know why *you* dropped them. Because of Terry, right?'

'Yeah and I didn't want Katie dragged into a witness box.'

Katie was fast asleep on the back seat, Terry buried in his Gameboy.

'But why should *Fromby* drop the charges? That's not like him.'

'It's a long story.'

'Tell me.'

He gave her the short version: Roberta Peel, Fromby, Eric Marsden, the tapes, the files, the knife.

'My God,' said Andi. 'And you've kept them all these years?'

'Just as well I did.'

'Why have you never told me?'

'You didn't need to know.'

'And where are they now?'

'You still don't need to know.'

Mickey turned up the radio. Ricky Sharpe was agreeing with a caller who wanted asylum-seekers rounded up at gunpoint and put on the first plane out.

'Has he been drinking?' asked Andi.

'Usually. But not until he's finished broadcasting.'

'What's got into him this morning?'

'Meaning?'

'Well you heard him on Friday, taking the piss out of that fella who wanted to send the Romanians home. Ricky's always been a bit of a soft liberal.'

'Up to a point.'

'But he's never been a deporter, or a hanger, or a flogger.'

'Maybe he's got a bad hangover.'

'He's your mate, you know him best.'

'Something's happened at the weekend.'

'He sounds grumpy. Angry.'

'Maybe.'

'You heard what he said during the news.'

'What about?'

'At the end of it, that stuff about Eastern European gangs in central London, robbing people of their last £250, all the money someone had for a week. That didn't sound like part of the regular news bulletin.'

'And you think that someone might be Ricky, don't you?'

'Stands to reason.'

'So that's why he's changed his tune.'

'You know what they say.'

'What?'

'A reactionary is a liberal who's been mugged.'

# Twenty-six

'I am a racist.'

The four hundred delegates to the Policing Diversity and Social Deprivation in a Multi-Cultural Environment drew breath. Many looked uncomfortable.

'That's right. I *am* a racist.'

Deputy Assistant Commissioner Roberta Peel paused and hung her head in mock shame.

The hall exploded in rapturous applause.

'Each day I look inside myself and confront my own racism. I am riddled with subtle prejudice, preconception and indirect discrimination.

'My racism may be unwitting, it may be unconscious. But it is racism. I am guilty.

'I have myself been a victim of discrimination, of the institutionalized sexism that runs through the body of the police service in Britain like a cancer. I was a victim, but at the same time I have been guilty of victimization.

'Thanks to the Macpherson Report I have been able to come to terms with my racism and the institutionalized racism which pervades our entire society.

'There has been a collective failure of our organizations to provide an appropriate and professional service to people of ethnicity and gender and social disadvantage because of institutional prejudice, ignorance, thoughtless and disadvantageous stereotyping of minorities.

'We must bring about a paradigm shift in social awareness and challenge the parameters of our accountability, transparency and sensitivity.

'In our inner cities we must stop seeing crime as a

145

problem and look upon it as a challenge. A challenge to all of us. I am a racist, yes, but I am also an oppressor.

'Our unequal society is to blame. When we are confronted with a young offender we should not be seeking to punish but to understand the pernicious forces of conservatism that stigmatized him.'

More rapturous applause.

'The Prime Minister has spoken bravely about the forces of conservatism preventing our nation from becoming a modern and progressive 21st-century European democracy.

'Those same forces of conservatism are at work in the police service. They must be confronted and defeated.

'We must first confront those forces within ourselves.

'That's why I say to you today – and challenge you to say the same:

'I am a racist.'

The applause lasted for a good thirty seconds before it was spent.

Roberta milked it.

The last handclap bounced off the walls and died.

There was a low hum of conversation.

Roberta stepped back towards the microphone.

She placed both hands on the dais and said: 'I can't hear you.'

All eyes were upon her.

'I said I can't hear you. Is this just to be another self-congratulatory seminar? Have these speeches we have heard here today been just empty words?'

From the body of the hall, a male voice called out: 'I am a racist.'

'That's good.'

'I am a racist.'

'Come on.'

'I am a racist,' more voices joined in.

'I AM A RACIST. I AM A RACIST. I AM A RACIST.'

'BETTER,' shouted Roberta.

'I AM A RACIST. I AM A RACIST. I AM A RACIST.'

They chanted, over and over again, as Deputy Assistant Commissioner Peel looked on approvingly, part headmistress, part evangelist, admiring herself on the giant TV screens suspended around the hall.

'Now go from this hall and build a police service of which we can all be proud,' Roberta commanded.

The delegates filed out to spread the gospel.

Roberta stepped down from the podium. A grey man in a grey suit approached from behind the stage.

'Magnificent, my dear, if that's not being sexist.'

'Not at all, Home Secretary.'

'You're the future of policing in Britain, Roberta.'

'I'd like to think so.'

'I don't want to be presumptuous; after all these things aren't wholly in my gift.'

'I understand.'

'But it won't have escaped your notice that the old man is due for retirement.'

'Indeed not, Home Secretary.'

'Well, in the normal course of events the succession would pass to his immediate deputy.'

'Of course.'

'But we, the Prime Minister, too, feel that in this case, good man though Jarvis is, he is, um, perhaps a little 20th-century.'

'And?'

'We thought it would be best all round if we were to skip a generation.'

'I see.'

'Look here, Roberta, what I'm trying to say, and this isn't official, but the job's all yours.'

'Home Secretary, I'm flattered.'

'Flattered you may be, my dear. But not wholly surprised.'

'Modesty forbids.'

'No need to be modest. I've studied your career, from Bramshill, through the ranks, your crime management initiatives, your inclusivity strategies, your anti-sexism and anti-racism programmes, your pioneering bridge-building with the gay community, your zero-tolerance of motoring offences when you were at county.'

'We must not be judgemental. We must be pro-active as well as reactive, but always with compassion. I encountered a great deal of resistance in those early days.'

'You're pushing on an open door now.'

'Thank you, Home Secretary.'

'Thank you, Commissioner.'

'It's still *Deputy Assistant* Commissioner, for now.'

'For now, yes. But you'd better get used to it, Roberta. Goodbye.'

'Goodbye.'

The Home Secretary headed for his official car.

Roberta packed her briefcase and turned to go.

Her car was waiting, too.

As she left the building, a young PC saluted. She acknowledged his salute.

There was a vibration in her pocket.

She took out her pager.

'Ring JF, pronto.'

Her driver had the rear door of the Rover 75 already open in anticipation. She settled onto the back seat and pressed the stored number on her mobile. After three rings, Fromby answered.

'Yes?'

'You left a message.'

'Something has come up. We need to talk.'

'Tonight?'

'Yes.'

'My place.'

'OK.'

'Bring a bottle, we've got something to celebrate.' Roberta sounded excited, like a schoolgirl.

'Sure.'

'Talk, you said. Anything urgent?'

'Er, not right now. It'll keep.'

# Twenty-seven

'You're nicked, chummy.

'I said, you're NICKED.

'You are not obliged,

'You are NOT obliged,

'Oh my god,

'Oh my GOD!

'But it may harm your defence if, JEESUS!

'It may harm your defence . . .'

Roberta breathed deep, hard, straining against the police-issue handcuffs manacling her wrists and ankles.

'It may harm your defence if you do not mention, AAAGH!

'Something which you later RELY ON IN, IN, IN!

'OH GOD, OH GOD!

'later rely on in court. Anything you DO SAY!

'will be taken. TAKEN, TAKEN, TAKEN!

'CHRIST!

'taken down, DOWN! DOWN! and may,

'SLOWLY, DAMN YOU, SLOWLY.

'taken down and may be used,

'OH SHIT, OH GOD!

'May be used in, in, IN, IN, IN, IN, IN!

'HARDER, HARDER, HARDER!

'May be used in EVIDENCE!

'SLOWER! NO, FASTER!

'FASTER! HARDER!

'May be used in evidence AGAINST YOOOOOU!

'OH MY GOD! PUSH! HARDER! FUCK YOU! FUCKING FUCK FUCK FUCK FUCK JEEEEESUS! FAAAAAAAAA-AARK!'

The handcuffs dug deep into Roberta's flesh. The police helmet she was wearing thudded into the bedhead and was forced down over her eyes as her body arched a full eighteen inches above the pillows supporting her arse and her lower back.

She thrashed around and convulsed as if strapped into an electric chair, then collapsed into a sweating, panting heap.

The man standing at the end of the bed gently withdrew the police truncheon.

Roberta lay motionless, her movement constrained by the handcuffs, which had drawn blood as they fought to contain the ferocity of her violent orgasm, her body pegged out like Gulliver on the white bed sheets.

The man was naked, except for a balaclava, borrowed from the Black Museum at Scotland Yard and rumoured to be the former property of one of the Great Train Robbers.

He took a key from the night stand and, one by one, unlocked the handcuffs restraining Roberta.

She drew her knees up to her chest and purred contentedly.

'You can take that off now.'

Justin Fromby removed the balaclava and threw it onto a chair.

'I thought you were going to come quietly,' he laughed.

No chance.

The bust of Karl Marx stared back from her dressing table.

Since she discovered the delights of Marx all those years ago, as a young WPC, no ordinary man could satisfy her.

During her weapons training, she pleasured herself regularly with the steel barrel of a Smith & Wesson handgun.

She still, occasionally, dusted off Karl, smothered him in baby lotion and gave him a run-out for old times' sake.

But nothing compared to the old-fashioned police truncheon she was first issued with at Tyburn Row.

She kept the mahogany surface lovingly polished and lubricated with KY Jelly.

She called the truncheon Dixon.

At first she would always fly solo, but later persuaded Justin to come along for the ride, as co-pilot.

She'd experimented with bondage, but the necessity of leaving one hand free to manoeuvre the truncheon spoiled the effect.

Justin adored Roberta but was glad that Dixon relieved him of the obligation of rising to the occasion.

He sat on the bed next to her.

She stroked his thigh with her index finger.

He failed to respond. Neither of them expected him to.

'I really wish that I could, you know,' Roberta said.

'Shhhh. I've told you a thousand times, there's no need. Just so long as you're fine.'

'Good old Dixon. I just wish that I could return the compliment.'

'Not necessary. Never has been.'

Roberta rolled over and pulled up the duvet. She drained the last of the champagne Justin had brought over.

She hadn't been able to wait to tell him about the conference and her conversation with the Home Secretary.

'It's what we've always worked for.'

The excitement of the day demanded a sexual release. Dixon was soon on the case.

'Justin?'

'Hmm.'

'Have you ever?'

'Have I what?'

'You know, with another woman?'

'Don't be daft.'

'Another man, then?'

Justin sipped his champagne.

'Justin?'

'What?'

'Is that it?'

151

Justin tapped the side of his nose with his finger and smiled.

Roberta prodded him in the ribs.

'Come on, tell me, I wouldn't mind.'

'Nothing to tell.'

'I thought we agreed that there would never be any secrets between us,' she teased.

'I'm glad you raised that,' Justin changed the subject.

'Secrets?'

'We did agree that there would never be any secrets between us, right?'

'Of course.'

'Then why didn't you tell me about Tyburn Row?'

'What about Tyburn Row?'

'That night, Trevor Gibbs and that fat, racist cop. Remember?'

Roberta's face dropped in blank, terrified uncertainty.

'Guess who I bumped into at the weekend,' said Fromby.

'Who?'

'An old friend. An ex-PC from Tyburn Row. Ring any bells?'

'Oh shit.'

'You do remember.'

'PC French. Mickey French.'

'Correct.'

'Where? How?'

Justin told her the full story. Wayne 'Monkey Boy' Sutton, Mickey French, Jez Toynbee. Goblin's. The knife, the files, the tape.

'Why on earth didn't you tell me?'

'You asked me to do it.'

'That's not the point. You didn't tell me that French caught you in the act.'

'I panicked.'

'You also didn't tell me that he'd got the whole lot down on tape. You should have kept your mouth shut. Denied everything.'

'I'm sorry.'

'It's a bit late for that.'

'I didn't think he'd ever use it. After all, he was implicated, too. The moment he failed to report me, he became part of a criminal conspiracy. He had just as much to lose as we did.'

'Had. Past tense. He's out of it now.'

'I know. Took a bullet.'

'Lincoln Philpott.'

'You came up against him then, didn't you? You got Philpott off.'

'One of my better days.'

'So why didn't French expose it back then? He had a motive, he had a grudge.'

'He was still in the force. And Marsden, the racist Plod, was still alive and living on a police pension.'

'French is still implicated.'

'But now he's angry and he doesn't give a shit.'

'He's still got a family to support. Shall I talk to him, try to reason? We always got on well.'

'That was over twenty years ago. Have you ever come across him since?'

'Briefly, when he was on weapons at Hendon.'

'I remember the Smith & Wesson.'

'That's beside the point. Whatever problem he's got is with you. Why should he want to do anything to harm me?'

'Can you think of anything?'

'Off the top of my head, no.'

'You realize this could destroy everything. I mean *absolutely* everything. You, me. The Commissioner's job. Everything we've ever worked for. Everything we ever wanted. This could jeopardize the whole Project. Shit, it could mean prison.'

'Do you think he's still got the tapes, the knife, the rest of the stuff?'

'He was pretty convincing if he hasn't.'

'He wasn't bluffing, then.'

'I've come across enough chancers in court. No, I'd say he wasn't, for certain.'

'But there's nothing in it for him.'

'We can't take the risk. We have to recover the evidence.'

'We don't even know where he's got it hidden.'

'His house has to be favourite.'

'So what do we do? Just walk in and ask him politely to hand it over?'

'Funnee.'

'I could always get a warrant, tell a magistrate we're acting on information received, in connection with stolen property. We could search the house.'

'No. We, you, can't be anywhere near this.'

'What then?'

'Leave it to me. I'll think of something.'

# Twenty-eight

The Scorpio left the motorway and joined the B-road, passing a sign reading, 'You are now entering Heffer's Bottom. Please Drive Carefully.' Mickey stuck to the speed limit religiously. He'd had enough grief to last him a lifetime, let alone a weekend.

'Not bad, all things considered,' Mickey said. 'Four and a half hours. Probably a new Commonwealth record.'

Andi smiled. She was glad to be going home.

In the rear mirror the suburban sprawl disappeared behind a hedge. The road dipped down and narrowed and the constant hum of the M25 petered out.

If you didn't know better, you'd think you were in the middle of the countryside, even though this was less than twenty miles from Charing Cross.

Heffer's Bottom was situated in the no-man's-land created by the Green Belt, the demilitarized zone between Essex and north-east London.

It fell within the Metropolitan Police area but was due to be handed over to Essex as part of yet another reorganization. The village police house had long since closed and the local bobby withdrawn and transferred to Edmonton.

Mickey drove past the 16th-century church and turned into the High Road. The village cricket pitch had been colonized by travellers six months ago.

They'd already looted the pavilion and burned it down, as a basis for negotiation.

About a dozen caravans were dotted around. The wicket, once tended lovingly by a local groundsman, had been desecrated. Where generations of amateur cricketers had

155

lived out their fantasies, imagining themselves Trueman or Tyson, Bradman or Botham, there were the charred remains of a stolen builders merchants' lorry.

Piles of scrap metal and pirate wooden pallets littered the site. Children and dogs ran wild. There were a few horses tethered to a fence and a couple of trotting carts.

Half a dozen battered trucks were parked up, none of them with valid tax discs, most of them run on illegal red agricultural diesel, stolen from local farms.

And, beside each caravan, a gleaming 4x4 off-roader. Landcruisers, Shoguns, Discoveries, even a brand-new Mercedes ML430.

These pikeys didn't do badly for themselves, Mickey thought. Considering that they're all supposed to be skint, scraping a living from old bits of scrap and flogging lucky heather door-to-door.

Since the pikeys arrived, there had been a spate of burglaries in the village and surrounding district. Garden sheds had been ransacked, lawnmowers, motorbikes, cars stolen. A few residents had reported break-ins. The French residence had already been a target.

They were after what they called 'smalls' – portable pieces of valuable jewellery.

The rule of law didn't so much run in these parts as walk on by. That was if it bothered turning up at all.

The caller who rang the Ricky Sparke show complaining about police attitudes to rural crime and burglary struck a chord with Mickey. Collier St James was the next village away, across the county border.

On the rare occasions the cops did arrive, they always protested that there was nothing they could do unless they caught the culprit in the act.

Some residents said they had watched stolen vehicles being driven onto the travellers' camp and could see their own property standing there in broad daylight in the middle of the old cricket pitch.

Individual officers sympathized but said they had been

ordered to handle the pikeys with kid gloves as part of the Met's Policing Diversity and Sensitivity Strategy.

Someone had identified the pikeys as an oppressed minority, which made them pretty much a protected species. Police patrols had orders not to enter the illegal settlement.

The truth was simpler than that, Mickey knew. The Old Bill were shit scared of pikeys. Always have been.

Travellers were invariably armed and unafraid to use whatever weapons came to hand.

So they were left alone, save for the DSS van arriving every fortnight to hand out the Giros.

These days the police policed those who consented to be policed, and that was about it, Mickey reckoned. Cowardice, moral and physical, was the order of the day.

Community policing extended to that part of the community likely to offer serious violence to the police.

The only time most of the taxpaying, law-abiding majority ever came into contact with the police was when they were nicked for doing 34 mph in a 30 mph zone or pulled over for a random seat-belt check. And would you mind blowing into this, sir.

Or when their car was nicked or their house was burgled and they were greeted with an indifferent shrug and offered a note for the insurance.

As the Scorpio passed the gypsy camp, a group of men watched it go by.

Word had got round that Mickey used to be Old Bill. The pikeys were suspicious of him.

Twice he had confronted them, the second occasion only ten days earlier, when he caught two of their number, a man of about twenty-three and a boy of fifteen, breaking into his garage and attempting to have it away with his golf clubs.

Mickey had taken a blow to the shoulder with a pitching wedge, but he'd managed to wrestle back his golf bag and his clubs.

That night a gang from the camp had arrived on his door-step. He had faced them down with his ex-police revolver, which he had a licence to own, despite the post-Dunblane clampdown. They didn't frighten him.

'Next time I catch any of you fucking thieving pikeys on my property I'll blow your heads off. I'll round you up and shoot you like rats in a barrel. Understand?'

They understood. They always understood violence and the threat of violence. They had a grudging respect for Mickey.

Now they also had a grudge against him.

There had been another run-in in the local pub a couple of days later. To a loud chorus of approval from the regulars, Mickey had repeated his threat to shoot anyone he caught breaking into his property.

On neither occasion had the police been called. What was the point?

Mickey and Andi had discussed moving again. But where? They'd moved to the village to escape the inner city and give the kids a better chance in life.

Maybe this was as good as it got.

Mickey swung the Scorpio into the driveway.

The garage door was ajar.

'Wait here.'

'What is it, Mickey?'

'Might be nothing. Just stay in the car.'

'Did you leave the garage door open?'

'No, I'm certain. Just hang on.'

'Wotsup, Dad?' asked Terry.

'Stay put, son.'

Mickey reached under his seat and retrieved the metal Crook-Lok, a two-foot steel rod which fitted across the steering wheel when parked to deter thieves. He got out of the car and walked the five yards to the garage, a grey, prefabricated structure with a corrugated-iron roof. It had been put up in the Thirties by the original owners to house a black Austin Seven and a BSA motorbike and sidecar.

The Chubb padlock Mickey had installed to secure the doors had been wrenched open.

He instinctively opened the door with the end of the Crook-Lok. His police training had instilled in him the preservation of the crime scene. You never knew. There may be prints.

The lawnmower. Gone.

The kids' bikes. Gone.

The golf clubs. Gone.

Mickey backed out and turned to Andi sitting in the car.

'Mickey?'

'Yep.'

'All of it?'

'Just about.'

'Our bikes?'

'Sorry, son. I'll replace them.'

'That's all right, Dad,' said Katie, who had stirred from her slumbers. 'I've grown out of mine.'

Andi made to get out of the car.

'Just hang on, love.'

'You don't think?'

'I'll go first. You stay here with the kids.'

Terry opened the back door.

'Son, I said stay here,' Mickey insisted.

He walked down the pathway, towards the house. The front door was hidden from view by a porch.

The frame was splintered and the door hanging by a single hinge. The resistance offered by the deadlock and the chain had proved futile. Mickey stepped inside.

There was shattered glass on the doormat and the hall table had been smashed.

Mickey opened the door of the cupboard under the stairs. The alarm box had been ripped off the wall and the bell disconnected.

Mickey hadn't bothered plumbing it into a monitoring centre. He figured that by the time the Old Bill arrived, the thieves would already have been long gone.

He pushed open the door to the family room.

Carnage.

And the stench.

God, the stench.

The furniture had been slashed and the walls smeared with shit, like the H-blocks in the Eighties.

Picture frames containing family photos were strewn about the floor and crushed underfoot.

Mickey bent down and picked up Katie's first school photo, gap-toothed, pigtailed innocence. The glass had been shattered and there was a yellow stain on her face.

Someone had pissed on it.

Someone had pissed on his daughter.

Someone had pissed on his family and smeared shit on his walls.

In the cracked mirror above the York stone fireplace, Mickey could see the distorted reflection of some crude lettering.

He turned to inspect it.

In what looked like blood-red spray paint was written:

### NEX TIM ITS YOU COZZER

Bastards.

'MICKEY!'

Andi stood in the doorway.

'I told you to stay in the car.'

'What's that smell?'

'Just get out of here, please.'

'Is it what I . . . Jeesus, Mickey.'

'Please, love, just take the kids outside.'

But Andi ignored him.

She ran upstairs to the bedroom. Her jewellery box lay open on the quilt. It was all gone.

Not valuable, but sentimental.

Her gran's engagement ring. Her dad's watch. Mickey's dad's antique fob.

At least they hadn't trashed the bedroom.

She walked back downstairs, clutching the empty jewellery box.

Mickey walked towards her and hugged her tight.

'Everything?'

'Oh, God.'

Terry said nothing, just turned and walked out of the house. Katie's eyes began to stream. Mickey reached out and embraced her, pulling her close.

Utter desolation.

'Just go and get back in the car.'

'But I've got to clear up. We can't leave it like this.'

'It's a crime scene, love.'

'It's our HOME, Mickey.'

'I know. Just, please, do as I say. I'll call it in.'

'It was those, those bloody travellers, wasn't it?'

'A million.'

'I'll put the kettle on.'

'I'd rather you waited in the car.'

'Mickey, I'm not being forced out of my own kitchen by those animals.'

'OK. I'll come with you. Let me go in first.'

Mickey pushed open the kitchen door.

It appeared to be unscathed.

Thank God.

Andi filled the kettle and plugged it in.

She went over to the fridge and stooped to retrieve a bottle of milk.

Next to the fridge was a dish of cat food, untouched.

Funny, they'd left her enough for three days.

From the next room came a piercing shriek.

'DADDY! DADDY! DADD-EEE!'

Katie.

Mickey and Andi rushed back to the family room.

Their daughter was frozen to the spot, her delicate hands clasped to her cheeks.

'Why aren't you in the car?'

'Daddy, look, oh, look, oh, no.'

Delayed shock, Mickey thought.

He put his arm round his daughter and began to manoeuvre her out of the room.

'Don't worry, precious. It'll clean up. It'll be all right. I promise.'

'No, Daddy. It's, it's Tammy.'

'What about Tammy?'

'Look, Daddy. There. Loook.'

There, on the carpet, beside the sofa, in a pool of red, lay Tammy, the family Siamese. Mickey turned her over with his toe. Her throat had been cut.

'NEX TIM ITS YOU COZZER.'

It wasn't written in blood-red paint.

It was written in blood.

# Twenty-nine

Mickey handed Andi the keys to the Scorpio, told her to take the kids to her mum in Palmers Green and stay there.

Her protests were muted. She knew he was right.

The police would be here soon. Mickey would handle everything.

Terry sat in front with his mother. As the car backed out of the driveway they all waved, mechanically.

Andi lowered the window.

'Are you going to be OK?'

'Fine, yeah. Call me when you get to your mum's.'

'You coming over later?'

'Nah, I'll stay here tonight. The glazier can't get here until tomorrow morning. We're going to need a new lock, too. I'll sort it. You just look after the kids. Give my love to your mum. Sleep tight.'

'God bless.'

As the Scorpio rounded the corner, a police jam-sandwich turned into the road and pulled up outside the house. It was almost an hour since he'd dialled 999.

Two young coppers got out. Mickey didn't recognize either.

'Evenin' all,' said Mickey, sarcastically.

'Good evening, sir. Sorry we're . . .'

'Late?'

'Yes, sir. Sorry. We got here as quick as we could. We've only got two cars covering the whole of the north-eastern sector tonight. There's been a bit of a set-to in a boozer in Waltham Abbey. Fortunately we were in the car park checking tax discs when it all went off.'

'Now there's a surprise.'

'Burglary, is it?'

'Correct.'

Mickey examined the two cops.

Christ, they didn't look much older than Katie. Was I like that once?

He led them into the house and showed them the damage. He explained the background.

There had been a wave of break-ins since a gang of 'travellers' set up on the municipal cricket pitch.

'Mustn't jump to conclusions, sir,' said the younger cop, blonde hair, freckles, NHS-style specs. Dead spit for the Milky Bar Kid.

'Look, son. I'm an ex-DS. Twenty-five years in. Trust me. I know the patch. I've had trouble with them before.'

'That's as maybe, sir. But we can't rule out the possibility that this was an opportunist attack.'

'So what the fuck do you make of that, Sherlock?'

Shit on the walls and 'NEX TIM ITS YOU COZZER'.

'Smack of motive to you, does it?'

'Why would they do that?'

'I've had a couple of run-ins with them.'

'Did you report them?'

'What was the point?'

'We take all such incidents very seriously.'

'Oh, do me a favour. If that's the case why don't you just steam in with a warrant and search the site?'

'There are procedures, sir.'

'Procedures, my arse. There's always been procedures. Procedures never caught a real villain. I'd have given them a kicking until they put their hands up to it, fucking thieving dids. I dunno why I even bothered calling you. I might just as well go round there myself and sort it.'

'Sir,' said the pimply young Plod with a hint of condescension in a voice that had barely broken, 'I wouldn't recommend that. We can't have anyone taking the law into their own hands.'

'Don't patronize me, son. I was in the Job when you were a fucking tadpole.'

'Now you listen to me, Mister, that's right, MISTER French,' snapped back the Milky Bar Kid. 'You're not in the Job any more. Things are different now, what with PACE and Macpherson. And if you ask me, all the better for it. We're a community force these days, we have to respect ethnic diversity and multi-culturalism. Members of the travelling community have the right not to be smeared as common criminals.'

'Rights?' Mickey laughed. 'Don't give me rights. Don't give me multi-fucking-culturalism. The only culture these fucking pikeys have is thieving. Whose side are you on, son?'

'It's not a question of sides. Look, for what it's worth, I agree.' It was a million that the pikeys – er, sorry, the members of the travelling community – were behind the burglaries. But it was more than his job was worth to investigate further, otherwise he'd have the equal opportunities committee, the local police liaison working group and the ACC (Diversity) down on him like a ton of hot horseshit. And what would that do for his career?

Precisely, Mickey thought. This little boy was on the fast track, the up escalator, through Bramshill to the very top. He'd come across his sort before. This kid reminded him of a WPC he'd worked with at Tyburn Row for a few months in the late Seventies, soft hands, soft politics, straight out of the LSE via Hendon. Always talking about 'crime management' and community relations.

Now look at her. Tipped as the next Commissioner of the Metropolitan Police.

'You'll go far, son.'

'We'll notify CID and get the scenes-of-crimes officer over as soon as we can.'

'I'm going to have to clean up.'

'You know the drill, Mr French.'

'Of course I do, but I can't live with this a minute longer.'

'But we need to preserve the scene.'

'OK,' said Mickey. 'Hang on.'

He went to the kitchen and returned carrying a spatula and an empty, cracked, earthenware dish.

'Go on then.'

'Go on what?'

'Samples. Evidence.'

'I think we should wait for the SOCO.'

'Squeamish?'

'It's not that.'

'Oh, no?'

'I really do think we should wait.'

'Here, allow me.'

Mickey walked over to the wall and scraped off a piece of dried shit. He tapped the end of the spatula and tipped the flaky, brown excrement into the dish.

'People's exhibit one.'

'What do you want me to do with that?'

'Oh, I dunno. Maybe you could go onto the gypsy camp and ask everyone for a stool sample. Then all you've got to do is match it up and Bob's the live-in lover of your mum's boyfriend's half-sister.'

Mickey handed the dish to the Milky Bar Kid.

'Just about sums it up.'

'What does?'

'Life's a crock of shit. And so is this case. Admit it, no one's getting felt for this.'

'I still think we should let CID make that decision.'

'I've had enough of this,' Mickey said, retreating once again to the kitchen.

He came back bearing a scrubbing brush and a bucket full of soapy water. He unscrewed the top of a bottle of Domestos, tipped it in and began scrubbing furiously.

'Mr French.'

'What is it now, son?'

'I don't think –'

'Look, five gets you ten this is dog-shit. And you won't be getting any prints off the cat, will you?'

'Perhaps you're right. I'll give you a crime number, just in case. For the insurance.'

'If you must.'

'I'm sorry about what's happened, sir. Really, I am. I just wish we could have got here sooner.'

Mickey stopped scrubbing.

'I'm sorry, too, son. It's not you. It's not your fault. It's the whole rotten system.'

'We don't make policy, Mr French.'

'I know. But I'll tell you one thing.'

'Yes?'

'If those fucking pikeys come anywhere near me, my family or my house again, I'll blow their fucking heads off.'

# Thirty

The scenes-of-crimes officer arrived about half an hour after Milky Bar and his mate left, called to an illegally parked skateboard in Chingford.

She went through the motions but told Mickey not to hold his breath. The CID didn't turn up at all.

Mickey scrubbed the wall back to the plaster.

He carried the cat into the garden and buried it under a rose bush.

He couldn't stand the cat, if truth be known. It was Andi's pet. But he wouldn't have wished the manner of its demise.

Mickey opened a bottle of scotch and poured a slug into a chunky, cut-glass tumbler. He drank it down in one and refreshed it.

He dragged the furniture into the hall, rolled up the light brown Berber carpet, with its dried puddle of cat's claret, and carried it into the back garden.

He went to the garage to fetch a can of petrol he used to refuel the mower. The pikeys had stolen that, too.

Fortunately, they'd overlooked the barbecue lighter fuel. Mickey doused the carpet, allowed it to soak for a couple of minutes, then set fire to it with a long-handled safety match.

The flames leapt into the night sky. Mickey poured another drink and watched it burn.

When the fire began to dampen, Mickey went back into the house. He took a black binliner from under the sink and started collecting the debris. The hall table was beyond repair. That could go on the fire. So could the broken wooden picture frames.

The metal frames had stood up well; the glass was smashed, but could be replaced.

Mickey picked up the picture of Katie, defiled and yellowed by piss.

He walked outside to where the carpet was still glowing. He stoked the fire with the broken hall table.

As the flames revived, he took the photo of his daughter and dropped it on the pyre.

He watched as the yellow picture turned brown and shrivelled.

He thought of the little girl in the photo, her first school photo, and the ordeal she had endured that past weekend.

The heat from the fire was intense, but Mickey shivered. He stared into the flames.

From the house, the telephone interrupted his frigid contemplation.

Mickey walked inside and answered.

'Hi, lover.'

'Hi. You OK?'

'Uh-huh.'

'The kids?'

'They've had a bath and gone to bed.'

'Your mum?'

'A bit hysterical. She's taken it badly.'

'Have you told her about Goblin's?'

'Not tonight. That can wait.'

'Look, I want you to stay away from here for a while.'

'Why?'

'There's stuff I have to do.'

'I've got to come back. I haven't even got a change of clothes.'

'Tell me what you want. I'll bring everything over.'

'But you haven't got the car.'

'OK. I'll pack, you can come and collect it.'

'I'll come now.'

'No, tomorrow. I'll ring first.'

'Fair enough.'

'You fine?'

'I'm a big girl, Mickey. I miss you.'

'You've only been gone a few hours.'

'A few hours too long.'

'See you tomorrow.'

'Love you.'

'Me, too.'

Mickey put down the phone and poured another large one.

Sleep was out of the question.

He climbed the stairs and opened the hatch to the loft. He pulled down the ladder, switched on the light and hauled himself inside.

There it was. What he was looking for.

Mickey took the two cans of white emulsion downstairs and emptied them into a decorator's tray. He took a paint-brush from a jar full of turps under the stairs and set about his task.

```
NEX TIM ITS YOU COZZER
NE   M   S  OU COZ
N        S  U   Z
            U
```

Half a dozen strokes with the broad brush and it was gone. Using a roller, Mickey painted the entire room white. He gave it two coats and finished the bottle of scotch.

By morning, there would be no trace.

By morning?

It was morning.

Mickey looked at his watch. Almost nine.

The doorbell rang.

'Mickey?'

'Theo, son.'

'Got your message. Fucking animals. Soon have it fixed.'

Theo Panthos, handyman, distant cousin of Andi, dumped

his tools in the hall and fetched a piece of frosted glass from his van.

'You're a star, Theo,' said Mickey, hugging him.

He was exhausted, but the booze had mellowed him.

Theo fixed the pane in the front door, replaced the hinges and fitted a new lock.

'I'll come back later and put you an extra deadlock at the top. Next time it'll make it harder for them.'

'Next time? There's not going to be a next time. Next time they're dead.'

'Right on, Mickey. But better safe, eh?'

'How much I owe you?'

'We'll work something out later. I'll be back.'

'Cheers, mate.'

Theo drove off just as the phone rang again.

'Hi, it's me.'

'Andi, sorry love. I was going to ring. Theo's been here.'

'Has he fixed the door?'

'Good as new.'

'I'm coming back to clean the rest.'

'No need. It's done.'

'Whadya mean?'

'You'll see.'

'I'm coming back anyway, for some clothes, at least.'

'Sure, how long?'

'I'll come straight away.'

'Come alone.'

'Why?'

'The kids will be all right with your mum.'

'Yeah.'

'There's something I want to talk to you about.'

'What?'

'Just hurry over. You'll see. It's nothing bad, honest.'

'About an hour then.'

'Great.'

Mickey dragged the furniture back into the sitting room. The distressing carnage of the previous night had been erased. Bar the lack of a carpet, it could have been a bad dream. Soon sort that.

Mickey dialled an old school friend.

'Regal Carpets.'

'Brian, Mickey French.'

'French, you old bastard. How are you?'

'Don't ask. It's been a bad few days.'

'Sorry to hear that. What can I do?'

'Have you still got our carpet in stock?'

'Berber wasn't it? Light brown? Should have. If not the next best thing.'

'Have you still got the measurements?'

'They'll be here on file. Why? It hasn't worn out already, has it?'

'No, I burned it.'

'I thought you'd given up smoking.'

'No, I burned it in the garden.'

'Eh?'

Mickey gave him the short version.

'It'll be done by tonight, just as soon as the lads get back from doing a house in Chigwell. Stand on me.'

'You're a star, Bri.'

'I know. See you later.'

Mickey showered, shaved and changed. He climbed back up to the loft and crawled into the corner where an old tea chest was nestling behind the paint tins.

Mickey reached inside. It was still there.

He took out the dusty plastic documents case handed to all Police Federation reps at the Worthing Conference in 1981.

He slid back the flimsy fastener and reached inside. First he took out a sheaf of papers, then a cassette tape, then a rolled chamois leather. He unrolled the chamois. A knife fell out. The knife Trevor Gibbs had been found with at Tyburn Row all those years earlier. The knife, the tape, the juvenile records which Roberta Peel had tried to dispose of on Justin Fromby's instructions.

Mickey put them back in the case and went downstairs.

He took out the cassette, stuck it in his Panasonic tape deck and pressed PLAY.

It hissed and crackled into life. The first voice he heard was his own. Younger, higher, but recognizably him.

'Found what you were looking for?'

'Er, yeah.'

'And what are you going to do about it?'

'What do you mean?'

Roberta Peel sounded younger, too. Plummier, more Home Counties. More the vicar's daughter. Not at all like the classless New Establishment he had heard her affect on television recently.

'I've been talking to Eric Marsden.'

'And?'

'Fromby's trying to fit him up on an assault on the prisoner.'

'I reckon he did beat him.'

'Eric denies it. Says he got the injuries in the fight outside the chip shop. Sounds about right. I nicked Gibbs the last time. He's a nasty little fucker. You going to charge him?'

'Mr Fromby says that if we charge Gibbs, he'll make a formal complaint against Marsden.'

'If this caution comes to light, you've got no option but to charge him.'

'What should I do?'

'That's up to you, girl.'

'Fromby knows about the previous. He wants me to lose it. And the knife.'

'What, this one?'

'Where did you get that from?'

'Never you mind. What are you going to do with the previous?'

'The way I see it is that everybody wins here. Fromby gets what he wants, Marsden's off the hook. Everybody's happy.'

'And what if I don't give a fuck and turn you in? Give me that. You're a lucky girl.'

'Lucky?'

'There's two copies still in here. Usually we keep one and send the other to central records at the Yard. This hasn't gone off yet. I must have forgotten.'

'So what happens now?'

'You're a silly fucking cow. Old Eric Marsden may be a cunt but he's only got a year left to his pension.'

'So?'

'So why wreck anyone's career here. Eric Marsden's or yours?'

'What about the sergeant?'

'He is the original wise monkey. He sees nothing, hears nothing, says nothing. He doesn't want to know. No charge, no paperwork. He's sweet. Fromby's hardly going to say anything. The boy certainly won't object to being released. Eric will stay shtoom and he'll put the frighteners on the skinhead who picked him out. He'll tell the sergeant that Gibbs is being released pending further inquiries. That'll be the end of it.'

'And you? What's in it for you?'

'I don't want Eric going down the shitter and I reckon you've got a big future.'

'What are you going to do with all this – the knife, the file, the tape recording?'

'I haven't thought about it. Nothing, maybe. Who knows?'

Mickey stopped the tape and pressed REWIND.

The doorbell disturbed him.

A key rattled in the lock.

Mickey opened the door.

Andi was standing there with the key in her hand.

'Theo's changed the lock.'

'That explains it.'

'Come here.'

174

Andi fell into his bear-hug.

She threw down her bag. It hit the deck. The hall table wasn't where she was expecting it.

'Oh, God. I forgot.'

'Everything's going to be fine. Come on through.'

'Wow! You must have been up all night.'

'I had no one to sleep with.'

Andi smiled.

'Mickey, you're, you're, oh you're fantastic. I could have helped.'

'You needed to be with the kids.'

'Thank you, Mickey.'

'It's not perfect.'

'It's wonderful.'

'Brian's putting the carpet down later.'

'Have you taken it up to clean it?'

'No, I burned it.'

'Where?'

'In the garden. I figured it would be best. Nothing cleanses like fire.'

'And Tammy?'

'Under the rose bush.'

'Thanks. I know you couldn't stand that cat.'

'We'll get you another one.'

'No need.'

'Cup of tea?'

'I'll make it. By the way, I thought I heard voices.'

'Voices?'

'It sounded as if you'd got a woman in here.'

'My bit on the side?'

'Stop it, Mickey. I distinctly heard voices.'

'On tape.'

'Tape?'

'Yeah. Remember? I told you about it in the car. Fromby, Tyburn Row.'

'Where have you been keeping it?'

'Up in the loft with all my old Federation stuff.'

'Can I hear?'

Mickey put the tape back in.

'You sound so young.'

'It was a long time ago. Pity we didn't have video then. I'd look a damned sight younger, too.'

'So that's her?'

'Yep.'

'I see what you mean. It's dynamite, Mickey.'

'Told you.'

'But you can't ever use it.'

'I didn't have to. I only had to threaten to. It frightened off Fromby.'

'Does he really think you've got it?'

'Dunno. He can't afford to take the risk.'

'Do you think he's told her about it?'

'She already knows.'

'What are you going to do with it?'

'I'm hanging on to it.'

'But if he knows you've got it. This could finish him, end her career.'

'They're gambling that I won't use it. I'm compromised, too.'

'You'll have to get rid of it, Mickey.'

'We'll see,' said Mickey, putting the cassette back in the plastic case.

'Please.'

'I said, we'll see. I need more time to think.'

'Once the carpet's down, I'll go and get the kids.'

'No. That's what I wanted to talk to you about.'

'What?'

'This weekend has been a hell of a lot for them.'

'For all of us.'

'They need a holiday.'

'We all need a holiday.'

'I'm glad you agree.'

'And?'

'Call Auntie Olive, in Florida. She'd love to see you. The weather will do you all good.'

'What do you mean, you?'

'I'm not coming.'

'Oh, no. I'm not going without you.'

'Please, Andi. I'll come out in a couple of weeks. There's stuff I have to do here, first.'

'You sure?'

'Positive. Now go and pack. I'll run you to your mum's. We'll sort some tickets out. Ricky's cousin's got a travel agent's. He'll fix you up. I'll call him. Now go pack.'

Andi disappeared upstairs.

Mickey called Ricky. He was fresh off-air.

'Hello, mate. Did we have a belter this morning? A bloody riot.'

'Sorry, Rick, didn't hear it.'

'Traitor.'

'Been busy. Tell you about it later.'

'Fine. Spider's.'

'About eight?'

'Great.'

'While I'm on, give us the number of your cousin with the bucket shop.'

Ricky reeled it off the top of his head.

'Going away?'

'Not me. Andi and the kids.'

'She's finally leaving you, then?'

'Piss off. See you later.'

Mickey rang Ricky's cousin, gave him a credit card number and confirmed three seats, BA, Gatwick to Orlando, 11.10 the next day.

He walked over to the dual tape deck, unwrapped a blank C60. He took the Tyburn Row tape back out of the Federation case, placed it into the adjoining cassette slot and pressed FAST DUB. When it was complete, he repeated the process.

He was finished by the time Andi came back downstairs.

'All fixed.'

'I wish you were coming, Mickey.'

'Now then. When I'm done here. I promise. I'll run you to Gatwick first thing. I'll call Uncle Tom later. He'll meet you at Orlando. You'll have a great time.'

'If you say so, Mickey.'

'I want you to look after something for me.'

He took one of the duplicate cassettes and placed it in her left hand.

'Is this what I think it is?'

'It's a copy.'

'What for?'

'Insurance. Take it with you.'

'Mickey French, I hope you know what you're doing.'

'Who me?'

They both chuckled.

'Come on, I'll take you to your mum's then come back and let Brian's boys in. I've got to see Ricky later, but I'll join you at mum's later, say about eleven.'

Mickey locked the door, opened the boot and dropped the bags inside.

As they sat in the front of the car, Andi threw her arms around Mickey's neck and kissed him on the cheek.

'Whatever you're up to –'

'I'm not up to anything.'

'Whatever it is, just promise me you'll be careful.'

'I promise.'

# Thirty-one

'You're late.'

'I know.'

'He's on his second bottle,' said Dillon, wiping a wine glass on a tea-towel and handing it to Mickey.

He found Ricky Sparke sitting at a corner table, clutching protectively a bottle of Chilean Chardonnay and doing the crossword in the last edition of the *Evening Standard*.

Spider's was quiet. A few afternoon drunks were sleeping off their long lunches. A couple of leathery ex-Windmill girls were sipping sherries at the bar and remembering past glories.

There was always a lull early evening. Spider's didn't really start to rock and roll until pub chucking out time. It was normally still heaving at two-thirty in the morning, with bar, restaurant and theatre staff unwinding after another night on the West End hamster wheel.

'You're late.'

'I've already had that from Dillon,' said Mickey. 'Sorry, it's been a bastard of a day. Bastard of a weekend, come to that.'

Ricky poured the last of the wine into Mickey's glass.

'I can't stop too long, mate. I'm on a three-line whip.'

'I was just thinking,' mused Ricky. 'You know how they say you can tell someone's personality?'

'How?'

'For instance. Take a bottle of wine. An optimist sees a half-empty bottle as half-full. A pessimist sees a half-full bottle as half-empty.'

'So what's your point, Bertrand Russell?'

179

'Well my bottles are either full or empty. And even when they're full, I can see them empty. So what does that make me?'

'A piss artist.'

'Almost. A thirsty piss artist,' he laughed, draining his glass.

'OK, I can take a hint,' said Mickey, signalling in Dillon's direction.

Dillon had anticipated their requirements. He walked over to the table, dressed, like his hero Johnny Cash, all in black. He was clutching two, already opened, bottles of Chilean Chardonnay.

'I dunno about two,' said Mickey.

'Shall I take one away?'

'No, no, no. That won't be necessary,' Ricky insisted. 'I'll make sure it goes to a good home.'

'Slate?'

'Mine,' volunteered Mickey.

Ricky refilled their glasses.

'Half-full?'

'Half-fucking-empty,' said Mickey.

'Like that?'

'Not many.'

'Tell your Uncle Rick.'

Dillon went into the room behind the bar and changed the CD. Spider's had the best muzak in London. Like Rocktalk 99FM without the phone-in plankton and phoney mid-Atlantic DJs.

Where else would you get the soundtrack from *Mean Streets* at half-eight on a weekday evening?

Smokey was doing 'Mickey's Monkey'.

'Oi, they're playing your song, old son.'

'Me Mickey. You Monkey.'

'Bollocks.'

'These days I've Got to Dance to Keep from Crying.'

'You could get on the radio with stuff like that.'

'That's your department, Rick.'

'Transport, law and order, that's mine. Or at least I used to think it was.'

'Come on, spit it out.'

Mickey recounted the trials and tribulations of the last weekend. The lot. The roadblock, the gyppoes, the speed traps, Goblin's, the burglary, the damage, the shit, the piss, the cat. The whole nine yards.

Every so often, Ricky would interject.

'A fucking ELF?'

'You are KIDDING?'

'Holy SHIT.'

By the time Mickey had finished, so were the two bottles. Ricky went to attract Dillon's attention.

'No more for me, mate. I'm under starter's orders. I've got an early off. If I don't get the overground to Palmers Green, I'll have to get a black cab, if I'm lucky.'

'No motor tonight?'

'I drive for a living. Have you forgotten? A couple of gallons of Dillon's Chilean Chardonnay and that's my licence.'

'Sure.'

'Look, I've got to have it on my toes. I'm taking Andi and the kids to Florida tomorrow.'

'You're going to Florida?'

'No, *I'm* not. *They* are. I'm taking them to the airport. That's why I wanted your cousin's number. Ta. He did me a deal.'

'Why aren't you going?'

'Reasons. I dunno. We'll talk about it tomorrow. I'll pick you up from the radio station.'

'But you haven't heard about my weekend yet.'

'Let me guess. Rolled by a couple of Eastern Europeans. Last £250. Getting warm?'

'How did you know?'

'I heard you ranting on the wireless. It sounded personal.'

'Too right. It got a massive response from the callers, too. I seem to have hit a raw nerve.'

'Right. I'm off. Do me a favour, will you?'

'Anything, as long as it doesn't involve bestiality, Scottish country dancing or eating Pot Noodles.'

'Nothing like that. I just want you to look after this for me.'

Mickey took a package from the poacher's pocket in his outback jacket and put it on the table.

'What's this? It's not my birthday.'

'Just look after it for me, will you?'

'Sure. But what is it?'

'Important is what it is. Dynamite, you could say. What's in here is more lethal than Semtex.'

'It's not going to go off in my hand, is it?'

'You're safe enough. There are some people who would love to get their hands on it, though.'

'Who?'

'A couple of very important people.'

'Am I to be told who they are?'

'Tomorrow. I'll tell you everything. Just guard it with your life. Outside the family, you're the one person I trust. Just don't get pissed and leave it on the tube.'

'Don't worry. I'll call it a night, too. It won't do me any harm. I'm on air at nine.'

'Very wise.'

'Go on, run along. Give my love to Andi and the kids.'

'Remember what I said. Guard it with your life.'

'Have I ever let you down?'

# Thirty-two

*'Those were the latest headlines. Coming up in an hour, Ricky Sparke. Stay tuned to Rocktalk 99FM. This is Squeeze.'*

Georgia Claye stirred under the duvet. She reached out her right hand and hit the off button on the clock/radio.

What time had she gone to bed? She didn't recall.

The inside of her mouth tasted like a tramp's trainer. An empty red wine bottle nestled beside her on the pillow.

The blinds were open, the window closed. The atmosphere inside the bedroom was fetid.

Georgia rubbed her eyes. The black mascara she'd forgotten to remove smeared off on her knuckles.

She eased herself upwards on her elbows. She was still wearing her bra. Her knickers were marooned on her left ankle. She must have passed out while undressing.

Her breasts drooped apologetically, like two supermarket carrier bags half-filled with water. They rested on her beer gut, which sagged onto her thighs as she leant forward.

Georgia rolled towards the edge of the bed and attempted re-entry. As she hoisted herself up, she caught a glimpse of her body in a full-length mirror.

Fifty looming, flabby and forlorn. She had legs like Popeye's trousers, pitted with cellulite and varicose veins. Her long, lank, once black hair had turned grey. She looked like the Witches of Eastwick's ugly mate.

She'd been considered something of a beauty when she arrived in England from Gary, Indiana, in the 1970s, to study journalism. Fell in love with a handsome Italian student doctor training at Bart's. They married after a whirlwind romance, but it didn't last. He left her for a man he met at a Tom Robinson gig when Georgia was seven months pregnant and was last heard of heading an AIDS project in central Africa.

She had considered going back home, but was caught up in the metropolitan whirl, the excitement of pub rock and punk, so decided to stay in London and bring up her son.

Georgia contracted a doomed second marriage to a scaffolding contractor who used her as a punch-bag. She dabbled with lesbianism, too, but her heart wasn't in it. A succession of unsuitable 'uncles' passed through her son's life.

Now the boy was gone, too, running a pioneering gay bar in Dumfries.

Georgia threw on a dressing gown and made her way unsteadily downstairs. Back in the Eighties, she'd gone all open-plan and dispensed with the stairwell and the banisters after her second husband had taken a lump hammer to them in a fit of drunken rage. She kicked him out and somehow never got round to replacing them, making an architectural feature out of their absence.

This morning she had cause to regret it. She had nothing to cling onto as she negotiated the precarious incline. She dared not look down. She froze to the spot, fearful of falling forward. If she fell, it could be days before she was discovered.

There was only one way down. She sat on the steps and slid down on her arse, jarring the base of her spine, effecting a soft landing on the pile of newspapers which had been pushed through the front door.

She had to move. A flat would be nice. Ground floor. No stairs. But she was loath to leave her little piece of Holloway. Georgia struggled to her feet and made her way to the kitchen. She filled the kettle and plugged it in. She opened the fridge, retrieved a bottle of cider and poured it into a glass.

Halfway down it kicked in.

She picked up the papers and sat at her desk in the open-plan lounge, knocked through by a couple of moonlighting McAlpine's Fusiliers in exchange for £500 in their hand and three-in-a-bed with Georgia. The threes-up was Georgia's idea.

The room looked like a skip. There were old newspapers and empty bottles everywhere.

The walls were decorated with yellowing cuttings and cartoons, documenting Georgia's passage from unpaid contributor to *Puke*, a small punk rock rag, to occasionally paid Fleet Street freelance.

She currently had a sort of contract with the *Clarion*, a soft-left, small-circulation daily broadsheet. But her contract wasn't worth the paper it wasn't written on. She hadn't had anything published for a couple of months.

On her desk was the only award she had ever won. The Golden Spike. It stood nine inches high on a wooden base and was given to her by the Publish and Be Damned Association in recognition of the number of articles she had written which an assortment of editors had refused to publish.

Georgia liked to believe that her bold exposés of female circumcision and police corruption were simply too hot to handle. The Publish and Be Damned Association, a self-congratulatory collection of disaffected and embittered radical hacks, certainly thought that.

In truth, most of Georgia's work ended up on the spike because it was complete bollocks.

Which is why she struggled to get anything published. So she supplemented her meagre stipend from the *Clarion* as a rent-a-gob pundit on bear-pit television shows and two-bob radio stations.

Such as Rocktalk 99FM.

As she drained her cider, the phone rang.

'Georgia?'

'Speaking.'

'Hello. Timmy, here. I'm a researcher on the Ricky Sparke show, Rocktalk 99FM.'

'Hello, Timmy.'

'We were wondering, Ricky was wondering, if you'd like to do our newspaper review this week.'

'Usual time?'

'That's right, ten till eleven am.'

'Let me check my diary.'

Georgia put her hand over the mouthpiece and opened her diary. Blank.

'Ten till eleven, you say?'

'Uh-huh. We'd need you here by ten forty-five.'

'Well, I do have a couple of rather important engagements.'

'That's a pity.'

'But I suppose I could try to rearrange them.'

'Could you? Oh, that would be super.'

'Will you send a car for me?'

'I could do, but only if you waived your fee.'

'Is there a fee?'

'Not if you want a car.'

'What if I find my own way in?'

'We could probably run to fifty quid.'

'Hmm.'

'And we'll make sure there's plenty of hospitality.'

'Such as?'

'A couple of bottles of wine. A few crisps. Ricky likes to let his hair down occasionally.'

'OK, I'll do it. I'll take the tube.'

'See you.'

'Bye.'

Georgia opened another cider and made a mental note not to get shit-faced the night before the show.

Fifty quid was fifty quid.

And there would be wine.

# Thirty-three

'Your boy's in number three, sir,' said the custody sergeant. 'Bag-snatching, on the tube.'

'Thank you, sergeant. I'll see my client now,' said Justin.

'If you don't mind me saying, Mr Fromby, sir, this is a bit beneath you, isn't it?'

'I'm sorry?' Justin gave the sergeant a reproving look.

'I mean, bag-snatching. Small time.'

'I was taking my surgery at the law centre when we got the call informing us that you were holding a refugee in custody and that he was in need of legal assistance. There's no ceremony, no hierarchy at the law centre. Cabs on a rank, sergeant. No injustice is beneath me, as you put it. Everyone is entitled to the best possible defence.'

'If you say so, sir.'

'Oh, I do say so.'

The sergeant unlocked cell three and showed Justin Fromby inside.

'Would you like me to wait outside, sir?'

'That won't be necessary.'

'Very well.'

'Oh, sergeant. Shut the door, will you?'

Ten minutes later, Fromby emerged from the cell and informed the sergeant he would like to speak with the arresting officer.

The young undercover detective constable, name of Collins, was summoned from the canteen.

'You haven't charged my client, yet.'

'We are going to, sir. All in due time.'

'Witnesses?'

'Myself and my partner, sir. We caught him bang to rights.'

'And the woman?'

'Woman?'

'You know perfectly well who I mean, detective constable. The owner of the alleged stolen property. The woman whose handbag was allegedly taken by my client. Surely she is also a witness.'

'Oh, her, you mean?'

'Yes. Do you have her witness statement?'

'Actually, sir, the woman in question is a police officer. She will be making a statement in due course.'

'A POLICE OFFICER?'

'British Transport Police. It was a joint operation.'

'*Operation?*'

'Operation Artful Dodger, sir. Targeted at robbery on the transport network.'

'I'm sorry, constable,' said Justin, with the emphasis on cunt. 'What we have here is a clear case of entrapment.'

'That's bollocks. This was a lawfully constituted operation, sanctioned at the highest level. The arrest was done by the numbers.'

'I can't accept that. In my opinion, my client was enticed into a compromising situation. This was a highly dubious arrest. I wish to see your superior officer.'

'That's not possible.'

'Not possible.'

'All senior officers are away attending a diversity training seminar. There's no one here above the rank of sergeant.'

'In that case, I must insist that you release my client immediately.'

'I can't do that, Mr Fromby.'

'SERGEANT!' Fromby called.

The custody sergeant came shuffling through, clutching a polystyrene cup of decaffeinated coffee substitute.

'You rang, sir?'

'Sergeant, I must insist on my client's immediate release.

188

Now that I have been acquainted with the circumstances of this arrest, I realize that we are looking at entrapment and this station and the Commissioner of the Metropolitan Police are looking at a substantial suit for damages. The *Clarion* will have a field day. Undercover cops prey on stateless, vulnerable refugees, that sort of thing. Should be able to get *Panorama* interested, too.'

The sergeant paused for reflection, sipped his coffee substitute and scratched his balls.

'I can't release a prisoner without an address.'

'He has got an address. He's staying at a hostel in Tottenham.'

'But there's no one to stand bail for him. I can't accept his own recognizance.'

'I shall stand surety for him.'

'You, sir? That's highly irregular.'

'Nowhere near as irregular as this arrest.'

'Sarge,' pleaded the young DC.

'Sorry, son. I'm not having this landed in my lap. Mr Fromby, I will release your client on police bail into your custody, provided you agree to return here with him in fourteen days.'

'Thank you, sergeant.'

Justin led the slightly bewildered young Romanian from the police station and hailed a taxi, which was loitering alongside an illegally parked black Mercedes S500.

# Thirty-four

The taxi drew up outside Justin Fromby's house in Dartford Park, a substantial but discreet Edwardian villa a few hundred yards from the eastern fringes of Hampstead Heath, probably built for a City banker around the turn of the century, less than a mile away from the north London bedsit he used to rent as a student.

Justin and Ilie Popescu got out and walked up the half dozen stone steps to the front door. Ilie noticed there were three doorbells.

Although Justin occupied the whole three storeys and the basement, he'd had three doorbells installed so that people thought the house, like most of its neighbouring properties, had been divided up into flats. They were numbered 37A, 37B and 37C, but they rang the same bell.

Justin had paid £1.75 million for the house, but through a shell company. Even though, in a good year, he pulled in seven figures, he was careful to hide his wealth.

The Consolidated Union of National Trades Societies paid Fromby more in brief fees than fifty of their minimum-waged members earned in a year.

'You can wait in there.' Fromby showed Ilie into the drawing room. The mundane Edwardian exterior of the house disguised a minimalist interior, a riot of white paint, bare surfaces, chrome, steel and leather, and stripped floorboards, a homage to Philippe Starck.

Ilie sat down on an angular chaise longue, slightly bewildered. He had thought about bursting out of the taxi but had heard the deadlocks on the passenger doors engage when the meter started running.

'Why have you brought me here?' he asked Fromby, in deliberate, broken English.

'Would you prefer still to be in a police cell?' Justin replied. Pretty boy, he thought to himself.

'No, of course. But my girl, she will be worried.'

'Where is she?'

'She's at the hostel. In Tottingham.'

'Tott-en-ham,' Fromby corrected him.

'Yes. Tott-EN-hem. Sorry. My English.'

'That's OK. I'll get you back to Tottenham in due course.'

'Will I have to go back to the police station?'

'Perhaps. Don't worry.'

'Why are you helping me like this?'

'I am a lawyer. I believe in human rights. I simply want to understand more about your plight. You say you have applied for asylum?'

'Yes, when I arrived in Britain.'

'Have you any relatives here?'

Ilie hesitated.

'Is that important?'

'It could be.'

Ilie thought hard.

'No. No one.'

'I see.'

'Can you help?'

'Perhaps.'

'I have no money.'

'I don't want money.'

'But how can I repay you?'

Justin smiled, walked over and placed his hand on the young Romanian's shoulder.

'We might be able to think of something.'

He patted Ilie on the head, like a collie. 'You must be hungry.'

Ilie shrugged.

'A drink? A sandwich?'

'Thank you.'

Justin opened the door and called up the stairs.

'WAYNE!'

Moments later a boy, about fifteen, shuffled into the room, pulling on a blue Adidas T-shirt.

'Wot is it?' the boy grunted, chipping away at his ear wax with an elongated, nicotine-stained fingernail.

Justin scowled but disguised it with a thin-lipped smile. He slipped his right arm loosely around Wayne Sutton's slim waist.

'We have a guest, Wayne,' he said, indicating the olive-skinned visitor.

Ilie rose and offered his hand but said nothing.

'Awright,' grunted Wayne.

'Would you please be kind enough to get our friend here something to eat and drink, please, Wayne?'

'Wot?'

'I don't know, anything. Do you like tea?'

Ilie looked blank.

'Vodka? Wodka?'

Ilie's eyes lit up.

'Wayne, pour our guest a glass of vodka. There's Polish, Russian, Finnish? Which would you prefer?'

'I drunk the Russian last night,' said Wayne.

'Polish OK? Wyborowa?'

Ilie nodded. A line of coke might be nice, too, he thought to himself.

Wayne poured a slug into a Waterford glass tumbler.

'Just one for now, mind,' said Justin. 'We don't want our guest getting drunk. We have much to do.'

Much to do? wondered Ilie.

'How about something to eat?' Justin asked.

'I'll take him out for a burger,' said Wayne.

'No, no, no. Rustle him up a cheese sandwich,' Justin interjected. 'We can't have our friend going out anywhere. Not just yet.'

He turned to Ilie. 'Just make yourself comfortable. If there's anything you want just ask Wayne. I have to check my messages in my study. I'll be back shortly. Come along, Wayne. The kitchen. Our friend must be hungry.'

They left the room. Ilie heard the key turn in the lock.

In the hallway, Justin grasped Wayne's right wrist and handed him the key.

'He is not to leave. Understand?'

Wayne nodded.

'What do you want with him? You've got me here,' Wayne asked anxiously.

'It's nothing like that,' Justin reassured him with a gentle kiss on his left cheek. 'I might have a job for him. Just make sure he stays put.'

'What kind of job? I could do it.'

'No. Please, Wayne, for once just do as you're told. No more questions, OK?'

'OK.'

Inside the drawing room, Ilie studied his new surroundings and wondered if there was anything worth stealing. He could probably overpower the old man, but there was the boy and two against one was risky.

He had heard the key turn in the lock and could see through the micro-blinds that the windows were fitted with the concertina steel grilles erected by the 21st-century London gentry to protect themselves against burglary, the New Age Plague.

Ilie poured himself another Wyborowa and considered the odds. Sure, for now, he was a prisoner.

But an hour ago he'd been in a police cell. Somewhere out there, somewhere, the men from Moscow were looking for him.

Ilie savoured his spirit.

There were worse prisons.

# Thirty-five

Justin closed the door of his study. In contrast to the Philippe Starck drawing room, the study was more like a 1970s student bedsit. The only clue to the elevated status of the occupant was an antique partner's table and captain's mahogany and leather chair, both circa 1852 and bought from an exclusive dealer in deepest Essex.

Otherwise the room was strewn with papers, pamphlets, law reports, back copies of the *Clarion* and a notice board studded with yellowing clippings of the golden days of industrial action – the siege of Saltley gates, Orgreave, Grunwick.

On the walls, limited-edition plates commemorated historic working-class struggles long before Justin was born – the strike for the Dockers' Tanner, the Battle of Cable Street.

In his adult lifetime, Justin had been involved on the fringes of just two major industrial confrontations, Wapping and the Miners' Strike of 1984/85.

On both occasions he was on the losing side.

These defeats had served to further convince him that the only way to change the system was from within, to make sustained progress through the corridors of power, even if it took a quarter of a century. The long march through the institutions was all but complete. Now the great prize he and Roberta had worked for was within their grasp, Commissioner of the Metropolitan Police.

But first he had to deal with the one man who had the evidence which could destroy them.

Mickey French.

He picked up the phone and dialled a mobile number.

'Peel.'

'It's me. Where are you?'

'I'm in the office.'

'Can you speak?'

'Yes.'

'I think I may have found a solution to that matter we were discussing the other night. But first I need you to check a name.'

'Go on.'

'Gica Dinantu. G-george, I-iris, C-charlie, A-apple. New word, D-dog, I-iris, N-nuts, A-apple, N-nuts, T-tommy, U-uncle.'

'Anyone could tell you'd never served in the police or the armed forces.'

'What?'

'U-uncle,' she laughed.

'You what?'

'No, U-uniform.'

'What are you talking about?' Justin said impatiently.

'Well, it's U-uniform, for a start. N-november, T-tango.'

'OK, so I'm a complete charlie uniform november tango. Have you got it?'

'Gica Dinantu.'

'Good.'

'Who is he? I take it he's a he?'

'Yeah, Romanian. Asylum-seeker. Twentyish, I'd guess.'

'What do you want to know about him?'

'Everything.'

'Why?'

'I'll tell you later. Can you do it?'

'Should be simple enough. I'll get back to you.'

'I'm at home. I'm here all evening. Can you come round?'

'Should be able to. I'll ring you before I leave.'

'See you later.'

'Ciao, baby.'

Roberta knew Justin would have a good reason. She

logged on to her PC, swiped her ID card, and clicked on the hyperlink to the immigration service computer.

She entered the name Gica Dinantu.

His bare details appeared on the screen. Photograph – so that's what he looked like. Pretty boy. Name, country of origin, port of entry, age. Age? Sixteen? Justin had reckoned he was around twenty. Asylum application number. Last known address, Tottenham, London N17. A hostel. That was about it, though he had been fingerprinted at Croydon. A routine precaution but many of the overworked, stressed-out immigration officers simply didn't bother.

Roberta accessed the Scotland Yard central database. A Gica Dinantu had been arrested at Tyburn tube station earlier that day on a charge of robbery. That was quick. Computerization had transformed the police service. Not always for the better, Roberta thought. These days prisoners' particulars went straight into the system. Files couldn't simply vanish as they did in the old days. She reflected on what might have happened had computers been around back at Tyburn Row in the 1970s. And she shuddered. Best not to think about it.

Back to the screen. Gica Dinantu. No further details. Bailed to the custody of, that explains it, Mr Justin Fromby, of Fromby, Hind & Partners.

But why? What was Justin up to?

Roberta swiped her card again and punched in a new password. It took her into the Interpol computer.

She carefully typed in the name Gica Dinantu and waited a few seconds until it downloaded.

Roberta opened the file. Several keystrokes later she knew what little there was to know about Gica Dinantu.

It wasn't exactly what she had been expecting.

Then she double-clicked on the link to known associates.

One name.

It was flagged.

Please contact an Inspector Freund, Hamburg, Germany.

Curious.

She scrolled down the file.

Curiouser and curiouser.

She printed off the file, shut down her PC and called Justin.

The constable on the door saluted as she left New Scotland Yard. 'Goodnight, ma'am.'

Roberta, normally always one to acknowledge the other ranks, completely ignored him.

Outside, her driver was waiting. He leapt out of the Rover and opened the rear passenger door.

'No, no thank you, Frank. That will be all for tonight.'

'Can I drop you somewhere, ma'am?'

'Er, no, no thanks,' she said, distractedly. 'I'll take a cab.'

'Will you be wanting me to collect you from home in the morning?'

'What? Sorry.'

'From home. Tomorrow, ma'am,' said the driver.

'No, that's fine. I'll make my own way in.'

'Very well, ma'am. Goodnight.'

But Roberta was gone, hailing a cab outside St James's Park Underground station.

'Dartmouth Park,' she said.

Twenty-five minutes later the cab pulled up outside Justin's house.

She handed the driver a £20 note for a £14 fare.

'Keep the change.'

'Thank you very much, ma'am,' said the cabbie. 'Don't I know you? Aren't you that lady superintendent or something on the telly the other night?'

'No,' said Roberta.

'I could have sworn. It's just that picking you up outside the Yard and like.'

'You must be mistaken. Good evening.'

She turned and walked up the stone steps and pressed the second of the three doorbells – the one which rang in Justin's study.

Justin answered the door and showed her in.

She took off her coat. Underneath she was still wearing her uniform.

'Good. Nice touch,' he said approvingly.

'What?'

'It makes it more official,' he said.

'Now just hold on. You'd better read this.'

Roberta handed him the Interpol file. Justin seized it excitedly.

'This is better than I hoped,' he exclaimed.

'Better? Better for what?'

'How did you get this?'

Roberta explained that the Interpol file on Gica Dinantu had been closed some months earlier.

When he'd been killed during a lorry hijacking in Hamburg.

Justin drew breath. He took a bottle of Glenmorangie from the top of a filing cabinet and poured them both a large measure.

'So who's the guy in the photo?'

'His name is Gica Dinantu (deceased), formerly of the Tigani, Romania.'

'But that's not the Gica Dinantu in the other room,' he said.

'Try him,' said Roberta, pulling another photograph from an envelope.

'*That's* him,' confirmed Justin.

'No, *that's* the man who was with Gica Dinantu when he was killed. It was thought that he had been incinerated in the crash which resulted from the high-speed chase and shoot-out in which the real Gica Dinantu died. But they couldn't be sure, so they posted this picture on the Interpol website. It seems there's at least one detective, an Inspector Freund, who thinks he escaped.'

'He's the cop who flagged the name?'

'Presumably.'

'You've not called him?'

'Of course not.'

'Will he know you've been into the file?'

'Unlikely.'

'You don't think there's been a mix-up?'

'In what sense?'

'Like getting the photos back to front?'

'You've read the file. You're the lawyer. You work it out,' she said.

Justin paced across the room. He stared through the steel bars destroying the symmetry of the elegant sash window.

'As I said, this is even better,' he declared.

'Are you mad?'

'Maybe. But this could work to our advantage.'

'Come on. What's on your mind?' Roberta pressed him.

'When I walked into that cell I knew there was more to him. Forget the language difficulty. He didn't strike me as your run-of-the-mill bag snatcher. There was something else. I felt he was hiding something. I had no idea what he was hiding.'

'So you brought him back here. But why?'

Justin brushed her aside. 'It was always going to be a risk, but this guy's a professional. Car-jacking, suspected involvement in drugs. Interpol thinks the Russian mafia are after him. He's a resourceful fellow. Obviously a born survivor.'

'So if he's Public Enemy Number One, if he's so brilliant, how did he end up in a north London police cell, charged with bag-snatching?' asked Roberta.

'Providence, my dear Ms Peel.'

'Cut the Avengers act, Justin.'

'It was also providence which caused me to be on duty at the law centre the very day he was arrested. And of all the police cells in all the world, I had to walk into his.'

'For God's sake. Justin. First the Avengers, now *Casablanca*.' Roberta poured herself another shot of whisky into a mug with Tony Blair's famous five pre-election pledges printed on the side. 'And when are you going to do something about this study? The rest of the house is like an *Ideal Home* spread. This room reminds me of that bedsit in Tufnell Park.'

'It's supposed to. I like it like this. Reminds me who I am. What I'm doing here. You should remember that more often. High office has gone to your head. It's Home Secretary this, Chief Constable that.'

'That's what I do, remember,' Roberta was becoming increasingly tetchy.

'Of course I do. That's what we're doing here. That's what our little Romanian friend next door is doing here.'

'Now we're getting somewhere.'

'We're going to retrieve the Tyburn Row tapes. The files, the evidence. Everything.'

'And how, exactly, are we going to do that?'

'We are going to burgle Mickey French. Or, more precisely, our friend in the next room is going to burgle Mickey French.'

'We can't do that, Justin.'

'*We* can't. But *he* can.'

'You're forgetting I'm a deputy assistant commissioner in the Metropolitan Police.'

Justin grabbed her by the shoulders and stared deep into her eyes. 'And if you want to be Commissioner – and my God, you do – then you will listen to me. If we don't do this and French goes public it's all over. Not only will you not be Commissioner, you won't even be a copper. You will be finished. I will be finished.'

'But I can't get involved in a criminal conspiracy. And that's what this is.'

'You should have thought about that twenty-five years ago, back at Tyburn Row. That was a criminal conspiracy, too.'

Roberta slumped onto a corduroy sofa.

Justin settled beside her and slid his arm around her. He pulled her close. 'Darling, this is for us. For you. We have no alternative.'

Roberta sat forward and took a deep breath. 'Right, let's think this through.'

'OK, that's better.'

'For a start, what makes you think our, er, Romanian friend will go along with it?'

'What choice has he?'

'He could simply do a runner.'

'Where would he go? He's got the German police and, very probably, the Russian mafia out looking for him. He's gone to extraordinary lengths to conceal his identity. We're the only friends he's got in the world,' said Justin.

Roberta laughed. 'How do we convince him?'

'You're the one in the uniform. Does he want the Met on his case too? We hold all the cards, especially since we now know his true identity.'

'All right, but burglary?'

'French must be keeping the evidence in the house. I've got his address, from that incident at Goblin's.'

'But how can we be sure our man will find it? He doesn't know what he's looking for,' said Roberta.

'You've got a point. There is another way. At least then we could be fairly certain the evidence would be destroyed,' mused Justin.

'Out with it.'

'Arson.'

'*ARSON?* You are mad.'

'It's a damn sight easier than burglary.'

'Justin, I don't know. I really don't know. I *am* a police officer. Whatever I went into the Job for, this wasn't it. Bending the rules is one thing, commissioning arson is quite another.'

'So what's your suggestion?'

Roberta stared at the floor.

'There you go. Are we going to do this thing, or what?'

Roberta stood up and finished her drink. She straightened her skirt, buttoned her jacket, fixed her neckerchief, smoothed her hair and said:

'Come on then. You'd better introduce me.'

Justin and Roberta crossed the corridor. Wayne was walking from the kitchen carrying a tray of bacon sandwiches.

'I'll take those, Wayne,' said Justin. 'Here's twenty pounds,' he said, handing Wayne a note. 'Why don't you go to the movies or something? Make yourself busy. And stay out of trouble.'

Wayne took the cash and disappeared.

Justin unlocked the door.

'It's OK. Don't be frightened,' Justin said as the young Romanian leapt to his feet in a blind panic at the sight of the formidable lady police officer.

Ilie's mind was racing, his eyes searching for an exit. What the fuck was all this about? Had they come to take him back to prison?

'Bacon sandwich?' offered Justin. 'Oh, I'd like you to meet a friend of mine. Deputy Assistant Commissioner Roberta Peel, from New Scotland Yard. She's a very important lady. Very high up in the police force.'

Roberta looked the young man up and down. She approached him, hand outstretched in greeting.

'That's right, Deputy Assistant Commissioner Peel. Pleased to meet you, Ilie Popescu.'

# Thirty-six

*'It's ten o'clock. You're listening to Rocktalk 99FM. I'm Ricky Sparke and these are the latest headlines.*

*'It was revealed today that asylum-seekers are receiving free artificial insemination treatment on the NHS.*

*'Hang on a minute. Let me run that by you again. Asylum-seekers are receiving artificial insemination treatment on the NHS?*

*'Someone in the newsroom must be pulling my plonker. Who wrote this?'*

'Ricky, just get on with it. Read the fucking news,' his producer yelled in his earpiece.

'That's all right. Let him go,' said a familiar voice. Charlie Lawrence had entered the control room.

Mickey looked up from the script to see his Antipodean boss grinning from ear to ear and giving him the thumbs-up.

*'Sorry about that, ladies and gentlemen. I am reliably informed by my producer that this item is not a complete wind-up. It is absolutely true. I give up. No doubt plenty of you will have a view on that, especially if you're among those couples who have been waiting years for fertility treatment. Call me now on the usual number.*

*'It's not often I'm left speechless, but this is one of those rare occasions. Frankly, I don't think I'll bother with the rest of the news. How do you top that? Who gives a monkey's what's going on in Sierra Leone, anyway. I'll get back to your calls just as soon as we've heard from Elvis Costello.'*

While Elvis was presenting a reasonable case for giving Chelsea a wide berth, the Rocktalk 99FM switchboard went into meltdown. For the next two hours Charlie Lawrence rolled up the sleeves of his Ralph Lauren cotton Oxford button-down and helped man the phones.

At the end of the show, Ricky, Charlie and the rest of the team were exhausted.

'Fucking brilliant, mate,' declared Lawrence. 'Top stuff. I only came in to give you the latest figures. Look at this.'

He handed Ricky a sheet of A4 containing a jumble of numbers.

'Leave off, Charlie. I do words, not numbers. What does it all mean?'

'Ricky, mate, you are now doing numbers. We're up thirty per cent over the past week. Shit, if it carries on like this we might even make a profit before we're very much older. You've really struck a chord lately. You should get mugged more often, mate.'

'I dunno,' said Ricky, with a sardonic shrug.

'Listen, mate, you've really struck a fucking chord with all this asylum kick. This is hot-button, heart of the nation. A Number One, top of the fucking heap.'

'Yeah, yeah.'

'Ricky, this is sensational. Look on it as doing a public service. You don't get anything like this on any other station. You're telling it like it is. The public loves it.'

'I know, but the public would love public executions, too.'

'So what's your point?'

'Some of the fucking idiots we get on the phone, that's what.'

'They're our customers, Ricky. They pay your fucking wages.'

'I know, Charlie, but there are degrees.'

'Of what?'

'You ever heard of the Duke of Wellington?'

'Young's pub, nice barmaid.'

'Not the Duke of Wellington, the Duke of fucking Wellington. A person not a pub.'

'Never met the bloke. I don't get invited to those kind of posh Pom parties.'

'Hardly surprising. Anyway, he died a couple of hundred years ago.'

'Where's this going?'

'During the Napoleonic wars the Duke was commanding the English forces at Waterloo. No, *not* the station, before you say it. Anyway, he took one look at our troops and said something to the effect that he didn't know what effect they had on the enemy, but they scared the shit out of him.'

'So?'

'That's how I feel about some of our listeners. Sometimes the show sounds like a fucking National Front rally.'

'That's not your fault.'

'I'm the fucking host. I choose the topics.'

'Right, mate. And you keep hitting the bullseye. You might choose the topics but you don't choose the reaction. That comes from the listeners themselves.'

Ricky rubbed his eyes and sighed. 'Yeah. I guess you can pick your enemies but you can't always pick your friends.'

'Fuck me, mate, philosophy, too. You are on a roll.'

'That's all you give a toss about, isn't it?'

'That's my job, mate. And your job is to drive audiences. Right now you're doing it brilliantly. The Ricky Sparke show is the hottest, most talked-about show in town. So what if the fuckwit liberals hate it? The listeners love you. Just keep on doing what you're doing.'

'And what do I do next – invade Poland?'

'You're tired, mate. Piss off and relax. You've earned a few tinnies.'

'Something tells me I am about to be taken unexpectedly drunk.'

'Just make sure you're sober in the morning,' Charlie reminded him.

'Will anyone notice the difference?'

Outside the Rocktalk 99FM studios, Mickey French was waiting in the car. Ricky opened the passenger door and leaned inside.

'Dump the motor in the underground car park. We've got an appointment with Dr Smirnoff.'

Mickey needed no persuasion. Andi and the kids had arrived safely in Florida and he'd never been much of a one for his own company.

After half a dozen large ones and a couple of Cumberland sausage sandwiches in the nondescript drinking barn, a former car showroom, over the road, they took a cab to Soho.

The door of Spider's was locked.

'Where the fuck's Dillon got to?' asked Mickey.

'I'm right behind you boys,' a soft Irish brogue answered.

'You're late. You're supposed to open at three.'

'It's my club. I'll open when I like. I didn't get away until five-thirty this morning. Why don't you go and have one in the French? I haven't even cleaned up yet.'

'We'll give you a hand,' said Mickey.

'OK, come on then.' Dillon unlocked the door and the three of them abandoned the broad daylight of central London and descended into an Orphean cellar, full of glasses, empty, half-empty and broken, scattered everywhere. A couple of stray coats and a lost handbag but no casualties.

'I'll tell you what, boys,' said Dillon. 'You missed a great night.'

'Give us a livener, then,' said Ricky. 'Oh, and stick some music on, too.'

Dillon poured three generous measures of Stolichnaya and selected a Louis Jordan CD.

What's the use of getting sober, they all sang along, if you're gonna get drunk again?

Mickey and Ricky collected the glasses, righted the tables and chairs while Dillon sluiced the floor, fumigated the khazi, washed up the empties and replenished the optics.

When some semblance of order had been restored, they took their respective places on either side of the bar. Dillon pulled the cork from a bottle of Chilean Chardonnay and plonked it in front of Ricky and Mickey.

'On the house, boys. Thanks.'

'Gawd bless yer, guv. You're a toff and no mistake.' Mickey tugged his forelock.

'Ever think you're getting old?' Ricky asked of no one in particular.

'We're all getting old,' said Dillon.

'It's just that sometimes I look round me and think to myself, this does not compute. The older I get the more I hanker for the past. I miss the old days.'

'Such as?' said Mickey.

'You know, when the pubs shut at three and didn't open again until five-thirty. That's when I first started coming here.'

'But you campaigned for all-day opening,' Mickey reminded him.

'Yeah, I know, but it's not the same. I hate pubs. That's something I never thought I'd hear myself say.'

'Me neither,' said Mickey. 'Considering how you spend half your life in boozers.'

'That's not what I mean. It's not pubs, it's what they've become. Laser karaoke discos with stupid names like the Ferret and Sea Slug, full of kids drinking alcopops from the bottle and foreign tourists in garish anoraks ordering halves of warm beer they don't like and then wondering why the barman won't bring it to their table.'

'You're not wrong, Ricky,' nodded Dillon. 'That's why this place has survived. I thought all-day opening would be the death of me. Quite the opposite.'

'This is what drinking should be about. Dank, subterranean, full of like-minded people.'

'Oi, less of the dank,' chided Dillon.

'You know what I mean. And it's not just pubs, it's everything.'

'Here we go,' said Mickey. 'This is going to get deep and it's not four o'clock yet. Better open another bottle.'

'Take today. I've just done a couple of hours on artificial insemination for asylum-seekers on the NHS. I must have sounded like Dr Goebbels. But I'm not the one who moved the goalposts.'

'What do you mean?'

'I've never been against immigration. Or genuine refugees. My own gran was a Russian Jew who fled here after the first war. Take your missus, Mickey, and her family. All genuine refugees from Cyprus. Good as gold. And your lot, Dillon. I guess they came to, what, work the railways, dig the roads, stuff like that.'

'Correct. My family practically built the A40 single-handed,' confirmed Dillon.

'Well, there you go.'

'But that's not what we're dealing with here. There's a full-scale international smuggling racket, gangs of fucking criminals from Eastern Europe and Kurdistan and the government is rolling out the red carpet. Yet raise the question and you get shouted down as some kind of racist.'

'Change the subject, someone. This is getting depressing,' said Mickey.

'Oh, by the way, your bird was in the other night,' said Dillon.

'Whose bird?' asked Mickey.

'Georgia Claye.'

'She is not my fucking bird.'

'You brought her down here, introduced her to the club.'

'So?'

'She's a fucking menace when she's pissed.'

'She's *always* pissed.'

'Practically fell down the stairs and started picking arguments with anyone who would listen. I had to put her in a cab. She's barking.'

'Dagenham East, more like,' said Ricky.

'Eh?' said Dillon.

'Four stops past Barking.'

'I drove her home once, after I'd dropped you off, remember?' Mickey reminded Ricky. 'She made a pass at me.'

'You didn't give her one?'

'Fuck off. Not with yours. I've smelt her breath, I hate to think what the rest of it smells like. Anyway, I'm a happily married man. And that reminds me, better make this the last. Andi's ringing me from Florida at seven our time. I'd best get home. She'll only worry if I'm not in.'

'Fair enough, son,' said Ricky. 'I might just stay on.'

The club was beginning to fill up with the usual suspects, out-of-work actors, unpublished authors, barmen on their afternoon breaks and a handful of Fleet Street's finest. Ricky nodded acknowledgement as they walked in.

'That's it. The crew of the Starship *Enterprise* have just arrived. I'm off,' said Mickey.

'A toast before you go, my good man,' announced Ricky.

He emptied the dregs of the bottle, raised his glass and saluted his best mate.

'To family.'

'Family.'

# Thirty-seven

As his cab weaved through the north London suburbs back to Tottenham, via Highgate, where his brother lived, down the hill to Crouch End, up again through Alexandra Palace and park, over the railway line, past the tube station at Wood Green, Ilie Popescu's mind was racing. He couldn't take it all in. His brain was churning, considering the angles, the options, the upside, the downside.

Was he going to wake up back in his prison cell? This was beyond surreal. He ran it through the memory bank again.

The Fromby guy. Some kind of hot-shot lawyer. The woman cop. Assistant something or other. Big noise at Scotland Yard.

He'd heard of Scotland Yard. Everyone had heard of Scotland Yard. The English, so incorruptible, so he thought.

Ilie had come across bent cops before. He'd bought a few bent cops in his time. He thought back to that sap Freund, in Hamburg.

Yet this big-time lawyer and seriously senior woman police officer had asked him to commit a crime. To torch someone's house. This isn't how things are done in England, Ilie thought. Is it? Romania, sure. All those freelance Securitat gorillas for hire. Russia? You bet. He could even believe it of the Germans, after his dealings with Freund.

But senior police officers at Scotland Yard just don't pick complete strangers off the street and ask them to commit arson. Do they?

Weird. Fucking weird.

Yet a few hours ago he was behind bars. Now he was free

and on his way back to the hostel. And Maria. Christ, Maria. The thought of Maria sent the blood coursing through his dick, which began to strain against his designer denims. He put her to the back of his mind. Concentrate, Ilie. Concentrate. Pros, cons.

How did it go again?

Deputy Assistant Commissioner Peel. Pleased to meet you, Ilie Popescu.

It was the first time he'd heard his own name since he fled Romania, apart from his brief encounter with his brother. He thought he'd covered his tracks.

Ilie couldn't read much of the file Deputy Assistant Commissioner Peel had handed him in the drawing room of Fromby's house. But he understood enough. Interpol, for a start. Freund, for another.

The pictures clinched it. Gica, poor, stupid Gica. Ilie almost felt a moment's remorse, but he brushed it aside. Gica knew what he was getting into. That could have been Ilie dead instead.

They knew everything. Fromby had summarized Ilie's options. They weren't attractive.

Ilie thought about going to the authorities and throwing himself at their mercy. But these people *were* the fucking authorities. Even if he could find anyone to listen, who would believe him?

Option one was to do as they wanted. Fromby would take care of the bag-snatching charge and Ilie would be free to resume his life. If he refused, he could be placed back under immediate arrest and Deputy Assistant Commissioner Peel would pick up the phone to Freund. Ilie would be deported back to Germany to face trial and almost certainly a sentence of life imprisonment.

There was another course of action available to Fromby and Peel. These were well-connected people. His file could accidentally fall into the hands of the Russian mafia in London. The head of the Russian mafia was rumoured to be living a few streets away from Fromby, in a large mansion on the eastern fringes of Hampstead Heath. The Russian trade mission was closer still, just up West Hill, in Highgate.

Germany meant a life sentence. The Russians meant a death sentence.

And if he tried to go missing, or reneged on the deal, his picture would be posted on every police noticeboard in London and on the front page of every newspaper. Deputy Assistant Commissioner Peel would lead the hunt.

Ilie had to hope the police found him before the Russians, but Peel couldn't guarantee it.

Either way, he was fucked. He was a free man or a dead man. You choose, Ilie.

You'll do it? You will.

Our survey said, top answer.

'We're here, guv.' The cabbie's voice jolted Ilie back to reality. 'That's fifteen quid exactly.'

Ilie peeled three five-pound notes from a wad Fromby had given him for expenses. Walking-about money, he'd heard the Londoners call it.

'Fifteen quid. Exactly,' repeated the cabbie, expectantly.

Ilie stared at him.

'That's what's on the meter,' the cabbie said.

'I give you fifteen,' said Ilie.

'Fucking gyppoes,' muttered the cabbie, deciding to call it a night. He wasn't going to get a decent fare in Tottenham at this time of night, let alone a tip. More than likely he'd get rolled for his takings.

Ilie ignored him and walked into the hostel. Maria was waiting for him in his room, sitting on the bed, red-eyed, worried, scared.

She flung her arms around his neck.

'Where have you been? Tell me.'

Ilie fastened her jaw in his right hand and forced their mouths together. He felt her tears on his face. Hot, moist, passionate.

'Not now,' he said.

He pushed her back onto the bed, lifted her skirt, seized her damp gusset in his fist and tore off her pants. He unzipped his jeans and drilled his cock inside her.

Ilie came instantly, convulsively. As the tensions of the day surged from his body he emitted a visceral scream, like a wolf caught in a trap.

It would have woken the dead, let alone the family of five Somalis in the next bedroom.

Maria had become accustomed to brief, brutal love-making, ever since their first adrenalin-fuelled coupling up against a wall at the side of Euston railway station. Ilie was not big on foreplay. She didn't complain. She loved him. When he was asleep she would finish herself off, drawing her knees together, gently squeezing her lips, massaging her clitoris with her index finger, lubricated by the warm semen Ilie had left behind.

Tonight was unlike any other time they had made love, however. There had been no thrill, no excitement, no sug-gestion of love. This was raw sex in its literal sense. In other circumstances it would have constituted a violent rape.

But she had consented. She wanted him.

She needed to be close to him. He was all she had in London. She would hold him tight all night. Perhaps they would make love again. Maria stroked Ilie's head.

He got up from the bed, folded his sticky, detumescent dick into his Y-fronts and zipped up his jeans.

He bent over and kissed Maria gently on her forehead.

'I have to go out,' he said.

'No. Stay, please stay,' she pleaded.

'I have to go. There is something I must do.'

'Can't it wait? You have just come in.'

'No, it has to be now.'

'Tell me what it is you have to do.'

'I can't. Not tonight.'

'When?'

'Sometime, maybe. I have to go.'

Ilie had formulated his plan in the cab on the way back

to Tottenham. Fromby and Peel had told him what he had to do but had not stipulated when he had to do it.

The sooner it was done, the better. No time like the present, Ilie figured.

Tomorrow he would get his life back.

Ilie pulled the address and directions from the back pocket of his jeans.

With luck, he could be back in bed with Maria in an hour and a half, maybe two hours, tops.

Ilie left the hostel and walked a couple of blocks. He turned into a side street behind Tottenham Hotspur football ground.

He needed a car which would not attract attention. He saw it immediately. A black London taxi. The police would not think of stopping a black cab.

Using the skills he acquired in Hamburg, he was in the driving seat in seconds. The owner hadn't even bothered fitting an alarm. Who was going to half-inch a black cab, for heaven's sake?

The diesel engine clattered into life. Ilie selected Drive and eased the car out of the side street and onto Tottenham High Road, heading east towards the North Circular.

As he approached the junction with White Hart Lane, he noticed a drunk waving furiously at him, beckoning him to pull over. Ilie switched off the yellow For Hire sign.

He would need petrol, not for the cab, but to start the fire. He pulled into an all-night filling station and checked the boot. There was a fuel can, full of diesel. No good. It had to be petrol. He emptied the diesel in the gutter and walked over to the pumps. He put a gallon of four-star in the can, approached the window and offered a ten-pound note in payment.

'You do know you've put regular petrol in there?' said the young West Indian cashier, helpfully.

Ilie regarded him with contempt. Lippy schwartzer.

'I mean, your cab runs on diesel, doesn't it?'

Ilie ignored him and walked away.

'Just trying to help, mate.'

Ilie turned and walked back to the cab.

'Fucking gyppo,' the cashier spat, thinking that he'd never seen a gyppo driving a black cab before and noticing that he hadn't bothered to pick up his change. That would buy him a drink later.

Nice motor, the cashier remarked to himself as Ilie turned back onto Tottenham High Road.

He was admiring the car which pulled away from the kerb and glided into position roughly fifty yards behind the taxi driven by Ilie Popescu.

The black S500 Mercedes.


The big man in the front seat of the Merc studied a sheaf of Polaroids.

'He went back to the house with the guy, after they left the police station. That's them going inside,' said the man in the back.

'He can't resist it, Popescu, can he? Small-time crook. Fucking bag-snatching. That's a long way down from stealing half a million dollars,' remarked the big man. 'Who's he, the other guy?'

'Lawyer, I guess.'

'And the woman?'

'She turned up at the house later.'

'Wife?'

'Don't think so. She didn't seem to have a key. She rang the doorbell. Some kid let her in. That's him there, going out about twenty minutes later.'

The big man glanced at the photo of Wayne Sutton and discarded it. The last few shots were of Ilie Popescu leaving the house with the man and woman standing in the doorway.

'He left alone?'

'Alone.'

'Stop anywhere?'

'No. I never lost sight of him. He went straight into the building, hostel, I guess. That's when I phoned you.'

'Was he followed?'

'No. Only by me.'

'Were you followed?'

'Absolutely not.'

'Excellent.'

The big man dialled a Moscow number on his cellphone.

# Thirty-eight

Curiosity got the better of Ricky Sparke. Back at his flat, he went to his desk drawer and retrieved the package Mickey French had handed to him in Spider's.

Guard it with your life, Mickey had implored him.

A bit dramatic, Ricky thought. Could have been the booze.

He'd meant to ask Mickey about its contents in Spider's but, one way and another, events and several bottles of Chilean Chardonnay had overtaken them.

Mickey hadn't raised it, even though he had promised to tell him, he must have forgotten, too.

Ricky poured himself a nightcap, drummed his fingers on the desk, picked up the package, shook it next to his ear, squeezed it, juggled it between his hands, weighing it up.

Mickey hadn't actually told him not to open it.

And he had a perfect right to find out what it was he was meant to guard with his life.

Ricky eased open the package and tipped the contents onto the desk. A cassette tape and some official-looking police documents concerning a juvenile called Trevor Gibbs. Didn't ring any bells.

Ricky took the cassette from its case and inserted it into his state-of-the-art Nakamichi tape deck.

He hit PLAY. The tape crackled into life. It was pretty lo-fi, devoid of Dolby compression, flaws all amplified by his digital Meridian active loudspeaker system.

Ricky sat back and listened.

A man's voice. It was Mickey.

Younger, but still Mickey. And a woman.

Ricky rewound the tape, listened to it a second time, then picked up the phone and punched in Mickey's number.

Engaged.

Ricky tried several times over the next half-hour. Permanently engaged.

Eventually the number rang out.

Mickey answered.

'I thought you'd taken the phone off the hook,' said Ricky.

'I've been talking to Andi, in Florida,' said Mickey.

'Shit, of course. Sorry, mate. I forgot. Everything OK?'

'They're all fine.'

'Look, why don't you just piss off and join them? It'll do you good to get away.'

'Next week, maybe. The week after,' said Mickey, non-committal.

'What's keeping you?'

'I've got a lot of thinking to do.'

'Would it have anything to do with the package?' Ricky asked.

'Yeah. Sort of.'

'Who's the bird?'

'What bird?'

'The bird on the tape,' Ricky said.

'You've listened to it, then?'

'What do you think?'

'I thought you might. You've always been a nosy fucker. Never mind. I meant to tell you this afternoon, but, you know, one thing led to another.'

'One bottle led to another, as I recall,' Ricky elaborated.

'Yeah, right. Sorry, mate, I've got a lot going on inside my head right now.'

'So who's the bird?'

'She's called Roberta Peel. She was a young plonk when I was at Tyburn Row.'

'I know that name. Isn't she the bird they're saying is going to get the Met?'

'The very same,' Mickey confirmed.

'I saw her on TV the other night. Nice tits.'

'Always has had.'

'You didn't?'

'Oh, do leave off.'

'I heard Fromby's name. Conceited wanker. If you don't mind me saying, what I heard on that tape didn't exactly strike me as kosher.'

'It's called perverting the course of justice, old son,' said Mickey.

'Oh dear, oh dear. That would be seriously embarrassing for a couple of people, for instance, a celebrity lawyer and a high-flying lady cop.'

'Got it in one. How do you think I got out of that spot of bother at the holiday camp?'

'Aha. It fits.'

'I threatened to go public, with the tape. Fromby backed off.'

'I don't blame him.'

'Trouble is he now knows I've still got the evidence.'

'No, *I've* got it,' Ricky reminded him.

'You've got *copies* of the original documents and the tape,' Mickey said. 'I've still got the originals and the knife.'

'Why don't you let me look after them, too?'

'I don't want to involve you if I don't have to.'

'Mickey, I *am* involved,' Ricky stressed.

'They don't know that. They needn't ever find out.'

'Who else is in this loop?'

'There's one other copy of the tape.'

'Where's that?'

'Florida.'

'I should have guessed. Andi knows all about it, then?'

'No secrets in this house, Ricky.'

'So what are you going to do?'

'Dunno. Thought I'd clean my guns.'

'*What?*'

219

'Helps me relax. I always try and clean the shooters when the kids are out of the house.'

'I didn't know you still had your guns.'

'Yeah, I'm still a licensed marksman. If you've been in the Job, sensitive areas, diplomatic protection, Branch, that sort of thing, they let you keep them.'

'I thought the government banned handguns, after Dunblane,' said Ricky.

'They did, except for terrorists, criminals and Old Bill.'

'Yeah, I wondered why since they banned guns the number of armed robberies and drive-by shootings had gone through the roof.'

'Another triumph for British justice,' said Mickey.

'By the way, who's the other bloke I heard mentioned. Marsden, was it?' Ricky enquired.

'Yeah, Eric Marsden. Old-school copper. Bit of a heavy-handed cunt, but he got the job done. He's dead now. His son's a DI out this way, Angel Hill. Bright lad. I knew him as a boy and came across him a couple of times when I was still in the Job.'

'And Gibbs, was it?'

'Trevor Gibbs. Good family, lovely parents, but he was a complete tearaway. Got into drugs, bit of blagging. Runs with the Yardies these days. Nasty piece of work.'

'And he was the real beneficiary of this little arrangement?'

'I've often thought about that over the years. If we'd have put him away then, who knows? Fucking Fromby.'

'Yeah, but you went along with it,' Ricky reminded him.

'For the sake of old Eric Marsden, really. And, well you heard it on the tape, I thought the girl, Peel, had a big future. Why fuck her career over some little toerag and a charge which might never stick?' Mickey said.

'You're still implicated. You're not thinking of going public?'

'As I said, dunno.'

'Think they might come after you or are they banking on you staying shtoom?'

'They can't be sure what I'll do. Neither can I.'

'If you do blow this, could you go down?'

'Possible.'

'Don't do it, mate,' Ricky implored him. 'For Andi's sake. And the kids.'

'Look, I'm not going to do anything rash. You just look after that little package, OK?'

'Trust me.'

'I have thought about destroying them, but . . .'

'But what?'

'I dunno if I can play that card again.'

'You've *threatened* to do it, but you haven't actually done it. They can't be sure whether or not you'll ever pull the trigger,' Ricky reasoned.

'We'll all just have to wait and see, won't we? I'll pick you up tomorrow.'

'The car's at the radio station,' Ricky reminded him.

'I'll get an early train, swing by and collect it. See you usual time.'

'Brilliant. Oh, and Mickey.'

'What?'

'Careful with those guns.'

# Thirty-nine

Mickey French fondled the short barrel of the .38 Smith & Wesson model 36, Metropolitan Police standard issue during the 1980s. He knew the specs by heart.

Barrel: 1.9 inches, snub nose. Weight: 21 oz unloaded. Stock: smooth combat wood. Ramp front, rear notch fixed. Five shot, single or double action. Ammunition: .38 steel-jacket, 110 grain, hollow point.

Easily concealed in either a shoulder holster or the hip holster which lay on the table in front of Mickey. Weapon of choice for personal protection officers.

Mickey knew the weapon inside out. Light pressure on the trigger for single action, roughly 4.5 lb pressure for double action – double tap in police parlance.

One shot normally was enough to stop the target, take him down, straight away. They called it the knock-down effect.

The .38 Smith & Wesson packs a powerful punch for a small pistol. Mickey had a particular affection for this gun. It was the first he had ever been issued with.

Together with its companion model, the .38 Number 10, a six-shot revolver with a 4.5-inch barrel, the Smith & Wesson Number 36 formed the core of the Met armoury up until 1987.

It was a Number 10 which PC Trevor Locke managed to conceal under his raincoat after being taken hostage in the Iranian Embassy siege in 1981. Mickey was there for five straight days, providing armed back-up.

Mickey put the Smith & Wesson back in its holster and fastened the safety clip.

Although still in use around the world, the .38 was becoming something of a museum piece.

The new generation of automatic and semi-automatic handguns had replaced the trusty old revolvers.

Like the Glock 17 which Mickey now held in his right hand. Calibre: 9mm. Barrel: 4.5 inches. Weight: 24.8 oz unloaded. Stock: polymer. Sights: fixed and adjustable, optional night sights. Features: unique safe action system with three internal devices that disengage as the trigger is pulled and re-engage automatically. A tough, lightweight gun. The only metal parts other than the bullets are the barrel, trigger mechanism and slide.

Now the most popular handgun in the Met, the Glock's magazine holds seventeen 9mm parabellum hollow-point bullets for rapid fire at 1,350 feet per second. It's said to be virtually idiot-proof. The safety catch is on the trigger and the weapon can be carried locked or unlocked.

This was the gun with which Mickey had been issued for home protection and still held a licence to keep. Ex-cops, particularly those who had served in the anti-terrorism or weapons divisions, were vulnerable to revenge attacks even after retirement.

Mickey kept the Smith & Wesson in his metal gun safe at all times. Unless he was away from the house, in which case it, too, was under lock and key, he kept the Glock in a drawer with the magazine of ammunition close to hand.

Habit, really.

Mickey poured himself a large Jameson's. He was missing Andi and the kids. Hearing her voice on the telephone cheered and saddened him simultaneously. As the smooth blend swilled round his mouth, Mickey reflected on the travails of the immediate past.

The ambush, the Goblin's incident, Fromby, the burglary, the dead cat. He'd been able to sort the Goblin's business, he'd dealt with the aftermath of the break-in but he'd been powerless to prevent any of it happening in the first place.

His family had been exposed to danger and trauma. And it wasn't his fault, but it was his responsibility.

He felt pretty damn useless, impotent. Twenty-five years in the Old Bill, commendations for bravery, and for what? He couldn't even keep his own family safe, except by sending them 4,500 miles away.

Fuck it. Mickey poured another Jameson's and turned down the lights. The darkness outside matched the darkness descending upon his soul, the haunting images of his frail, sobbing daughter; the bovine, defiant expression on Wayne Sutton's face; the snarling, scavenging beggars; the smug, self-righteous Justin fucking Fromby.

Sod it.

Mickey drained the bottle, switched off the lamp and closed his eyes.

No point going to an empty bed.

# Forty

The black cab came to rest in a lay-by, next to a sign reading, 'Heffer's Bottom. Twinned with Reinaldo-sur-Mandy'. Ilie Popescu engaged the handbrake, turned off the headlights and shut down the engine. He took a swig from a half-bottle of vodka he'd brought with him from the hostel.

He retrieved the crumpled scrap of paper containing Mickey French's address and rough directions from his jeans pocket. He pulled out an *A–Z* from the side of the driver's seat.

Ilie reached into his jacket pocket and took out a small ziplock envelope of white powder. He peeled off one of the five-pound notes and rolled it into a tube. He propped the *A–Z* on the steering wheel and levelled it with his left hand.

Ilie tipped the cocaine onto the shiny surface of the *A–Z* and, using the sharp edge of the ziplock packet, fashioned it into two roughly equal lines.

Expertly holding the rolled-up note in two fingers and blocking his left nostril with his thumb he snorted one of the lines. Ilie waited a few seconds and then repeated the exercise, this time inhaling through his left nostril while blocking his right with his other thumb.

Ilie took another swig of vodka, turned the engine back on, released the handbrake and headed for his target.

Heffer's Bottom was as it had been described to him, even in the dark. This was as deep into the English countryside as Ilie had ever ventured.

He drove past the church, then a field full of caravans, old lorries, horses, some rather impressive 4x4 off-roaders.

225

Once his mission was complete, Ilie thought to himself, he might dump the noisy, sluggish black cab and steal one of the off-roaders for the journey back to London.

The loosely tethered Alsatians and free-roaming Rottweilers made him reconsider.

There were burning embers in the field and piles of scrap metal dotted everywhere. It reminded him of his home village in the Tigani, back in Romania.

Ilie passed the post office and the pub and turned into Mickey's street. The house was on his right.

Ilie drew up thirty yards further on. There were houses on only one side of the street. Opposite were fields, a farm track, a small copse, overgrown hedgerows. The road was quiet, dark. There were half a dozen street lights but only one was actually working. Ilie got out of the cab and walked slowly towards his target.

There were no lights on in the house. No car in the drive. Staying close to a privet hedge which separated Mickey French's house from the adjoining property, he peered into the garage through the small window in a side door. No car in there, either. Excellent.

Ilie crept into the back garden. No lights in the back, either. No windows open back or front.

Chances were there was no one inside. Who sleeps with the windows shut in this weather?

Ilie noticed he was sweating profusely. Beads were running down his neck. The back of his shirt was sopping and the perspiration ran down the crack of his arse. He suppressed a sneeze brought on by the cocaine. His mouth was parched. The vodka was dehydrating him.

Ilie returned to the black cab, parked a hundred yards away.

He took the petrol can from the boot, checked the cigarette lighter in his jacket pocket and walked back towards the house.

An owl hooted, a cat screeched.

A fox ran out in front of Ilie, startling him.

He approached the house stealthily and listened. No lights, no movement, no sound, no sign of life.

Ilie decided the best way in was straight through the front door.

If there was anyone in the house, which was unlikely, they'd be asleep.

Worst-case scenario, he'd have time to scatter the petrol, start the fire and be out of there before they knew what was going on.

And if there was anyone there and they fried, fuck 'em.

Ilie placed the petrol can at the side of the garage.

He walked up to the front door and checked the security.

No deadlock, just a Yale.

Piece of piss.

Not much of a door either. Couple of good blows should take it down, if he hit it right.

Ilie retreated onto the lawn, took a run at the door and launched himself at it, feet first.

It yielded instantly, coming away at the hinges and crashing into the hallway.

Ilie's momentum took him through with it.

Mickey French still had the barrel of the Glock on his lap when he heard the crash.

What the fuck?

The pikeys. They said they'd be back.

Mickey grabbed the magazine from the side table and jammed it into the stock of the gun. It was a fluid movement. He'd done it a hundred times in training.

Mickey somersaulted forward and sprang to his feet.

Fuck it. He could feel his back giving way.

It was pitch black. By the pale backlight from the street illuminating the hallway, through the open living-room door, Mickey could see a dark shadow advancing.

He took aim and fired. Two shots, by the book.

Double tap.

The bullets hit Ilie Popescu at a speed of 1,350 feet

per second, sending him spinning backwards through the front door.

The momentum carried Ilie into the garden, the shock of the impact anaesthetized by the cocktail of cocaine and vodka coursing through his system.

Mickey, temporarily blinded by the muzzle flash, stumbled after him, tripping, falling flat on his face.

He'd been trained for this kind of situation. But the sound of gunfire, the muzzle flash, the surprise all served to disorientate him momentarily.

Ilie Popescu staggered onto the lawn. He felt as if he had been hit by a sledgehammer. But where?

He clutched his upper left arm, his chest, his shoulder. The narcotics were distorting his nervous system.

Fuck. I've been shot, it dawned on him. Run. Get away.

He could see the cab. If only he could make it.

As Ilie turned, two more bullets thudded into his chest, exploding his heart, like a duck egg in a microwave.

Ilie was killed instantly. As he fell on the lawn, a trickle of blood seeped from his mouth.

Mickey heaved himself to his feet and limped towards the body, gun clutched in both hands, pointing towards the corpse on the lawn.

His back was in agony. Mickey felt as if he was the one who'd been shot.

He walked over to the body and prodded it with his foot.

Brown bread.

Mickey stood in the middle of the lawn and looked to the heavens. Thank God Andi and the kids were in Florida.

What the fuck was happening to his life? On top of everything, he'd just killed a man.

He'd been trained to kill. He was no stranger to death.

He just never thought he'd have to shoot an intruder in his own home.

Mickey's heart was pumping. The adrenalin rush flushing the day's booze from his system. He had to think clearly.

Mickey knew what had to be done. Call it in, preserve the scene.

He'd probably spend all next day answering questions, but this was a clean shoot. It was self-defence, any way you cut it.

They wouldn't question his version of events. Not his word against a lying, thieving pikey. Not Mickey French, ex-cop, twenty-five years in, commendations, took a bullet for Queen and country.

One of the good guys.

Mickey felt no remorse. Not a flicker. He felt nothing for the young man lying dead on his front lawn.

He walked back into the house and dialled 999.

'Police,' he told the operator, knowing his call would be switched through to Scotland Yard central despatch.

'This is ex-detective sergeant Michael French. I wish to report a sudden death.'

He gave the operator the address and a few brief details.

Mickey replaced the Glock on the table in the living room and removed the magazine.

He went to the kitchen, filled the kettle and waited, quite composed.

The two young PCs in the area car took the call. They drew up about fifteen yards from the house and reported their position. They were told to await armed back-up.

Fifteen minutes later, a convoy of police vehicles swept into the village. Armed officers surrounded the house, taking up positions behind cars and in the hedgerows. Ilie Popescu's body lay undisturbed in the middle of the lawn.

A helicopter hovered overhead.

Mickey heard the commotion and wandered to the front door, clutching a mug of tea.

He was temporarily dazzled by the flashing blue lights. He looked down to see his chest peppered with red dots from the night laser sights fitted to the police weapons.

Mickey heard a voice over a megaphone.

'This is Detective Inspector Colin Marsden, Angel Hill

CID. You are surrounded by armed police. Put your arms above your head and walk slowly towards the middle of the lawn.'

Mickey had been here before, just not on the receiving end. 'It's all right lads. I know the drill. Take it easy.'

'Just do as you are told,' barked the voice. 'Walk to the middle of the lawn. Stop. Lie on the ground. Face down, hands behind your back. No sudden movement.'

Mickey held his mug of tea at arm's length and placed it on the window sill next to the front door. 'I'll drink that later. It's a bit hot, anyway.'

'Just do it,' said the voice.

Mickey walked slowly to the middle of the lawn.

'Stop now,' the inspector ordered as he drew level with the body of Ilie Popescu.

'On the ground.'

Mickey complied, painfully. His back was killing him.

He knelt first, then slowly eased himself forward, lowering his left arm to take his weight.

'Hands behind your back, where I can see them,' the inspector ordered.

Mickey may have known the drill, but for the first time in his life realized how it was virtually impossible for anyone in his situation to comply with proper police procedure. How do you lower yourself face down with your hands behind your back?

His question was answered immediately.

Mickey felt a boot in his back.

'Do as you are fucking told,' another voice yelled. 'Down, down, down.'

Mickey slumped forward.

'Take it easy, lads,' he appealed to them.

'Shut the fuck up,' he heard the young firearms officer behind him scream. '*SHUT. THE. FUCK. UP. All right?*'

Mickey felt the nozzle of a rifle press hard against his neck. His hands were yanked backwards, his wrists bound with the new-fangled nylon hand restraints which were rapidly replacing the traditional metal cuffs. His back was alight.

Mickey's face was pressed to the ground. He turned his head to breathe more easily. He was no more than five feet from Ilie Popescu.

The young man's eyes were still wide open, staring. Mickey had seen that look before. Five got you ten he was on coke. There was blood running from his mouth.

Mickey thought he'd seen that face before.

But where?

Looked familiar. Gyppo certainly. But more Eastern European than pikey. Who the fuck was it?

What was he doing kicking in Mickey's front door in the middle of the night?

Burglary, probably.

But how did he get here? Who was he with? Where were they now?

Mickey felt a hand on his collar.

'Right, you. Up.'

'There's no need for all this. I called it in,' Mickey said.

'I'm DI Marsden. You are not obliged to say anything but it may harm your defence if . . .'

'. . . you fail to mention something which you later, yeah. Yeah,' Mickey completed his sentence. 'I know the score.'

The young DI thought the prisoner looked vaguely familiar.

'Marsden?' said Mickey. 'Eric Marsden's boy?'

'That's right,' said the DI.

'Mickey French. Served with your dad at Tyburn Row.'

'Right. Of course. But this is no time for a walk down memory lane. What the fuck has been going on here?'

Mickey talked him through it, briefly.

'Who's the victim?' Marsden asked.

'Fuck knows,' said Mickey. 'Look, is it really necessary to truss me up like a fucking turkey?'

'Suppose not,' said Marsden. 'Standard procedure. Sergeant, free the prisoner, please.'

The sergeant cut Mickey loose.

They walked into the house.

'The gun's there. On the table,' he said, pointing to the Glock.

Marsden took an evidence bag from his pocket, slipped on a pair of latex gloves, picked up the gun between his thumb and forefinger and dropped it into the bag.

'No need for that, son,' said Mickey. 'I'm not denying it. Fancy a cup of tea? It was fresh made just before you got here. Might still be warm.'

'You're taking this very calmly, for someone who's just shot a man dead,' Marsden remarked.

'It's how I was trained to react. Weapons, close protection squad. Anyway, this was clean. The gun's licensed. I'm a qualified police marksman.'

'*Ex*-police marksman,' Marsden corrected him.

'OK, ex-police. But I'm still permitted to keep the gun for personal protection. This guy broke into my house in the middle of the night. I felt my life was threatened. Self-defence.'

'You killed him. We've checked the body. He was unarmed,' Marsden said.

'I wasn't to know that. Reasonable force. That's all I used,' Mickey insisted.

'Reasonable force.'

# Forty-one

A small crowd, woken by the commotion, had gathered by the time Mickey was escorted from the house to the waiting police car.

'Mickey, you all right?' called Mrs Baines, from number 23.

'Mickey, son, what's going on?' Sid, the pub landlord, shouted from a distance.

'Everything's fine, Sid. Don't worry,' Mickey reassured him.

A group of travellers from the illegal encampment on the village cricket pitch had also been attracted by the excitement.

Amidst all the activity, no one noticed a black London taxi parked a hundred yards down the street being driven slowly away.

Police were too busy sealing off the immediate area and asking questions of the assembled crowd.

As the body of Ilie Popescu was being carried towards the ambulance, Mickey noticed a tall, greying-haired man in a donkey jacket, jeans and cut-off wellington boots talking to a plain-clothes cop.

He recognized him as Seamus Milne, so-called 'king of the gypsies'. Milne's polished aluminium caravan dominated the camp in the village, like a medieval monarch's tent on a battlefield.

The plain-clothes cop halted the stretcher-bearers in their tracks as they were about to negotiate the steps to the back of the ambulance. He lifted the blanket covering Ilie Popescu's face and nodded at Milne.

The gypsy king gave the corpse a casual glance, looked back at the cop and shook his head.

Not one of ours, his expression said.

Who was it, then? Mickey asked himself.

A uniformed officer pushed Mickey's head down as he climbed into the back seat of the unmarked CID car.

'OK, son. Careful,' Mickey said, impatiently.

As the car headed away from the scene, Mickey remarked to Colin Marsden that he had been expecting a Chief Inspector at least.

'I'm *acting* DCI,' said Marsden. 'My governor's on second-ment to the Home Office. Some working party on turning a blind eye to drug dealers,' he added.

'Sounds as if you don't approve, son,' Mickey observed.

'I neither approve nor disapprove. I just go along with it. I do my job. I'm not a politician. I'm a thief-taker, like my dad.'

'And I'm not a thief.'

'No, but you are a killer.'

'Self-defence.'

'That's for someone else to decide.'

The car swung into the yard of the local nick. Mickey was escorted inside to the custody suite.

'Who have we got here then, Colin?' asked the sergeant, not looking up.

'Evening, Ted,' said Mickey. He and the sergeant went way back.

'Mickey, what the fuck are you doing here?'

'Little local difficulty, Ted.'

'That shooting. It was you.'

'Sorry to interrupt this little reunion,' said Marsden. 'If it's all right with you, Ted, I'd like to book the prisoner in.'

'Of course, guv,' said the sergeant. 'Sorry. Full name?'

'Michael Edward French,' said Mickey.

'What's the charge?' asked the sergeant.

'Murder,' said Marsden.

'WHAT?' Mickey froze.

'Murder? You sure?' the sergeant checked.

'This is going to be done by the numbers. We've got an unarmed victim. A shooter who admits it.'

'I haven't admitted anything,' said Mickey, backtracking.

'That's not what it sounded like to me back at the house. What was it you said, "I'm not denying it"?'

'I wasn't denying it was my gun. I haven't admitted murder. I told you, self-defence. Reasonable force.'

'I assume he's been read his rights?' asked the sergeant.

'I cautioned him back at the house,' Marsden confirmed.

'Well then, Mickey. If you want my advice, I'd keep your mouth shut.'

Mickey clammed up.

'Sarge, I'm only going on the facts as they stand right now. I need time for further investigations. We don't even know who the victim is, yet. I'm having him fingerprinted at the hospital. Once we've got those, we can run him through the computer. Meantime, I'd like Mr French here detained on suspicion of murder.'

'Do you want to call anyone, Mickey?' asked the sergeant.

'Not right now, Ted. Thanks.'

'OK. Empty your pockets.'

Mickey took his wallet from his rear pocket. The sergeant examined the contents. Thirty-four pounds in cash, assorted credit cards, Spider's membership card.

'You're not still drinking in that dive?' he asked Mickey.

'Not since this afternoon,' Mickey said.

Three photos. Andi, Terry, Katie.

'Your eldest has blossomed, Mickey.'

'Fifteen, now.'

'Pretty girl. And your boy. He's a big lad. Like his old man.'

'Yeah. Look, Ted, can't I keep them?'

'You know the score, Mickey.'

'Fair enough, Ted.'

Mickey was shown into a cell.

Marsden followed him in.

'Look, I know you're an old mate of my dad's,' said the young DI. 'But you know what the Job's like today. Climate of fucking terror. This investigation has to be spotless. But I will get to the truth, wherever that leads.'

Mickey smiled at him. 'I wouldn't want it any other way. Just do your job.'

Marsden stopped as he left the cell.

'I will promise you this, though. I'll keep you informed.'

'I appreciate that.'

The sergeant appeared at the door.

'Cup of tea, Mickey?'

'No thanks, Ted. I've just put one down.'

# Forty-two

Ricky Sparke's alarm woke him at 6.30 am. He yawned, stretched, scratched his balls and swung his legs out of bed. He shaved, showered, washed down his daily dose of Milk Thistle with a can of V-8, dressed and headed downstairs.

No Mickey.

That wasn't like him.

Ricky knew he was pissed last night but he distinctly remembered Mickey telling him he'd swing by the radio station, retrieve the motor from the underground car park and collect him usual time.

Ricky gave it five minutes.

No sign.

He called Mickey's cellphone.

*'The posaphone you are calling has not responded. It may respond if you try again,'* said the automatic message.

Ricky tried again.

*'The posaphone you are calling may be switched off. Please try later.'*

Maybe Mickey had slept in. He'd had a skinful last night, too.

Ricky dialled Mickey's home number.

A standard BT answering message kicked in.

After the tone, Ricky spoke. 'Hey, French. If you're there get your arse out of bed and pick up the phone.'

Nothing. Ricky heard the tape run out. He switched off the phone.

Mickey would turn up later. No doubt with a sore head.

Still, he hadn't ever failed to show before.

Ricky walked to the main drag and hailed a black

cab, slipping on his Ray-Bans and hoping he wouldn't be recognized. The provisional wing of the LTDA still had a fatwah out on him.

Ten minutes later he arrived at Rocktalk 99FM.

'Morning, Harry,' he greeted the security guard. 'Any sign of Mickey yet this morning?'

'Morning, Ricky. No. I was just wondering about him myself.'

'Oh yeah?'

'Yeah. His motor's still in the car park. Been there all night.'

'He said he'd stop off and collect it before picking me up.'

'Maybe the trains were fucked up again.'

'Yeah, maybe,' said Ricky.

That might explain it. The trains were always fucked up. Strikes, suicides, leaves on the line, wrong kind of snow. Wrong kind of twats running them, more like.

Still, he would have expected Mickey to ring.

'Any messages?' he asked his production assistant.

'Usual bunch of nutters,' she said.

'Any word from Mickey?'

'Nothing.'

Ricky poured himself a coffee and scoured the papers in preparation for that morning's show.

'Usual parcel of bollocks,' he said. 'What the fuck am I going to say to get them going today?'

'Petrol prices?' suggested his producer.

'Been there.'

'Speed cameras.'

'Done that.'

'Asylum-seekers.'

'You're not serious. We did that yesterday. What is this, *Groundhog Day*?'

'Sorry, Rick.'

'Isn't anything happening anywhere in the world?' asked Ricky.

His producer shrugged.

Just before nine o'clock, Ricky took up his position in the studio.

As the theme music began to roll, his producer rushed in with the latest headlines.

'Sorry, Ricky. This is just off the wires.'

Ricky didn't have time to rehearse his reading of the news. The theme music faded and the red ON AIR light indicated that his mike was live.

*'Good morning everyone. You're listening to Rocktalk 99FM. I'm Ricky Sparke. And these are the latest headlines.*

*'Reports are coming in of a shooting overnight. Police have confirmed that a burglar has been shot dead . . .*

*'GOOD!'*

Ricky interjected with genuine delight. Commenting on the news as he was actually reading it out had become Ricky's trademark. The listeners loved it.

*'As I was saying, a burglar has been shot dead in the village of Heffer's Bottom.'*

Heffer's Bottom. That's where Mickey lived.

Ricky composed himself.

*'A man is helping police with their inquiries. We'll bring you the latest details just as soon as we get them. More news later. Your calls next. First, here's the Buzzcocks.'*

'Ricky, what happened to the rest of the headlines?' his producer yelled in his ear. 'What about the weather forecast?'

'In a minute,' Ricky said. He switched on his mobile phone and dialled Mickey's number again. Nothing.

It was him. It had to be him.

'RICK-EEE!' his producer screamed. 'The record's finished.'

*'I'm sorry, ladies and gentlemen. I've just been trying to get some more information on that shooting in Heffer's Bottom. That's really the only story which interests me this morning.*

*'I had a look at the rest of the headlines while you were listening to the Buzzcocks and, quite frankly, I wouldn't blow my nose with them.*

*'Incidentally, if you want to know what the weather's like, I suggest you look out of the window.*

*'Let's go to the phones. Pete, in Wisbech.'*

*'All right, Ricky?'*

*'Sweet as a nut, Pete. What can we do for you?'*

*'It's about that burglar being shot.'*

*'What about it?'*

*'I think it's bloody brilliant, if you'll pardon my language.'*

*'We're all grown-ups, Pete. I've heard worse. Just make sure I don't hear any worse on the air, OK?'*

*'Sorry, Ricky. Like I was saying, I've been burgled six times in the past two years. The police have done nothing. These burglars are vermin. If I'd have had a gun and I'd caught someone in my house, I'd have blown his head off.'*

*'Thanks, Pete. You're not with Amnesty International, by any chance?'*

*'Do what?'*

*'Never mind, Pete. Keep those calls coming in. Here's the Kinks.'*

'Listen,' Ricky said to his producer on the talkback. 'I want everything, repeat everything on this burglary. Got it?'

'Sure.'

Ricky's excitement at this fantastic breaking story was tempered by his concern for his mate. Last time they'd spoken, Mickey said he was cleaning his guns. What with the no-show, it had to be Mickey.

'Get on to the local nick and find out the name of the man they're holding,' he told his producer. 'Second thoughts, don't bother. Ring the local boozer, the Keep & Bear Arms. It'll be in the book. I think the landlord's called Sid.'

'How do you know?'

'Just do as you're fucking told. OK? And when you get him, tell him to make like he's never met me. Right?'

Terry and Julie had crossed the river and Raymond Douglas Davies was in paradise.

*'I never get tired of that song. One of our greatest living Englishmen. Ray Davies, the Kinks, "Waterloo Sunset".'*

'Line one, Ricky,' his producer prompted him.

*'More now on that shooting. On the line now is the landlord of the local pub in Heffer's Bottom, Sid, isn't it?'*

*'That's right, Ricky. It's Sid Allen, here.'*

*'You hear everything, Sid. What can you tell us about this shooting?'*

*'Early hours this morning it happened. It seems one of our locals, Mickey French, was disturbed by an intruder. I don't know too many details but I saw them take Mickey away in a police car. And they loaded a body into an ambulance. One copper told me he was dead. They thought he was a burglar. Wouldn't surprise me, we get a lot of that here, ever since the pikeys . . .'*

*'Members of the travelling community, you mean?'*

*'Oh, yeah, right. Anyway, we've had all kinds of burglaries and things going missing.'*

*'Don't let's jump to any conclusions, Sid. What's going on right now?'*

*'Well, Ricky, there's Old Bill, sorry, policemen, crawling all over the place. I believe Mickey, Mr French, that is, was taken to Angel Hill nick.'*

*'Thanks, Sid. Well, there we have it. More on that story later in the programme. After we've heard from Counting Crows.'*

'I had no idea,' Ricky's producer said on the talkback. 'You OK? I thought you handled that well. In the circumstances.'

'Thanks.'

'Did you know it was Mickey?'

'I had a hunch, soon as I heard it was Heffer's Bottom.'

'You OK to carry on?'

'I'm fine.'

*'Counting Crows, Omaha, somewhere in Middle America. Meanwhile, somewhere in Middle England a burglar has been shot dead. I've got to be fairly careful about what I say, because of the law, sub judice and stuff like that. It's early days yet. We still don't know all the facts of this case.*

*'We'll find out more about what happened as the show, the day, the days, the weeks, maybe, go on. And, I can promise you this, you'll hear it first on Rocktalk 99FM. This is Warren Zevon. "Send Lawyers, Guns and Money". Sounds just what Mickey French needs right now.'*

In his office down the corridor, Charlie Lawrence, programme director, punched the air.

# Forty-three

Acting Detective Chief Inspector Colin Marsden was at his desk early. He'd slept briefly and fitfully.

At thirty-five, his dark hair was already greying at the temples and thinning. He looked older. Years of snatched meals in police canteens had played havoc with his digestion and his waistline.

His marriage, to a young nurse called Denise he'd met while on duty, had gone west a few years ago. As Princess Di once remarked, there were always three of them in the marriage.

Colin, Denise and the Job.

He had never wanted anything other than to be a police officer, like his father, grandfather and two of his uncles before him. His younger brother, Billy, had also followed in the family footsteps and was now a DS with the drugs squad.

Colin remembered his dad talking about Mickey. Good copper. Brave. Dependable.

Now he had Mickey French downstairs in the cells on a charge of murder. And he still didn't know who the victim was.

The fingerprints and preliminary post mortem report would be with him in a couple of hours.

Marsden buttoned his shirt collar, fixed his tie, put on his chain store jacket and beckoned his sergeant to accompany him to interview the prisoner.

Strangely, for a man facing a murder charge, Mickey French had slept soundly.

It wasn't the first night he'd spent in the cells. When he

was a rookie cop at Tyburn Row on the night-shift, he'd often get his head down for a couple of hours.

His own reaction surprised him. He was concerned about Andi and the kids but convinced himself he'd be out in a few hours, once the facts had been sorted. Marsden seemed a decent sort. Straight-up.

There was an inner calm about Mickey. It was as if the shooting had been an act of catharsis, evacuating the pent-up stresses of the recent past – the ambush, the Goblin's incident, the burglary.

All that troubled him was the identity of the man he had shot. He had assumed it was one of the pikeys. But from what he could gather as he was being put into the police car, that wasn't the case. The chief pikey, whatever his name was, had shaken his head.

Marsden collected Mickey from the cells and walked him to the interview room. He introduced his sergeant and inserted two blank tapes in the cassette recorder. He reminded Mickey he was still under caution.

Mickey had waived his right to legal advice. He would speak for himself.

Painstakingly, Mickey took him through the incident.

He had been sitting in his living room, in his own home, cleaning his guns, which he was legally entitled to possess, when he had been disturbed by an intruder. Fearing for his life, he loaded the gun and fired in self-defence, as he had been trained to do by the Metropolitan Police.

'Who was he, anyway?' Mickey asked.

'We still don't know,' Marsden said. 'Once I've got the prints I'll run them through the system. If he's got form, we'll soon find out.'

'It's a million he's got form.'

'Maybe,' said Marsden.

'Not one of the pikeys, then?'

'What made you think it would be?'

'We've got history. Check your records.'

'Enlighten me.'

244

Mickey ran him through the background, starting with the attempted robbery of his golf clubs right up to the assault on his home.

'They topped the cat?' said Marsden incredulously.

NEX TIM ITS YOU COZZER.

'So you see how I was in fear of my life?'

Marsden cracked his knuckles and stretched.

'Hmmm. My problem is that whoever the victim is here, he is *not* one of the men you believed had made threats against you.'

'Victim? *I'm* the fucking victim here.'

'Technically speaking, no, you're not. You see the difficulty,' said Marsden.

'Crystal,' said Mickey. 'Look, I'm not trying to be difficult.'

'This is a very difficult situation.'

'Tell me about it. I still maintain that whoever the intruder is, correction, was, I only used reasonable force under the law.'

'We haven't found a weapon,' said Marsden.

'I was entitled to assume he was armed, given the background,' said Mickey.

'You're not entitled to assume anything, you should know that,' said Marsden.

'I was trained to assume the worst.'

'Just talk me through your day again,' said Marsden. 'Then we'll knock it on the head until I've managed to ID the victim and had some more scenes-of-crimes reports.'

'What's that got to do with the *prix de poisson*?'

'Humour me. I need to build up a picture of your frame of mind at the time of the shooting.'

Mickey smiled. He could see where this was leading. It would boil down to intent when push came to shove.

'Let's get one thing straight. When I sat down to clean my guns, I had no intention of using them. The Glock was unloaded when I heard the intruder. I reacted instinctively. Standard police procedure.'

'You're not a police officer any more.'

'It's like riding a bike. I acted automatically.'

'You made no attempt to establish whether the intruder was armed.'

'No time. It was dark. I was under attack. Threats had been made against my life. I defended myself.'

Marsden got up, walked round the room and sat down again.

'There was an empty bottle of Jameson's,' he said.

'What's your point?'

'Had you drunk the whole bottle?'

'Half, maybe,' said Mickey.

'You're a driver now, right?'

'What about it?'

'There was no car at the house.'

'I left it in town.'

'Oh?'

'I had a couple of drinks at lunchtime.'

'How many is a couple?'

'Nothing heavy.'

'Be more specific,' Marsden entreated him.

'Four or five large ones, drop of wine.'

'Drop of wine? How much is a drop?'

'Couple.'

'Couple of what, glasses?'

'Bottles.'

'I'm impressed.'

'Years of training,' said Mickey.

'Yeah, my dad told me. These days drinking on duty is a non-runner,' said Marsden.

'Always was,' said Mickey. 'Never enforced, though.'

'Now it's a hanging offence. They don't even like you drinking off duty. It's even been mooted that they're going to conduct random breath tests when officers start their shifts.'

'Fucking hell. If they'd done that a few years ago there wouldn't have been a copper on the beat anywhere in

London,' said Mickey. 'Not that there is now,' he added. 'All sitting behind hedges in jam sandwiches waiting to nick some poor sod doing 35 mph.'

'We're not here to discuss the finer points of policing policy,' said Marsden. 'It does seem to me that, even by the standards of the Sweeney, you'd had rather a lot to drink.'

'I can handle it.'

'Four or five large ones, a couple of bottles of wine, half a bottle of Irish whiskey. I'd have been unconscious. You must have been pretty drunk.'

'Oh, I get it. So pissed I didn't know what I was doing when I pulled the trigger. Come off it, you saw me at the scene. Did I strike you as drunk?'

'Not particularly. But I'm not a doctor. I'm going to have to ask you to provide a blood sample.'

'What for?'

'I told you, I'm doing this by the book. In duplicate, triplicate, copperplate.'

'What will a blood sample prove?'

'Something or nothing. I'm just covering all the bases.'

'And if I refuse?'

'Come on, Mickey, if you're arguing your innocence it's not going to help you if you come over unco-operative.'

'OK. Let's get it over with.'

'I'll see if the FME's in,' said Marsden, using police abbreviation for doctor. 'We'll continue the interview once I've made a few more inquiries.'

'Can I make my phone call first?'

'Sure,' said Marsden. 'Just one more thing for now.'

'Yep?'

'You left the car in town, right?'

'Underground car park.'

'So what was a can of petrol doing by the garage?'

'Can of petrol? Dunno.'

Can of petrol? wondered Mickey.

# Forty-four

Ricky Sparke's mobile rang as he was leaving the studio.

'Sorry about this morning, mate,' said Mickey. The sergeant let him use the phone in his office. He shut the door and told Mickey to take all the time he needed.

'What the fuck have you got yourself into?'

'Nothing I can't handle. Anyway, what do you know?'

'I know you've shot a man dead and you're in Angel Hill nick. I spoke to Sid, from the Keep & Bear Arms. What happened, for Christ's sake?'

'Pretty much what you know. I'm sitting at home, guy breaks in, I shoot him. I can't go into much more detail right now.'

'What's going on?'

'They've got stuff they have to do. I'll be here a while.'

'Got a brief?'

'Nah, don't need one. I'm fine. I know the drill.'

'I'm coming out there,' said Ricky.

'Don't. They won't let you see me right now. I've still got to make a formal statement.'

'Is there anything you need?'

'I'm OK. I know the station sergeant, he'll look after me.'

'This is up and running now. You know how these things get out. The phones went mad this morning. Everyone's on your side. The papers are on the case. They'll soon put us together. Want me to deal with them?'

'If you like. Do what you have to.'

'What about Andi and the kids? Want me to call her?'

'No. Whatever you do, don't do that. I don't want her worried. Anyway, when I spoke to her last night she said they were going down to Palm Beach for a couple of days, staying overnight. I told her to book in at the Breakers, give herself a treat. By the time they get back to Zero Beach, I'll be out of here.'

'If it's clear-cut, why are they still holding you?'

'Loose ends, mate.'

'Such as?'

'For a start, we still don't know who the fucker is.'

'Who?'

'The dead guy.'

'What? I just sort of assumed it was one of the pikeys, you know, after everything.'

'Me, too. Not so, apparently.'

'Are they charging you?'

'Dunno. I'm arguing self-defence. You know, reasonable force.'

'Sounds reasonable to me.'

'Not to them, though.'

'What do you mean?'

'It's a bit complicated.'

'In what way complicated?'

'The guy, the intruder, he was unarmed.'

'So what? He'd broken into your house in the middle of the night. You had every right to shoot him.'

'That's not how they see it. Not yet.'

'What aren't you telling me here?'

'They are holding me on suspicion of murder.'

'MURDER? What the fuck?'

'Calm down, Ricky. It's a formality. They have to do everything by the numbers, especially with me being an ex-cop.'

'I don't like the sound of this. You being fitted up?'

'Nah, don't think so. The cop on the case, the DI, acting DCI, Marsden, I knew his dad, seems sound. He's got to cover all the angles.'

'Marsden. That was the cop you were talking about on the tape, Tyburn Row.'

'His dad, Eric, yeah.'

'He know anything about that business?'

'I don't even know if Eric knew anything about it. He didn't need to know. Even if he did, he never mentioned it again. Look, I'm going to have to go. The doctor's here. I've got to take a blood test.'

'Blood test. You weren't driving last night.'

'Routine.'

'Sure there's nothing you want?'

'No. I'll call you later.'

'Be lucky, Mickey.'

What makes me think I'm going to need some luck? Mickey thought to himself.

As Ricky switched off the phone, he saw Charlie Lawrence bounding down the corridor.

'Ricky, boy. That was fantastic. Brilliant show. Fucking brill-eee-ant, mate!'

'Yeah, sure, thanks,' said Ricky, his mind elsewhere.

'We've got to keep this one going.'

'Eh?'

'This is the big one, Ricky. State of the nation stuff.'

'It's my mate we're talking about here. Mickey. You know, Mickey French,' said Ricky, deliberately. 'He's practically on the payroll here.'

'I know, mate. That makes it even better. We're going to get him the best lawyer money can buy.'

'He says he doesn't want one. He reckons he'll be out soon. Self-defence.'

'It isn't going to go away though. Use your journalist's instincts. This is huge. Massive. You heard the callers this morning. Mickey's a hero. He shot dead some scumbag burglar. That's what they'd all love to do. This is going to be one of those cases which really make a difference. And we're, you're, right at the very heart of it. Fuck the sub judice crap. Let me worry about that. Just go for it. Think what it will do for the ratings.'

'You cynical bastard,' said Ricky. 'I'm more concerned about Mickey.'

'Me too, mate. Me too. But don't let's lose sight of the bigger picture. It's fantastic radio. Today's show was a brilliant listen. Rock and fucking roll. You'll win awards for this.'

'If you say so, Charlie.' Ricky shrugged, unimpressed.

'I know so, mate. And in your heart of hearts, you know so too. Think about it. People have been waiting for something like this to happen. And it's fallen into our lap. Ricky Sparke and Rocktalk 99FM just caught fire. Big time.'

Ricky knew Charlie Lawrence was right. What had Mickey said? Do what you have to do?

'Charlie, you're a complete cunt, you know that,' he said.

'That's MISTER Cunt to you, mate,' Lawrence laughed. 'And just to prove I'm a cunt to myself, too, I'll tell you what I'm going to do.'

'Go on.'

'Every percentage point we go up in the ratings, I'm going to increase your wages by ten grand. Ten per cent up, that's a hundred fucking grand. Twenty per cent up, well you work it out for yourself.'

Ricky could do the numbers. Mickey's a big boy.

And you know what they say.

Every cloud.

# Forty-five

Wayne Sutton gripped the edge of the antique partner's desk, his eyes closed, his face pressed sideways down, his earring digging into the embossed leather surface. He chewed gum, nonchalantly.

His T-shirt rode up exposing his spotty back. His pants and tracksuit trousers were pulled down around his ankles.

*Thwack!*

Wayne felt the rolled-up newspaper smack against his pale, spotty little arse.

*Thwack!*

Again.

Justin Fromby raised the first edition of the *Evening Standard* above his head and brought it down again.

*Thwack!*

It never took long.

*Thwack!*

Wayne heard Fromby groan on the sixth stroke. The beating stopped.

That would be that until tomorrow. Fromby never harmed Wayne. Never used a cane, or riding crop, or anything which might hurt Wayne and leave a mark.

Never asked him for a blow job. Not even a wank.

Fromby seemed content to bend Wayne over his desk, or the kitchen table, or the sofa, administer six of the best while tossing himself off at the same time.

Fromby sometimes spanked him with an oven glove, other times with a warm, damp towel. But most of the time it was a rolled-up copy of the *Evening Standard*, first edition usually. City Prices.

Then he'd sit down and read the paper as if nothing had happened.

'Can I get up now?' Wayne asked.

'Just stay there a second,' said Fromby, studying Wayne's bare arse more intently than usual. The newsprint had come off on his buttocks. Maybe Fromby had hit him harder than usual.

'Oh, shit,' said Fromby.

'Wotisit?' asked Wayne.

'OH, SHIT!' repeated Fromby.

'Mr Fromby? Wossamatter?' said Wayne, looking over his shoulder.

The lettering was reversed but you didn't need a mirror to make out the front-page headline, now faithfully reproduced on the nether regions of Wayne Sutton.

EX-COP KILLS BURGLAR

Fromby slumped back in his captain's chair and unfurled the *Standard*.

Wayne pushed himself away from the desk and rearranged his clothing.

'Wossup, Mr F?' he asked again.

Fromby waved him away. 'Go and put the kettle on or something Wayne, there's a good lad. And shut the door on your way out.'

Fromby studied the paper.

EX-COP KILLS BURGLAR.

Fromby knew what was coming next.

A former policeman is believed to have shot and killed an intruder at his home in the village of Heffer's Bottom.

The incident happened in the early hours of this morning.

Police are refusing to reveal either the identity of the dead man or the suspect, who is currently helping with inquiries at Angel Hill police station.

But Sid Allen, the landlord of the local pub, the Keep & Bear Arms, told Rocktalk 99FM today that Mickey French, who lives in the village, had been taken away by police.

Mr French is understood to be an ex-Metropolitan Police officer, who served in the weapons division.

The victim is believed to be a burglar. Mr Allen said there had been a number of burglaries and thefts in the area, which has become a magnet for travellers.

The rest was a cobbled-together cuttings job on Heffer's Bottom, a quick recap of the latest burglary figures and a non-committal quote from Scotland Yard. By five o'clock it would fill half the paper.

Justin Fromby re-read the report half a dozen times. This couldn't be a coincidence. He hadn't thought Ilie would go straight out and do it. This had to be him.

Think, Justin.

Police are refusing to reveal the identity . . .

Did that mean they didn't know the identity of the victim? Or they did know, but weren't saying?

Justin grabbed the phone and called Roberta on her private line at Scotland Yard.

'I'm in a meeting,' she said.

'Then get out of it. Right now,' Fromby said.

'Excuse me,' she said to the three members of the community relations council sitting opposite her, cupping her hand over the mouthpiece.

'Just get out of whatever you're in the middle of and call me straight back on the mobile,' said Fromby. 'It's raining shit.'

Roberta's smile hardened, like an Olympic synchronized swimmer.

'Of course, Home Secretary,' she said.

Her guests sat forward and looked at each other. They were impressed.

Roberta replaced the receiver, entwined her fingers to steady her shaking hands, and spoke to her guests.

'I really am so awfully sorry, ladies and gentlemen. I'm afraid something has come up. I think we had just about finished our business for today, anyway, hadn't we?'

They all nodded in agreement.

'In that case, I do hope you'll be good enough to excuse me. That was, well, you heard, didn't you? Please forgive me, but when duty calls,' she said, rolling her eyes upwards and pointing her finger towards the ceiling.

They all smiled. She showed them out.

'Thank you so much for coming.'

Roberta asked her secretary to show her guests out and hold all her calls.

She shut the door and called Justin.

'What the hell is it now?'

'Have you seen the *Standard*?' he barked.

'Of course not. I've been in meetings all morning.'

'Is this line secure?'

'Is any line?' she said.

'Can you get away?'

'I suppose so. When?'

'Half, no make it three-quarters, of an hour.'

'Where? I've got to be in town for a meeting at the Home Office later this afternoon.'

'The Two Chairmen?'

'You know I can't been seen in pubs, not with the no-drinking policy. Anywhere round here someone would recognize me.'

'Lincoln's Inn Fields, then.'

'It's full of dossers. Anyway, you'd be clocked in thirty seconds.'

'You're right. I wasn't thinking. Get on the tube to Euston. Meet me on the concourse, main line, by the entrance to the underground.'

'Fine.'

'And buy a *Standard*.'

She'd read the paper by the time she arrived at Euston. Justin was waiting for her.

'Well?' he said.

'It has to be him, right?'

'You're the police officer.'

'I told you it was risky.'

'It's too late for any of that,' said Justin. 'We have to think clearly and quickly. When it says they are refusing to reveal his identity, what do they mean?'

'Routine,' said Roberta. 'Even if they know, they have to notify next of kin.'

'He hasn't got any. Not that he told us. Do you think they do know who he is?'

Roberta looked about her. Passengers milled around them on the concourse. No one took any notice of a middle-aged couple deep in earnest conversation.

'I don't know. It depends if he was carrying anything to identify him, papers, for instance.'

'He wasn't carrying them when he was arrested,' Fromby said.

'Fingerprints,' Roberta said. 'They didn't fingerprint him at the nick, but they did when he entered the country, remember? That's how I traced his real identity.'

'Shit. Is there anything you can do?'

'He's in the system,' she said. 'I can't do anything about the immigration service computer. But that's no problem. They'll turn him up as asylum-seeker, mark him down as a burglar.'

'What about when they check the Yard computer?' Justin said.

'I might be able to deal with that.'

'We've been down this road before,' said Justin, remembering Tyburn Row.

'I think I can lose it. If not, I can classify it.'

'Can you?'

'I'm pretty confident. He's not been charged, though the arrest has been logged.'

'And my involvement?'

'I should be able to wipe the file. Worst case, I'll just put a block on it. Need to know, that sort of thing.'

'Will anyone be able to get at it?'

'Not without going through me.'

'Won't that look suspicious?'

'Give me twenty-four hours. This could all work to our advantage,' she said, patting his cheek.

'Don't patronize me.' Justin recoiled. 'What are you talking about?'

'Listen. Last time I let you think of something, look where it got us. Now it's police business.'

'What are you up to?' asked Justin.

'Not now, darling,' said Roberta. 'No time. I've got to go. I have to get back to the Yard before they've identified the body. I've got a lot of work to do.'

# Forty-six

It was late afternoon before the file containing the scenes-of-crimes report, the preliminary post mortem and the fingerprints landed on acting DCI Colin Marsden's desk.

Let's find out who he is first, Marsden thought.

His sergeant had run the prints through the Scotland Yard computer. No match.

Try the Home Office, immigration, Marsden told him.

The corpse wasn't a local gypsy, they knew that now. But he had that Romany look about him. Could be foreign, Eastern European, maybe. Looked a bit like that lad who played for Chelsea.

The sergeant wasn't hopeful.

Just do it, Marsden had ordered him.

No stone and all that.

His perseverance paid off.

Someone at Croydon had done his job properly. A perfect match.

He was called Gica Dinantu. Country of origin, Romania. Port of entry, etc. Age sixteen. Asylum application number. Address given as a hostel in Tottenham, London N17.

That would figure. Marsden knew there had been a spate of crimes committed by asylum-seekers in north London. A team of them regularly turned up in Angel Hill, knocking on doors, begging. Young men, women in headscarves and shawls, babes in arms. It had got nasty a couple of times and the woodentops had moved them on.

Maybe this Gica Dinantu was one of that bunch.

But they worked in teams, during the day.

And this had happened in the early hours of the morning.

What was he doing in Mickey French's house at that time of night?

How did he get there?

The begging gangs usually travelled by train. And the trains would have long since stopped for the night.

Maybe his accomplices had done a runner.

If he was a lone burglar, he would at least have had a bag with him. And a few tools. And some way of getting there. And getting away.

Nothing.

Marsden tipped the dead man's belongings onto his desk. A dodgy Rolex, a gold ring.

He picked up the watch. Hang on, this wasn't one of those moody kettles you could buy in the pubs in Cable Street for a fiver. This looked kosher.

There was an evidence bag, too, full of money. It had already been counted. Over £400. Cigarettes, a lighter.

But no papers, no ID.

No problem. No need. Marsden now knew who he was.

He opened the post-mortem report.

Death by gunshot wounds.

Tell him something he didn't know.

Male, aged twenty-one to twenty-four, smoker, had drunk approximately half a bottle of vodka in the two hours before he had died, evidence of recent cocaine use. Also evidence of recent sexual activity.

Half-pissed, coked-up and fresh from a leg-over.

So what the fuck had this Gica Dinantu been doing in Mickey French's house in the middle of the night? Marsden asked himself again.

And there was something else troubling him.

Immigration had his age down as sixteen. The post-mortem puts him between twenty-one and twenty-four. The medics were usually spot on.

Was this the same guy? Were these the right prints? Had there been a fuck-up?

259

Anything known?

Marsden turned on his desktop computer, logged on and punched in the name Gica Dinantu.

File not found.

Marsden studied the typed-up reports from the scenes-of-crimes officers and the detectives who had been drafted in to do house-to-house. When he was ready, he had Mickey brought from the cells to the interview room.

'Dinantu. D-I-N-A-N-T-U. Gica Dinantu. Ring any bells?'

'Not a clue,' said Mickey.

'He's, was, Romanian.'

'Nice for him.'

'You don't seem to realize what a serious predicament you're in here,' snapped Marsden.

'Oh, I realize, son. I realize better than you know. But I've told you what happened. What else is there?'

'Motive, for a start.'

'Self-defence, the best motive there is,' Mickey replied. 'Man breaks into my house, middle of the night, I feel my life threatened, use reasonable force to stop him. End of fucking story. What does it matter who he is?'

'He's an asylum-seeker.'

'So what was he doing in my house in the middle of the night?'

'I've been asking myself that question over and over.'

'Are you going to charge me or let me go?'

'I've applied for an extension, further inquiries.'

'I'm not going to do a runner, for fuck's sake.'

'I told you,' said Marsden, matching Mickey's glare. 'This is going to be done dead straight. I'm not going to be blamed for bailing a murderer.'

'*Alleged* murderer. There you go again, Colin. Rushing to judgement.'

'I'm not rushing to anything. That's what I keep trying to tell you. There are aspects of this case with which I am not comfortable. I have further inquiries to make before I can charge you, before I know what to charge you with, or

260

decide whether I'm even going to charge you. Until then you'll remain in custody,' Marsden said.

He knew that this was going to end up way over his head. The CPS – Crown Prosecution Service, or Criminal Protection Service, as it was known within the police force – would take the final decision as to the charge.

There was a chance, what with Mickey being an ex-cop, and a weapons man to boot, that the investigation would be taken out of his hands.

He didn't want that happening. He was still only *acting* DCI.

If he handled this well, got a result.

This could be his big chance.

# Forty-seven

This could be my big chance, Roberta thought.

She'd rushed back to the office, logged in to her computer and checked the Gica Dinantu file.

No one had visited it since her.

Good.

She trashed it out of her own queue.

There was still the central record.

Using the skills she'd gained on a three-month computing and data course and the privileged security access her rank permitted, she tracked the file back through the system, carefully deleting every mention of Gica Dinantu.

She was able, finally, to enter the internal system of the nick to which Ilie had been taken after his arrest at Tyburn tube station and remove the original file.

No one would know he had ever been inside a police station, even if they bothered to check.

And you know what these local CID boys are like. Bone idle.

She imagined the DCI at Angel Hill. Probably in his fifties. Sclerotic, alcoholic, disillusioned, all ambition long since spent, counting the days to his pension, anxious to get the case off his book.

Once he'd established the identity of the body, interviewed the locals, talked to the folk back at the hostel and realized there was no next of kin, he wouldn't dig much further.

With Mickey French being ex-Job, he wouldn't be keen on prosecuting him, either.

In fact, the more Roberta thought about it, this hick

detective, whoever he was, would probably be absolutely delighted if someone from Scotland Yard pulled rank and took the entire case off his hands.

Roberta was home in bed with Dixon before the identity of the corpse at Heffer's Bottom leaked out in time for the late television news.

She woke early.

Fleet Street's finest had spent the previous day crawling all over Heffer's Bottom and the story dominated the first editions.

GUN COP SHOOTS BURGLAR – The *Daily Mail*.

BULLSEYE! – The *Sun*.

VIGILANTE MURDERS REFUGEE – The *Guardian*.

News of Mickey French's encounter led the bulletins on all radio and television channels.

Other talk show hosts picked up where Ricky Sparke left off. It monopolized the early-morning phone-in shows.

Roberta Peel was back in her office at 7.30 am. She called the Home Secretary at his private residence at 7.31 am.

'I hope I haven't disturbed you,' she apologized.

'Not at all. I'm due on the *Today* programme in about half an hour. The radio car's setting up outside. The latest asylum figures,' he replied.

'That's partly why I needed to talk to you. I think that we have to consider the wider political implications of this shooting in Heffer's Bottom,' she said. 'There are certain considerations here, Home Secretary, not least for the Metropolitan Police Service and, you will appreciate, for the government itself.

'The shooter in this case is an ex-police officer. We must be seen to prosecute him without fear or favour.

'The victim is a refugee from oppression. We have to demonstrate that all are equal under British law. You will, of course, be alive to the possible repercussions at a time when the government's, if I may say so, enlightened

263

approach to asylum is under assault from the forces of conservatism.'

The Home Secretary listened intently and murmured agreement.

'I believe,' Roberta continued, 'that the strategic sensitivity of this case demands the involvement of a senior officer. I would be happy to take that responsibility upon myself, if that is what you would wish, Home Secretary.

'In light of our conversation at the anti-racism seminar the other day, I thought it only appropriate to run this by you before I spoke with the Commissioner.

'The way in which we handle this case will put down a marker for the future of policing in Britain, indeed the entire development of the culture of law and order and race relations for decades to come.'

The Home Secretary mulled it over and gave her his answer.

'Thank you, Home Secretary,' cooed Roberta. 'So you'll call the Commissioner yourself? Excellent, Home Secretary. So much better coming from you. Oh, and Paul, give my love to Mary, won't you?'

Roberta replaced the receiver.

Three minutes later, the phone rang.

'Yes, sir. If you think that would be appropriate. I'll make the necessary arrangements and clear it with division. It would be an honour, sir. Thank you, Commissioner.' She smiled.

Roberta buzzed through to her secretary.

'Get me Angel Hill police station, please. Acting Detective Chief Inspector Marsden.'

# Forty-eight

Mickey French spent a comfortable night in the cells. He knew quite a few of the local lads. They'd sent out for pizza for him and let him use the showers. The sergeant had told one of the PCs to fetch Mickey a change of clothes from the house.

Today the custody extension would expire and they'd have to charge him or bail him.

Even if they did charge him, whatever they charged him with, he was confident of making bail before a magistrate.

No reason not to grant him bail. Unblemished record, clear-cut case of self-defence.

He'd be home before Andi rang from Florida.

How would he explain it to her? She'd be worried.

Still, no great cause for concern.

Mickey rubbed the sleep from his eyes and splashed cold water on his face.

No cause for concern? Out of here by lunchtime.

Hang on, who was he kidding?

Start thinking like a cop, Mickey.

Put yourself in Marsden's place.

Look at it from a police perspective.

They've got a dead kid, an asylum-seeker. Unarmed.

They've got a trained marksman, full of booze, playing with his guns in the middle of the night.

Forget what the kid was doing in the house at that ungodly hour.

What was Mickey doing cleaning his guns in the early hours?

How convenient that the magazine of bullets just happened to be at hand.

When he saw the kid lying there, stone dead, he showed no remorse, nothing. Not even when the cops arrived.

What were they going to read into that?

Maybe he could have overpowered him. He was only a kid, after all, not much older than Katie, not much bigger than Terry.

Would he have acted differently if he'd been stone-cold sober?

Couldn't he have shot low? Brought him down.

Did Mickey really have to shoot to kill?

It was how he'd been trained, sure. But trained to deal with blaggers, terrorists, men in balaclavas with sawn-off Purdeys.

Not fucking kids.

Was it because he was angry, because of what the pikeys had done to his house, to Katie's photo, to the cat?

Did this kid pay for all that?

*Reasonable* force?

*Reasonable?*

Was it really *reasonable* to shoot dead an unarmed intruder?

Mickey, what the fuck have you done?

Too late for that. Too late for what if?

More a case of what next?

Until this moment, it had felt as if everything which had happened to Mickey and his family over the past couple of weeks had been cleansed in gunfire.

Mickey had been telling himself that, finally, it was all over.

Now cold reality dawned.

It was only just beginning.

# Forty-nine

Marsden was re-reading the house-to-house reports and checking them against the newspapers.

Fleet Street seemed to have found out a damn sight more than his own officers.

Marsden supposed the papers could have made half of it up, but they certainly made themselves busy. What did they know that he didn't?

Each newspaper coloured the facts with the prejudices of its own readers.

You paid your money and took your choice.

They ran the gamut of bigotry.

Mickey French was either hero or villain. Avenging angel or cold-blooded murderer.

Gica Dinantu was either thieving, scrounging vermin or a slain innocent.

Right or wrong.

Black or white.

Colin Marsden bought none of it. His world comprised dozens of shades of grey.

Still, he would crack it.

This case had national significance.

His big chance.

Marsden's concentration was disturbed by the telephone.

He'd been half-expecting the call.

Deputy Assistant Commissioner Peel on the line.

'Ma'am,' he said, sitting to attention.

'We do have everything under ... I see ... yes, completely, ma'am ... indeed I will ... of course, ma'am ... look forward to working with you,' he lied.

Big chance, eh?

What did this ball-breaking bitch know about investigating murder? He'd read a profile of her recently.

Bramshill, fast-track, community relations, anti-this, anti-that, all men are rapists, that kind of bollocks. Her career had been one long committee.

Still, she was the future, like it or not. And he didn't.

But it was a long time to retirement. And look on the bright side, Colin, it could all work out for the best.

She was tipped for the very top. If he made the right impression, she might take him with her.

He'd always fancied a job at Scotland Yard.

Bite your lip, Colin.

By the book, remember?

Colin Marsden tipped another spoonful of sugar in his coffee. To help the medicine go down.

It was still his case, he told himself.

Not that he really believed it.


Marsden had faxed all the relevant paperwork to Roberta before she left the Yard. She read herself in on the way. She had plenty of time. On a good day, the journey from Victoria to the Essex borders could take an hour and a half. This was a bad day.

Roberta instructed her driver to take her directly to Heffer's Bottom. She wanted to inspect the scene.

The house was taped off when she arrived. Forensic had been and gone. There was a patrol car outside and a WPC on the door.

As her car drew up, she could see the WPC talking into her personal radio. They had been expecting the DAC, but not at the house. Not just yet.

The young woman cop stiffened and saluted as Deputy Assistant Commissioner Peel approached the house, carrying a briefcase, and introduced herself.

'I've informed inspector, sorry, acting DCI Marsden, of

your arrival. He will be here directly, ma'am,' she said.

'And who told you to do that?' barked Roberta.

The poor girl reddened.

'The acting DCI, ma'am.'

'I see. Get him on your radio will you please?' Roberta asked.

The WPC contacted Angel Hill control, which patched her through to Marsden.

'I was just leaving, ma'am. I'm sorry. We were expecting you at the station, first,' he said.

'That won't be necessary. I can find my own way around. I'm sure the WPC here can help me with anything I need to know,' Roberta said.

'I'm not sure she's competent, um, in that regard. I really think –' Marsden stalled.

'I am merely here to familiarize myself with the crime scene, inspector,' Roberta informed him, with an abrupt air of authority. 'I'm already up to speed. Your preliminary report is excellent,' she said, gently releasing her command structure grasp of Marsden's balls.

At the other end of the line, Marsden breathed a sigh of relief. Perhaps this wasn't going to be too bad, after all.

'I'll be fine, inspector. I've got your drawings, your notes. I'll take a quick look round and join you shortly.'

'Very well, ma'am.'

Roberta smiled as she clipped the personal radio back above the WPC's left breast.

'Don't worry,' she said. 'I don't bite. I was a young Plonk once, believe it or not,' she reassured the petrified girl, who laughed nervously.

'Er, ma'am, would ma'am like me to accompany her inside?' the WPC asked.

'No, I'll find my own way. You just stay here and keep everyone else out. Understand?'

'Yes, ma'am,' said the WPC, not daring to make eye contact.

The door still lay in the hallway, where it had been kicked down.

Roberta picked her way into the living room and closed the door.

She would have to be quick. Maybe twenty minutes, tops.

Where would Mickey French keep it?

She rested her briefcase against the sofa. Her eyes darted round the room. She checked the drawers in the dresser, careful to replace everything.

She rifled through the cupboards in the kitchen, putting everything back as she went.

Roberta opened the kitchen door and stepped into the garden. The shed. A real possibility. Men kept all manner of secrets in their garden sheds.

She went inside. Weedkiller, a few old garden tools, seed packets and a chipped workbench. She opened the drawer in the bench. An old copy of *Playboy*, a yellowing *Sporting Life*, a rusty pair of scissors, an empty half-bottle of scotch.

Nothing else.

Roberta made her way back into the house.

She opened the cupboard under the stairs. The usual collection of boots, trainers and family junk. And a gun safe.

Maybe he kept it in there.

Too obvious. But then again. She looked through the drawers in the living room again, searching for keys.

She found a bunch at the back of a drawer full of videos.

One by one she tried them in the lock of the gun safe.

Bingo.

The safe eased open.

A Smith & Wesson .38. Police standard issue back in the 1980s, she recalled. A box of ammunition and a firearms certificate.

But no knife, no documents, no tape.

Roberta was busting for a piss.

She went into the downstairs cloakroom and squatted. As she looked up, she could see an assortment of photographs of Mickey French in police uniform, receiving commendations, passing out at Hendon.

At Tyburn Row.

The team photo. Mickey, middle row, dead centre. Eric Marsden, front row, extreme left.

And there she was, in the back row, third from the left. Fresh-faced, probationary WPC Roberta Peel.

She remembered it being taken. Not long before. Well, not long before. And here she was taking a piss in Mickey French's downstairs cloakroom, in the middle of a highly irregular search for evidence which could destroy her career.

Mickey French himself was banged up in a cell on suspicion of murder. And Eric Marsden's son was on the case.

Small world.

It was her world now.

Running out of time. Try upstairs.

Kids' room. Highly unlikely.

Master bedroom.

Roberta checked the bedside table. Cufflinks, credit card receipts, petrol bills, business cards. Mickey must sleep this side.

The drawer below, a couple of novels. Carl Hiaasen, Keith Waterhouse. Box of Kleenex.

Roberta walked round to the other side of the bed. Top drawer, nail clippers, nail file, old lipsticks.

Bottom drawer. Locked.

Roberta went to the dressing table. Make-up, underwear, socks, necklaces, that kind of stuff. At the back of a drawer full of Janet Reger lingerie she found a small key.

She walked back to the bed and tried the lock.

It turned.

Roberta pulled open the drawer. Was this where he kept it?

She reached inside, took out a box, like a cigar box, and lifted the lid.

No knife, no papers, no tape.

Just a magnificent set of vibrators, ranging from twelve inches down to thimble-sized.

And a tube of KY Jelly.

Roberta shuddered. She could feel herself moistening.

She thought fondly of Dixon. Good old Dixon. Hard, shiny, dependable Dixon.

And Karl Marx.

She pressed her knees together and drew them up towards her chest.

Stop it, woman, a voice inside her screamed.

Roberta snapped out of it. She closed the lid, put the box back in the drawer and locked it. She replaced the key in the underwear drawer and plumped up the duvet where she had been sitting.

This was getting her nowhere.

Where else could she look? Where did he keep it? That's if he really had kept it.

Five more minutes and the WPC would be getting suspicious.

Where else was there to look? She checked the bathroom cabinet but knew in advance that would be a non-runner.

Roberta stood on the small landing. She looked up. A trap door. The loft, of course. It was worth a try.

She took a chair from the bedroom, stood on it and eased open the hatch. An aluminium sliding ladder dropped down.

Roberta climbed up the ladder and turned on the light.

Tea chests, an old train set, suitcases, half-used boxes of floor tiles. Where should she start?

There were three boxes in one corner, partly covered in sheets and layers of dust. There was dust everywhere.

In the far corner, there was another chest, behind some paint cans.

Roberta stooped under the eaves and made her way over. Someone had been here recently. The dust had been disturbed.

Under some newspapers she found a plastic documents wallet marked 'Police Federation. Worthing. 1981.'

Roberta opened the wallet and felt inside.

A small oblong cassette case. A sheaf of documents. A chamois leather.

She unrolled the chamois leather. The knife fell out. Trevor Gibbs's knife. The blade was blunt now. The polished ivory handle was about five inches long and had an unusual ribbed finish, swelling upwards from the blade into a bulbous tip.

Pay dirt.

She held the papers up to the light. The juvenile records relating to Gibbs's arrest.

Roberta examined the cassette box.

There was a tape inside.

On the casing, two words, handwritten.

Tyburn Row.

The Holy Grail.

Roberta's heart was pounding.

She hurried down the ladder, switching off the light as she went. She pushed the ladder back in its frame, shut the trap door.

Roberta carried the chair back into the bedroom and carefully replaced it in the exact spot she had found it.

As she turned to go, she hesitated.

Roberta looked out of the bedroom window. The panda car was still there. Her driver was leaning on the Rover, stubbing out a cigarette with his left foot, savouring the final draw. He kept mouthwash and air-freshener in the glove compartment, knowing how much his boss hated even the merest suggestion of stale cigarette smoke.

She could see the WPC taking two paces forward, two paces back, relieving the tedium.

Otherwise there was no activity.

Roberta put the documents wallet with its priceless contents down on the chair and went to the dressing table.

She retrieved the key from the Janet Reger drawer and unlocked the bedside cabinet.

Roberta re-examined the vibrators, cosseted in their case like a set of miniature Purdeys.

She closed the lid and took the Federation wallet from the chair. The knife tumbled onto the duvet. Roberta wrapped the blade in the chamois leather. She lay back on the bed, hoisted her skirt and bit hard on her knuckle to suppress her squeals of triumphant ecstasy.

# Fifty

Roberta settled back onto the leather rear seat of her official Rover 75, her briefcase beside her.

'Everything OK, ma'am?' asked her driver.

'Perfect,' she replied.

'Where to now?'

'Angel Hill. And put the radio on, would you? I'd like to catch the news. And find out what the reptiles have turned up today on this case.'

'I bought a *Standard* from the newsagents on the corner,' said the driver, handing her the paper. 'I thought you might be interested.'

'Thanks,' said Roberta, scan-reading the first few pages. 'Nothing much here we don't know already.'

As they pulled away from the house, Ricky Sparke's voice filled the car.

'. . . that was Squeeze, "Pulling Mussels from a Shell". You're listening to a specially extended edition of the Ricky Sparke show on Rocktalk 99FM. You'll remember that yesterday we broke the news that police were holding an ex-cop, Mickey French, in connection with the shooting of an intruder in the village of Heffer's Bottom.

'As you have probably heard on our news bulletins today, and as you may have read in your morning newspapers, it has now been confirmed that the dead man is an asylum-seeker from Romania.

'We've been getting your reaction all morning. Now Rocktalk 99FM can bring you a world exclusive.

'I'm joined on the line now by the man himself, Mickey French.

*'Good morning, Mickey. You're live on Rocktalk 99FM.'*
*'Hello, Ricky. Hello, everyone.'*


Roberta sat bolt upright, almost decapitating herself with her seat belt.

'Turn that up. And pull over,' she snapped. 'And get me Angel Hill. Get Marsden. RIGHT NOW!'


*'Mickey, before we start, I think I should just make it clear that when I said the other day we were launching a new competition, Shoot a Burglar and Win a Million, I was joking, mate.'*

*'I hadn't planned to be the first contestant.'*

*'Mickey, seriously, everyone's talking about what happened. Can you tell us about it, in your own words.'*

*'I was sitting at home, cleaning my guns, when I heard a crash.'*

*'Let's get this clear, Mickey, you're an ex-cop, right?'*

*'Yeah.'*

*'And you had a licence to keep these guns?'*

*'Absolutely. They're perfectly legal.'*

*'Go on.'*

*'I saw this figure advancing towards me in the dark. I feared for my life. Using my police training, I loaded my gun and fired. The intruder, burglar, whatever, spun backwards, stumbled out onto the lawn and fell. I went over to the body, confirmed he was dead and called it in.'*

*'YOU called the police?'*

*'Sure. I used to be a police officer. I was comfortable with what I had done. I'm not proud of shooting him, but I do think I used reasonable force in self-defence. I was in my own home at the time and did what I thought, how I had been trained to react, was necessary in the circumstances.'*


Marsden came on the phone.

'Yes, ma'am.'

'Don't you dare "yes ma'am" me. Are you listening to this?'

'What, ma'am?'

'Your prisoner. Live on the radio.'

'Sorry, ma'am?' Marsden was confused.

'Mickey French, talking live on Rocktalk 99 F-*fucking*-M.' Roberta could swear like a trooper when she had to, for effect. 'From your police station.'

Oh, my god.

'Are you sure, ma'am?'

'You think I'm imagining it. Put a stop to it. *Immediately*.'

Marsden dropped the phone and rushed off to the custody suite. The interview continued.


'*Mickey, tell us why you thought your life was in danger.*'

'*Threats had been made against me and my family. There have been other incidents at my house.*'

'*Do you know who was responsible?*'

'*There's a camp of pikeys, sorry, travellers, down the road. Been there a coupla months. Nothing but trouble since they moved in. They trashed our house, killed our cat.*'

'*Your CAT?*'

'*Yeah. They said it would be me next.*'

'*Why on earth would they do that, Mickey?*'

'*I'd had the odd run-in with them.*'

'*And you thought this intruder was one of them?*'

'*That was my first reaction.*'

'*That's perfectly understandable, Mickey. But we now know that it wasn't anyone local.*'

'*So I've been informed.*'

'*Do you know this Gica Dinantu?*'

'*Never heard of him.*'

'*Can you give us any good reason why he'd be breaking into your house in the middle of the night?*'

'*Burglary, I guess.*'

'*Now, Mickey, I know you're still at the police station. Have you been charged?*'

*'No, just cautioned. But they're talking about murder.'*

*'MURDER?'*

*'That's what they're saying.'*

*'I'm sure all our listeners will be shocked to hear that, after what you've just told us. Let me ask you this, Mickey. Any regrets about what happened?'*

*'Of course I regret that someone is dead.'*

*'But would you do it again?'*

The door of the sergeant's office burst open and Marsden and three officers stormed in. Marsden grabbed the phone and terminated the call.

'You're taking the piss, Mickey. You can't do this,' he said.

'I just did.'

'You're in deep shit. Fuck it, *I'm* in deep shit,' yelled Marsden. 'Get him out of here. Back in his cell. And lock it.'

Marsden glared at the custody sergeant, who glared at Mickey.

'I'll deal with you later,' Marsden said to the sergeant. 'Your job's on the line here. *My* fucking job's on the line here.'

Mickey looked sheepishly at the sergeant as two burly PCs led him away.

'Sorry, Ted,' he apologized.

'Just fuck off, Mickey,' said the sergeant, shaking his head, anticipating his future career prospects as a security guard at the Bluewater Shopping Centre.

*'Mickey, hello, Mickey. Mickey, you there? It appears we've lost the line to Mickey French. I'm sorry, ladies and gentlemen. But at least he managed to shed some light on what happened.*

*'You heard him say it, live and exclusive on Rocktalk 99FM. They're talking murder here.*

*'How can that be? Whatever happened to an Englishman's home is his castle? A man has a right to defend himself in his own home.*

'If you ask me this, this burglar, this intruder, this asylum-seeker, this CRIMINAL, and that's what he is, ladies and gentlemen, a CRIMINAL, deserved everything he got. Death by misadventure, maximum, you tell me.

'He was in the wrong place at the wrong time. Tough.

'Call your MP. Get down to Angel Hill nick and demonstrate. Let's get Mickey out. Let's strike a blow for Middle England, for justice.

'The Mickey French is Innocent campaign starts right here. Make your voice heard. Register your support.

'Who you gonna call?

'Rocktalk 99FM, that's who. Rocktalk 99FM, your OFFICIAL Mickey French radio station.'

Ricky Sparke just put fifty grand on his wages.

# Fifty-one

Hurricane Roberta hit Angel Hill nick gathering Force Nine and rising.

'What the hell were you thinking of?' she demanded of the custody sergeant.

'Ma'am. I take full . . .' Marsden piped up.

'Damn right, you do, inspector.'

Oh dear, *inspector*, was it? Not acting detective *chief* inspector. Not even *acting*. Marsden's sphincter tightened.

'But for the moment, I'd like to hear what the sergeant has to say for himself. I want his last day here to be a happy one,' said DAC Peel, sitting behind Marsden's desk.

'Ma'am, Mickey, the prisoner, French, that is, asked to make a phone call. He is entitled, under PACE,' explained the terrified sergeant.

'Why wasn't someone with him?'

'We assumed, what with the custody extension and everything, that he had decided to call a solicitor.'

'Did you ask him?'

The sergeant shuffled and stared at the floor. 'Not specifically, ma'am.'

'Not *specifically*?'

'Not at all, ma'am.'

'Why the hell not? You're supposed to dial the number for him.'

'I know, ma'am. But I thought, in the circumstances, like.'

'What circumstances?'

'Well, you know, with Mickey, the prisoner, being one of us,' the sergeant said.

Roberta pushed the chair backwards, stood up and leant forward, hands on the desk. Marsden thought he noticed what looked like a fresh bite mark on her left knuckle.

'Let's get one thing *absolutely* straight, so there can be no misunderstanding. Michael Edward French is not, repeat *not*, one of us. He is entitled to no special privileges, no special treatment. That's exactly what the critics of the police service are looking for. That's what *I'm* doing here. To ensure that French is treated like any other prisoner. We have to be especially sensitive. May I remind you that what we are looking at here is a suspected murder with a possible racial motive. Haven't any of you out in this god-forsaken backwater even *read* Macpherson?'

Marsden cleared his throat. 'I think I can assure you that as far as the arrest and the procedure are concerned, everything has been done by the book, ma'am.'

'Then what the hell was he doing live on the radio? From *inside* this police station? What is this – Radio Plod? Dial 999 and ask for Mickey?'

The sergeant spoke up. 'We had every reason to believe he was conferring with his solicitor. We had no idea he was ringing the radio station.'

'That's enough, sergeant. I am viewing this as a serious breach of discipline. You've made the Metropolitan Police Service a laughing stock. You are suspended from duty, on full pay, pending a full disciplinary hearing. That will be all.'

'Ma'am,' said the sergeant, clicking his heels and turning like a dismissed squaddie on his way to the glasshouse.

Roberta sat down in Marsden's chair.

'I'm sorry, ma'am. This wasn't my fault, but it was my responsibility. He was my prisoner. I can only apologize,' said the acting DCI.

'You can't be held entirely responsible for the actions of a sloppy custody sergeant,' said Roberta, her attitude softening.

'Ted's a good man, ma'am.'

'Ted's an imbecile, inspector,' she corrected him. 'I can see from your initial report and the thoroughness with which you have conducted your inquiries thus far that you can see the wider picture.'

'Just doing my job, ma'am.'

'You appear not to have been affected by sentiment, like some other people.'

'With respect, ma'am, it's understandable why old hands like Ted would cut Mickey, French, that is, a bit of slack. He was a good copper.'

'I believe your father served with him,' said Roberta, failing to mention that she, too, had once worked in the same nick as Marsden senior.

'Yes, ma'am.'

'Do you know French?'

'I've come across him a couple of times, ma'am. But I wouldn't say I know him.'

'Let me ask you this, Colin. You don't mind me calling you Colin, do you?'

'Not at all, ma'am.'

Roberta could smell the resentment the second she walked into Angel Hill. She needed an ally. Marsden was younger than she'd imagined, quite good-looking, but gone slightly to pot, prematurely aged. It was an occupational hazard. She could spot a CID officer at a hundred paces. They all had that same, untidy round the edges, world-weary look about them. Ground down by the system.

Marsden seemed different. His paperwork was impeccable, which was a good sign. And he didn't carry with him the air of defeatism which infected so many detectives.

'Colin, the eyes of the whole nation will soon be on this case. Difficult, not to say unpopular decisions will have to be made. What I need to know from you, here and now, in this office, is simply this – are you prepared to follow this through? Wherever it leads?'

Marsden took a deep breath and looked Roberta straight in the eye.

'Wherever it leads, ma'am.'

'Excellent. We'll interview the prisoner shortly. Perhaps you could get me a cup of coffee from the canteen, Colin. I'm parched.'

Marsden wasn't quite sure that a detective chief inspector should be running errands to the canteen. Not even an *acting* detective chief inspector. But what the hell, he was off the hook. He could do with the walk.

'My pleasure, ma'am. Milk and sugar?'

'No thanks,' Roberta smiled, patting her stomach. 'I have to watch my figure.' She could be quite coquettish when she felt like it. For a Deputy Assistant Commissioner.

Marsden looked properly at DAC Peel for the first time. Nice tits, he thought.

# Fifty-two

Roberta dialled Justin on his mobile. She caught him on his way from a meeting at the Smith Square headquarters of the Consolidated Union of National Trades Societies.

His phone rang as he was walking past a pub called the Marquis of Granby, a notorious den of political plotters.

'Where the hell have you been?' he said, grumpily. 'I've been trying to call you. I kept getting unobtainable.'

'I've been busy. I switched the phone off. I didn't want to be disturbed. Anyway, reception isn't great out here,' she said.

'Out where?'

'Angel Hill.'

'Isn't that where . . . ?'

'Correct.'

'What are you doing out there?'

'I am leading the Mickey French murder investigation.'

'You're *what*?'

Justin stopped in his tracks and ducked into a doorway.

'I'm on the case.'

'How the hell did that happen?'

'The Commissioner asked me to oversee the investigation after a request from the Home Secretary,' she explained.

'And I can guess where the Home Secretary got the idea from. Roberta, what on earth are you playing at?'

'It's called damage limitation.'

'It's called insanity.'

'No, Justin, we've tried insanity. That was your idea. Now we're going to do things my way.'

'But French has still got his Get Out of Jail card.'

'Not any more.'

'*What?*'

'I'll explain later.'

Fromby didn't push her. Walls have ears. And so do the Funny People. Justin was convinced his calls were constantly monitored by the security services. He'd seen *The Conversation* once too often. Students' Union paranoia.

Still, just because you're paranoid, it doesn't mean they're not out to get you.

'You know the media are trying to turn French into some kind of hero. He was on the radio this morning, pleading his innocence,' he said.

'Don't remind me. There's a custody sergeant downstairs filling out an application to join Group 4.'

'I hope you know what you're doing,' Justin fretted.

'Oh, yes,' said Roberta. 'I know exactly what I'm doing. I'm filling out *my* application to be the next Commissioner of the Metropolitan Police.'


Marsden retrieved Mickey from the cells and led him along the corridor towards the interview room.

'What the fuck were you thinking about, Mickey?' he asked.

'Survival,' said Mickey. 'I can see the way this one is going. Decided to get myself some outside help.'

'Why didn't you just phone a brief?'

'I don't need a brief. I know the law inside out. I did twenty-five years in the Job and spent my convalescence studying law.'

'So why the phone call to the radio station?'

'I only intended to call Ricky, keep him up to speed. I'd forgotten he was on air. You lose all track of time in here. His producer put me through while a record was playing – Lovin' Spoonful, I think it was – and Ricky just talked me into it. Next thing I was on live.'

'Come off it, Mickey. You know the rules on sub judice.'

'Sure, they're designed to prevent any public comment which could prejudice my defence,' Mickey said.

'Any comment which may prejudice any aspect of the case,' Marsden corrected him.

'Whatever. But it's my neck on the line. I just thought the world should know the facts before the system has had a chance to twist them.'

'You'll get your day in court,' Marsden said.

'I'd rather take my chances in the court of public opinion,' said Mickey.

'You've probably cost Ted his job,' said Marsden.

'Yeah, I'm sorry about that. Look, let me talk to the Chief Super, uniform, I'll put in a word, explain it wasn't Ted's fault.'

'I'm afraid it's gone way beyond that,' said Marsden, showing Mickey into the room. 'Sit down.'

'What do you mean, beyond that?'

'You'll find out soon enough,' said Marsden.

At that moment, Roberta walked into the interview room.

Mickey was amazed to see her, but didn't show it.

Marsden introduced her. 'This is Deputy Assistant Commissioner Roberta Peel.'

'Hello, Bobby,' said Mickey.

Bobby?

No one had called her that for years. Not even behind her back.

'I take the full Roberta,' she reminded Mickey.

'So I've heard, love,' Mickey chuckled.

For a split second, they were back in the canteen at Tyburn Row.

Marsden didn't know where to look. He was sure Roberta blushed.

'For the purposes of this interview, you can call me Deputy Assistant Commissioner, Ms Peel, or ma'am,' she replied.

'I'll call you whatever I like,' Mickey said.

286

'Let me remind you this is a police station,' said Roberta, formally.

'And let *me* remind *you* that I am no longer a police officer, Bobby, my precious. That's what everyone keeps telling me.'

'And let *me* also remind *you* that *you* are still under caution and that this is a murder inquiry. Can we proceed?'

Marsden switched on the dual tape deck and went through the formalities.

'You don't deny shooting Gica Dinantu,' Roberta said.

'No.'

'You maintain you acted in self-defence?'

'Correct. Look, I've been through all that with him,' said Mickey, nodding in the direction of Marsden.

'I am now running this investigation,' Roberta informed him.

'Why you, Bobby?'

'It was decided that the case should be handled, with no disrespect to the acting detective chief inspector, by a more experienced officer.'

Mickey threw back his head and roared with laughter.

'What's so funny?' Roberta said.

'What have you ever done? Be honest, Bobby. Hendon, Bramshill, bit of juvenile, domestic, community relations, a couple of years signing exes and shifting desks around a division. Secondment to the Home Office, a few policy committees, rape, sexual harassment. Oh, yeah, I nearly forgot, the rubber heels, CIB. Investigating other coppers. You enjoyed that, didn't you, sweetheart? Put a few pips on your sleeve.'

'If you've quite finished. I am running this interview,' she interrupted him.

'Not quite. Tell me this. Which was the last murder case you investigated?'

Roberta sat silent, stony-faced.

'I thought so. This kid here,' said Mickey, pointing to Marsden, 'what are you, son, thirty-five, thirty-six?'

287

Marsden, too, stayed silent.

'This kid has investigated more proper cases in his lunch-hour than you have in twenty years. He's good, too.'

Marsden shrivelled inside with embarrassment.

Roberta decided to let it pass. But she'd made up her mind. She was going to hang Mickey French.

She used to have a soft spot for him, all those years back at Tyburn Row. He hadn't buried her when he could have done.

Now he'd just humiliated her in front of a junior officer. A male junior officer.

And his Get Out of Jail card was safely locked away in her briefcase. He couldn't hurt her any more.

For a man facing a murder charge and a possible life sentence, Mickey was enjoying himself.

'OK,' he said, 'I buy the senior officer bit. But why you, Bobby?'

'The Commissioner asked me to take over the investigation.'

'No, you're not hearing me. Why not a DCS, from division? Or even a Commander from the Yard? Why *you*?'

Marsden had been wondering the very same thing. What the fuck was a DAC doing out here at Angel Hill?

'Let's get on with this, shall we?' said Roberta.

'Fire away, pet,' Mickey invited her.

'The day in question, you had been drinking heavily.'

'I'd had a few.'

Roberta picked up Mickey's earlier statement.

'Four or five measures of spirits,' she began to read.

'Large vodkas, splash of tonic, plenty of ice, no lemon,' Mickey enlightened her. 'And one for yourself, love.'

Roberta refused to rise to the bait.

'Two bottles of wine. We also found an empty bottle of whisky in the house, isn't that right, inspector?'

'Yes, ma'am,' Marsden confirmed.

'How much was in the bottle when you started drinking the whisky?'

'I forget.'

'I'm not surprised. This is what you call "a few", is it?'

'On a quiet day,' said Mickey.

'I have here the results of your blood test, back-timed at the lab. Your blood-alcohol content was nine times the legal drink-drive limit. Enough, apparently, to kill some people.'

'I wasn't driving.'

'No, but you were handling guns.'

'I wasn't pissed. Ask him. He was there.'

Roberta ploughed on.

'According to the medical reports you were clinically dead, never mind intoxicated.'

'Bollocks.'

'Let's leave those to one side for the moment,' Roberta said. 'And consider motive.'

'The only motive I had was protecting my own life.'

'What made you think it might be in danger?'

'Do we have to go over this again? I've already told him,' Mickey said, once again darting his eyes towards Marsden. 'Threats had been made against my life, my home had been trashed, my cat had been killed, for fuck's sake. This is all on record. Your boys attended. Read the reports.'

'I have,' said Roberta.

## NEX TIM ITS YOU COZZER

'The problem we have here is that the man you killed was not one of those you claim made the alleged threats against you,' Roberta said.

'Alleged?'

'Yes, alleged.'

'If it wasn't the pikeys, who the fuck was it?'

'You don't like members of the travelling community, do you?' asked Roberta, her eyes down, studying her papers.

Mickey paused. He could see where this was leading.

'In fact, you don't like gypsies, full stop.'

Mickey said nothing.

'Let me read this to you. *"If those fucking pikeys come anywhere near me, my family or my house again, I'll blow their fucking heads off."* Do you deny saying that?'

Mickey remained silent.

'It's all here, on paper. We haven't exactly been sitting around on our backsides while you've been in custody. We've been knocking on doors, talking to local people. It's called police work. You may remember it. We have built up a fascinating picture. Do you deny saying it?'

Mickey cracked his knuckles.

'Let's try again.' Roberta read slowly and deliberately, without emotion, like the Speaking Clock. 'Try this. *"Don't give me multi-fucking-culturalism. The only culture these fucking pikeys have is thieving. I'd have given them a kicking until they put their hands up to it, fucking thieving dids. I dunno why I even bothered calling you. I might just as well go round there myself and sort it."* It's all here, in PC, er . . .' Roberta hesitated.

'Smith,' Marsden prompted her. 'PC Ramsay Smith.'

'Thank you. In PC Smith's report. Do you deny saying any of this?'

'What's your point?' said Mickey, knowing perfectly well what her point was.

'What this says to me is that I am looking at a racist with violent tendencies who had made previous threats to kill.'

'You *are* taking the piss?'

'I have never been more serious in my life,' said Roberta.

'What has any of this got to do with this case?'

'Admit it, Mickey, you're a Romaphobe,' snapped Roberta.

'A *what*?'

'A *Romaphobe*.'

'Oh, very good. Just think that up, did you, pet? The Home Secretary will be proud of you.'

Roberta ploughed on. 'You clearly have an irrational hatred of gypsies. The dead man, Dinantu, is a gypsy. You couldn't believe your luck when he walked into your house. An ideal opportunity to "blow his fucking head off".'

'Hang on a minute.' Mickey was getting agitated.

There was a fit-up underway. A subtle fit-up, but a fit-up nevertheless. Careful, Mickey.

'It was dark. How the hell was I supposed to know he was a gypsy?'

'You assumed he was one of the "pikeys".'

'Sure.'

'And that's why you killed him. Because you thought he was a "pikey"' – pause for emphasis – 'and you had previously threatened to kill any "pikey"' – pause again – 'who came anywhere near you or your family.'

'But he wasn't a fucking pikey,' Mickey reminded her.

'No, he may not have been what you refer to as a "pikey",' said Roberta, holding the word as far away from her nose as possible. 'But he was a guest in our country, a member of a persecuted minority. And he was an innocent victim of your vendetta against the travelling community. You were drunk, we've already established that, and you were driven to murder out of racial hatred. I'm treating this as a hate crime. Classic Romaphobic behaviour.'

'I've heard it all now. You people have got a category for everyone, a slogan for every occasion. Fucking *Romafuckingphobia*. Do me a favour. What the hell was this *innocent* character doing crashing into my home in the middle of the night? Ask yourself that. Come to borrow a cup of fucking sugar?' Mickey rose to his feet and slammed the palms of his hands on the table.

'For the tape, prisoner rises to his feet aggressively,' said Roberta.

'Listen, let's kill this *Romaphobic* bollocks stone dead right now. We're not talking Raggle Taggle Gypsies here, roasting hedgehogs round the campfire, flogging lucky heather and a packet of pegs. We're not even talking *"tarmac yer droive, sor"*. We're talking so-called "travellers" who never travel any further than the DSS and the nearest off-licence. And others who'll travel a hundred miles from home to burgle an antiques dealer. Organized criminal gangs, outlaws.'

Mickey was on a roll. 'As for so-called *hate crime*? Let me tell you something, sweetheart. I don't *hate* anyone because of their race, creed, colour, whatever. I'll tell you who I *do* hate, though. I hate scavenging, thieving bastards. I hate burglars. I hate people who make other people's lives a misery. Most of all I hate people who break into my house, kill my cat, threaten me and my family. And in this case they just happen to be pikeys. Satisfied?'

'Sit down, French,' Roberta commanded him.

Mickey composed himself.

'Anyone else you hate?' she asked casually.

Self-righteous bastards like you, Mickey thought.

'Very well,' said Roberta. 'Let's return to the facts of this particular shooting, shall we? You gunned him down in cold blood, gave him no opportunity to identify himself or retreat from the situation.'

'How many more times?' said Mickey, in exasperation. 'I did what I was trained to do. You know the law. Criminal Justice Act 1967. "A person may use such force as is reasonable in the circumstances in the prevention of a crime; when force for a purpose is justified by that purpose."'

'That is for a jury to decide. I am satisfied that I have enough to charge you with murder. You will be formally charged shortly, re-advised of your rights and brought before a magistrate in the morning,' said Roberta. 'Is there anything else you would like to say before we conclude this interview?'

'I suppose a fuck's out of the question?' said Mickey.

# Fifty-three

Marsden led Mickey back down towards the cells. As they rounded a corner at the foot of the stairwell, he stopped and pushed Mickey into the gents' toilet.

Checking, double-checking, treble-checking traps one, two and three, until he was confident they could not be seen or overheard, Marsden spoke.

'Stand there and make like you're having a piss,' he told Mickey.

Mickey did as he was told.

'You don't do yourself any favours, do you?' said Marsden.

Mickey shrugged.

Marsden continued, in hushed tones: 'You went out of your way to antagonize her.'

'Just my way of being friendly,' Mickey said, saturating a stray dog-end in the urinal. He thought he might as well make the most of it.

'It's about time you started taking this seriously. She's going to charge you with murder.'

'Maybe, maybe not.'

'You heard her in there. Murder, racial motive.'

'What do you think, Colin?' asked Mickey.

'She's got a lot going for her – the blood-alcohol level, the previous threats you'd made. It doesn't look good. She's going to squeeze your bollocks until your eyes pop out. And you're handing them to her on a silver platter.'

'What do you care?'

'I told you,' Marsden said, 'I was always going to play this by the numbers. Straight down the middle. I booked you in on suspicion of murder because that was the right thing to do. But, between us and these four shit-house walls, I couldn't see anything over and above manslaughter at best.'

'And?'

'I didn't know it was going to turn into a witch-hunt.'

'Welcome to the bonfire party, inspector,' said Mickey.

'There's something here you're not telling me. Something I don't know,' said Marsden. 'What is it?'

'Fucked if I know,' said Mickey.

'It doesn't add up.'

'Go away and do your sums again, then, inspector, because I can't help you. Find out more about this Dinantu character, for a start. What he was doing at my house.'

'We're on to it.'

'Oh, one thing I can tell you,' Mickey said.

'What?'

'Well, you said you found a can of petrol outside the house?'

'Yeah, that's been puzzling me.'

'It definitely doesn't belong to me.'

'Can you explain how it got there?'

'Not a clue,' said Mickey.

'I've sent it to the lab, for dabs, anyway,' said Marsden. 'Another thing. What was all this "Bobby" business?'

'We've got history,' Mickey said, 'me and the DAC.'

'I'd deduced that much for myself.'

'We worked together, donkey's years ago. I was a Plod and she was a probationary Plonk . . .'

'Where was that?'

'Tyburn Row.'

'Tyburn Row? That was where you and Dad served together.'

'Correct. She didn't tell you she knew your dad, did she?'

'No,' said Marsden, puzzled.

Why not?

*     *     *

Half an hour later, Deputy Assistant Commissioner Roberta Peel strode into the custody area and asked to see the prisoner in his cell.

Alone.

The new custody sergeant thought it might be some kind of test. He told Roberta that under the Police and Criminal Evidence Act a prisoner could not be interviewed in his cell.

If she had more questions to put to the prisoner she would have to book him out of custody and into a formal interview room.

'You're absolutely correct, sergeant,' she said. 'I'm glad to see someone here follows procedure.'

The sergeant looked relieved.

'However, I don't want to reinterview French, merely verify a couple of details.' Roberta smiled.

'I don't know, ma'am, with respect. Perhaps you should speak to the inspector.'

'He's not in his office, sergeant. I just came by. It was empty. I will take full responsibility.'

'I'll make a note in the custody record, ma'am.'

'That won't be necessary. As I said, this is completely informal.'

'Very well, ma'am, if you insist,' he said, still unsure.

'Thank you, sergeant.'

'I'll have to leave the door open,' the sergeant said.

'Oh, *absolutely*,' Roberta insisted.

The sergeant unlocked the cell door and stood back two paces.

'That's OK, sergeant. I won't be a minute. I'm sure you have some paperwork to attend to. I'll call you when I'm ready.'

The sergeant could take a hint.

Mickey was sitting on his head with his hands folded behind his head and his legs straight out in front of him.

'Hello, Bobby, you changed your mind then?'

'Changed my mind?' said Roberta.

'Yeah. You know, when I said "I suppose a fuck's out of the question?" I didn't expect you to take me up on it.'

'Just shut up and listen,' said Roberta, exasperated.

'Yes, *ma'am*,' Mickey saluted, sarcastically.

'You disappoint me, Mickey. I really thought that you were better than the other canteen clowns.'

'And I once thought that you'd make a good cop,' said Mickey. 'Look at yourself now. A fucking social worker with scrambled egg on her hat. I should have dropped you in it when I had the opportunity. Done the world a favour, stopped you and your boyfriend in your tracks.'

'Oh, but you didn't, Mickey.'

'To my eternal regret. How's that Rod Stewart song go? *I wish, that, I knew what I know now, when I was younger.*'

'Too late, Mickey.'

'It's never too late, Bobby, my love.'

'Oh, but it is.'

'Are you forgetting?'

'Certainly not. But you'll never be able to use it.'

'What, you think, because I'm implicated? I'm already looking at murder. What difference is a bit of withholding evidence twenty-odd years ago going to make?'

'That's not what I meant.'

'What, then?'

'You'll never be able to use it. None of it.'

'What are you getting at?' Now Mickey was getting curious.

'It's amazing what you turn up when you search a crime scene, thoroughly. You come across all sorts of things – knives, cassette tapes, official documents.'

Roberta flashed him a sweet, sarcastic smile.

'Oh, incidentally,' she said, 'how was Worthing in 1981?'


By 5.30 pm about thirty people were picketing the main entrance of Angel Hill police station, carrying Free Mickey French placards and wearing Rocktalk 99FM T-shirts.

They were outnumbered by photographers, reporters and television camera crews.

At 7.35 pm, the Press Office at Scotland Yard announced that Michael Edward French had been formally charged with the murder of Gica Dinantu.

# Fifty-four

'My god, you sound completely different,' said Justin.

'I was so much younger then. We all were.' Roberta sipped a glass of chilled Premier Cru Chablis.

They'd come a long way from the rough, screw-top red wine of their student days.

Justin had been about to open a bottle of vintage Dom Perignon but Roberta cautioned against premature celebration.

'Not just younger. You were much plummier,' Justin teased her.

'You can talk.' Roberta laughed. 'There's not a trace of the Nottinghamshire coalfields in your accent these days. When I knew you, you sounded like something out of D H Lawrence.'

'We all adjust, darling,' said Justin, camping it up. His modern accent was a model of glottal stops and dropped aitches, sometimes David Mellor, other times Tony Blair, occasionally Mick Jagger. He could switch effortlessly from Estuary to Etonian, sometimes in the course of the same sentence.

They were reclining on the sofa in Justin's study in Dartmouth Park, listening to the Tyburn Row tape.

'I still can't believe you had the nerve,' he said.

'She who dares, darling.'

'But weren't you worried about being caught?'

'Why should I have been? I had a perfectly legitimate reason to be there. I am a high-ranking police officer leading a murder inquiry at the personal behest of the Commissioner and the Home Secretary. It is quite natural that I would want to conduct a thorough search of the crime scene,' Roberta said.

'Even the attic? How would you have explained that? Looking for Anne Frank?'

'It doesn't matter. I found what I was looking for. We're in the clear.'

'You sound confident,' said Justin, 'but what if French starts shouting his mouth off, making wild accusations?'

'Who would believe him? He's just been charged with murder. What good would it do him? He doesn't know anything about our . . .'

'. . . our involvement?' Justin prompted her.

'He never will. Only three of us know what Dinantu, Popescu, whoever he was, was doing there. Two of us aren't saying and the other one is dead,' Roberta continued.

She poured them another glass of wine.

'Did Wayne have any idea who he was?' she asked.

'Not a clue. Just another client, as far as he was concerned.'

'In which case, there's absolutely nothing to link us to the body,' said Roberta, draining the glass.

'And now, thanks to you, nothing to link us to Gibbs, Marsden, French, Tyburn Row,' he said. 'But let's make absolutely sure of that.'

He walked over to the cassette deck, turned to Roberta and asked: 'Want to hear it once more for old times' sake?'

'I don't think so.'

Justin pressed the erase button and wiped away the past.

He took the documents from the wallet and fed them into his shredder.

'What about the knife?' asked Roberta.

'I'll dump it tomorrow. Drop it in Highgate Ponds or something.'

'No don't do that, darling,' she purred, fondling the handle, running her tongue over the ivory surface. 'I've become quite attached to it.'

\*　　\*　　\*

Twenty minutes later they returned from the bedroom. Justin opened another bottle of Chablis and Roberta rubbed a little Savlon into the handcuff burns on her wrists and ankles.

'How strong is his reasonable force defence?' asked Justin.

'You tell me, you're the lawyer.'

'It's a moot point. It could go either way. You know as well as I do that householders are allowed to use reasonable force when confronted by an intruder or to protect their own lives. But what is "reasonable"? The law isn't precise. Consider the two most famous cases. Kenneth Noye, a career criminal, killed an undercover policeman in the grounds of his home and walked. Tony Martin, a farmer with no previous, killed a burglar and was convicted of murder. It depends on the vigour with which the police choose to prosecute, the attitude of the trial judge and, of course, the jury. Then there's the inquest verdict, too. That can have a bearing.'

The inquest would come first. Once Mickey had been charged, the formal coroner's inquiry into cause of death would be opened and adjourned.

'The police will prosecute this with extreme vigour,' Roberta assured him. 'The judge? That can probably be arranged. The jury?'

'I've tried a couple of cases out at Angel Hill,' said Justin. 'Unpredictable. It's still quite a tight-knit community. Lots of emigrants from the East End and north London. Predominantly white, aspirational working class. They all voted Thatcher in the Eighties. It's a fair bet most of them would sympathize with French. They've more than likely been burgled themselves a few times. You've heard the reaction on the phone-ins already. A quick trial and my money would be on an acquittal. Best try and drag it out for a year or so and get the case moved to the Old Bailey. Once the heat has gone out of it, everyone will have forgotten about Mickey French and you're in with a chance. The prosecution will get more help from a judge at the Bailey than a circuit judge.'

'There's a powerful head of steam building up behind French,' said Roberta. 'When I left Angel Hill tonight there was already a demonstration outside. We're drafting in more officers for the magistrates' court tomorrow.'

'All of this influences a jury. And the tabloids are having a field day,' Justin said.

'Then we're just going to have to redress the balance. We mustn't let the French camp make all the running.'

'What about sub judice?' said Justin, the lawyer in him ringing alarm bells.

'Technically, the whole case became sub judice the moment French was arrested. But he's the one who waived his rights when he went live on the radio, pleading his innocence.'

'I'm not sure a judge would see it like that. He'll stamp on anything which could prejudice a fair trial.'

'We'll cross that bridge when we come to it. All I want to do is even up the odds a bit. What's to stop you, for instance, in your capacity as a member of the Oppressed Peoples' Refugee Association Hotline expressing your concerns about the rise of racism directed at asylum-seekers?'

'Nothing,' said Justin.

'Right. Well, put yourself about a bit. Call in a few favours. Get yourself on the BBC tomorrow. I've got another idea. Throw me the phone book.'

Roberta flicked through the pages of the north London telephone directory and found the number she was looking for.

After half a dozen rings, a woman's voice answered.

'Georgia?' said Roberta.

'Whoozat?'

'Georgia Claye? It's Roberta here. Roberta Peel.'

'Hang on.'

Roberta could hear coughing at the other end. 'Georgia?'

'Oh shit, fuck it.'

'Georgia, are you all right?' asked Roberta.

'Yeah, yeah. I just set fire to the wastepaper basket. Sorry.'

'Georgia, how are you?'

'Wozallzisabout? I don't hear from you for, I dunno, fuck knows how long, and now you're ringing at this time of night – what time is it, anyway? – to inquire after my health.' She sounded pissed off. And pissed.

'I'm so sorry, Georgia. If it's not convenient.'

'No, it's fine. Just hang on a minute.'

Roberta could hear a gentle *sksssshhh*, as the ring pull released the pressure from the can.

Georgia took a slug of extra-strength cider.

'Now then,' Georgia said, as equilibrium returned to her alcohol stream. 'To what do I owe this honour after all these years?' she asked her old university classmate.

'I know we sort of drifted apart after I . . .' Roberta began.

'. . . sold out is the expression you're looking for.'

'. . . after I joined the police service,' Roberta ploughed on. 'I just wanted to say that though we haven't seen much of each other, I have been following your career with great interest. I really admire your work. Some of your articles in the *Clarion* have absolutely reflected my own thoughts.'

What the fuck does she want? thought Georgia, taking another slug of Olde Bowel Loosener.

'Your exposés of police corruption have been invaluable,' Roberta flattered her.

Eh?

Roberta continued. 'I know you may find this hard to believe, but we are on the same side, you know. While you have been toiling away on the outside, I have been working hard on the inside to reform the police service and stamp out corruption. Your articles have been invaluable to me.'

Fuck me sideways, Georgia thought to herself. But she was always up for a bit of praise, from whichever direction it came.

'That's very kind of you, Roberta,' she said. 'But that's not why you've rung me up in the middle of the night, is it?'

'Indirectly, yes it is, actually,' said Roberta. 'As I said, your work has been very helpful to me and I'd like to repay the compliment. I think I have something which may be very helpful to you.'

'Go on.' Georgia put down the can of cider. She was getting excited. She needed a big break.

'Well, you are familiar with this shooting out at Angel Hill?'

'The ex-cop and the asylum-seeker?'

'Yes.'

Mickey French. She'd invited him indoors one night, made it clear what was on offer, when he gave her a lift back from Spider's. Georgia seemed to remember trying to give him a blow job as he was driving her home, along Upper Street, Islington. But he wasn't having any of it. Fuck him. Or not, as it turned out.

'Yeah, I know what I've read, what I've heard.'

'Look, Georgia, I can trust you?'

'Of course.'

'There's much more to this story. I just thought you, the *Clarion*, might be interested in a bit of background.'

'Absolutely,' said Georgia.

'Perhaps I could drop round in, say, half an hour?'

'Er, yeah, why not,' Georgia agreed, wondering how she was going to tidy up the debris in thirty minutes.

'Great, I think you'll find it worth your while.'

'I'll, er, put the kettle on,' Georgia said, unconvincingly.

'Please don't go to any trouble,' said Roberta. 'Oh, and you do know?'

'Know what?'

'This is all background. Deep background.'

'Absolutely. I know how it works.'

'Strictly off the record.'

Off the record, off the wall, off the fucking Richter Scale. Any way Roberta wanted it. Georgia Claye, investigative reporter, was back in business.

Big time.

# Fifty-five

Mickey sat on the hard bench in the back of the Black Maria handcuffed to a uniformed PC.

'What's with the cuffs?' he'd asked Marsden.

'She insisted,' was the reply.

Mickey had shaved, but shower privileges had been withdrawn on the orders of DAC Peel. His clean shirt was now two days old. He stank of prison cell, a mixture of perspiration, boiled cabbage and stale piss.

He'd lost count of the number of times he'd made this kind of journey. Over the years, he'd been handcuffed to armed robbers, terrorists, murderers. At Paddington he'd spent the best part of a fortnight handcuffed to an Arab hijacker.

Now he was handcuffed to a police officer. And he was the one being accused of murder.

The young cop to whom he was joined at the wrist was apologetic. Mickey told him not to worry.

Maybe he shouldn't have made that phone call to Ricky, gone live on air.

Too late.

He was going to have to get out of this somehow.

Andi. The kids. Shit, she must have tried ringing.

Still, he'd get bail. Certain.

Certain?

Yeah, sweet.

The magistrates would know he wasn't about to do a runner. Ex-cop, distinguished service record.

He'd call Andi just as soon as he got out. Explain everything.

As the van approached Angel Hill court, Mickey heard a familiar voice.

*'Good morning, everyone. This is Ricky Sparke coming to you live from the Rocktalk 99FM mobile outside Angel Hill magistrates, where in a few short minutes Mickey French will appear on a charge of murder, simply for defending himself and his property from a violent intruder.*

*'I'm delighted to say we are joined here this morning by dozens of loyal Rocktalk 99FM listeners determined to protest about Mickey's detention and demand his release.'*

Until last night, Rocktalk 99FM had not possessed a mobile outside-broadcast studio.

Then Charlie Lawrence had a brainwave. He hired a flat-bed pick-up truck, hastily decked it out with Rocktalk 99FM decals and bunting and bunged a BT engineer a monkey to set up an ISDN digital phone line in the pub opposite Angel Hill magistrates' court.

The pub had been there since the 17th century, an old coaching inn, badly refurbished, strewn with garish banners advertising the delights of all-day happy hours, 'pubbe grubbe', 'kwiz nites' and karaoke evenings.

The magistrates' court opposite shouted at the surviving vernacular. It was a ghastly Seventies concrete edifice, scarred by the elements and two decades of exhaust fumes. Filthy grey net curtains with cigarette burns in them dangled apologetically at the windows. Twenty-five years ago the architect won an award for it.

Angel Hill had escaped the Blitz largely unscathed, despite the tonnes of Luftwaffe bombs aimed at the local bike factory, switched to munitions manufacture in 1940 for the duration.

Where the Fokkers had failed, the planners had succeeded in fucking things up, obliterating a once distinguished market town, just as they had throughout England. Cobbles had been dug up and replaced with little red herringbone-pattern bricks, the new municipal acne. Fake Victorian pillars and posts and bus shelters littered the pedestrianized high street. Butchers, bakers and candlestick-makers had given way to video stores and takeaways.

In the middle of a media scrum, Ricky was standing on the back of the truck, dressed, he thought, like a prize prat in Rocktalk 99FM Spandex bomber jacket and Rocktalk 99FM baseball cap. He was clutching a microphone. Cable stretched across the car park, through the gents' toilet window and connected to the temporary line installed behind the bar, where the signal was fed back to the Rocktalk studios in central London, before being relayed into the car park over two enormous loudspeakers.

Cutting-edge technology it wasn't. But it worked.

*'Let's hear from some of those listeners right now. Madam . . .'*

Ricky was joined on the back of the truck by an over-weight, peroxide blonde, wearing a tight denim skirt, white trainers and a replica Leyton Orient football shirt. She was waving a Rocktalk 99FM placard bearing the message: FREE MICKEY FRENCH.

*'What has brought you here this morning, er . . .'*
*'Kaylee.'*
*'Yeah, Kaylee. Why are you here?'*
*'We want Mickey out. He done nuffink wrong. He just defended hisself against some thieving gyppo. 'Bout time some-one done sommink.'*

In front of the truck, facing the court, about fifty Rocktalk listeners, predominantly mums and kids with badly scribbled placards, wearing assorted Rocktalk freebies, caps, T-shirts, badges, handed out by Charlie Lawrence's personal assistant, chanted:

*Free Mickey French.*
*Free Mickey French.*
*Free Mickey French.*

Rocktalk 99FM broadcast their chants across the airwaves. Mickey could hear it all quite clearly, though he could see nothing out of the obscured windows of the police van.

He couldn't see the counter-demonstration, either, organized by the Oppressed Peoples' Refugee Association Hotline and the Anti-Fascist League. But he could hear their chants, too.

The leader of the Anti-Fascist League, a bespectacled, greasy-haired man in his early thirties, unstructured suit and collarless shirt clambered onto a wall and hollered into a portable megaphone in the general direction of the Free Mickey French fraternity:

> *Dumb, dumb,*
> *Racist scum.*
> *DUMB, DUMB,*
> *RACIST SCUM.*

It was taken up by the forty or so OPRAH and AFL demonstrators.

> *DUMB, DUMB,*
> *RACIST SCUM.*
> *DUMB, DUMB,*
> *RACIST SCUM.*

A line of about twenty police officers linked arms and strained to keep the two factions apart.

> *FREE MICKEY FRENCH.*
> *FREE MICKEY FRENCH.*
> *FREE MICKEY FRENCH.*

Ricky was encouraging his side from his vantage point on the back of the Rocktalk mobile.

In the Black Maria, Mickey wasn't quite sure what the hell was going on.

Outside, a few placards were now being thrown along with the insults. And a few fists. Then a few bottles. TV cameras began to roll. Flashguns fired like a fashion shoot.

As the Black Maria pulled up into the yard outside the court, the AFL crowd surged towards it. Orchestrated by the man with the megaphone, the demonstrators began banging on the side. Mickey and the young cop were jolted forward.

> *DUMB, DUMB,*
> *RACIST SCUM.*
> *DUMB, DUMB,*
> *RACIST SCUM.*

Officers with riot shields peeled off, waded in and began pulling bodies out. The line broke and the pro-Mickey faction charged through.

A ferocious-looking woman in a pink Ellesse tracksuit was rugby-tackled by a stout WPC.

A large and especially ugly skinhead in a brand-new Rocktalk 99FM T-shirt headbutted a student waving an AFL banner.

Rocktalk FM faded to music.

'Babylon is Burning'.

The Black Maria was rocked this way and that, Mickey and the young cop steadying themselves.

Two mounted officers from the stables at Angel Hill helped restore order. The rival factions were driven back and separated, contained behind riot shields.

A uniformed inspector clambered onto the flat-bed of the Rocktalk mobile.

'Calm this fucking lot down or I'm nicking you for incitement, conspiracy and anything else I can think of,' he shouted at Ricky, who was enjoying himself.

'This is Ricky Sparke, coming live from the Rocktalk 99FM mobile at Angel Hill. While you've been away we've had a bit of a situation here. The van bringing Mickey French to the court has been viciously attacked by a gang of Trotskyite agitators.

'I would ask our Rocktalk 99FM listeners who have travelled here today to show solidarity with Mickey and not to rise to the provocation. We're here to see justice done, people. Let's keep it peaceful.'

The crowd responded and the inspector appeared mollified. The rear doors of the van swung open and Mickey found himself being bundled out. Everything went dark. Someone had thrown a blanket over his head.

What the fuck was all this about? Identification wasn't an issue. He tore off the blanket. He wasn't being smuggled into court like a fucking nonce, a child-molester or something.

Mickey's appearance was greeted with cheering and abuse in equal measure.

> One Mickey French,
> There's only one Mickey French.
> ONE MICK-EE FRE-ENNCH!
> There's only one Mickey FRENCH.

The big skinhead led the singing.

> Say, WE, WANT, MICKEY OUT.
> SAY WE WANT MICKEY OUT.

Call and response.

> DUMB, DUMB,
> FASCIST SCUM.

In the confusion, no one saw the bespectacled man in the unstructured suit light the rag in the neck of the milk bottle filled with petrol and hurl it towards the Black Maria.

309

It exploded on impact, showering petrol and broken glass and spitting fire.

The young cop pulled Mickey towards the door.

The crowd surged again.

A small child with a banner with FREE MICKY FRECH scrawled on it was trampled underfoot.

A woman's dress caught fire. She ripped it off, screaming, to reveal her uncoordinated underwear, red bra, black knickers. Both needed a wash.

The man in the unstructured suit slipped away.

Ricky Sparke's driver had seen enough. He jammed the flat-bed truck into gear and stamped on the accelerator pedal.

Ricky was thrown backwards, smashing his head on a loudspeaker column. The live link to Rocktalk 99FM was wrenched out of the gents' toilet window as the lorry careered out of the car park, bouncing off a police van.

The crowd scattered in all directions. The cops withdrew behind their riot shields. The big skinhead smashed a bay window at the side of the pub as he made good his escape.

Outside the court a mother cradled her crushed daughter and cried for an ambulance.

Mickey French was bundled inside and the doors barricaded behind him.

From an upstairs window, Deputy Assistant Commissioner Roberta Peel surveyed the battleground.

It was all going rather well.

# Fifty-six

Mickey stood in the dock and entered a formal plea of not guilty.

The magistrate, a kindly-looking woman of a certain age in white blouse and tailored jacket, invited him to sit.

'I understand you are representing yourself, Mr French,' she said.

Mickey rose.

'Yes, ma'am, that is correct.'

'Are you making an application for bail?'

'Yes ma'am.'

'This is a very serious charge, Mr French. You are accused of murder. Bail is not normal in such circumstances.'

'Ma'am, I am aware of that,' said Mickey, showing all due deference. He could give evidence in court in his sleep, not that he'd slept much lately. But this was the first time he'd addressed the bench from the dock. 'I would humbly argue that there are grounds for granting my application in these present circumstances.'

'Go on, Mr French,' said the lady magistrate.

'I am a former police officer, ma'am. I will address the charge I am facing in due course, but I would just like to record the fact that the deceased was an intruder and I was in my own home at the time of the alleged offence. I have no previous record of violence and would submit that I can not be considered in any shape or form to be a threat to the community.'

'Thank you, Mr French,' said the magistrate. 'Does the Crown have any objection to bail?'

Roberta got to her feet.

'May I address the bench, please, your worship?' she asked.

'And you are?'

'Deputy Assistant Commissioner Roberta Peel, from Scotland Yard, ma'am. I am leading the investigation.'

'Very well.'

Roberta took her place in the witness box.

'Ma'am, given the seriousness of the charge, the Metropolitan Police would most strongly oppose the granting of bail in this case. This is a murder inquiry with racial implications. It has already aroused strong public feeling and division, as your worship will have witnessed outside this very court this morning. We are very concerned about the consequences for public order.'

'I see,' said the magistrate.

Roberta continued. 'There are other reasons for opposing bail, quite apart from the seriousness of the charge.'

'Enlighten me, Deputy Assistant Commissioner.'

'We are also concerned about the safety of Mr French, the defendant.'

'On what grounds?'

Yeah, on what grounds? thought Mickey.

'It has come to our attention that there are people who wish Mr French harm. We learned this morning that a contract has been put out on him.'

'You *what*?' Mickey interjected.

'Mr French, please,' said the magistrate. 'Ms Peel, pray continue.'

'We have been told by an informant that a bounty of £50,000 has been placed on Mr French's head.'

'And who the hell would do that?' Mickey snapped.

'Mr French, I won't tell you again,' the magistrate chided him. 'Let me get this straight. You are saying, Ms Peel, that someone has offered £50,000 to anyone who kills Mr French?'

'That is precisely the situation, your worship.'

'Ma'am?' said Mickey, regaining his composure.

'Yes, Mr French?'

'May I be permitted to ask just who is supposed to have put a contract out on me? This is the first I've heard of it.'

'Yes, of course. I'd like to know, too. Ms Peel.'

'I am not at liberty to name our informant, obviously,' said Roberta. 'But I can say that the contract has been placed within the travelling community.'

Gyppoes?

'And why would they do that?' Mickey asked.

Roberta ignored Mickey and spoke directly to the bench. 'Ma'am, reporting restrictions are in place here?'

'Of course,' said the magistrate. 'I would remind the Press of that fact.'

'Ma'am,' said Roberta, 'without wishing to sound prejudicial, there is a history of violence between Mr French and the travelling community.'

Mickey shook his head. He could see where this was leading.

'But my understanding, Ms Peel, is that the deceased in this case was of Romanian origin, an asylum-seeker,' said the magistrate.

'That is correct, your worship.'

'So why, exactly, would the travelling community wish Mr French harm?'

'He has made threats against them in the past.'

'Hang on,' Mickey interrupted. 'I'd like to point out that death threats have been made against *me* by those you refer to as members of the travelling community.'

'Precisely,' said Roberta. 'And that is one very good reason for the police opposing bail in this case.'

'I'm confused, Ms Peel,' said the magistrate. 'Mr French is accused of murdering a *Romanian* asylum-seeker. Why would the travelling community put a bounty on his head?'

'It will be the Crown's intention to prove that when Mr French shot Gica Dinantu he believed he was, in fact, shooting a member of the travelling community, as he had previously threatened to do,' Roberta stated.

The fit-up was well and truly under way, Mickey thought.

'Mr French?' The magistrate turned to Mickey.

'Ma'am, I was just wondering why the Deputy Assistant Commissioner had not seen fit to tell me about this mythical contract.'

'There is nothing mythical about it,' said Roberta. 'It has only just come to my own attention. I haven't had an opportunity to convey the information to the defendant.'

'I see,' said the magistrate.

'Excuse me, your honour,' said an Australian accent from the back of the court.

'Yes?' replied the magistrate. 'Who are you?'

'Could I approach the bench?' asked the man in the designer suit.

'Are you a lawyer?'

No he fucking isn't, Mickey said to himself. And what the fuck is *he* doing here?

'The name's Lawrence, your holiness. Charles Lawrence, everyone calls me Charlie.'

'I shall call you Mr Lawrence,' said the magistrate, concerned that her courtroom was becoming a three-ring circus. 'I repeat, are you a lawyer?'

'No, your highness,' said Charlie, stooping like a third-rate Uriah Heep.

'I am not your highness, your holiness, or your honour. This is not Buckingham Palace, the Vatican or *Perry Mason*. Who are you and what do you want?'

'I am the programme director of Rocktalk 99FM, your, er, um, madam. Mr French drives for one of our presenters, Ricky Sparke. You may have heard of him.'

'No, I haven't,' scowled the magistrate.

'Nine till twelve, weekdays, very popular.'

'Get on with it, or I shall hold you in contempt.'

'Well, fine, it's, er, like this, your, er. Anyway, that sort of makes Mickey here, Mr French, a kind of employee of the radio station and in that regard I am authorized to offer £1 million bail.'

'A *million pounds*?' spluttered the astonished magistrate.

'Yeah, I've got a cheque right here in my briefcase. Just tell me who I make it out to.'

Mickey sat speechless.

'Ma'am,' interjected Roberta, 'this is highly irregular. This, this, stunt, changes nothing. For all the reasons I have stated, the Metropolitan Police urges you not to grant bail in this case.'

'Mr French, have you anything to say?' the magistrate asked.

'Only to reiterate what I said earlier, ma'am. I have no intention of absconding and I present no threat to the public.'

The magistrate consulted her papers.

'I appreciate that, Mr French. But taking into consideration everything Deputy Assistant Commissioner Peel has said and given the continuing threat to your own safety, I'm afraid I'm going to have to turn down your application. Bail is denied. You will be remanded in custody. Take him down.'

Mickey slumped forward. He'd convinced himself he'd be freed on bail. What about Andi? What about the kids? He had to talk to her.

Roberta looked on triumphantly as Mickey was led down the steps to the cells.

The court was adjourned. Charlie Lawrence took out his mobile and broke the bad news to Ricky, now parked up in a layby a couple of miles away, nursing a gashed head.

Mickey sat in his cell, awaiting transport to Paxton, the nearest remand prison, contemplating his next move. He hadn't planned for this eventuality. He'd been certain he'd make bail.

He could apply to a judge in chambers. But that would involve a brief. Mickey wanted to keep it simple. And, anyway, he couldn't afford silk and he knew he wouldn't get legal aid.

Rocktalk 99FM would probably pay for a lawyer. They

were milking it for all it was worth. But Mickey wasn't sure Charlie Lawrence's million-pound bail stunt had done him any favours.

He decided to sit tight overnight. The inquest would be opened and adjourned tomorrow. He'd take a view after that.

If Peel was right, he'd be safer behind bars. But where had the death threat come from?

Why hadn't she mentioned it? Why would the pikeys put a price on his head? It didn't make sense, despite the best efforts of Peel to rationalize it in court. He needed to talk to Marsden.

There was a game going on here and Mickey was already well behind on away goals.

His thoughts were not for himself, but for his wife and family. They say ignorance is bliss, but in this case ignorance of Mickey's predicament would have Andi worried sick.

They hadn't spoken for several days. She'd have tried home, she'd have tried his mobile. She'd have tried her mum too. What if her mum had seen it on the news? Maybe she'd tried Ricky. Would Ricky have told her Mickey was in jail or wouldn't he want to alarm her?

Ricky would be sure to visit him in Paxton. They'd work something out. He didn't want the kids told and he wanted Andi to stay put. There was nothing she could do and, with the Press sniffing round everywhere, she'd be well off out of it, tucked up in Zero Beach, Florida.

The cell door opened and in walked Roberta.

'I don't recall ordering room service,' said Mickey.

'I thought you might like a cup of tea,' she said with a sarcastic smile.

'Cut the crap, what do you want? Come to gloat, have you?'

Roberta surveyed him.

'You should be thanking me for opposing bail. I may just have saved your hide,' she said.

'Oh, yeah. So where did this alleged death threat, this contract, come from then?'

'That's confidential. All I can say is from a reliable police source.'

'That's bollocks. Anyway, contract or no fucking contract, I don't give a shit. I can look after myself,' Mickey said.

'And look where looking after yourself has got you, Mickey. You don't seem to realize what a serious position you're in. You're looking at life,' Roberta reminded him.

'I know what I'm looking at, thank you very much.'

'You could make it easy on yourself.'

'What, cop a plea? Manslaughter?'

'It's an option. By the time it comes to trial, you might get away with time served,' Roberta said.

'Piss off. I'm not pleading to anything. There isn't a jury round here would convict me. They'd all love to do what I did. If the police did their job properly, instead of playing politics and hiding behind bushes with radar guns, the fucking burglars would be inside and I wouldn't be in this mess.'

'Who said anything about a jury round here? This one's got Old Bailey written all over it. Could be months, a year maybe, before it comes to trial. That mob outside, your so-called supporters, will have long forgotten all about Mickey French and have moved on to hounding paedophiles or shoving shit through the letterboxes of Asian shopkeepers. The radio station will soon get bored,' she said.

'Don't bank on it, Bobby,' said Mickey, defiantly. 'I could take you and your boyfriend down with me.'

'Ha,' she laughed, mockingly. 'I thought you'd got the message. There's no evidence.'

'Oh, I heard you, all right. I got the message, loud and clear. You think you're out of the woods, don't you?'

'Out of the woods, across the field, down the road and safely snuggled up in front of the fire,' she said. 'In any event, without the evidence, it would be your word against mine. A desperate man facing a murder charge against a respected high-ranking police officer. Without the tape, without the file, you've got nothing.'

Mickey stood up and leaned forward, whispering softly in Roberta's ear.

'How do you know I didn't make copies?'

Roberta's triumphalism stalled. Her face petrified.

'But I only found the one set. There were no others. I searched the house thoroughly. You're bluffing,' she gabbled.

Mickey smiled.

'Am I?'

# Fifty-seven

Georgia Claye sat on her stool in the Keep & Bear Arms watching Justin Fromby being interviewed on the lunchtime news on the television above the bar.

*'Obviously, I can't comment on the circumstances surrounding this particular case. As you have just reported in your bulletin, a man has now been formally charged and remanded in custody.*

*'But what I can say in general terms is that all of us at the Oppressed Peoples' Refugee Association Hotline are becoming increasingly concerned at the rising number of racist attacks on refugees who have braved terrible hardships to seek asylum in this country, a safe haven from fear and intimidation, a chance to rebuild their scarred lives.*

*'The Little Englander violence is a stain on our nation. It was only a matter of time before one of these unfortunate refugees was slaughtered in cold blood.*

*'The courts must hand out exemplary sentences to anyone convicted of violent hate crimes against asylum-seekers.'*

'I notice he didn't mention that this poor little asylum-seeker was actually burgling someone's home at the time,' remarked Sid Allen, landlord of the one remaining pub in Heffer's Bottom. 'Same again, love?'

Georgia drained her extra-strength cider, 9.5 per cent alcohol by volume, and put the glass down on the mahogany bar top.

'No. Make it a red wine this time,' she said.

'Glass?'

'Bottle. House red will do.'

Sid unscrewed the top of the Moroccan Merlot and handed her the bottle.

'I suppose all this business has really put Heffer's Bottom on the map,' Georgia remarked.

'Oh, sure. I was on the wireless myself, day after it all happened,' said Sid proudly.

'Really?'

'Course, I wish it had been under different circumstances. He's a good man, Mickey. Terrible thing to happen. We all hope he gets off.'

'Drink in here, does he?' Georgia asked.

'All the time. Likes a drink, does old Mickey. You should see him pack it away. Holds it well, though. Typical copper, you know. They all drink like fishes, don't they?'

Georgia laughed. 'Nice village.'

'Still is, just about. Shame about them pikeys, though. You should see what they've done to the cricket pitch and bowling green. And ever since they arrived, there's been all sorts of crime. That wasn't the first time Mickey's been turned over, either.'

'Oh?'

'No, he's had a few run-ins with the gyppoes. Said he'd blow their heads off if they ever bothered him again. Not that, I mean, well, you know. Only talk like.'

'Oh, absolutely,' said Georgia.

'Rats in a barrel.'

'Pardon?'

'Rats in a barrel,' repeated Sid. 'That's what Mickey said. He pulled a gun on them once, when he caught them breaking in. He said he'd shoot them like rats in a barrel. Only words, though. Only talk.'

Georgia nodded. She took the bottle and withdrew to a corner table. She opened her bag and began to read the documents Roberta Peel had dropped off the previous evening. It was a copy of PC Ramsay Smith's report of an incident involving burglary and criminal damage at the home of Mickey French.

*'Don't give me multi-fucking-culturalism. The only culture these fucking pikeys have is thieving. I'd have given them a kicking until they put their hands up to it, fucking thieving dids. I dunno why I even bothered calling you. I might just as well go round there myself and sort it.'*

Georgia was building up her own psychological profile of Mickey. The landlord had confirmed what she suspected, what was in the police report.

Georgia drained the bottle, put out her cigarette, thanked Sid and headed for the railway station.

She bought a ticket to Tottenham.

Forty-five minutes later she was standing outside the hostel at the address given her by Roberta Peel.

She walked up the steps, in through the front door and made for the TV room.

The set was re-running footage of the mini-riot outside Angel Hill magistrates. The room was empty, but for a slight, pretty dark-haired girl.

Georgia approached her.

'I'm looking for anyone who knew Gica Dinantu,' she said.

The girl looked up, stared at Georgia, gazed back at the TV screen and began to cry.

'I'm sorry,' said Georgia, squatting on the arm of the sofa beside her. 'Please don't cry. I mean you no harm.'

'Police?' asked the girl.

'No, no. Not the police. Reporter.'

'Reporter?'

'Yes,' said Georgia, picking up a discarded copy of the *Sun*. 'Reporter. I write,' she said, making a scribbling motion with her hand, 'for newspaper.'

'My English, not good,' said the girl.

'That's OK? Did you know Gica?'

The girl nodded.

'I'm Georgia, what is your name?'

'Maria,' replied the girl.

'Pleased to meet you, Maria. Cigarette?'

Maria took one from the packet Georgia was offering her and lit it.

'So you knew Gica?'

'Yes,' said Maria, suspicious of this woman, who smelt strongly of drink. Even though Maria's English was not good, she could tell this woman's English was slurred.

'How long?'

'A few weeks, two months maybe.'

'You were friends?'

Maria nodded again.

'Tell me about him.'

'He was beautiful.'

'Why did he come to England?'

'To get away, like everyone. To start again. Men, they killed his father.'

'That's awful,' said Georgia. 'What men? Secret police. Is that why you're frightened of the police?'

'We all frightened of police in our country.'

'What can you tell me about Gica?'

Maria looked puzzled.

'What did he do?' asked Georgia.

'He was good man.'

'Of course.'

'He study,' said Maria, feeling her way.

'Study what?'

'He was very clever. Very kind.'

'He would have made a good doctor, I'm sure,' said Georgia, busking, searching for a good human-interest angle. Doctor would sound good.

'Very good doctor, yes,' Maria agreed.

'How did he spend his time in England?'

'He want to work, to get money.'

'So you think that's what he was doing when he was, when he, er, died?'

Maria dropped her head and wept uncontrollably.

'He was knocking on doors, asking for work, to pay for his

322

studies, as a doctor, when he was gunned down,' Georgia prompted her.

Maria was beyond words. Tears streamed down her cheeks.

'You were obviously close to him?' asked Georgia.

Maria nodded again.

'Very close?'

Maria wiped her eyes and tried to compose herself. She stood up and patted her stomach.

'I'm having his baby.'

# Fifty-eight

Paxton prison was scheduled for closure in 1972. Somehow the Home Office never got round to it.

Mickey had visited the jail many times, but never before in the back of a Black Maria.

Standing in prisoner reception, Mickey felt like Norman Stanley Fletcher. He was relieved of his belt, his wallet and £34.57 in cash.

'E-wing,' said the senior prison officer.

'E-wing?' Mickey wondered.

'E-wing,' said the officer. 'You're on Rule 43.'

'That's the fucking nonce wing,' Mickey reacted angrily.

Section 23. Solitary. Prisoners liable to harm themselves or at risk from other prisoners.

'Why the fuck am I on Rule 43?' asked Mickey.

'Look, son,' said the old-sweat officer. 'I do what I'm told. The powers that be consider you to be in danger from other prisoners. Think about it. You probably put some of the bastards in here. If there's one thing they hate it's a bent copper.'

'I'm not a fucking bent copper,' Mickey protested.

'Bent's not the word. Sorry. But you are ex-Old Bill. Half of our regulars would top you soon as look at you. Either that or you'd find yourself touching your toes in the showers like that fat bloke in *Deliverance*, pinned down while some armed robber shoves a pound and a half of throbbing John Thomas up your jacksie, just for the hell of it.'

'Not with my Farmers.' Mickey tried to make a joke of it. 'I've got piles like dreadlocks. It would be like trying to get into a Chinese restaurant, circa 1974.'

'E-wing,' said the senior officer.

Mickey was led away, along the corridor, up the steel stairs, down a landing, across a suspended walkway.

The smell was familiar. Shit, piss, sweat, fear, boredom, disinfectant.

'Welcome to Fraggle Rock,' said the screw who showed Mickey into his cell. 'I won't introduce you to the neighbours just now. You've got a serial rapist on one side and a bloke with HIV who specializes in dragging little boys off the street and buggering them senseless on the other.'

Nice people.

The screw left and locked the cell door.

Mickey lay back and considered his options. He didn't have any. The events of the past week rolled through his mind in glorious Technicolor, like a Pathé newsreel. The back of his eyes hurt. Mickey closed them, clenched his fists and drew himself into a fetal position, desperate to escape the nagging, suffocating sensation.

Despite himself, he fell into a deep sleep.

What seemed like hours later, actually only about ninety minutes, the cell door swung open.

'You've got a visitor,' said the screw. 'This way.'

Mickey was led back across the steel bridge separating Fraggle Rock from the main body of the prison, down the stairs, along the corridor and into a room containing metal tables and chairs, fixed to the floor with six-inch steel bolts.

Men in prison grey uniforms with tattoos and earrings sat in awkward conversation with peroxide blondes with bad teeth and white shoes.

Funny how their missus always looks the bleedin' same.

'Cool for Cats'.

Squeeze.

At a table in the corner sat Ricky Sparke.

Mickey sat down opposite him.

'You need a lawyer,' said Ricky. 'Charlie says the station will pick up the bill.'

'No thanks. There's nothing a lawyer can do for me that I can't do myself. And, anyway, Charlie's done me enough favours for one day.'

'Best intentions, mate. We'll get you out of here.'

'Have you heard from Andi? She'll have been trying to ring me.'

'Want me to give her a bell?' Ricky asked.

'Leave it till tomorrow. The inquest is being opened. I'll get out for that. Might even have another crack at bail.'

'Tell you what, there's a right little bandwagon rolling. The boyfriend, Fromby, has been popping up all over the place, denouncing racial violence directed at asylum-seekers. They're stoking the pyre.'

'Brilliant.'

'But you've got plenty of support. Our audience figures have gone through the roof. By lunchtime our Free Mickey French phone line had notched up more than 250,000 calls.'

'At 38p a minute, no doubt,' Mickey said witheringly.

'That's show business. Don't knock it, it's paid off my mortgage arrears.'

'That's all right then,' said Mickey.

'Look, there's money here for you, too. Are you sure you won't let Charlie hire you a lawyer? The bail bond offer still stands.'

'I'll think about it.'

'What happens now?'

'They'll open and adjourn the inquest tomorrow, at Angel Hill. Cause of death, post mortem, that kind of thing.'

'Great, we'll turn up with the mobile o/b unit. Get a bit of a demo going,' enthused Ricky.

'Do me a favour,' said Mickey, grasping Ricky's left wrist. 'No more favours. That fucking stunt outside the court got well out of hand. I heard a kid got hurt.'

'She's fine. A few cuts and bruises, that's all.'

'Did they find out who threw the petrol bomb?'

'Nah. My guess, one of the Trots.'

'Figures.'

'Mind you, you've got some right toerags in your corner, too.'

'Great. Look, Ricky, I think I can beat this. I know the law. I appreciate everything you're doing, but it may be counterproductive, long term.'

'We can't just pop the genie back in the bottle,' Ricky said.

'Maybe not.' Mickey shook his head.

'Anyway,' said Ricky, 'haven't you got a bit of leverage with the Deputy Assistant Commissioner? Haven't *we* got something on her. And Fromby?'

'She thinks not.'

'Eh?'

'She spun the drum when I was banged up. She found the tape, the papers, the knife.'

'Does she know you made copies?'

'She's not sure.'

'What do you mean?'

'I sort of, well, you know, intimated.'

'Does she know I've got the tape?'

'Not as such. But it's put her on the back foot a bit.'

'Wanna go public?'

'Not just yet,' said Mickey.

'At some stage you're gonna have to consider the nuclear option.'

'I know, but let's get tomorrow out of the way first. There's something here not quite right.'

'What?'

'I dunno, copper's instinct, I suppose. You get a feel for things. I haven't worked out the full SP yet.'

'You got anyone in your corner, apart from Rocktalk 99FM and the great unwashed?'

'Not in my corner, so to speak, but the DI, acting DCI, who arrested me, Marsden, seems like a bang-up kind of guy. He'll do what he has to, though. And I dropped a station sergeant head first in the brown stuff when I made that call to you, on-air.'

'Casualties of war, old son,' said Ricky.

'Maybe, but I regret it. He deserved better.' Mickey shrugged.

'Look, I'm going to get kicked out in a minute. Anything you need?'

'Not right now.'

'I'll see you at the inquest,' Ricky said, rising to his feet.

'Yeah. Might shed a bit more light.'

'Hey, think again about the lawyer, Mickey. Even up the odds a bit.'

Mickey nodded. 'I'll sleep on it.'

# Fifty-nine

Georgia Claye woke in her usual condition, having completely forgotten her pledge to herself not to get shit-faced the night before she was due on the Ricky Sparke show.

What the hell, she had something to celebrate. The *Clarion* loved her Mickey French scoop. Champagne was called for. She had no idea what time she'd left Spider's, although she vaguely remembered propositioning a Jamaican chorus boy, who turned out to be gay. At least that's what he told her. It's what most men told her.

The *Clarion*. My God.

Georgia took a swig from the glass of water on the bedside table. Except it wasn't water.

The vodka hit the back of her throat like napalm.

Georgia threw on a dressing gown and managed to descend the stairs on two feet, steadying herself on the party wall with her right hand.

No need for the human toboggan run today. She can't have been that bad last night, after all.

She retrieved the bundle of newspapers lying on her front door mat and spread them out on her desk.

There it was. Page one. Page fucking one. Page one lead. Splash headline. Exclusive. By Georgia Claye.

She went to the fridge for a can of extra-strength cider to drink in her triumph.

Exclusive. By Georgia Claye. The truth behind the Heffer's Bottom shooting.

The ex-policeman charged with the cold-blooded murder of a young asylum-seeker is exposed today as a drunken racist with a violent hatred of gypsies.

Michael French had previously threatened to round up members of the travelling community and shoot them 'like rats in a barrel'.

Sid Allen, landlord of the Keep & Bear Arms, in Heffer's Bottom, said that French was a notorious alcoholic.

Confidential information obtained by the *Clarion* indicates that on the night he gunned down 16-year-old Gica Dinantu, a refugee from Romania, French's blood-alcohol level was nine times the legal drink-drive limit – enough to kill a normal person.

Police sources confirm that French had made threats to kill gypsies on earlier occasions.

The *Clarion* can also reveal today that Dinantu, who fled Romania after his father himself was murdered by the secret police, hoped to become a doctor and was soon to be a father.

He was in Heffer's Bottom knocking on doors pleading for work to earn money to finance his studies.

His devastated fiancée, Maria (pictured left), who is expecting his baby, choked back tears as she remembered her beloved Gica.

She described him as 'beautiful' and 'good'.

Deputy Assistant Commissioner Roberta Peel, who is leading the investigation, said that the Metropolitan Police was determined to tackle racism and press for maximum sentences for offenders.

There was more in this vein, carried over onto pages two and three. Technically, it was all sub judice. But as far as the editor of the *Clarion*, Harold Potter, was concerned, French had forfeited his right to protection from prejudicial publicity the moment he went live on Rocktalk 99FM to protest his innocence.

On the editorial pages, Clarion Call, the newspaper's leader column, warned of the rising tide of racial violence which was turning Britain into the new Nazi Germany.

Alongside, the paper carried a signed article by the celebrated lawyer Justin Fromby, chair of the Oppressed Peoples'

Refugee Association and Hotline (OPRAH) demanding further restrictions on handguns, with the exception of those held by paramilitary groups involved in the Northern Ireland peace process, and calling for an end to all immigration controls.

Georgia wallowed in her triumph. Soon, she told herself, there would be other awards to stand alongside the Golden Spike on her desk.

She poured herself another slug of vodka to chase down the cider and opened a tub of Pot Noodles before showering and leaving for her scheduled appearance on the Ricky Sparke radio show.

# Sixty

'That was Tom Robinson and this is the Ricky Sparke show on Rocktalk 99FM, your official Free Mickey French radio station. My producer has just informed me that the number of calls in support of Mickey on our special phone line has just passed 300,000. Well done everyone. Keep them coming in. My guest on the programme this morning is the, er, distinguished journalist Georgia Claye, here to review the newspapers for us. Morning, Georgia. You're looking a bit rough this morning. Another night on the batter, was it?'

'I'm sorry?'

'Just joking, Georgia. Have another glass of wine. Why don't we start with the Clarion; you're all over the front page today.'

'Yes. I've written an exclusive report on the Mickey French case.'

'And may I just say, on behalf of Mickey and all of us here at Rocktalk 99FM, what a complete parcel of nonsense it all is.'

'I beg your pardon?'

'Your scurrilous little exclusive. Total bollocks, Georgia.'

'You can't say that on the radio.'

'I just did, my love. You should be ashamed of yourself.'

'I didn't come here to be insulted.'

'If you can't take a bit of constructive criticism you're in the wrong job, petal.'

'My report in the Clarion today is one hundred per cent accurate, the result of exhaustive investigative journalism. Mickey French is a drunken racist who deserves to be behind bars.'

'He also happens to be a friend of mine. And 300,000 loyal Rocktalk 99FM listeners disagree with you.'

Outside the studio, Ricky's producer had handed Georgia a tumbler of red wine to calm her nerves and steady her hands.

After the news she was shown in and sat opposite the presenter. Ricky gave her the thumbs-up.

Ricky had taken the top off a bottle of Beck's and was working his way down it.

There was a full bottle of red and a full bottle of white in front of Georgia. She drained the tumbler and replenished it instantly.

Georgia topped up her tumbler, tipping white wine upon red in her irritation.

> '*I don't care what your listeners think.*'
>
> '*Well, that's typical of you and your bunch of treacherous subversives at the* Clarion, *isn't it? The people, the paying public, can get stuffed. You're always right.*'
>
> '*In this case, I am right. The* Clarion *is right. We have the full support of the learned Mr Justin Fromby and Deputy Assistant Commissioner Peel from Scotland Yard.*'
>
> '*This whole case stinks of fit-up. Mickey French is a brave, former police officer, defending his own property against a thieving scumbag, another bogus asylum-seeker, here to leech off the British taxpayer.*'
>
> '*That's not true. Gica Dinantu was here fleeing from the secret police in Romania, who had murdered his father. He was about to become a father himself. Training to be a doctor.*'
>
> '*Oh, yeah. Then what was he doing miles away from his hostel, in Mickey French's house?*'
>
> '*Looking for work to pay for his studies at medical college.*'
>
> '*In the middle of the night? Get real, Georgia. Let's hit the phones. Stuart, line one.*'

A mobile telephone crackled into life. Ricky spoke.

> '*Fire away, Stuart. We're all ears. What do you want to say?*'

'Well, Ricky, I'm boiling mad listening to that old bag you've got in the studio sticking up for this robbing git. He got what he deserved.'

Georgia was apoplectic, spitting red wine everywhere. She retaliated.

'How can you say that? He was a young man, a boy, cruelly slaughtered in the prime of his life by a murdering, drunken racist.'

The caller, Stuart, fought back.

'He shouldn't have been burgling, should he Ricky?'
'Absolutely not, Stuart. As far as I'm concerned once someone puts themselves outside the law, they forfeit the protection of the law.'

Georgia butted in.

'So what you're saying is that you should be free to shoot anyone who comes into your house?'
'Got it in one, pet.'
'I don't believe this. He was a boy, a bay-bee, a BAY-BEE!'
'Get a grip, Georgia.'

Georgia rose to her feet and started wailing like a banshee, flailing her arms around, knocking over what remained of the wine, screeching at the top of her voice.

'AAAAAAARRRRGGGGGGGHHHHHH! I don't BELIEVE this! You're as bad as he is. You think it's right to kill BAY-BEES. To gun them down like RATS IN A BARREL! BAY-BEE KILLER. BAY-BEE KILLER!!!!'

Stuart on line one was speechless. Ricky took a swig of his Beck's and sat there with a bemused expression on his face.

Downstairs, Charlie Lawrence beamed and decided to jack up the advertising rates.

The staff in the control room were stunned. Georgia had completely taken leave of her senses, howling like a stuck pig.

The producer was about to fade to music when Charlie Lawrence walked in.

'Leave it,' Charlie ordered. 'This is great radio. A great, great, great listen.'

On the other side of the glass panel, Georgia was jumping up and down, banging her fists on the control console, like something out of *One Flew Over the Cuckoo's Nest.*

*'BAY-BEE KILLER!!!!! BAY-BEE KILLER! AAAAAARR-RRRRGGHH!!!!!'*

Georgia lost control of her mind, her emotions, her coordination, her voice and, tragically, her bowels.

Ricky placed the bottle of Beck's by the microphone, leant forward and spoke, gently.

*'Ladies and gentlemen, this might be an appropriate time for some more music. I'm afraid my guest has just followed through.'*

# Sixty-one

'*The posaphone you are calling may be switched off. It may respond if you try later.*'

Funny, Mickey normally kept the phone switched on, Andi told herself. Maybe he was hanging around the studio, waiting for Ricky. Five-hour time difference; it would be lunchtime in London.

He could be in the underground car park at Rocktalk 99FM. Cellphones didn't work down there.

More likely, he was in the pub over the road. Or in Spider's with Ricky. Dillon barred all mobile phones from the premises. The punters had to surrender them at the door.

She hadn't spoken to Mickey since, how long, three, four days? Of course, she'd been down to Palm Beach, taken the kids on day trips to Sea World and Disney, got back late, middle of the night London time.

Strange how the answering machine at home wasn't working. Mickey had probably forgotten to turn it on.

She'd try again later.

What with the roadtrips to Palm Beach and Orlando, Andi had lost touch with events at home.

The kids were lying by the pool at the condo block off State Road A1A.

Andi decided to take a walk. Zero Beach had been named the friendliest small town in Florida three years running. The old downtown was straight out of *The Last Picture Show*. Even though the old movie theatre, the Zero Beach National Bank and the Hiawatha apartment building now housed upscale restaurants and yuppie lofts, if you squinted hard enough you could imagine Cybill Shepherd tiptoeing her way dustily along the railroad track.

It also had a sizeable British expat community – retired agricultural machinery salesman, writers, men who made their money shipping citrus back to England.

Which is why the Zero Beach News Stand sold fifteen copies a day of the *Daily Mail*, transmitted by satellite from London, printed on the Orlando Sentinel presses, aimed at the expats and the Disney hordes, and on sale, same day, at 8 am throughout Florida.

Andi strolled along the boardwalk connecting the Dunes Café with Atlantic Drive, past the pastel buildings, packed with realtors, designer dress shops. At the local candy store, Andi stopped and bought herself a double pecan and amaretto waffle cone, which she needed two hands to tackle.

She sat on a bench, staring out at the ocean, finished her ice-cream, walked onto the beach and rinsed her hands in the sea.

She missed Mickey. He always said Zero Beach was the one place in the world he could really relax. Andi remembered them making love under the boardwalk on their first visit, twenty years earlier, before the kids were born. It was hardly *From Here to Eternity*. Mickey managed to get sand under his foreskin and it was one of the most uncomfortable fucks they'd ever had. But, hey, that's romance. And the thought of that night still made her tingle. Which sure beat the hell out of the saddle sores she'd suffered for days afterwards.

Where was Mickey right now? He said he'd join them. Soon, he'd promised. He always kept his promises.

Maybe when he arrived they'd leave the kids with his aunt and take a couple of days alone somewhere.

Andi strolled to the Zero Beach News Stand to buy a copy of that morning's *Daily Mail*.

Cass, the hippy retread working behind the counter, handed Andi the paper.

Andi turned to the front page.

There on page one was a picture of Mickey, her Mickey, alongside a story which began:

A petrol bomb was thrown and a child trampled underfoot as violent scenes erupted outside the magistrates' court where a former police marksman was remanded in custody charged with the murder of a burglar.

Police with riot shields and on horseback restored order after fighting broke out between rival factions when Michael Edward French was brought to the court in the back of a Black Maria.

He entered a formal plea of not guilty. An application for bail was rejected and French was remanded to Paxton prison.

'Hey, are you OK?' asked Cass.

Andi was riveted to the spot, she went weak at the knees, the newspaper shaking in her hands.

'Sit down a moment. I'll make you some herb tea.'

Andi slumped back into a wicker chair. Through glazed eyes, she read on.

Oh, Mickey, what have you done? She knew he'd made threats, but they were words, just words. She didn't think he'd ever really go through with it.

Cass handed her a camomile and ginger infusion.

'I could do with a strong, sweet Typhoo,' Andi said. 'Thank you, anyway. You're very kind.'

'Is everything all right?' asked Cass.

Andi sipped her tea and said nothing, reading and re-reading the report in the *Daily Mail*.

'I'll be fine, really, thanks,' she eventually replied.

'Someone you know?' Cass inquired, leaning over.

'Someone I thought I knew.'

Andi composed herself and hurried back to the condo.

'All right, Mum?' asked young Terry, lying by the pool, spotting his mother's red, raw eyes.

'Oh, yeah, fine. I think I got a mosquito in my eyes. I've been rubbing them. I'll be OK.'

She shut herself in the bedroom, dialled Mickey's mobile again.

Silly cow, if he's in prison he's not going to answer.

Think, woman. She tried her mum. No answer.

Ricky. Ricky would know.

She delved into her handbag, flicked through the pages of her address book.

By Ricky Sparke's name there were several numbers, most of them scrawled out. Numbers of flats he'd been evicted from, cellphones repossessed.

She tried the number marked *(s)* for studio. A young woman answered.

'Ricky Sparke show, hello.'

'Is Ricky there?'

'Are you a listener?'

'No, I mean yes, sort of.'

'Sort of?'

'I'm a friend.'

'They all say that.'

'Look, I'm Mickey French's wife. Andi French.'

'Oh, why didn't you say so, Mrs French?'

'I just did. Look, is Ricky there?'

'The show's just finished, he's already left. You wouldn't believe what happened on-air . . .'

'Right now, I'm not interested. I have to talk to him.'

'He's on his way to the inquest.'

'Inquest?'

'On the burglar Mickey shot. I thought you'd know?'

'No, look, I'm away. I've just heard.'

'Everyone's on Mickey's side. We've had thousands of calls, people pledging money. The ratings have gone through the roof.'

'I don't care about your blasted ratings. I want to talk to Ricky.'

'You could try him on the mobile.'

The girl gave Andi the number. She scribbled it down on a magazine cover using an eyeliner pencil and replaced the handset without bothering to say thank you.

She punched in Ricky's number.

'The cellphone you are calling may be engaged. Please try later.'

She tried again. And again. And again.

Fourth time lucky.

'Vigilantes'R'Us, how can I help you?' said the voice at the other end. Ricky was feeling chipper. Georgia Claye had shat herself on-air, the Free Mickey French bandwagon was rolling at warp speed, the Ricky Sparke show was the hottest property in town and his wages had just gone up fifty grand.

'Ricky?'

'Who's that?'

'Andi.'

'Shit, sorry, Andi. I wasn't expecting. I mean, I was going to ring, but Mickey said, and well, um, how are you?'

'I'm going out of my mind here, Ricky. I've just read the *Daily Mail*. What the hell has been going on?'

'There's nothing to worry about, Andi, honestly. It's all going according to plan.'

'According to plan? According to fucking plan, Ricky Sparke? My husband is in prison on a murder charge, I'm halfway round the world and no one thought fit to tell me, and you say everything is going according to plan?'

'Calm down, Andi,' said Ricky, trying to comfort her. 'Everything's going to be fine. We're on the case. Mickey has massive public support, it's not his fault, it was self-defence, you know, reasonable force.'

'He's still in prison.'

'We're working on it. Trust me.'

'Why do I want to check the contents of my jewellery box and make sure I'm still wearing my knickers when I hear you say "Trust me"? You forget I've known you too long, Ricky. You're a fully paid-up member of the

I'll-only-put-it-in-a-little-way school. You're not the one banged up in Paxton. What's in this for you?'

'Andi, *please*, Mickey's my best mate. I've been to see him inside; we're doing everything we can.'

'And the ratings are going through the roof.'

'Well, yeah, but that's not the point. This is about truth and justice.'

Andi laughed, sarcastically. 'Trust me, I'm a journalist, eh?'

Ricky could see her point.

'Look, I'm on the way to the inquest right now. We're working on it.'

'I'm coming home, tonight.'

'I don't think that's what Mickey wants right now. He doesn't want you and the kids involved.'

'How do I know what Mickey wants? I can't speak to him. How does Mickey know what he wants? He needs *me*. I need to be there.'

'But what about the kids?'

'They need to know nothing. Olive and Tom will look after them. I'll just say I've got to fly home to sign some papers or something and I'll be back soon, with Mickey. There's plenty for them to do here, watersports, the lot. They'll be fine.'

'Well if you . . .'

'I do, Ricky. I can get a flight out of here tonight. I'll be at Gatwick tomorrow, around seven. Can you get me picked up?'

'I won't be able to come, Andi, but I know a man who can.'

'Right, how will I know him?'

'You'll find him.'

'See you tomorrow and, Ricky, give Mickey all my love.'

'It goes without saying.'

'No, I want it said. OK?'

'OK, promise,' said Ricky. 'Oh, and, er, Andi, have you, um, still got that tape Mickey gave you?'

'You know about that?'

'I'm his best friend, remember?'

'Sure, it's here.'

'Bring it home, OK?'

'Yeah,' said Andi. 'Seven, Gatwick, tomorrow morning. Don't go on to Spider's, get pissed out of your skull and forget.'

'Trust me.'

'And don't, just don't, say "Trust me" again.'

Andi put down the phone and called the airport.

She threw some clothes into a bag and carried it into the hallway, just as Olive was returning from her manicure.

'Where are you going?' asked Olive.

Andi pulled her into the bedroom.

'I have to go back, back to England. Mickey's in trouble.'

'Trouble?'

'Big trouble. I need a lift to the airport.'

'What's happened?'

'I'll tell you on the way. The kids absolutely mustn't know. Get it?'

'Sure,' said Olive. 'But I don't understand.'

'I'll explain. Just, please, can you look after them for a few days?'

'They're no trouble, honest. But what if they ask?'

'As far as they are concerned, I've got to go home to sign some papers. I'll be back soon, with Mickey.'

'Whatever you say.'

The kids were lying by the pool. Andi hugged them in turn and explained she wouldn't be gone for long, no, the papers couldn't be faxed, or Fed-Exed, they had to be signed in the presence of a solicitor by both her and their dad.

What papers? Are we moving, or something like that?

Something like that. It's a surprise.

Dad will tell you all about it when he comes back with me.

Can I have a bigger bedroom?

Calm down. First things first.

'Has anyone seen a cassette tape lying around?' Andi asked.

'What, that new one on your bedside table?' replied Katie.

'Yeah. Where is it?'

'I'm listening to it,' said Katie.

'*Listening to it?*' Andi snapped.

'Yeah, I taped some Dixie Chicks off a CD that girl I met on the beach loaned me.'

'*You did what?*'

'Wossup, Mum? It was a new tape. There was nothing on it.'

'There *was* something on it.'

'There was nothing written on it.'

'*Oh, Katie.* Why didn't you *ask*?'

'I didn't think you'd mind. I'll buy you another one if it's that important to you.'

Andi did not want to lose her temper. It wasn't Katie's fault. She didn't want to leave on a sour note.

'No, that's fine, darling. I should have written on it. You weren't to know.'

'Know what, Mum?'

'What was on the tape,' Andi said.

'What *was* on the tape?'

'Oh, nothing. Really, nothing.'

It was only a copy, after all, Andi reassured herself.

# Sixty-two

'He's bluffing,' said Justin Fromby, spearing a baby arti-
choke. 'Has to be.'

'I'm not sure,' replied Roberta, toying with a bowl of
squid ink pasta.

She'd sent Marsden to the inquest and taken a couple
of hours to meet Fromby at a new highly fashionable
restaurant in Hoxton.

'Run it by me again. What exactly did French say?'

'He said,' Roberta repeated, 'he said "How do you know
I haven't made copies?", that's what he said.'

'And?'

'Well that was about it really.'

'There has to be more,' Justin pressed her.

'Not really. I just accused him of bluffing and he said "Am
I?" That was it.'

'So he didn't actually say he *had* made copies.'

'Not in so many words.'

Justin sipped his Pinot Grigio.

'OK, let's assume he has got copies. Why hasn't he used
them?'

'He hasn't got access to them?'

'Of course he hasn't, not in Paxton jail. But even if he did
have copies, how could he use them? He's been charged,
remanded, it's gone beyond back-scratching deals, surely.'

'He might decide to take us down with him, just for the
hell of it,' said Roberta.

'But he would have to have the evidence. You didn't find
any copies. Where would he keep them? Bank? Under the
floorboards?'

'Not a bank, I wouldn't have thought.'

'Who does he trust?' asked Justin. 'He hasn't even hired a lawyer.'

'He's had one visitor, yesterday, at Paxton.'

'Who?'

'That disc jockey, the one on the lorry outside the court yesterday. Ricky Sparke.'

'Ricky Sparke, eh? What do you know about him?'

'Piss artist, bounced around Fleet Street for years, never lasted long anywhere, then shipped up on the radio. Georgia Claye was due on his show this morning. I must find out how she got on.'

'We can't take any chances,' said Justin. 'There's too much riding on this.'

'Tell me about it,' said Roberta, juggling the ice in her mineral water. 'My future, for a start. We need everything to be watertight. French must go down. We need a clean result, here. The government – I was talking to the Home Secretary this morning – are wobbling on this. They've been shaken by the strength of the public backlash. The tabloids are going crazy, Middle England has adopted French as some kind of a hero, and that's all anyone wants to talk about on the radio phone-ins. The backbenchers are getting fidgety. The government is seen as weak on asylum, and weak on crime. And that reflects badly on the police service. And on me, by extension. That's why we have to nail French.'

'My contribution must have helped, in the *Clarion*. And Georgia Claye's story was extremely useful.'

'Yeah, but while it gets the right kind of spin in the public domain, the *Clarion* is preaching to the converted. Try and put pressure on our friends at the BBC and Channel 4. See if we can't demonize French a bit more. Have a word with Everton Gibbs, at the Commission for Racial Equality. See if he can help.'

'We have to be careful,' said Fromby.

'Why?'

'Well, let's assume, for the sake of argument, that French does have access to copies of the, er, sensitive material. If he thinks he's going down for life, no remission, murder one, as our American friends like to call it, then he's got nothing to lose. If, however, on the other hand he still thinks there might be some kind of deal to be done, a word here, a word there, he might hold back.'

'I've tried that,' said Roberta. 'I don't think there's much chance of him responding to me.'

'What about the local chap, Marsden, isn't it?'

'Colin Marsden.'

'Sound?'

'Not part of the Project, but honest.'

'How does he get on with French?'

'OK, I guess.'

'Fine. Look, I'm not telling you how to do your job, but pull back here, arm's length. Let Marsden deal with it for a while.'

'And what am I supposed to do with my time?'

'Keep up the PR offensive and meanwhile we keep on looking.'

'Looking for what?'

'Well, you said yourself that French may have made copies. So, if he has, and he doesn't have them, who does?'

'You tell me,' said Roberta.

Justin put down his fork and wiped his chin.

'Ricky Sparke would seem to be an obvious candidate.'

# Sixty-three

Mickey French spent an uncomfortable night in Paxton prison, sleeping fitfully, kept awake by the ramblings and tappings of his fellow inmates on Fraggle Rock.

He was relieved when the escort arrived to take him back to Angel Hill for the formal opening of the inquest.

The convoy left Paxton jail three hours early for the twenty-minute journey. They were expecting more trouble and weren't taking any chances.

The coroners' court shared a building with the local magistrates' court. When the Black Maria carrying Mickey arrived, sandwiched between two patrol cars, one armed response vehicle and four motorcycle outriders, crowds were already beginning to gather. The metallic chatter of radios, all tuned to Rocktalk 99FM, filled the air, an impromptu PA system.

> 'What I wanted to say, like, was that this is a diabolical bleeding liberty, banging Mickey French up like this. The geezer he shot is the one what should've been in jail.'
>
> 'I'm a first-time caller, long-time listener, and I think these Ruritanians should all be sent back to Ruritania.'
>
> 'Shooting's too good for them, if you ask me.'
>
> 'Great show, Ricky, keep it up son. Let's get Mickey out and these scroungers deported.'

On air, as he brought his show to a close, Ricky Sparke thanked his callers and apologized for the fact that, on police advice, the Rocktalk 99FM mobile outside broadcast vehicle would not be appearing outside Angel Hill coroners' court that afternoon.

*'That doesn't mean you can't go down there and protest. This is still supposed to be a free country. Let's make our voices heard, people. The campaign goes on. Free Mickey French.'*

The crowd outside the court took up the chant with enthusiasm.

> *FREE MICKEY FRENCH.*
> *FREE MICKEY FRENCH.*
> *FREE MICKEY FRENCH.*

They waved their banners and blew their whistles as the van carrying Mickey back to court swung off the main road.

> *DUMB, DUMB,*
> *RACIST SCUM.*
> *DUMB, DUMB,*
> *RACIST SCUM.*

The OPRAH/AFL contingent were back in force, too, waving their own banners and copies of that morning's *Clarion*.

So were the police. Everyone entering the Angel Hill shopping was shaken down and searched. DAC Peel had decreed that while peaceful protest would be allowed, there was to be no repeat of the previous day's violence. A dozen mounted officers were on duty, more than a hundred policemen and women with riot shields kept the factions a hundred yards apart and a cordon sanitaire was thrown around the court building itself. Around the corner, at the back of the Territorial Army centre, five coachloads of cops in full riot gear were held in reserve.

Inside the building, all was calm, though you could smell the tension. Mickey sat in a cell sipping tea. He had to wait two and a half hours before being shown into the courtroom.

Mickey took his place, still handcuffed to a uniformed prison officer. Marsden sat on the desk opposite, next to the coroner's officer, a veteran PC approaching the end of his career.

Mickey looked behind him, surveying the ranks of Press, the line of policemen guarding the double doors. He could see Ricky Sparke, sitting at the back of the court, next to Charlie Lawrence and a fearsome-looking, pinstripe-suited woman he didn't recognize. Ricky winked at Mickey.

Ricky must have hot-footed it to Angel Hill the moment the show finished. Now what was he up to?

Into the courtroom came the coroner himself, a local solicitor who also served as clerk to the magistrates.

Under English law, the coroner is one of the most powerful figures in the judicial system, with terms of reference far exceeding those of justices of the peace or even High Court judges.

Mickey knew that while, technically, the purpose of an inquest is to establish the cause of death, the coroner can, and does, probe all the circumstances. In a criminal court, there are strict rules of evidence. In a coroners' court, the coroner himself is sovereign. He can investigate anything he chooses. The coroner decides what is relevant and what is not and his decisions and those of an inquest jury can have a serious bearing on any subsequent prosecution.

There was no jury. The coroner would empower a jury once the cause of death had been established and recorded. The purpose of today's hearing was simply to open the proceedings and adjourn to a later date.

The coroner's officer briefly outlined the facts, name of the deceased, location of incident, time of incident. Investigating officer, status of investigation. Time life pronounced extinct and so on.

The coroner then asked the pathologist who had conducted the post mortem for his initial findings.

Proceedings in a coroners' court are more informal than in a criminal court. Witnesses do not have to take an oath and they can deliver their evidence while seated.

The pathologist, a balding, slightly overweight Pakistani, about Mickey's age, thanked the coroner and began to read from his notes.

He had conducted a post mortem on the body of a young man, aged between twenty-one and twenty-four, at Angel Hill District Hospital.

The deceased's stomach contained small traces of food, but he had not eaten a heavy meal. There was, however, a significant measure of alcohol present in the bloodstream and evidence of regular and substantial narcotics use. There were traces of cocaine in the nasal cavities.

Mickey did hear the pathologist detail the exact alcohol/cocaine/blood reading but forgot to jot it down. The precise medical expression, he thought, was a fucking shed-load.

The deceased had been in general good health, though he had suffered a recent injury to his left forearm, a knife wound, most probably. The pathologist also noted that there was also evidence of sexual activity during the four hours prior to his death.

The coroner raised his eyes. He thought he heard chuckling at the back of the court.

'At least the fucker died happy,' Charlie Lawrence whispered to Ricky. The young woman with them did not look amused.

Neither did the coroner, but he let it pass.

As for the cause of death, the coroner said the deceased has suffered four gunshot wounds, one to the upper arm, one to the shoulder and two to the chest. His heart had literally exploded and he had died instantly.

Mickey looked puzzled.

'Is there something you would like to ask the pathologist, Mr French?' said the coroner.

Mickey rose to his feet, hands on the table in front of him.

350

'That won't be necessary, Mr French. You may remain seated.'

'Thank you, sir,' said Mickey. 'Much obliged to you. Doctor,' he addressed the pathologist, 'did you say that the deceased suffered four gunshot wounds?'

'That is correct,' confirmed the doctor, re-consulting his notes. 'One to the upper arm, right arm, to be precise, one to the right shoulder and two to the chest cavity.'

'Thank you, doctor,' said Mickey.

'Will that be all, for now, Mr French?' asked the coroner.

'Just one more thing, sir,' said Mickey.

'Yes?'

'Doctor,' said Mickey, 'you said the deceased was aged between twenty-one and twenty-four. Did I hear you correctly?'

'Indeed you did.'

'I am obliged to you, doctor,' said Mickey.

'Are those all the questions for now?' asked the coroner.

'Detective inspector?' he said, looking in the direction of Marsden, who looked vaguely distracted. What was Mickey's game?

'Inspector?' repeated the coroner.

'Acting Detective *chief* inspector, actually, sir.'

'If you insist. Do you have anything to add at this juncture?'

Marsden half rose. 'Not at this stage, sir.'

'Very well. I find that the cause of death in this case was heart failure due to gunshot wounds. This case is adjourned for seven days. Thank you for your attendance.'

'Sir, may I speak?' the woman with Ricky and Charlie Lawrence interjected.

'What is it, dear lady?' asked the coroner.

'Sir, my name is Polly Kettle, sir. I am a solicitor with Kettle, Potts, Black & Partners. I represent Mr French.'

'This is the first I've heard of it,' said the coroner.

The first I've heard, too, thought Mickey, gazing inquisitively in Ricky Sparke's direction.

Was this another of Charlie Lawrence's damn-fool ratings-building stunts?

'Sir, I am engaged by Rocktalk 99FM, Mr French's sometime employers. This is Mr Lawrence, programme director.'

'G'day,' smiled Charlie.

'Sir, I have just come from a hearing before a judge in chambers at which an application was heard to overturn yesterday's decision by the Angel Hill magistrates to refuse bail. That application has been successful and I have here papers authorizing Mr French's immediate release on bail.'

'This is highly irregular,' the coroner said. 'Inspector?'

'I have no knowledge of this, sir.'

Me, neither, thought Mickey.

'The prosecution and the prison service have been informed,' said Polly Kettle. 'A solicitor from the Crown Prosecution Service was present at the hearing. The decision may not yet have been communicated to the prison service or to the inspector here.'

*Acting Chief* fucking inspector. Marsden was getting irritated.

'Has DAC Peel been informed?' asked Marsden.

'That is not our responsibility,' said Miss Kettle.

She's not going to like it, Marsden cringed inwardly.

'Sir,' said Miss Kettle. 'I can assure you the papers are in order. I have copies here for the inspector, for the prison service and one for your good self.'

The coroner inspected the documents.

'These appear to be perfectly correct,' he said to the prison officer. 'Mr French is to be released into the custody of Miss Kettle and Mr Lawrence of Rocktalk 99FM, whom I see has put up one million pounds surety.'

'That's correct, your worthiness. The same deal we had on the table yesterday,' beamed Charlie.

The prison officer nodded and unlocked the handcuffs. Ricky and Charlie walked up and shook hands with Mickey, who was stunned, speechless. He was free, for now.

'Told you we were on the case, mate,' said Ricky, arm round Mickey's shoulder. 'Someone had to make your mind up for you.'

'Thanks,' was all Mickey could mumble.

'Mr French,' said the coroner, half-wearing his clerk of the court hat, 'under the terms of your bail you are to report back to Angel Hill magistrates in six days' time and to this coroners' court in seven days. You are also to notify the police of your whereabouts at all times, surrender your passport and not venture within five miles of the crime scene at Heffer's Bottom. You understand?'

'Yes, sir. Thank you, sir.'

Colin Marsden approached the happy throng, as the assembled Press core rushed away to file their stories.

'Mickey, could I have a word?'

The fearsome Miss Kettle stepped between them.

'Mr French, my client, is not obliged to say anything to you.'

'That's OK, pet, give us a minute,' said Mickey.

Polly Kettle wasn't sure she liked being called 'pet', but £1,000 a day of Rocktalk 99FM's money should compensate for a bit of sexist banter.

Colin guided Mickey into a corner.

'I knew nothing about this,' Mickey said.

'Yeah, me neither. That's not what I want to talk about.'

'No, I didn't think so. I was going to ask to speak to you, anyway.'

'What was with those questions, to the doctor?' asked Marsden.

'I knew something didn't add up,' said Mickey. 'You heard him. He said the deceased was between twenty-one and twenty-four. You told me he was sixteen.'

'That's what it says on his immigration papers,' Marsden said, though he'd wondered about that, too, when he'd read the initial report.

'You're saying the doctor got it wrong?'

'No. Not at all.'

353

'Right, then, hear this. If he was older than we thought he was, how do we know he is who you say he is?'

Marsden bit his lower lip.

'And here's another thing,' said Mickey. 'He was hit by four bullets.'

'That's right.'

'You never mentioned that to me,' said Mickey. '*Four* bullets.'

'You fired the fucking bullets,' said Marsden. 'You should know.'

'I'll tell you what I do know. I only fired *twice*. Two shots. Double tap.'

'There were four missing out of the cartridge clip.'

'It wasn't fully loaded. I always leave two empty.'

'How convenient.'

'Look, I've admitted shooting him. If I'd fired four shots I'd have told you.'

Marsden scratched the back of his head.

'Why should I lie to you?' asked Mickey. 'We're talking sheep and lambs here. Check the ballistics.'

'Well if you didn't fire the other two bullets, who did?' said Marsden.

'You're the fucking detective, *acting chief* inspector.'

# Sixty-four

'Why the hell wasn't I informed?' Roberta screamed into the telephone.

'I, er, ma'am. I wasn't either,' replied Marsden. 'The first I knew about it was when the solicitor acting for French came forward at the inquest. It appears they went before a judge in chambers at lunchtime and he overturned the order. A solicitor from the CPS was present at the hearing.'

'Someone is going to be singing soprano for the rest of their lives,' Roberta promised.

Marsden didn't doubt she meant it.

'Ma'am. I called you just as soon as I could.'

'I'm not blaming you. It is the damned incompetent CPS again. Thanks to them we've got a murderer back on the streets.'

'*Alleged* murderer, ma'am,' Marsden corrected her, then wished he hadn't.

'Whose side are you on, inspector?'

'Ma'am, I was just going to make the point that I don't think Mickey, er, French, the defendant, that is, poses any threat to the public. Quite the opposite. The public appears to adore him.'

'That's the point. That's the whole point. What kind of message do you think this sends out?'

'There's no question of him not answering his bail. Not with a million pounds of the radio station's money riding on it,' said Marsden.

'Yes, but this kind of thing is bound to influence a jury. He's already been on the radio pleading his innocence.

How's it going to look now a judge in chambers has given him bail?'

'Can't we appeal, ma'am?'

'On what grounds, inspector?' demanded Roberta.

'The contract?'

'Contract?' Roberta sounded puzzled.

'The contract to kill French. Put out by the pike – er, by the travelling community,' Marsden reminded her.

'Oh, *that* contract,' Roberta said, composing herself. 'I'm sorry, inspector.'

'Ma'am?' said Marsden, with trepidation.

'Yes?'

'The contract. It's just that I wondered why you didn't tell me about it. Before the magistrates' hearing. Where did it come from?'

'Er, I only heard about it at the last minute. There wasn't time,' stalled Roberta.

'Who told you?'

'Criminal intelligence, Scotland Yard,' Roberta blurted.

Oh, yeah, thought Marsden. 'I see. Who's behind it?'

'We're not certain. But we are investigating.'

'Anything I can do, ma'am? I'm not without contacts in that area, working out here for so long, as it were.'

'No, nothing,' Roberta cut him short. 'Just get on with your job. Prove the case against French. Is that clear?'

'As Waterford, ma'am,' said Marsden.

'I'll talk to you later. Good day, inspector.'

I've had better, Marsden told himself as he replaced the receiver.

The contract wasn't the only thing she'd kept back from him. Why hadn't DAC Peel ever mentioned that she once worked with his dad, at Tyburn Row? You'd think that would be a natural point of contact, an ice-breaker. You don't forget something like that. Mickey French hadn't.

Marsden sipped his coffee and reopened the file on Gica Dinantu. Name, port of entry, age. Sixteen.

Sixteen.

The pathologist clearly stated in the post-mortem report that the deceased was aged between twenty-one and twenty-four. He'd confirmed that to Mickey, on cross-examination.

So why should Dinantu tell the immigration authorities he was sixteen? Was it relevant?

Marsden popped an extra-strong mint in his mouth.

He'd heard that asylum-seekers often claimed to be under-age to avoid deportation. Nothing more sinister than that, probably.

But he'd run it through the computer again, out of curiosity. Maybe he'd punched in the wrong name last time. Worth another check.

He logged on to the Scotland Yard database.

G-I-C-A D-I-N-A-N-T-U.

File not found.

Now what?

The bullets. The post mortem recorded that the deceased had taken four bullets. Mickey French was adamant he'd fired only two. Why should he lie? He'd admitted shooting Dinantu, put his hands up to killing him. Two bullets, four bullets, what was the difference?

What was it Mickey French had said? Sheep and lambs.

Marsden called ballistics.

'You're sure there were four?' he asked the technician who had examined the bullets.

'Yeah, positive,' the technician replied.

'Are they all the same?' Marsden asked.

'In what sense?'

'Were they all fired from the same gun?'

'They appear to be. They're the same calibre.'

'But have you examined each and every one of them?' Marsden pressed him.

'No. It wasn't necessary. Look, we were given four bullets, all found in the corpse. They looked pretty much alike, same calibre; we ran the tests on one, confirmed it had been fired from French's gun, the Glock. We assumed they

357

were all fired from the same gun. No one told us to look any further.'

'Do something for me, will you?' asked Marsden.

'What?'

'Run all four bullets through your system. I need to know if they were all fired from the same gun.'

'It'll take a bit of time.'

'I can wait,' said Marsden.

What was Dinantu doing at Mickey French's house in the middle of the night?

Not knocking on doors looking for work to earn money to pay for his studies as a doctor, that's for certain. Marsden dismissed Georgia Claye's report in the *Clarion* as a parcel of bollocks.

Yeah, and that was another thing. Where had the *Clarion* got hold of those quotes from an official police document?

Marsden cracked his knuckles. He needed to know more about Gica Dinantu. Maybe he'd go to Tottenham, talk to the girl in the article, the one who claimed to be having Dinantu's baby.

Or had Georgia Wossername made that up, too?

The phone rang.

'There's some people in the front office to see you, sir.'

'Who?'

'A couple of pikeys, sir.'

Marsden walked downstairs. Seamus Milne, the 'king of the gypsies', was standing there with a scruffy young boy of about fifteen.

'It's about the shooting,' said Milne.

'In here,' said Marsden, indicating the interview room off the main reception.

'Come along, you,' said Milne to the boy.

'What can I do for you?'

'I've been thinking.'

'Yeah?'

'There's some stuff you need to know.'

'Such as?'

'OK, so we'd had some run-ins with that cozzer, but this weren't nothing to do with us.'

'I know that.'

'I don't mean the shooting. I mean this so-called contract. On French. Look, I knows everyone. I've been asking about. And there is no contract. Not from any of us travellers.'

Curious, thought Marsden.

'Thanks for telling me. Appreciate it.'

'There's more,' said Milne.

'More?'

'Go on, tell him,' Milne urged the boy.

'Tell me what?' said Marsden.

'There was this taxi, black cab, one of them official jobs. Outside the house. That night,' said Milne.

'Whose house? What night?'

'That cozzer's house. The night of the shooting.'

'How do you know about a taxi being there?'

'He nicked it, when they were bringing the body out.'

'Who did?'

'This little runt,' said Milne, shaking the boy by the shoulder.

'What do you mean, nicked it?'

'Drove it off, torched it next day. You ain't gonna charge him, are you?'

'I'm investigating a murder, not the theft of a taxi.'

'Good. There's something else you should know.'

'Go on.'

'There was another car in the village that night, around the same time. I saw it leaving, just after the shooting.'

'What kind of car?'

'One of them big Mercedes. S-class.'

# Sixty-five

The Chrysler Grand Voyager containing Ricky Sparke, Charlie Lawrence, Polly Kettle and Mickey French swept over the Thames and headed for the underground car park at Rocktalk 99FM.

Outside, about fifty well-wishers, kitted out in 'Free Mickey French' T-shirts, baseball caps and lapel badges, courtesy of the radio station, began to wave banners and cheer on cue.

There were film crews and Press photographers to record the event, all arranged by Charlie Lawrence.

The crowd pressed against the side of the people carrier, banging on the smoked-glass windows, shouting encouragement and support.

Photographers scrambled round the van, holding cameras in front of them, flashlights popping as the security barrier lifted.

'This is like going back into court,' Mickey said.

'You're a hero, Mickey. Enjoy,' said Charlie Lawrence.

'I never asked to be a hero, Charlie,' said Mickey.

'There's gratitude,' Lawrence teased him.

'Leave it out, Charlie,' said Ricky. 'Mickey's free, that's all that matters. You, we, got what we wanted.'

'What Mickey wanted, too,' said Charlie.

'Mickey can speak for himself, thanks very much,' grumbled Mickey. 'Look, I'm grateful, but I'm still under the cosh. I might be out on bail, but I'm still looking at a murder charge.'

'Detail, mere detail,' said Charlie, as they clambered from the van and took the lift to the third floor.

Charlie's secretary poured champagne.

'To freedom.'

To freedom.

'Right, let's do it.'

'Do what?' asked Mickey.

'Let's get you on-air. Your public awaits.'

'Now just hang on,' protested Mickey. 'I'm not sure. I got myself in enough trouble last time.'

Polly Kettle spoke up. 'I really must counsel against this. As Mr French's lawyer I am afraid that anything he may say now may exacerbate the situation.'

'Wooah, there, sweetheart,' Charlie stopped her. 'Your job was to get Mickey out of pokey. You did brilliantly. But we're running the campaign.'

'Campaign?' said Mickey.

'Yeah, mate, this is bigger than just you. We've touched a nerve here. The fucking government's trembling, the police are in retreat, the people are on the march. And Rocktalk 99FM is right slap-dab in the middle of it all. Shit, mate, we're up twenty-three points as of this morning. Ricky, you tell him.'

Ricky looked shame-faced. 'OK, Mickey, I can't deny there's a drink in it for all of us. But you've been around long enough, you know how things work. This is the fucking *big one*.'

'And it's my fucking life on the line,' said Mickey.

'And we've put up a million smackeroos to get you out of jail,' Charlie reminded him. 'Not to mention Mizz Kettle's refreshers.' He poured Mickey another glass. 'Anyway, what about thanking the listeners. They've been behind you all the way.'

'OK,' said Mickey. 'Five minutes, that's all. And I'll only do it with Ricky.'

'Good man,' said Ricky, patting him on the back. 'As soon as it's over, we'll fuck off to Spider's. Sink a few scoops.'

*'This is the drivetime show on Rocktalk 99FM. Here are the*

*headlines. After a stunning campaign by Rocktalk 99FM
listeners, Mickey French was freed today.*

*'Rocktalk 99FM is standing surety for Mickey's bail to the
tune of ONE MILLION POUNDS.*

*'More headlines later, but now I'm joined in the studio by
the man who has led the Free Mickey French campaign, our
very own Ricky Sparke, and the man himself, Mickey French.
Ricky, it's all yours.'*

*'Thanks, Pete. Hello, everyone. Mickey, what's it feel like to
be free?'*

*'Great, just great, Ricky. And I want to thank all the listeners
who have given me their support.'*

*'When we spoke on the programme the other day, Mickey,
you sounded as if you felt confident about beating this charge.
Still feel like that?'*

*'I hope so, Ricky. I don't want to go into it all again. I'm
just glad to be out.'*

*'We've got a couple of people want to say "hi", Mickey.
Steve, line two.'*

*'Yeah, all right, Mickey, all right, Ricky.'*

*'Good, Steve.'*

*'Hi, Mickey. I just wanna say that we're all glad you're out
and I want you to know we're going to make this right, we'll
get even with the bastards for putting you through all this.'*

*'Look, Steve, stay cool, mate. I don't want any fuss made,
right now. I'm out, that's all that matters. I'm happy to let
the law take its course.'*

*'The law's rotten, Mickey. You should know that. Look what
you've been through. Direct action, that's what we need now.'*

Mickey was glaring at Ricky, running his finger across his
throat, as if to say 'cut this guy off'. Steve ploughed on.

*'It's not just you, Mickey. We've all had enough. The decent
people of England can't take much more. I mean, if you can't
shoot a burglar who breaks into your own home, what's the
country coming to? It's payback time.'*

Ricky intervened.

*'Thanks, Steve, I understand that passions are running high but we can't comment on this case any longer. Just let's give thanks that Mickey is out and hope to hell that the politicians are listening to Rocktalk 99FM. I'm back here tomorrow morning, let's have some more music.'*

The red 'mic live' button went out and Mickey got up to leave. Ricky took off his headphones and followed.

'Top stuff,' enthused Charlie Lawrence.

'That's it, OK, until after the case,' said Mickey, uncompromisingly.

'Whatever you say, Mickey, mate.' Charlie nodded.

'Come on, let's get out of here.' Mickey motioned to Ricky. 'I need a drink. It'll be quiet enough in Spider's.'

As they walked out of the front door, Mickey was mobbed, autograph books pressed in his hand, punters pleading for photographs.

Ricky hailed a cab from the rank over the road, Mickey jumped in and barked: 'Soho.'

''Ere, you're that Mickey French,' said the cabbie. 'We're all with you in the cab trade, you know.' Ricky's previous had been completely forgotten.

'Yeah, ta,' said Mickey.

'They all mean well,' Ricky said over the first drink in Spider's, on the house.

'I'm not comfortable with this,' Mickey complained. 'I'm not Robin Hood.'

'See it from their point of view. You've struck a blow for the ordinary guy. They've had fucking political correctness, and asylum-seekers and burglary and fucking everything else, the whole justice system skewed in favour of the scum, terrorists back on the streets with a cellar full of Semtex and a pound from the poor box, foreign thieves and beggars and illegal immigrants jumping straight to the top of the housing queue. They've been robbed, shat on from a great height, seen toerags laughing their way out of court. Mickey, they've had it up to here. To them, you're the bloke who fought back.'

'I didn't do anything for *them*. I did what I had to. For me and my family. What I was trained to do, for Chrissakes. That's all. Fuck it, Ricky, I don't know what's happening to my life. In a couple of weeks, ambushed at the roadside in my own car, my daughter attacked in her room at Goblin's, burgled, turned over, the fucking cat topped. I've seen the inside of two police stations, spent the night at Nonce Central on Fraggle Rock and I'm still facing a fucking murder charge.'

'But you're free.'

'Yeah, for how long? It's all gone to shit, Ricky, all of it. None of it my doing. I've only ever wanted to do the right thing. I'm not perfect, but I put my neck out there, twenty-five years in the Job. Asked for nothing that wasn't my due. And now *I'm* the criminal. When did that happen? *How* did that happen? Who voted for that?'

'And you wonder why all those people, our listeners, the cabbie, whoever, you wonder why they think you're some kind of hero? Why they identify with you? You've just answered your own question. Because the system has turned us all into criminals, one form or another.'

'That's just it,' said Mickey. 'I may not be a villain, but I'm no hero, either. Let them find another knight with a shiny helmet.'

'Don't you mean shining armour?'

'Speak for yourself, ducky.'

'Let's have another drink.'

Dillon brought over another bottle.

'Anyway,' Mickey said, 'where am I staying tonight? I'm not allowed within five miles of the house.'

'You're staying with me.'

'If I've got to sleep in that tip, I'm gonna need another drink.'

'Take it easy,' said Ricky. 'I forgot to tell you. You've got an early start in the morning.'

364

# Sixty-six

'So who was the judge, in chambers?' demanded Justin Fromby, pacing his study.

'Roberts,' said Roberta.

'Mister Justice Andrew Roberts. I should have known. He should have been pensioned off years ago. He's senile. Talk about forces of Conservatism, the man's a fucking fascist. Pro-hunting, anti-abortion, anti-union. How the hell did he get the French bail appeal?'

'Just lucky, I guess.'

'I don't know how you can make light of this.'

'I am not making light of this. Roberts was the only judge on duty. He stays here all summer, never misses a Test match. Everyone we can rely on is swanning around Tuscany on the New Labour circuit. Anyway the CPS fucked up spectacularly. Most of them were off at a seminar in Majorca, boning up on the new European Human Rights legislation. They sent along some rookie lawyer, fresh out of law school.'

'Roberts would have eaten him for elevenses and washed him down with a bottle of claret. When this case comes to trial we'll have to make sure Roberts is kept well clear of it, otherwise French will walk. I'll talk to the Lord Chancellor. He'll fix it.'

'Need I remind you,' said Roberta, 'we have more pressing considerations.'

'It's in hand,' Justin snapped.

'What do you mean?'

'I said, it's in hand.'

# Sixty-seven

'Taxi, miss?'

Andi looked up from her trolley.

'MICKEE! Oh, Mickey, oh, thank God.'

Mickey wrapped her in his arms.

'But how? I mean, I thought. When I spoke to Ricky,' she spluttered.

'It's OK, everything's going to be fine. I'll explain on the way back. How are the kids?' he asked.

'They're lovely, they're fine,' Andi said.

'They don't know, do they?

'No, no. Nothing, nothing at all.'

'Then how did you, er, you know, explain this, you coming home suddenly?'

'I said I had some papers to sign. They think we're moving, because of the, you know, the cat business and all that.'

'They may well be right. I never want to see the place again. Which is just as well. I'm not allowed within a five-mile radius, bail conditions.'

They started to make their way across the concourse at Gatwick.

'Where are you staying? Where are *we* staying?'

'Ricky's putting us up.'

Mickey went over to the pre-pay parking machines and fumbled for a coin.

He could feel the man at the next machine staring at him.

'Oi, excuse me, you're that Ricky French geezer, topped that gyppo, aren't you? I signed your petition, rang the radio hotline ten times.'

'It's *Mickey*, actually.'

'Hey, everybody,' the man shouted, turning to the rest of the queue. 'It's Ricky French, you know, RICKY FRENCH, shot that scumbag, in all the papers.'

Mickey was surrounded.

'Sign this, Mickey, please, Mickey,' begged a young woman waving a copy of the *Sun* with Mickey's picture on page one.

'This way, Mickey, come on, smile, mate,' urged a man with a Nikon.

Soon there were about thirty people, pushing and shoving, poking and prodding, patting his back, forcing him into involuntary handshakes. A blowsy woman with a 46-inch bust planted a kiss on him, bang on his lips.

'MICKEE! MICKEE!' screamed Andi. 'What's going on? Let's get out of here.'

Mickey grabbed his ticket from the machine and barged his way through the mêlée. He seized the trolley, took hold of Andi's hand and began to run towards the car park, with the crowd in hot pursuit.

Mickey and Andi were cornered by the lifts.

'Come on, Mickey, just one picture. Is this the wife?'

Mickey shoved the luggage trolley towards the throng, catching a young woman on her ankle, gashing her leg. She let out a yelp of pain.

'Look, I know you mean well, but please, *please,*' Mickey clenched his fists by his sides and drew breath. 'Look, my wife's had a long flight, *please* won't you just FUCK OFF and LEAVE US ALONE!'

The crowd fell silent and began to disperse, mumbling to themselves.

The man who'd spotted Mickey at the parking machine turned to his wife and said: 'Well, that's bloody charming, isn't it? A bit of bloody fame and it always goes to their head. Who does he think he is? After all we've done for him.'

# Sixty-eight

'Protests have been springing up all over Britain about the flood of bogus asylum-seekers arriving daily in Britain. Fighting broke out at a march in Birmingham, there was further trouble in Worthing outside a hotel taken over by the local council to house immigrants and reports are just coming in overnight of an attempted arson at the government immigration centre in Croydon. Shots were fired during clashes between travellers and members of the Reclaim Essex Alliance on official gypsy facilities on the outskirts of Ilford. All police leave has been cancelled.

'The opposition home affairs spokesman said the situation had been inflamed by the Home Secretary's refusal to cut short his Tuscan holiday and return to Britain to take personal charge of the crisis. He said the recent, ongoing Mickey French case had focused public opinion on the way in which the law is now heavily biased in favour of criminals and against decent, law-abiding, home-owning taxpayers. He called for an immediate end to all immigration, for the armed forces to be mobilized to repel asylum-seekers at ports and for those involved in smuggling human cargo into Britain to be jailed for life.

'Everton Gibbs, from the Commission for Racial Equality, will tonight chair an emergency conference, which is due to be addressed by the top lawyer Justin Fromby and Scotland Yard's head of diversity, Deputy Assistant Commissioner Roberta Peel, who is leading the French inquiry and is tipped as the next Commissioner of the Metropolitan Police. You're listening to Rocktalk 99FM. Those were the headlines. Ricky Sparke will be here to take your calls after this, "Tommy Gun", from the Clash.'

368

Andi reached over and turned down the volume. 'I never could stand the Clash,' she grumbled.

Mickey had filled her in on the events of the past few days, sparing her a few of the gorier details.

'You can't turn your back for five minutes.' She tried to make a joke of it. 'What happens now?'

'What happens now,' Mickey said, as they crawled through south London, past boarded-up shop fronts and drug dealers openly plying their trade on street corners, 'is that we head for the radio station, pick up Ricky, get some lunch, then make for the flat.'

'Can't we go straight to the flat?' asked Andi. 'Ricky's not off the air for a couple of hours.'

'I haven't got a key. Ricky said he'd get one, a couple cut, one each.'

'Pity,' she said, running the fingers of her right hand along the inside of Mickey's leg.

Using both hands, she reached over and unzipped his flies. Mickey was already straining inside his Y-fronts.

'Not here, not in traffic,' he said, while offering no resistance.

'You just think of that song we used to sing when we were kids,' Andi whispered, 'about the little girls in the back seat kissing and a-hugging with Fred.

'Keep your mind on your driving, keep your hands on the wheel, and keep your beady eyes on the road ahead,' she sang, as she moistened her lips and lowered her head into Mickey's lap.

# Sixty-nine

Colin Marsden slept uneasily that night, random thoughts nagging his mind, a drip, drip, drip of doubts and contradictions, falling from the darkness like Chinese water torture.

He was back at his desk at seven, picking up his messages. The lab had confirmed the corpse's fingerprints were on the petrol can. And an e-mail was waiting for him from the overnight duty CID man at Tottenham.

Marsden had searched the Met computer system and discovered that a black taxi had been stolen from a street near Spurs' football ground some time on the night of the shooting. It was the only cab stolen throughout the whole of the Metropolitan Police area that week.

The e-mail told him the cab was still missing and that a petrol station attendant may have seen the thief.

Marsden decided he'd take a trip to Tottenham, after all. Talk to the petrol pump attendant, call in on the girl, Maria.

There was another e-mail message. Call a DS Collins, out at J-Division, the old Tyburn Row beat his dad had pounded. Wonder what he wants?

The canteen opened at 8.30 am. Marsden bought a bacon sandwich and a tea, three sugars, and settled down to read his newspaper.

Mickey's release on bail had been relegated to a single column on page one. There was a brief report of the inquest.

Marsden checked some of the other papers lying around the canteen. Mickey's release and the inquest had been relegated throughout Fleet Street, most of which was leading on the overnight violence in Birmingham and Ilford and the arson attack on the immigration centre at Croydon.

None of the reporters at the inquest had picked up on the significance of the two questions Mickey had put to the pathologist, so excited had they been at the dramatic news of his release on bail.

On the front of the *Clarion* there was a beaming picture of DAC Peel. YARD RACE CHIEF WRITES EXCLUSIVELY FOR CLARION. See page 28.

Marsden saw page 28.

Roberta was writing in much the same vein as Fromby the previous day. While she was prevented from going into too much detail about the Mickey French shooting, she emphasized that nothing could be read into Judge Roberts's decision to free him on bail, that the case was still being treated as a racist murder and was being given the highest priority. She deplored the violence targeted at vulnerable refugees and peace-loving members of the travelling community and hoped that the courts would hand out exemplary sentences to those convicted of hate crimes.

Marsden polished off his bacon banjo, stopped off for a stiff shit and was back at his desk by nine.

He called the J-Division number given on the e-mail.

'Collins,' said the voice at the other end.

'This is acting Detective Chief Inspector Marsden, Angel Hill.'

'Good morning, sir. Thanks for calling back. I'm sorry to bother you, but I think I might have something for you.'

'What might that be, constable?'

'It may be something, or it may be nothing.'

'Let me be the judge of that,' said Marsden.

'It's about your body, sir, the shooting at Heffer's Bottom.'

'When you say my "body", do you mean the deceased or the accused, Mickey French?'

'The, er, dead man, sir.'

'What about him?'

'I gave him a tug, a week or so back.'

'*What?*' Marsden sat bolt upright. 'Say that again.'

'I thought you might like to know.'

'You *can* say that again.'

'We were on a joint op with the dip squad from the British Transport Police. He tried to snatch a handbag from an undercover woman officer.'

'Are you certain it was him?'

'Yeah, I think so.'

'Only *think* so?'

'No, sir, I'm pretty certain.'

'Why are you telling me this only now? Why didn't you get in touch straight away?'

'I'm sorry, sir. I only caught up with it all yesterday. I've been away on leave, took the missus for a short break in Ibiza. Very nice this time of year, have you been?'

'Cut the fucking travelogue, detective. Get on with it.'

'Well, I saw the picture of the deceased and he looked like the same guy. And I remembered the name, Dinantu, specifically, because I checked the spelling when we booked him in at Tyburn Row and I had to type it into the computer twice.'

'Hang on,' said Marsden. 'You entered the arrest on the Met computer?'

'Yes, sir. And here's the funny thing, when I went to check yesterday it was gone. Maybe I wiped it by mistake. But I do remember him and his bloody lawyer.'

'*Lawyer?* He had a lawyer?'

'Yes, sir,' said Collins. 'And that struck me as odd.'

'What, that he had a lawyer?'

'No, sir, who his lawyer was. He's quite well known. He's just been on breakfast telly, he's never off the telly, talking about this case, banging on about racial crimes and immigration and such.'

'Justin Fromby?'

'Yes, sir.'

Justin fucking Fromby.

'What happened?'

'The usual, sir. Fromby claimed his client had been fitted up, started making noises about entrapment and complaints, going to the media, that sort of thing. The station sergeant took fright and bailed him to report back in fourteen days. He didn't want the rubber heels and the reptiles crawling all over the place.'

'Own recognizance?' asked Marsden.

'No, that was the other funny thing. Fromby said he'd stand surety. They left together.'

'Isn't there a record of that at the station?'

'No, sir. I've checked the computer on that, too. Nothing. It's as if he was never here, never existed.'

Marsden sucked on his pencil and dialled his brother, Billy.

'Drug squad, DS Marsden.'

'Billy, it's me.'

'My brother, the DCI,' laughed Billy.

'*Acting* DCI,' Colin corrected him, for once emphasizing the *acting*, not the *chief* bit.

'DCI's in the bag after this one, the French case,' Billy teased. 'You're in all the papers.'

'If you can find me lurking in the shadows behind DAC Peel,' Colin said.

'What can I do for you, bruv?' asked Billy.

'Coupla things.'

'Shoot.'

'You know all about computers, don't you?'

'More than you, at any rate. If knowing *less* than you is technically possible. Worked out how to programme the video yet?'

'Stop fucking about. I get by. I can just about fathom the Yard system,' Colin said.

'Then what can I do for you?'

'Something that should be there, isn't there.'

'What do you mean?'

'An arrest which was entered isn't there. The DC who tapped it in insists he entered it. But now it's gone. He thinks he could have wiped it.'

'Not possible. He might have wiped his own machine's memory, but a record is automatically entered on the central system at the Yard. He couldn't wipe that,' said Billy, confidently.

'I've searched the system, but I keep getting "file not found". Why?' asked Colin.

'Simple. Either this DC never did enter it, or someone else has wiped it.'

'Is that easy?' Colin inquired.

'Far from it. The whole system is designed to stop sausage-fingered Plods erasing stuff by mistake. Hence the automatic copy to central records,' Billy explained.

'But it's not there.'

'So if your DC mate is telling the truth, someone else has been into the system and wiped it off.'

'Could anyone do that?'

'You'd need the approved access.'

'Who would have that?' Colin pressed him.

'Systems guys probably, but there's tight security safe-guards,' said Billy.

'Who else?'

'Maybe top brass in the Branch, I'm not sure.'

'Outside of the Branch?'

'You're looking at DAC and above,' said Billy.

DAC and above, Marsden registered.

'Thanks, bruv, maybe the DC just fucked up and is telling porkies to cover himself,' Colin speculated convincingly, not wanting to involve his brother more than he had to.

'Sounds favourite,' agreed Billy.

'Thanks. Oh, by the way, can you access the Interpol computer at drugs squad?' Colin inquired.

'Not me, personally,' said Billy. 'But I know a man who can.'

# Seventy

'Holy shit, I've been burgled,' exclaimed Ricky.

'How can you tell?' asked Andi, surveying the devastation, papers and cassettes strewn everywhere, drawers half-open.

'Looks pretty much like it did when I left this morning,' remarked Mickey.

'Stop fucking about. I've been turned over. The video's gone, look. And the DVD, and that new MP3 player I bought a coupla weeks ago. It was still in its box. I haven't fathomed the instructions yet,' said Ricky, picking his way across the sitting room.

They'd skipped lunch and driven straight to Ricky's flat from the radio station as soon as Ricky had come off-air. Andi wanted to get changed and showered.

The plan had been to go on to Spider's for a reunion piss-up and a cheese sandwich.

That *had* been the plan.

Wayne Sutton had watched first Mickey, then Ricky, leave the flat, let himself in with accomplished ease and done what Justin Fromby had instructed.

He hadn't hurried. Fromby had told him he'd have several hours. The flat owner was on the radio all morning, that Ricky Sparke.

For a grin, Wayne had even rung the show, just to check it wasn't a recording. He'd even got on-air. Wayne on line three.

'*Morning, Wayne, what can we do for you?*'
'*It's about all this burglary what you've been talking about.*'

'Yeah?'

'I mean, there's probably I dunno how many burglaries going on right now.'

'You're right, Wayne. There's an epidemic out there.'

'I ain't talking about illness, I'm talking about burglaries.'

'Yeah, right, Wayne.'

'That bloke, that Mickey, what shot that burglar, I reckon he done us all a favour.'

'Glad you agree, Wayne.'

'Yeah, there's a lot of it about. For all you know, someone could be burgling your gaff while you're talking to me.'

Wayne had to cut himself off. He fell about laughing. If only the stupid old git knew.

He went about his work in exactly the way Justin Fromby had told him, scooping up anything which looked like an official document and emptying all the cassettes into a sports bag. Mr Fromby had told him to concentrate on the home-made tapes, the blank tapes. He didn't bother with the pre-recorded stuff. Wayne would have nicked them, too, but there wasn't anyone he'd ever heard of, just groups called things like Southside Johnny and the Asbury Jukes, whatever the fuck an Asbury Juke was. The Neville Brothers, they were footballers not pop stars, Wayne thought. Creedence Clearwater Revival, what kind of a fucking stupid name was that? Wayne slung them on the floor.

He helped himself to the video, the DVD and the MP3. Reckoned he deserved a drink, while he was at it, like.

Wayne let himself out, unnoticed, sauntered back to Victoria and caught the tube north to present his haul to Mr Fromby.

He was home and dry before Ricky Sparke walked back in.

'Anything else gone?' asked Mickey, as Andi immediately busied herself tidying up.

'Looks like they stole all the dishcloths and cleaning materials, too,' she remarked, retrieving a bone-dry, tea-stained tea-towel from the cupboard under the sink, where the wine was kept.

'Fuck it, look at my cassette collection. There was some rare stuff here. I'd taped all my old Stax, Volt and Atlantic singles off the old 45s. All fucking gone. It was priceless. They've had the lot. And been through all my drawers. At least there wasn't any money here.'

'Have they had all the tapes away?' asked Mickey.

'All except the pre-recorded stuff.'

'I think we can guess what they were looking for. Thank God I gave you that other copy, Andi,' Mickey said.

'Ah, yeah, I meant to tell you about that,' said Andi, sheepishly, walking out of the kitchen as Ricky scrambled around on the floor, muttering to himself.

'About what?' asked Mickey.

'The tape. I don't know how to, er . . .' Andi hesitated.

'Go on.'

'I'm sorry, love. But Katie, well, she taped over it, some pop group.'

'She did *what*?' Mickey spluttered, clasping his hands to his face.

'Don't be angry with her. It was my fault. I left it lying around. She wasn't to know. There was nothing written on it.'

'That's it, then, we're fucked,' said Mickey, with an air of defeatist desperation.

'BRILLIANT. FUCKING ACE!' hollered Ricky, still down on his hands and knees, surrounded by Wilson Pickett and Booker T tapes.

'Brilliant, just brilliant!' he repeated.

'I dunno what you're so jubilant about, Sparke. Haven't you heard what Andi just said about Katie recording over the only other copy? We're fucked.'

'Not quite,' beamed Ricky. 'You should have a little more faith in your Uncle Ricky.'

He tapped Mickey on the cheek with a cassette case. The tape rattled inside.

'I'm not a complete cunt. Sorry, Andi. Don't you think I worked out that if they'd turned your drum over they'd get round to me eventually?'

'I suppose,' said Mickey.

'Well, that's why I took precautions.'

Ricky opened the cassette box, labelled 'HOLD ON I'M COMING. Their Greatest Hits.'

He took out a blank tape, marked in felt-tip.

*Mickey*, it said.

'There you are, mate. Safe and sound. I'd make a couple more copies, but as you may have noticed, they've half-inched the old Nakamichi.'

'You mean?'

'Correct.'

'You switched the tapes?'

'Obviously.'

Andi threw her arms round him. 'Oh, Ricky, I could . . .'

'Steady on,' laughed Mickey.

Andi kissed Ricky on the cheek. Then snuggled up to her husband.

'Tell me,' said Mickey. 'What made you choose this particular cassette box?'

'It sort of sums up the difference between them and us. Between you and me, old son. And Roberta Peel and Fromby. What mattered when we were younger. What matters now.'

'In what way?'

'They got Marx and Engels. We got Sam and Dave.'

# Seventy-one

Justin sorted through the papers. Wayne had cleaned out Ricky's files.

Credit card receipts, gas bills, council tax reminders, income tax forms, phone bills, but nothing which looked like a Metropolitan Police juvenile bureau arrest sheet.

Roberta shuffled the tapes, meticulously taking each one and playing it on Justin's old Technics cassette deck, fast forwarding, rewinding, both sides.

Clarence Carter, Solomon Burke, Arthur Conley, Eddie Floyd, the Mar-Keys, the Bar-Kays.

Soulfinger.

*Da-da-da-da, da-da-da, da-da, da-da, da-da.*

Soulfinger.

'Turn that down,' barked Justin. 'Where do you think you are, Radio Luxembourg?'

'Patience,' urged Roberta. 'If it's here, I'll find it.'

There were dozens of tapes, all catalogued on the cases in Ricky's handwriting.

Stax/Volt tour. King & Queen, Otis and Carla. Rufus Thomas.

Roberta emptied the contents of the sports bag onto the sofa.

'There's nothing here,' said Justin. 'Just the usual domestic detritus. No joy?'

'This is the last one,' said Roberta.

A tape, label peeled off both sides of the cassette itself, nothing written on the box.

This might be it.

She took the tape out of the box, slotted it into the cassette deck, and pressed PLAY.

Justin and Roberta held hands and crossed fingers.

> *I want everybody to get up off their seat.*
> *And put your arms together and your hands together*
> *And give me some of that OLD SOUL clapping.*

And I thank you.

'I'm sure that's Sam and Dave,' said Roberta.

'I've always been more of a Hawkwind man, myself,' Justin remarked.

'Well, that was the last one.'

'What do you reckon?' Justin asked.

'I think you were right. French was bluffing.'

# Seventy-two

'Thought it was a bit odd, gyppo driving a black cab,' the young West Indian petrol station attendant told Colin Marsden.

'He only came in for a can of petrol. I can remember saying to him didn't he want diesel? I mean, that's what black cabs run on, isn't it? He just ignored me. Slapped the money down and buggered off. I was only trying to be helpful.'

'Is this him?' asked Marsden, showing the attendant the picture of Ilie Popescu taken at the immigration centre in Croydon.

'Could be. They all look alike to me. But I can do better than that. What day d'you say it was?'

Marsden reminded him.

'Hang on a minute,' said the attendant, wandering into the office. 'Follow me.'

He went over to a steel filing cabinet containing a box of video tapes.

'Here we are. This is the one. We keep them all for a week, just in case a cheque bounces or a credit card turns out to be stolen.'

He slid a tape into a combined TV/video player. 'Quite late, wasn't it?' he said, fast-forwarding through the time-coded recording. 'There you go. Here he comes now.'

Marsden watched, fascinated, as the security cameras caught Ilie Popescu driving the stolen cab onto the fore-court, filling the can with four-star, paying and driving off.

'What's he done, anyway?' the attendant asked.

'Oh, nothing, just routine,' Marsden said, shrugging off the inquiry.

He rewound the tape and re-viewed the action.

This time he noticed a second car pull into the kerb, twenty yards short of the filling station, dim its lights, then move off again as the black cab swung back out onto the main road.

A black S-class Mercedes.


Colin Marsden found the nearest available parking space, about forty yards from the hostel.

He reversed in between a 1987 3-series BMW and an untaxed Bedford van with a flat tyre.

Checking the address again, he got out of the car, pressed the remote and armed the alarm system.

Blip-blip.

The street was full of bags of rubbish and overflowing skips. Front gardens were cluttered up with old bikes, discarded prams with missing wheels, communal dustbins, fried chicken and pizza boxes, picked at by cats by day and urban foxes by night.

Honest Edwardian villas were decaying all around, the product of decades of neglect and ill-advised, botched 'improvements'.

Some of the houses still had the original wooden sash windows, now peeling and rotting. Others had nasty aluminium replacements, totally out of keeping with the character of the properties.

A few houses were boarded up. There were a couple of surviving, elegant Edwardian front doors, complete with stained glass. They were outnumbered by DIY-chainstore Mock Georgian, manufactured in ubiquitous uPVC and containing brass handles and inappropriate bullseye windows.

One property had windows clumsily obscured with black emulsion and an all-steel front door. Probably the local crack house, Colin figured.

This had been an expansive thoroughfare when it was

first built, warranting its elevated 'Avenue' status, lined with London plane trees, now wilting under the pollution.

Some trees had wreaked a terrible revenge on their violators, spreading their roots through the soft clay, causing widespread subsidence to the surrounding terraces, some of which now leaned like a fairground Haunted House, propped up with makeshift buttresses.

As Marsden went to cross the road opposite the hostel, between a double-parked builder's lorry and an abandoned Fiat 124, the force of the explosion lifted him off his feet, propelling him backwards over a crumbling garden wall and hurling him down a flight of steps leading to a pokey basement flat, carved out of an old coal cellar.

He wasn't sure how long he blacked out, but he came round under a larch-lap garden fence panel and the bonnet of the Fiat, which had been ripped off in the blast.

He had been showered with glass, his chin was cut, blood seeping down the front of his shirt, trousers torn, knees grazed, shaken, but otherwise, remarkably, in good shape.

Plumes of smoke hung over the street, car alarms pierced the air. Marsden scrambled free and hauled himself up the steps.

The hostel was ablaze, flames leaping from the roof and windows, water gushing from shattered bathroom pipes.

Cars were tipped on their side, like Dinky toys. Men, women and children wandered aimlessly, dazed and confused.

A Somali man dragged himself along the path from the hostel, clawing at the ground. His right foot had been severed, the stump leaving a dark red slipstream. Wailing uncontrollably next to him, his wife, clutching a limp bundle, a baby girl, killed instantly, dangling like a rag doll.

From out of the smoking doorway, Marsden could see a pretty young woman, aged around twenty maybe, dark hair, stumbling blindly towards the street.

As he crossed the road to go to her aid, a second explosion

forced him back. The girl was battered to the ground, her face hitting the pavement like a flipped pancake, forcing the bridge of her nose up into her brain, delivering the coup de grace.

In the distance, Marsden could detect the sirens of the first emergency vehicles alerted, now heading for the scene of devastation.

He waited one, two, three minutes, perhaps, crouching behind a skip, for fear of further explosions.

Satisfying himself that the immediate danger had passed, he picked his way through the carnage and approached the body of the young girl, lying face down on the path.

He knelt and stroked her hair, but didn't have the stomach to turn her over.

Marsden removed his jacket and draped it over her head and shoulders.

He heard movement behind him and looked up to see a swarthy, Eastern European man, mid- to late twenties, he thought, staring at the body, tears welling in his eyes.

'Maria,' the man said. 'They called her Maria.'

# Seventy-three

Everton Gibbs held his arms in the air, palms facing the audience, and called for order.

There was genuine, boiling anger in the hall.

Gibbs, a distinguished black man, lean, early sixties, greying at the temples, immaculately turned out, dark, tailored suit, white shirt, navy, spotted tie, buffed black loafers, had travelled far since his days as a community activist on the Parkgate Estate.

He had risen to lead Tyburn council, clashing constantly with the privileged young white Trots, favouring stealth, persuasion and evolution over confrontation and revolution.

His work had brought him to the attention of the Home Office and he had graduated to a position of great influence in the Commission for Racial Equality.

The Prime Minister was said to admire Everton's robust Christianity and his cool-headed, inclusive approach.

Everton Gibbs had been happily married for forty years. He and his wife had moved out of the Parkgate and into a rambling Victorian villa in Muswell Hill, which they had lovingly restored, and had raised four children.

The eldest son was now a doctor, the daughter a rising star in marketing and the youngest son doing a postgraduate degree in law.

Then there was Trevor. They didn't talk about Trevor much, other than to ask themselves where they had gone wrong. Like the rest of the Gibbs children he was brought up to fear God, know right from wrong, respect his elders and instilled with the work ethic.

But Trevor had fallen in with a bad crowd, brushes with the law early on, experimenting with ganja and then harder drugs. Everton didn't dwell on the thought, but it was rumoured that Trevor was now heavily involved with the Yardies, running drugs and guns out of Kingston, Jamaica.

Everyone reassured Everton that Trevor was no reflection on him, he had done his best and look at the way the other three kids had turned out.

But Everton still grieved for his middle son and felt guilty.

On the platform in the hall alongside him were Justin Fromby, whom Everton had known since the Parkgate; Roberta Peel – she, too, had come a long way since Tyburn Row – and, alongside her, the radical journalist, Georgia Claye, whom Everton thought looked a little flushed.

'Friends,' Everton addressed the three hundred people assembled before him. 'Thank you for coming. The tragic event at Tottenham this afternoon has given this meeting new impetus, reminding us all how we must be ever vigilant against the tide of racism engulfing our society. To open proceedings tonight, I call on an old friend and tireless campaigner, Justin Fromby.'

There was wild applause and cheering. Fromby was almost like a film star to the serried ranks of forty-something *Clarion*-readers comprising the bulk of the audience.

'Comrades, colleagues,' Justin began, running his fingers through his sleek mane. 'Before we continue, will you all please join with me in observing a minute's silence in respect of all our brothers and sisters who have perished at the hands of racists and Romaphobes, particularly the victims of today's cowardly atrocity in Tottenham. Let us, too, remember, poor Gica Dinantu, a guest in our country, a refugee from terror and oppression, gunned down in cold blood. His only crime was looking for work. We must congratulate the fearless Mizz Georgia Claye for her campaigning work in this area and also thank Deputy Assistant

Commissioner Peel, Scotland Yard's head of diversity, for taking personal command of this case, emphasizing the seriousness which the Metropolitan Police and, indeed, society, places on eradicating this type of dreadful smear on our national reputation.'

The audience rose for a minute's silence.

Halfway through, the respectful tribute was disturbed by the sound of snoring from the platform. Georgia Claye was standing up, but her head was slung back, her mouth wide open, doing a passable impersonation of someone trying to kick-start a tractor.

Roberta Peel nudged her.

'Er, uggh, waah, urrrgh,' bumbled Georgia, as she lost her balance, sashayed to the side of the stage and fell head-over-heels down the steps, her too-short skirt riding up to reveal a pair of voluminous red silk knickers.

The audience reacted with a mixture of indignation and titters. Roberta stepped into the breach.

'Please forgive our honoured guest, ladies and gentlemen. She has been working night and day to expose the true story behind the shooting of Gica Dinantu and it would appear that she has been overcome by tiredness.'

Nothing, obviously, to do with being overcome by six cans of Olde Bowel Loosener and two bottles of Beaujolais at lunchtime.

'May I suggest a brief adjournment,' said Roberta.

Everton Gibbs agreed.

'Comrades, we shall continue shortly,' he said. 'Meanwhile please enjoy our new Asylum Manifesto, copies of which you should have found upon your seats.'

At the side of the stage, Georgia was slumped unconscious, her stupor consolidated by a lump on the head sustained as she hit the deck.

Two stewards were called to assist her removal.

With head held high and feet held higher, Georgia was carried out.

# Seventy-four

Wayne Sutton sold Ricky Sparke's video, DVD machine and MP3 player to a fence in the Caledonian Road and what he didn't blow on skunk he fed into a fruit machine in an arcade in King's Cross, popular with rent boys and nonces.

Making his way back through Holloway in the early hours, munching a kofti kebab, he noticed the front door of a house wide open.

Well, Wayne reckoned, it would be rude not to.

He went inside and discovered an open-plan set-up, stairs leading off the main room, no handrail.

There was a leather coat draped across a Moroccan-style sofa, newspapers strewn everywhere and a television talking to itself.

Wayne surveyed the room. The video was an old model, one of those top-loaders, went out with the ark. The CD player wasn't up to much either, part of a cheap stacking system.

Wayne toyed with a few ornaments, largely African wood carvings and odd bits of stone.

There was a desk in the room, with an ancient Amstrad word processor and some kind of, well, he wasn't sure what it was.

Wayne picked it up. A thin piece of metal with a sharp point, a spike, about twelve inches tall, supported by a wooden base. There was an engraved plaque on the base. It read: 'The Golden Spike, for services to campaigning journalism.'

Wayne put it down. That was no good to him. He

checked the drawers for money, credit cards, stuff like that. Nothing.

Wayne wandered into the kitchen, opened the fridge and helped himself to a can of super-strength cider.

There seemed to be little else in the fridge, apart from three bottles of wine and a rancid carton of milk.

Wayne took a slug and decided to investigate further. Upstairs, might be a handbag or something.

There was a light on in a bedroom. Wayne pushed open the door. The bare arse was the first thing which struck him, like a giant, flabby, bruised peach, facing upwards, puckered in his direction.

About eighteen inches below the prow of the buttocks, Wayne noticed a giant pair of red silk knickers, half mast, stretched between Georgia Claye's spreadeagled knees.

She was face down on the duvet. Her cabbie had dumped her at the front gate. Somehow she had managed to drag herself indoors, upstairs and made the bedroom.

Her handbag was lying open at the foot of the bed. Wayne removed her purse, took out what was left of the fifty pounds she'd received for her incontinent appearance on the Ricky Sparke show – she insisted on cash – and stuffed it in his pocket.

As he looked up, his eyes were drawn to the cavernous arse, wobbling involuntarily as Georgia snored.

Georgia stirred and turned over, semi-conscious, spotting Wayne standing at the foot of the bed.

Georgia had to admit to herself that she didn't recognize the young man standing there, but it wouldn't be the first time.

She'd often woken after a night in Spider's or the local navvies' boozer with a strange man in her bed, a damp patch on the duvet and a nasty taste in her mouth.

Most of the time, she vaguely remembered meeting them, inviting them home. But not this one. He was a bit young. A bit of a result, actually.

Wayne began to back out of the bedroom, disgusted

by the ghastly sight of this flabby, wrinkled, marooned manatee.

'No, don't go, please stay. Come here, lie down. We haven't got to know each other properly yet,' called Georgia, pathetically.

Wayne turned on his heels and charged downstairs, heading for the front door. Her left foot caught in the strap of her handbag, her knickers constricting the movement of her right.

Georgia surged forward, like a Sumo wrestler. She tried to pull up her knickers on the move as she followed Wayne out of the bedroom onto the landing, stumbling, losing her balance at the top of the stairs.

She reached for the non-existent banister, slipped, bounced off the wall and flew through the air, hitting her desk face down, at speed, her one and only trophy puncturing her left breast and piercing her heart.

Georgia Claye's life ended, fittingly, like so much of her life's work.

On the spike.

# Seventy-five

Colin Marsden rubbed the bandage covering the three stitches he'd needed in his chin. His knee was raw and, generally, he felt as if he'd been kicked by a horse.

He'd hung around until the emergency services arrived, briefed the uniformed chief inspector and gone by ambulance to North Middlesex hospital, where his wounds had been treated but it had not been necessary to detain him. He'd made his own way to Tottenham nick, given a full statement and called DAC Peel on her mobile to inform her of what had happened.

He'd missed out the bit about the black cab and the petrol pump attendant, explaining merely that he'd wanted to find out more about the deceased, build up a bit of a picture, try and understand what he was doing in Heffer's Bottom at that time on the night of the shooting.

Just tying loose ends, ma'am, leaving nothing to chance.

Roberta had been in the back of her official Rover when he rang, on her way to address the anti-racism rally, convened by Everton Gibbs and the racial equality commission.

She was glad to hear that he had escaped relatively unscathed and said she hoped to be at Angel Hill some time the following afternoon.

Marsden had taken a sedative given to him at the hospital and had slept soundly. He woke, ravenous.

Only an Angel Hill canteen special would suffice.

He was there on the dot, for the full English, much to the surprise of his colleagues, who expected him to milk a few days' sick leave out of his ordeal.

No point sitting around moping, Colin figured, though he was haunted by the anguished look on the young girl, Maria's face in the split second before the secondary explosion.

He checked his e-mails. One from his brother, Billy, another from the ballistics lab.

He rang Billy first.

'DS Marsden.'

'Hi, Billy,' said Colin. 'Before you ask, I'm fine.'

'Glad to hear it. Why shouldn't you be fine?'

'You've not heard?' said Colin.

'About what?'

'The explosion, Tottenham. The hostel. I was there.'

'Shit. I mean, yeah, I heard, not until this morning. We were out all night, on an operation. All got a bit hairy. That's what I wanted, well one of the things, I wanted to talk to you about. Hey, are you OK?'

'I said, didn't I? Cuts and bruises, nothing fatal,' Colin reassured his kid brother. 'What have you got for me?'

'Coupla things. First, you were asking about getting into the Interpol system? Well, I rang the liaison guy at the Yard, he's an old mate, told him it was a drugs squad investigation, ran your man's name, Dinantu, past him.'

'And?'

'And he's dead.'

'I know that. I've seen the body. I was there, half an hour after French shot him,' sighed Colin.

'No, just listen.'

'Go on.'

'Gica Dinantu was killed in an abortive car-jacking in Hamburg, months ago.'

'What?'

'The name's flagged. Some Kraut inspector, called Freud, or Frend, or something. Seems this Dinantu character died in a shoot-out, a chase. But his oppo, the Krauts reckon the guy who masterminded it, may have got away.'

'So?'

'So my mate at the Yard contacted this Freund, Freud, character. Ran the picture of *your* Mr Dinantu by him, e-mailed it to him. And guess what?'

'Why do I think I know what's coming?' Colin anticipated the next piece of information.

'It wasn't Dinantu. It's his oppo. Your corpse is the accomplice, the other guy in Hamburg, name of Ilie Popescu. Romanian, car thief. Tied up with the Russian mafia, some suggestion of a falling-out. Over money. Seems the German police were right. He did get away.'

'And arrived here posing as an asylum-seeker, adopting the identity of his mate, who he knew was dead already, Gica Dinantu,' said Colin.

'Oh, and that's not all. My mate at the Yard tipped me the wink that someone else had been into the file, Dinantu/Popescu file, from this end, recently,' Billy added, tantalizingly.

'Did he say who?' asked Colin.

'No.'

'Didn't, couldn't or wouldn't?' inquired Colin.

'I've no idea, bruv. He said it was classified, that's all. Over his head. I don't know if that gets you any further,' said Billy.

'Thanks, Billy,' said Colin.

'Small world, though,' said Billy.

'Eh?'

'There was something else I needed to talk to you about.'

'Yeah?' said Colin, curious.

'Not on the phone, it's, er, a bit sensitive. Can you get over here, say lunchtime?' asked Billy.

'Yeah, should be OK. Though I shall have to be back later, the DAC, Her Ladyship, is paying another state visit. Meet you in the boozer, the Crown, about one?' said Colin.

'No, we can grab a pint later. Come to the nick first.'

# Seventy-six

'Police are still sifting through the rubble of the asylum hostel in Tottenham, destroyed by an explosion yesterday. Five people were killed, including one baby, and at least twenty more taken to hospital. The full casualty list has still to be finalized. No one has yet claimed responsibility.

'Scotland Yard has launched a top-level investigation into the blast, which is being treated as a racist attack. It has just been announced that it will be led by Deputy Assistant Commissioner Roberta Peel, the Met's head of diversity, who is also in charge of the Mickey French case.

'After addressing an anti-racism, pro-asylum rally last night, DAC Peel promised Rocktalk 99FM that the perpetrators of the Tottenham bombing would be brought to justice.

'Also at last night's meeting, the Clarion journalist Georgia Claye, was taken unexpectedly unwell. Her condition was described as "predictable".

'Elsewhere, in west London, a high-speed chase in the early hours, involving officers from the drugs squad, ended in a pile-up which is still causing traffic chaos in the Hanger Lane area. Police were pursuing three suspects who escaped on foot after their car left the road and crashed into a new digital speed camera at approximately 85 miles per hour. Shots were fired and a police spokesman today said that when they catch the driver he could be looking at a two-year ban.

'Meanwhile, in an effort to tackle pollution and cut the number of unemployed, able-bodied young men in London, the Deputy Prime Minister has announced a scheme to pave over the area from Euston Road to the Embankment, ban all traffic, including black cabs, and bring back sedan chairs

*and horse-drawn buses, thus creating thousands of job oppor-*
*tunities, and bringing a welcome boost to the farriers' trade*
*and the organic manure industry.*

*'The Deputy Prime Minister announced this initiative in*
*Trafalgar Square before boarding a helicopter for RAF Norwood,*
*where a private Lear jet was waiting to take him and his family*
*on holiday to the Monaco Grand Prix, as guests of the Formula*
*One Association.*

*'Those are the headlines from Rocktalk 99FM. Ricky Sparke*
*is next.'*

Ricky was feeling a little delicate. They had repaired to
Spider's, after clearing up the flat, and Ricky had stayed on,
sending Mickey and Andi on ahead to get reacquainted.

He'd let them have his bed and said he'd sleep on the
sofa. What he didn't realize is that the sofa upon which he
would spend the night was in Spider's.

Dillon let him crash there on compassionate grounds and
arranged an alarm call.

Several pints of dark, sweet coffee and a sausage and egg
baguette later, Ricky was ready for the fray. As the time
bell rang on the 'Sultans of Swing', Ricky faded up his mike
and spoke.

*'Good morning, everyone, welcome to the Ricky Sparke show.*
*And a very good morning, if he's listening, and if he's not*
*there's going to be trouble, to our very own Mickey French,*
*reunited with his child bride. Let's hope you got even less sleep*
*than I did, kiddywinkies.*

*'Phone lines are open now, call us on the usual number.*
*Your calls are already banked up back to Heston Services, so*
*don't let's waste any more time. Steve's on line one. Morning*
*Steve, what's your pleasure?'*

*'Morning, Ricky, I rung up the other day, when you had*
*Mickey on, like, Mickey French.'*

*'Yeah, right, Steve. Welcome back to the show.'*

*'Thanks, mate.'*

> 'What do you want to talk about this morning, Steve?'
> 'That explosion at Tottenham, Ricky.'
> 'Terrible business, Steve, terrible. What about it?'
> 'I dun it.'
> 'I'm sorry?'
> 'I dun it. I blew it up.'
> 'Stop messing about, Steve. This isn't funny.'
> 'It's not meant to be funny, Ricky. I'm dead serious.'
> 'You mean, you, you, er?'
> 'I planted the bomb, Ricky.'
> 'Come off it, Steve. Stop pulling my plonker.'
> 'I'm not pulling anything, Ricky. I got all the gen, like, on how to make the bomb off the internet. It was dead easy.'
> 'I'm not listening to any more of this. I'm going to cut you off.'

'You'll do no such fucking thing, mate,' Ricky heard Charlie Lawrence shout in his earpiece over the talkback. 'You keep him going. This is a real scoop. This is great radio.'

Steve ploughed on.

> 'Don't cut me off, Ricky. You're the one what started all this Free Mickey French business, on the radio.'
> 'Yeah, but, look, Steve, he's free.'
> 'Only on bail, Ricky. He's still charged with murder. I told you the other day, direct action, that's what's needed, until all the charges are dropped. That's what I did. Direct action.'
> 'People were killed yesterday. A baby, a young woman.'
> 'Casualties of war, Ricky.'
> 'That's it, enough. You're insane. We're tracing this call.'
> 'Don't bother, Ricky, I withheld the number. I'll be in touch.'

The line went dead.

Charlie Lawrence instructed the producer to stick on another record.

Ricky flung his headset onto the console and stormed out of the studio, into the control room.

'You're fucking mental, too,' he screamed at Charlie Lawrence.

'This is a fucking radio station, not the Samaritans,' Lawrence shouted back. 'Ratings are what matter, ratings. That was radio to die for.'

'An unfortunate turn of phrase, Charlie.'

'Look, mate. I dunno whether this Steve character was making it up or not, but think of it – a confession, on air. *Fabuloso!* We'll be beating the listeners off with a stick. Think of the figures, think of our deal, think of the money. You're a rich man, Ricky.'

'Think of twenty years inside for inciting terrorism,' yelled Ricky. 'You heard him. He got the idea from us.'

'That's bollocks, mate,' said Lawrence. 'We can't be responsible for every fucking nutter who rings up, decides to go round planting bombs.'

'Did you get his number?' Ricky asked the phone-op.

'No, I put him straight through.'

'We never put anyone straight through. We ring them back, check they're kosher,' said Ricky. 'Station policy.'

'*I* told her to put him through,' Lawrence interrupted. '*New* station policy. We were spending a fortune ringing them back. I decided to save a few bob.'

'And now we've got a lunatic running round out there,' said Ricky.

'We don't know that.'

The door burst open. Mickey and Andi barged in.

'What the fuck was all that about?' Mickey demanded to know.

'You heard?'

'In the car, on the way in, just now,' Andi said. 'Ricky, what is going on here?'

The record came to an end. The producer played a trailer, another commercial.

'Get back in there,' Lawrence ordered Ricky.

'Get to fuck,' Ricky said.

'Put on another record. *DO IT!*' Lawrence demanded.

'I didn't sign up for Vigilante FM,' shouted Ricky.

'And I don't want to be associated with this, either. I used to be a copper, or have you forgotten that?' Mickey protested.

'We've put up a million quid to get you out,' Lawrence reminded him.

'Then I'd rather go back to jail,' said Mickey.

'And I'd rather he was in there than have your mad listeners going round blowing up hostels, murdering babies and women,' screamed Andi.

'Fuck it, I'm not going back in there,' said Ricky. 'Where's my coat? I'm off.'

As Ricky turned to leave, the producer called out: 'No, Ricky, wait. Please, just wait while I print this out.'

He walked over to the printer and handed Ricky a sheet of A4. Ricky read it, hurriedly, threw down his jacket, pushed past a startled Charlie Lawrence and marched back into the studio.

He put the headphones back on, settled in front of the microphone and motioned to his producer to fade the music. Ricky spoke.

'*"The End of the World as We Know It"*, by REM, ladies and gentlemen. In case you're wondering, the reason I cut that song short was to bring you a newsflash, just in from the Press Association.

'It has just been announced in a statement from Scotland Yard that yesterday's explosion at an asylum hostel in Tottenham was caused by a gas leak, REPEAT, A GAS LEAK, and not a bomb as thought previously. Gas board and fire brigade investigators say they are satisfied the blast was an accident and not deliberate.

'I'm sure you will be as relieved to hear that as we all are here at Rocktalk 99FM. I can only apologize for our last caller. There are some sick bastards out there.'

# Seventy-seven

Colin Marsden shook hands with his brother, Billy, and, self-consciously, patted him on the shoulder.

'Good to see you, kid.'

'You, too,' said Billy. 'This way.'

Billy led Colin through the station, past the custody suite, and out towards the car park at the back of the nick.

'What's all this about, Billy?' asked Colin.

'You'll see.'

At the bottom of the ramp, a breakdown truck had towed in a black S-class Mercedes, front-end crumpled, otherwise intact.

'This the one on the wireless?'

'The very same,' confirmed Billy. 'We were out on an obbo, Bishops Avenue, Hampstead, one of those twenty-million-quid gin palaces, ownership registered in the Cayman Islands, shell company for the Moscow wise guys, according to the Funnies. We had a tip that they were bringing in drugs from Africa, the Middle East, part-paying them in stolen cars, Mercs, Porsches, Beamers, Rollers, stolen to order. So we're staking out this mansion, the gates open, this Merc drives out. Anyway, we decide to drop in behind, we're in the Omega, the one with the Lotus tuning. The Merc heads north, towards Henley's Corner. We keep our distance, as you do, not wanting to freak them. As we're passing through the east side of the suburb, you know, where the road narrows, the Merc starts pulling away, 50, 60, 70, speed cameras going off like the Blackpool illuminations.

'We stay with them, but hang back. At Henley's Corner,

they jump the lights doing about 75, right in front of a pair of Black Rats. Well, the traffic boys are going to have a bit of that, aren't they? The best thing that's happened to them all night.'

Colin laughed.

Billy continued. 'On go the blues and twos, off goes the Merc, straight through the next set of lights, the Golders Green turn, and hell for leather heading west, with our friends the Black Rats doing their Smokey and the Bandit impression. The Merc hits the Brent Cross flyover doing 90-odd, the Black Rat driver clatters a bollard protecting a hole in the road, cable works or something, loses it, and tips sideways on two wheels in the direction of Cricklewood.'

Colin shook his head.

'Anyway,' Billy went on, 'we think "fuck it", switch on the siren and give it some hammer. We're gaining on the Merc, past IKEA, under the railway line, past the Park Royal exit. As we approach Hanger Lane, the Merc swerves violently, hits a patch of oil or something, glides across three lanes and smashes straight into that new half-a-million quid's worth of digital traffic camera.'

'Yeah, yeah. Get on with it, Billy.'

'Well, you know what these Mercs are built like. Fucking tanks. Three geezers scramble out as we pull up behind. The next thing, we've taken a couple of bullets in the windscreen, no one hurt, thank God, we're head down and they're legging it off towards Hanger Lane tube station.'

'Did you go after them?' Colin asked.

'Me, a hero? You must be joking. We weren't armed. It started as just a routine stakeout,' said Billy. 'By the time the ARV arrived, they were long gone.'

'All very exciting, but what's any of this got to do with me?' Colin said, thinking that he didn't remember mentioning anything about a black S-class Mercedes to his brother. To anyone else come to think of it. But both the king pikey and the lad at the petrol station had seen one the night of the shooting. Colin had seen the Merc near the petrol station himself, on the security video.

'Come on, let's go up to the office,' said Billy.

The drugs squad room was deserted.

'Where is everyone?' asked Colin.

'The inspector's on holiday, Marbella. The DCI's away at Bramshill on some equal opportunities seminar. That leaves little old me in charge. Here, have a look at this. We found them in the boot. They left them there when they did a runner.'

Lying on the desk was a black briefcase and a gun, like a pistol, but with a shoulder extension, a night sight and a huge silencer. Colin didn't recognize the weapon.

'What is it?' he asked.

'It's called a Keltec Sub-9,' explained Billy.

'Never heard of it,' shrugged Colin.

'Former weapon of choice, KGB, East German Spetznatz, their SAS. Particularly popular with assassins. Folds away to sixteen by seven, easy to conceal, easy to assemble. Semi-auto, single action, ambidextrous. And here's the beauty of it. Accepts practically any 9mm pistol magazine. Dead silent, too.'

'How d'you know all this?' asked Colin.

'I did the weapons course, Hendon, remember? When I fancied joining the branch. Guess who my tutor was?'

'Mickey French.'

'Correct, Mickey French. As I said, small world,' Billy grinned, 'and it gets smaller.'

'Spit it out.'

Billy opened the leather attaché case. Alongside the compartment which had contained the components of the Keltec Sub-9, was a small Nikon camera, zoom lens. Lying on top was a brown envelope. Billy pulled a sheaf of photos out of the envelope. One by one, he handed them to Colin.

'Recognize anyone?' Billy asked.

'Shit, that's Dinantu, or Popescu, or whatever he's called. The dead guy. And that's, that's, fuck me.'

'Mr Justin Fromby,' Billy prompted him.

Collins, the dip squad detective had told Colin that Fromby had bailed Dinantu. Certain.

'Where were these taken?' Colin asked.

'Can't be sure, but they're time- and date-coded.'

The little white digits in the right-hand corner were quite specific.

'It gets better,' said Billy. He was enjoying this. It's not often he had one over his big brother.

'Give me the rest,' snapped Colin, reaching for the remaining photos.

'Oi, manners,' Billy chided him. 'You need to see them in sequence.'

A woman arriving at the house, hour or so later, raincoat. From the back, no clear ID.

'Who's the boy coming out?' asked Colin.

'Not sure,' said Billy. 'I've not had time to run him through the system. But you'll recognize this next one.'

Colin took the photograph in both hands.

Dinantu/Popescu climbing into a taxi, a couple of hours after arriving. At the door, Fromby and a woman he recognized only too well.

Deputy Assistant Commissioner Roberta Peel.

Colin sat down, put the picture on the desk. Staring, gaping.

What the fuck had he walked into?

Fromby, Peel and the dead guy, pictured together, according to the time and date code, just hours before Dinantu/Popescu was shot dead at Mickey French's house.

And round the Romanian's head, in felt-tip pen, someone had drawn a target, like you see through a gun-sight.

'Billy,' he said to his brother. 'You can't get involved in this.'

'I am involved, bruv. But in what, I'm not quite sure.'

'Me neither, not entirely. Look, can you let me take this lot, the gun, the photos?' Colin asked.

'I suppose, but you'll have to have them back here by the

end of the week, when the DCI gets back, else he'll have my bollocks.'

'Trust me.'

'Fine. But, Col,' said Billy, 'you be careful. Be very careful.'

# Seventy-eight

'But, Home Secretary,' protested Roberta. 'Paul, *please.*'

'Less of the *Paul,* if you don't mind, Deputy Assistant Commissioner. Home Secretary will do just fine.'

'Pau, er, sorry, Home Secretary, do we have to be so formal?' she inquired in her most coquettish voice.

'Yes, we bloody do, Roberta, Deputy Assistant Commissioner, rather. This is a very serious matter. I don't expect my holidays to be interrupted by phone calls from the Prime Minister. He is particularly concerned about the way in which things have been allowed to spiral out of control. And so am I. For Christ's sake, I've had to fly back from Tuscany. I'm not happy, not happy at all. What the hell do you think you have been playing at?'

'Doing my job, that's all,' Roberta said, anxiously twisting the cord of the telephone in her private office.

'Your *job*? Since when has your job been stirring up false anxieties, conjuring mad bombers out of thin air, scaring people half to death? I've had Everton Gibbs on. He thinks you've made a complete fool of him. Why the hell didn't you wait for the full report before announcing that the explosion at the hostel in Tottenham was a racist attack?' The Home Secretary sounded absolutely furious.

'But, but, all the evidence pointed to it,' Roberta blustered.

'*Evidence? Evidence?* What fucking *evidence*?'

'But, Paul, Home Secretary, sorry, given the background, I just assumed that . . .'

'*Assumed?* You're not paid to assume anything.'

'But look at the facts. The hostel was crowded with

asylum-seekers, foreign nationals, refugees. There've been threats made against the asylum community, only the other day, on the radio. What was I supposed to think?'

'That's the point. You are supposed to *think*!'

'I was only following government guidelines,' Roberta pointed out. 'Remember? All incidents involving minorities to be presumed racist. If someone thinks it is a racist incident, then as far as I'm concerned it *is* a racist incident.'

'But this was a *gas leak*, not fucking *Mississippi Burning*.'

'We weren't to know that. We had to treat it as a suspected racist bombing, especially after Soho and Brick Lane.'

'By all means *treat* it as a suspected racist incident. But don't stand in front of a rally and announce that it *is* a racist bombing and then go on television and radio and make the same wild allegations. Scaremongering and spreading terror is not part of your brief. You're doing the racists' job for them. They must be pissing themselves,' the Home Secretary barked into Roberta's ear.

'But, but . . .'

'Just *listen*.' The Home Secretary, in full rant, cut her short. 'You gave members of the ethnic minorities, vulnerable people, the impression that racist bombers were operating in London. There are barricades going up all over the place, in Brixton, Southall, Haringey. Everton Gibbs is trying to build bridges between the communities, and they're building fucking barricades. You've set back race relations fifteen years.'

'Now, I really must protest,' said Roberta indignantly. 'I've done more than any senior member of the Met . . .'

'You've made the Metropolitan Police Service a complete laughing stock. And the government. And, by extension, *me*.'

'*You?* How come?' asked Roberta.

'It was me who specifically asked the commissioner to make you head of diversity and give you complete command of the French business, the shooting in Heffer's Bottom. And that's another thing.'

'What?'

'You've made a right pig's ear of that, too,' the Home Secretary said.

'*I'm sorry?*' said Roberta, completely taken aback.

'I don't know why I let you talk me into it.'

'I thought you wanted me to handle it,' she said.

'I thought you *could* handle it.'

'I've done everything by the book. This *was* a racist murder, definite. He's charged and awaiting trial.'

'Yes, on bail.'

'I couldn't help that.'

'Maybe not, but you could have kept the temperature down, not stoked the fires,' the Home Secretary said.

'I thought you wanted this to be a demonstration of zero tolerance of racist violence,' she argued.

'But we didn't want a backlash. You could have kept the lid on it. First French turns up on the radio, while still *in custody.*'

'That wasn't my fault. I've dealt with it.'

'Then that *Clarion* piece, by barmy bloody Georgia. Were you behind that?'

'Absolutely not!'

'Then where did she get all the inside stuff from, the quotes from police reports?'

'I, er, she must have paid someone, at division.'

'Don't insult my intelligence any further,' said the Home Secretary, wearily. 'The Prime Minister is deeply, deeply disturbed at the way events have turned out. Especially the riot, outside the court. Angel Hill is a key marginal, you know. There's an election coming up. There are plenty of marginals like Angel Hill, all over the country. Haven't you seen the polls? Haven't you got any political antennae? French has nationwide support, you know. You've managed to turn him into a martyr.'

'*Me?* Turn him into a martyr? Now, hang on. You were all for this,' Roberta screamed into the phone.

'No, no, no. You were put in charge to establish the facts.

There are plenty of people who think French is the victim in all this. Perhaps he *was* in the right to defend his own home, use "reasonable force" I believe is the expression. That certainly seems to be the consensus.'

'I thought you wanted him hanged, drawn and quartered,' said Roberta.

'No, Deputy Assistant Commissioner. I have a record of our conversation. I seem to remember it was *you* who was all in favour of making an example of French. Perhaps you should have taken more time to establish the full facts, before rushing to charge him. I'm very worried about your lack of judgement, all round. We appear to have misjudged your leadership qualities.'

'You're not hanging me out to dry on this one, Paul.'

'I'm so sorry, I have to go,' said the Home Secretary. 'The Prime Minister's on the other line. Goodbye, Deputy Assistant Commissioner.'

You complete and utter shit, Roberta said to herself and began to wonder if Group 4 might soon have a vacancy for a Deputy Assistant Commissioner.

# Seventy-nine

Colin Marsden drove straight to the Home Office ballistics lab, opposite the Imperial War Museum, in Lambeth, south London, and introduced himself to the technician working on the bullets found in the Heffer's Bottom corpse.

'D'you get my e-mail?' the technician asked.

'No, sorry. It's been a bit, you know,' Marsden said.

'I heard you were caught up in that Tottenham palaver,' the technician said.

'Yeah, caught up, you could say that.'

'A couple of our guys were down there. They marked it as a gas main from the off,' the technician said, nonchalantly. 'Dunno what all the fuss was about.'

'You had to be there, so to speak,' said Marsden. 'What have you got for me?'

'Over here.' The technician led Colin to a table with an enamel, kidney-shaped dish containing four lead slugs.

'These the ones?' Marsden asked.

'The very same.'

'They all look alike to me.'

'Sure they do. They all looked alike to me, too, until you asked me to look a little harder. No one had ever mentioned anything about two guns,' the technician said.

He picked up one slug with a pair of tweezers.

'This was the first, the only one, originally, I examined. No doubt, fired from *this* weapon,' he said, tapping Mickey French's Glock. 'This one, too, was fired from this gun.'

'And these?' Marsden asked, pointing to the other two lead slugs, which were more badly distorted than the first two.

'Fired from a different gun. Same calibre, mind, but not the same gun.'

'These weren't fired from the Glock, you're certain?' Marsden pressed him.

'They might have been fired from *a* Glock, but not this one.'

'How can you tell?'

'Right, stop me if I'm getting too technical, but basically, these two, the first two, are your bog-standard, hollow-point, 9mm bullets, regular police issue,' said the technician.

'And the others?'

'They're 9mm, too, same calibre, almost identical unless you look hard. These are what they call soft-nose. The first two mushroom on impact. These sort of explode, which is why they're more badly mangled. But basically once they're inside the body they behave pretty much the same.'

'So how do you know the difference?' asked Marsden.

'I ran them through spectrographic analysis.'

'What?'

'You really don't need to know, unless you've got all day,' the technician said.

'All day is something I haven't got.'

'Good. There's another test. Police-issue bullets have steel jackets and leave no residue in the barrel. The soft-nose have no jacket and always leave behind them minute traces of lead,' the technician explained.

'And?' Marsden was riveted.

'The Glock barrel was clean. The second two could not possibly have been fired from that gun.'

'Positive?'

'Absolutely, stake my job on it,' the technician said.

'A bloke's life may be staked on it,' Marsden told him.

'I read the papers,' the technician said.

Marsden put the briefcase down on the desk and opened it. 'Something else for you.'

'Keltec Sub-9.' The technician recognized it immediately.

'Could those two,' Marsden said, pointing to the second pair of bullets, 'have come from this?'

'Entirely possible,' said the technician. 'I'll be in touch.'

# Eighty

*'You're listening to Rocktalk 99FM. I'm Ricky Sparke. These are the latest headlines. The Prime Minister flew back to London today amid growing unrest. There were clashes in Tottenham between asylum-seekers and local skinheads. One man was stabbed and three others taken to hospital. Police made four arrests, one for wounding with intent and three others for parking on a zigzag line.*

*'As barricades remained up during another night of looting in Brixton, the Prime Minister appealed for calm.*

*'The latest opinion polls show the government trailing the opposition by fourteen points in the Angel Hill by-election. Voters are expressing concerns about the government's perceived weakness over law and order and illegal immigration.*

*'The Home Secretary, in an exclusive interview with Rocktalk 99FM, emphasized that Britain would continue to provide a safe haven for genuine refugees but said the rules would be re-examined. He deplored the recent violence in the capital and said he had reminded the Metropolitan Police of their responsibility to the whole community. The Home Secretary would not comment on reports that the Crown Prosecution Service had been asked to re-examine the papers in the Mickey French case, but would say that the Prime Minister was personally concerned with redressing the rights of householders to protect their property.*

*'We'll bring you the latest developments throughout the day here on Rocktalk 99FM. In a few minutes I'll be joined by a very special guest and bringing you another Rocktalk 99FM exclusive. That's after we've heard from Bob Marley and the Wailers, from the Lyceum concert. "Burnin' and Lootin'".'*

411

Ricky Sparke's special guest was shown into the studio personally by Charlie Lawrence. As the Wailers faded, Ricky introduced him.

'Ladies and gentlemen, my special guest on the programme today, and it's a pleasure to welcome him, is Everton Gibbs. Mr Gibbs has risen from humble beginnings on one of London's most run-down estates to a position of prominence on the Commission for Racial Equality. A very warm welcome to you Mr Gibbs.'

'Everton, please.'

'Great. Everton, let me ask you, do you regret holding that rally the other night?'

'No I do not, Ricky. The purpose of the rally was to focus attention on the problems of racism in Britain, particularly the hostility towards asylum-seekers.'

'But the leader of the Council of Mosques himself has expressed his concern at the, and I know you're not going to like the use of these words, flood of bogus refugees arriving in Britain. This is something which concerns all British citizens, surely, of whatever ethnic origin?'

'I would agree with you there, Ricky. But we have to have a free and open debate.'

'It doesn't help when people like yourself hold rallies whipping up wholly unjustified fears about non-existent racist bombers roaming London.'

'That was not the purpose of the rally. I regret, I admit, I do regret, the impression that was given in some quarters.'

'From the platform, may I remind you, Everton. By a senior lawyer and a high-ranking officer of the Metropolitan Police. You constantly complain about racists being given a platform; what about what happened at your rally?'

'I've already said I regret that. I have made my views known to the Home Secretary. I'd like to use your programme to formally distance myself and my organization from those allegations and appeal to all sections of the community for calm.'

'You've just done that, live on London's No 1 radio station, Everton. And for that, we're most grateful. Can we talk, in *more specific terms, about the Mickey French case. I understand that was the original reason you called the rally, to, how did you put it?, to celebrate the life of Gica Dinantu.'*

*'I didn't ever use that expression, "celebrate", Ricky. I was concerned, as we all were at the Commission, that this case, as it has indeed proved, would become a focus of the hostility between the host community and the asylum community.'*

*'We're talking here about a common burglar, a thief. What about a man's right to defend his own home? In the bulletin, just now, we've heard the Home Secretary as good as admit that the balance between the householder and the criminal has tipped too far in the wrong direction.'*

*'I would remind you that members of ethnic minorities are far more likely, statistically, to be the victims of violent crime.'*

*'I'm glad you raised that, Everton. Where do you stand on the Yardies?'*

*'I condemn all crime, all violence, from whatever quarter.'*

*'Let me play you something, Everton.'*

Ricky Sparke motioned to the control room. Charlie Lawrence nudged the studio engineer, who pressed PLAY. The tape crackled into life.

*'Found what you were looking for?'*

*'Er, yeah.'*

*'And what are you going to do about it?'*

*'What do you mean?'*

*'I've been talking to Eric Marsden.'*

*'And?'*

*'Fromby's trying to fit him up on an assault on the prisoner.'*

*'I reckon he did beat him.'*

*'Eric denies it. Says he got the injuries in the fight outside the chip shop. Sounds about right. I nicked Gibbs the last time. He's a nasty little fucker. You going to charge him?'*

'Mr Fromby says that if we charge Gibbs, he'll make a formal complaint against Marsden.'

'If this caution comes to light, you've got no option but to charge him.'

'What should I do?'

'That's up to you, girl.'

'Fromby knows about the previous. He wants me to lose it. And the knife.'

'What, this one?'

'Where did you get that from?'

'Never you mind. What are you going to do with the previous?'

'The way I see it is that everybody wins here. Fromby gets what he wants, Marsden's off the hook. Everybody's happy.'

'And what if I don't give a fuck and turn you in? Give me that. You're a lucky girl.'

'Lucky?'

'There's two copies still in here. Usually we keep one and send the other to central records at the Yard. This hasn't gone off yet. I must have forgotten.'

'So what happens now?'

'You're a silly fucking cow. Old Eric Marsden may be a cunt but he's only got a year left to his pension.'

'So?'

'So why wreck anyone's career here? Eric Marsden's or yours?'

'What about the sergeant?'

'He is the original wise monkey. He sees nothing, hears nothing, says nothing. He doesn't want to know. No charge, no paperwork. He's sweet. Fromby's hardly going to say anything. The boy certainly won't object to being released. Eric will stay shtoom and he'll put the frighteners on the skinhead who picked him out. He'll tell the sergeant that Gibbs is being released pending further inquiries. That'll be the end of it.'

'And you? What's in it for you?'

'I don't want Eric going down the shitter and I reckon you've got a big future.'

'What are you going to do with all this – the knife, the file, the tape recording?'

'I haven't thought about it. Nothing, maybe. Who knows?'

Everton Gibbs sat stone still, incredulous. Ricky Sparke said nothing. He let his guest, the listeners, absorb the moment. Five seconds of dead air sound like a lifetime.

'Ladies and gentlemen, I apologize for the profanity. Mr Gibbs, Everton, recognize the woman's voice?'

'I, er, um, what?'

'You should do. She was on your platform, the rally, the other night?'

'Where did you get this, I mean, what, erm, well?'

'Fromby? Name ring a bell, Everton? And Gibbs, any relation, you think?'

Everton Gibbs sat opposite Ricky, dumbfounded, as if he'd seen a ghost.

'Let me tell you a story. Once upon a time there was a young tearaway called Trevor Gibbs. Stabbed a guy outside a chip shop, Tyburn Row way. Eric Marsden, dead now, the local beat copper, nicked him. Gibbs is represented by a hotshot young lawyer called Fromby, who dreams up some fake charge of assault against Marsden. Fromby prevails upon a young WPC, Roberta Peel, to lose the evidence. Trevor Gibbs, your son, Everton, walks. He's now one of the major villains in London, do you deny it?'

Everton Gibbs composed himself and replied.

'Whatever you've just done, it was a despicable trick. You got me here under false pretences.'

'Did you know that Peel and Fromby had conspired to pervert the course of justice in order to spring your son, let him walk on a stabbing charge?'

'Who was the other man on the tape?'

'That's not important right now. But I assure you the tape is genuine. Did you know?'

'I assure you, and your listeners, everyone, I have never heard this before. In the name of God, this is the first time. I knew nothing, you must believe me. Nothing.'

'Mr Gibbs, for what it's worth, I do believe you. I'm sorry. Truly I am.'

# Eighty-one

Ricky, Mickey and Andi had sat up, arguing, debating, long and hard about whether he should play the tape on-air.

'You can't let the bastards get away with it,' Ricky reasoned. 'These are bad people. They've got to be stopped.'

'But it'll incriminate me. You're not thinking of me. You're just thinking of your precious fucking ratings. How much have you made out of this already?' Mickey protested.

'OK, I never pretended there wasn't a drink in it. But that's not why I got into it. Fuck it, you've known me long enough. If that's what you think, what you really think, sincerely believe, then I won't do it. We can burn the fucking tape here and now. Gone and for ever,' said Ricky.

'I dunno,' Mickey said, swallowing another large Smirnoff.

'Look, Mickey, they're already fitting you up for murder.'

'I did shoot the guy, though,' Mickey reminded him.

'What happened to "reasonable force"?'

'Yeah, I know. But hey, look, I'm not proud of any of this.'

The last word went to Andi.

She put her arms round Mickey's thick neck, from behind.

'It's your decision, lover,' she whispered in his ear.

'What do you think I should do?' Mickey asked his wife, looking deep into her eyes.

'I can't make that decision for you, Mickey. You'll do what you have to, what you've always done. You'll do what's right.'

# Eighty-two

'Just what in God's name did you think you were playing at?' Everton Gibbs raged around Justin Fromby's Philippe Starck sitting room.

'We were only trying to help,' said Roberta.

'*Help? HELP?* Have you any idea of the damage, the enormity, the sheer wickedness of what you have done?' stormed Gibbs.

'But, Everton, please, calm down, we did what we thought was for the best,' Fromby implored him.

'The best for *who*? Not for me, not for my son, not for my family,' Gibbs yelled.

'But, but, we thought that if we could stop him getting a criminal record at his age . . .' said Roberta.

'Have you *seen* his criminal record lately?' said Gibbs.

'Everton, you know how things were back then. Rampant racism in the police force. He wouldn't have stood a chance once he'd got into the system,' said Fromby.

'*I* should have been the judge of what was best, not you. Who appointed you to be judge and jury? Why wasn't I told? You've made a fool of me,' Gibbs snapped back.

'That was never our intention,' Roberta said.

'He was, is, *my* son. Let me tell you something. I came here with nothing. Life was tough. But we brought up our children to fear God, to respect the law, to love this country. We tried to teach them right from wrong. Sure, Trevor went off the rails, early, fell in with a bad crowd. But we could have dealt with it, in our way. Getting arrested and hauled before the court might have been the best thing that ever happened to him. Taught him the wickedness of his ways.

Stopped him short. Instead, what does he learn, eh? He learns that if you've got the right lawyer, pull the right strings, you can get away with anything. You destroyed everything I had tried to teach him. *Everything.* And you have the gall to tell me that what you were doing was *for the best.* As if me, a simple black man from a sink estate, wasn't fit to make that decision. What do you expect? *Yes, Massa. Thank you, Massa?* You people are as bad as the real racist scum. At least with them we know what we're dealing with. With *you*? You patronize us, make allowances for us we don't need. It's just one big game to you people, using black people, racism, as a stepping stone up your ladder, with your quotas and committees and your fancy – what was it? – *Romaphobia.* We don't need your help. We don't *want* your help. I despise you. No, that's not true, I pity you. I really pity you. May God forgive you one day, because I never will.'

'The door was open,' said Marsden. 'I let myself in. Not disturbing anything, am I?'

'I was just leaving,' said Everton Gibbs. 'I must remember to wipe my feet on the way out.'

'What do you want, inspector?' demanded Roberta.

'It's acting *chief* inspector, ma'am. But then you know that, don't you? You just can't seem to get it right,' said Marsden.

'What are you doing in my house?' said Fromby.

'Brought you some photos, sir. Or may I call you Trotsky, like my old man did?' Marsden threw the sheaf of photos recovered from the boot of the Mercedes onto the glass-topped coffee table.

Roberta and Fromby thumbed through them, silently.

'Good, aren't they?' said Marsden.

'What are these supposed to prove?' said Roberta.

'Prove? They don't actually prove anything. But they link you to the man shot dead at Mickey French's house. You thought you'd covered your tracks, didn't you? You might be able to wipe a computer's memory, but a human's a little more difficult.'

'Say your piece and get out,' snapped Fromby.

'I don't expect you to admit to anything. But as I say, these link you to the man shot dead by French and that tape they played on the wireless this morning links you to French himself and establishes motive,' said Marsden.

'Motive for what?'

'How about arson?' said Marsden. 'I've got the fingerprints of the dead man, the same man seen with you in these photographs, on a petrol can found at the crime scene.'

'All circumstantial, no proof,' Roberta blustered.

'True, the Romanian's dead. So he's not talking. If he told the girl, she's dead, too.'

'So,' said Fromby, 'are you going to charge us?'

'I could read you your rights, for the hell of it.'

'Stop pissing around, Marsden,' said Roberta, getting visibly irritated. 'How far are you taking this?'

'Like I told you, first day we met, Angel Hill, ma'am.' Marsden smiled. 'Wherever it leads.'

# Eighty-three

The Angel Hill coroner tidied his papers and placed them neatly on the desk in front of him.

'Having heard all the post-mortem evidence and examined the new report from the ballistics laboratory, I am satisfied that the two bullets which killed Gica Dinantu, or, rather, Ilie Popescu, were not fired from Mr French's gun, the Glock.

'As to whether the shots were fired from the other weapon, the, er, Keltec Sub-9, the ballistics report is inconclusive, although I would place on record the likelihood on the balance of probabilities that this was indeed the gun which fired the fatal rounds.

'We have heard that Mr French discharged two shots, which hit the deceased in the shoulder and upper arm. I am further satisfied that Mr French, as a qualified police marksman, did not shoot to kill and indeed, in my opinion, was acting within the guidelines of "reasonable force".

'Further, I would venture that even if the shots fired by Mr French had proved fatal he still would have been acting within the definition of "reasonable force" established in the case of *Crown v Rungle* at the Old Bailey on 7 September 1951.

'For those of you unfamiliar with this judgment, I shall summarize it for your benefit and for the benefit of anyone who may be tempted to break into another person's home.

'*Crown v Rungle* concerned a Mr Rungle, who killed a burglar at his home with a garden fork. The judge, Mr Justice Codd, pointed out that burglary is, in itself, a violent felony. He stated that it is the right and duty of any householder, or any other honest citizen, who finds a burglar in a dwelling house to arrest him.

'Pursuant to that arrest, the honest citizen may, and, indeed should, use any force that he considers necessary and any weapon that is at hand to stop him. If the result is death, it is justifiable homicide, not murder, or even manslaughter. Mr Rungle was acquitted.

'In this case, I find that the deceased was killed by person or persons unknown and I understand police inquiries are continuing. As far as Mr French is concerned, I shall be recommending to the Home Office and the Crown Prosecution Service that the charges he is facing be discontinued.'

The coroner's verdict was received with relief and ecstasy. Mickey sat still, strangely passive.

'Incidentally,' said the coroner, having waited for the jubilation to subside, 'in the case of *Crown v Rungle*, Mr Justice Codd did add the caveat that the householder should shout "stop" first, if possible.

'He also recommended that, *obiter*, everyone should keep a garden fork by his bedside.

'Next time, Mr French, use a garden fork.'

# Eighty-four

As Mickey and Andi walked from the court, arm in arm, mobbed by well-wishers and Rocktalk 99FM's Free Mickey French barmy army, Marsden approached.

'Thanks, inspector, sorry, acting *chief* inspector,' said Mickey.

'Not necessary. And, by the way, it's no longer *acting*. I've been promoted to full DCI,' beamed Marsden.

'Your old man would be proud of you,' said Mickey, shaking him by the hand.

'Yeah. I'm being made up officially on transfer,' said Marsden.

'Leaving Angel Hill. Where you going?'

'CIB.'

'*Rubber heels?*' exclaimed Mickey.

'Apparently the Home Secretary himself liked the way I handled this business,' said Marsden.

'Good for you, son,' said Mickey.

'We're going to need to talk, Mickey,' said Marsden.

'I'd love to buy you a pint,' Mickey said.

'Yeah, right. But we'll need an official chat, too.'

'Official?'

'Yeah. First case, investigating a certain allegation of perverting the course of justice at Tyburn Row, twenty-five years ago,' said Marsden.

Mickey couldn't resist a grin. 'Should've seen it coming.'

Marsden turned to Ricky Sparke, who'd been earwigging the conversation.

'Mr Sparke, Ricky, I'm going to need that tape, I'm afraid. It's all the hard evidence I've got to go on. It seems DAC Peel destroyed the rest.'

'Sure,' said Ricky, compliantly, taking the tape out of his inside jacket pocket and handing it to Marsden. 'Always happy to assist the police.'

# Eighty-five

'This is Rocktalk 99FM. Here are the headlines. Rocktalk 99FM's Free Mickey French campaign achieved sensational success when Mickey walked from Angel Hill coroners' court without a stain on his character.

'Scotland Yard has announced that Deputy Assistant Commissioner Roberta Peel, the head of diversity, has been suspended on full pay pending an inquiry by the Police Complaints Authority into allegations believed to be connected to the Mickey French investigation and the subsequent riots in London.

'Officers also want to interview the celebrity lawyer Justin Fromby, who failed to appear for a number of scheduled television and radio appearances this morning. Reporters say the fashionable micro-blinds at his £1.7 million luxury home in north London have been closed all day.'

They laughed as they climbed out of the cab and descended the steps to Spider's, where Dillon was waiting with a bottle of champagne. A Captain Oates was on the horizon.

'Why'd you give Marsden the tape?' asked Andi over the first glass of bubbly.

'Good manners, you know me,' said Ricky.

'But it drops Mickey right in it,' she said.

'Nah, he'll be fine,' Ricky reassured her.

'How can you say that? You know what's on the tape.'

'That's how I can say it.'

'Eh?' puzzled Andi.

'I know what's on the tape.'

'What are you going on about?'

425

'The Miracles. Right now, Chief Inspector Marsden is probably listening to 'Mickey's Monkey'.

> *'Cat called Mickey came from out of town*
> *Dum-di-dum-di-li.'*

'You wicked bastard,' laughed Andi.

'Hey, Mickey,' shouted Dillon, waving the *Evening Standard*. 'You're all over the paper.'

Mickey took the *Standard* in both hands. The banner headline read: *'NEXT TIME USE A FORK, Coroner's amazing advice to man who shot a burglar.'*

But Mickey wasn't reading the splash.

His eye was drawn to a single column at the foot of the page.

### MONKEY BOY OFF TO THE SUN

A group of young offenders left Heathrow today for an adventure holiday in the United States.

The party included the notorious 'Monkey Boy' who has been convicted of dozens of offences of burglary, car crime and criminal damage.

The group, under the supervision of social workers, will spend two weeks surfing and sailing at the Florida resort of Zero Beach.